someone
else's child

BOOKS BY ALISON RAGSDALE

Her Last Chance

Dignity and Grace

The Liar and Other Stories

The Art of Remembering

A Life Unexpected

Finding Heather

The Father-Daughter Club

Tuesday's Socks

someone else's child

ALISON RAGSDALE

bookouture

Published by Bookouture in 2022

An imprint of Storyfire Ltd.
Carmelite House
50 Victoria Embankment
London EC4Y 0DZ

www.bookouture.com

ISBN: 978-1-80019-368-0
eBook ISBN: 978-1-80019-367-3

We are born of love; Love is our mother – Rumi

PROLOGUE

Two babies. Twin daughters. That's what was written in the stars for your dad and me, and when we lost sweet Faith, just hours after she and our darling Hope were born, we thought we'd never fill the gaping hole Faith left in our hearts. Nothing could have prepared us for the pain of holding her for only moments, before she was whisked away as the doctors tried to get her to breathe, to deliver Hope, then control my haemorrhaging.

I asked over and over why Faith wasn't crying, and as I faded in and out of consciousness, your dad held my hand so tight, his voice steady in my ear, 'Hang on, Cat. It's going to be OK,' until I passed out.

No more pregnancies. It didn't seem real when they said those words to me. We had fought so hard to have our family and in one fell swoop, at just thirty-six, I would carry no more babies. Your dad was my rock, and while he tried to hide it, I always knew that his heart was as wrecked as mine.

We'd been home only six weeks, trying to adjust to having one empty bassinet and an extra car seat, stored away in the garage, seeing the hollow space next to Hope in the double stroller, when, one afternoon, the adoption agency that we had registered with two years earlier called. They had a baby girl who needed a home, and after hearing nothing about our application to adopt, while focusing on multiple IVF cycles, we couldn't believe this was happening, now.

Your social worker told us you'd been born just two days after Hope and Faith, and the first time I saw a photograph of you, I knew you were meant to be ours. There was something in your big, turquoise eyes that captured my injured heart. It was like you were speaking to me, telling me that you'd come to rescue us.

It took only days to get the initial legalities sorted out and then we came to meet you at your foster home, in Glasgow. Your daddy held Hope while I took you in my arms, your little hands in tight fists, and your rosy mouth so like Faith's that I could hardly breathe. I knew I was going to do everything in my power to be the mother you needed and deserved. Hope had lost her twin, and we our precious first-born, and here you were, a serendipitous angel. Our saving grace.

We called you April, after the month of your birth, and when you came home with us, we finally felt ready to begin our lives as the family we had always expected to be. You quickly became as precious to us as Hope, and we couldn't imagine life without you.

You two would lie next to one another, on the big soft blanket in the living room, two sets of tiny fingers entwined as you stared at each other, like you were seeing yourselves reflected in one another's eyes. It was as if Hope recognised you, and you her, and it filled me with such peace.

I would watch you both for hours, the sounds of your gurgling and gentle, milky hiccups making my eyes fill.

Each day that passed, I missed my Faith so much it ripped me open, but you were here, the second daughter – meant to be ours. You eased our pain, comforted Hope, and needed me as much as I needed you.

Little did we know what lay ahead for us all, but, for a while at least, we were truly happy.

1

EIGHT YEARS LATER

Catriona stood at the kitchen window of the cottage and watched as Hope and April trotted in circles around one another on the back lawn. They wore their matching red anoraks, their yellow wellingtons a splash of sunlight on the otherwise overcast March afternoon.

To the far left of the property, beyond the gentle slope of the garden, behind the long ridge of gold-topped gorse, and the wooden fence that Duncan had installed when they'd moved in, the River Carron burbled. The brisk north wind was pulling up white peaks that arched away with the current as the river tumbled alongside the edge of the garden, then tipped into Loch Carron, the glistening body of water that lay directly in front of the house. The loch was dotted with tiny islands that added perspective to the ethereal beauty of the scene.

In the distance, beyond Lochs Carron and Kishorn, was the outline of the magnificent Cuillins, on the Isle of Skye, the amber-coloured slopes sweeping up to the towering, often snow-topped mountain peaks. To the right was the rugged profile of the Applecross peninsula, and Beinn

Bhàn, dominating the horizon, its purple-tinged summit shrouded in a misty shawl. The surrounding low coastal moorland, dotted with small crofts, sheltered bays and coral beaches, provided the most stunning scenery in the western Highlands.

As this breathtaking panorama glittered before Catriona's eyes, it reminded her of why they'd bought the cottage, eleven years earlier. Whenever she took it all in, she never failed to marvel at the magnificent landscape that hugged their home.

Outside, a cluster of noisy sea birds banked overhead as the wind whipped the girls' long hair around their flushed faces – Hope's a lustrous auburn, the same shade as Catriona's, and April's a rich chestnut. As her hair flew away from her face, April's widow's peak caught Catriona's eye, the distinctive V-shaped hairline that had developed soon after April's hair had begun to thicken.

As her daughters darted around, Catriona smiled to herself, the scene a gift of joy that she never took for granted. The pain of losing little Faith was as fresh now as it had been eight years earlier, and the only memento Catriona had, a soft pink hat that her baby had worn for only moments, lay wrapped in white tissue paper, tucked inside a shoebox at the back of the wardrobe in the master bedroom.

Every 30 March, Catriona would wait until Duncan had gone downstairs, then she'd unwrap the tiny hat, hold it up to her face and inhale, searching for any hint of the sweet baby girl who'd come into her life and then left, in what seemed like an instant. Then she'd pack the hat away, drag a brush through her long mane and wipe her sky-blue eyes before heading downstairs.

Duncan always knew what she'd been doing, and his

chocolatey eyes would glitter as he pulled her into a hug, his long arms circling her back as he whispered, 'You OK?' She'd nod, rise onto tiptoe to kiss him and run her fingers through his unruly dark hair. She'd then turn to her daughters and say, brightly, 'Right. Who's for pancakes?'

Snapping her back to the moment, the girls both squealed in delight as Hope caught up to April and grabbed her sleeve. 'You're it.' Hope threw her head back. 'Catch *me*, now.'

April spread her arms wide. 'Ready? Here I come.' She launched herself towards her sister, her toe catching in the grass, sending her crashing to the ground, face first.

Catriona instantly stiffened, then relaxed as she saw April lift her head, laughing into the wind as Hope rushed over and hauled her to her feet, then bent down and gently brushed the grass from her sister's knees.

Catriona couldn't hear what the girls were saying, but April was nodding as Hope straightened her coat for her, then they were off and running again. Their voices were high-pitched, transported by the breeze, as they raced across the lawn, one beautiful creature after the other, both halves of Catriona's heart, on the move.

Suddenly, April gave a joyful shriek that made Catriona wince, and she instantly cast her eyes to the conservatory, on her left, where Duncan was working.

They had added the glass-sided room to the back of the stone cottage when the girls were four. It had been intended as a playroom but had soon become Duncan's de facto office whenever he was home. It had a vaulted ceiling, a brick floor, and rows of low shelving under each of the wide windows that sat either side of French doors leading to the garden. The shelves were full of books on town planning, and photographic journals of suspension bridges, and ingenious construction projects from around the world. The girls would sometimes wander in there to read or play snap at the desk that sat in front of the window by the door, the stunning views across the loch simply a background to the devoted sisters, heads down as they lost themselves in their games.

Catriona used the conservatory for her lessons, the light in the room having a particular golden glow that she looked forward to, as the afternoons came around. She had started language tutoring when the girls turned six. Her aptitude for languages had first come to light while she and her parents were living in Gibraltar. At the age of five, she had picked up Spanish in under two months, and as her father was transferred to a new naval base, so she would soak in another language, chattering like a native and making her parents proud. She loved to speak French, Spanish or German, whenever she had the opportunity, and teaching had felt like a natural way of passing on her passion.

The west-facing conservatory offered the perfect spot to enjoy the spectacular sunsets over the loch. Catriona and Duncan would often linger in there of an evening. They'd sit close together on the narrow, wicker sofa along the back wall, their fingers entwined as they sipped their wine and listened for the girls, upstairs in their room.

Now, seeing Duncan's head snap up from his monitor, Catriona leaned forward and knocked on the window. Hope turned to face the house, her cheeks flushed and her glossy hair flying wildly in the wind, a sight of such beauty that Catriona momentarily held her breath. Having had a hand in creating this child, this luminous creature, was without doubt her greatest accomplishment.

Holding Hope's gaze, Catriona pressed her index finger to her lips and smiled behind it. Understanding,

Hope's shoulders came up towards her ears as she pulled a 'sorry' face, then she grabbed April's arm as she dashed past her, pulling her sister into her side and speaking close to April's ear. April turned towards the window and grimaced before her face melted into a grin, and then, in identical motions, both girls covered their mouths with their hands and tiptoed theatrically away towards the bottom of the garden.

Catriona laughed softly as, startling her, Duncan's arms circled her waist from behind. 'God, she's got a voice like a banshee, that one.' He dropped his chin into the soft flesh of Catriona's shoulder, and she caught a whiff of coffee on his breath. 'What a racket.'

Catriona set the kettle on the counter and switched it on, his tendency to immediately put April in the firing line irritating her. 'They're just as noisy as each other, you know.' She eased herself out of his arms. 'Partners in crime.'

Seeming to catch the slight correction in her words, Duncan stepped back and shoved his hands into his pockets. His dark flannel shirt was snug around his firm torso, his face and forearms slightly tanned from weekends working outside on the shabby wooden boat he was restoring, down in the ramshackle boathouse. The fine hairs on his arms matched the darkness of his head, and as Catriona focused on his broad wrists, the urge to touch him was, as always, overwhelming.

'Did you tell them to stay away from the riverbank?' Duncan frowned. 'I still need to fix that section of fence.'

'They know not to go down there.' Catriona rolled her eyes. 'I tell them every time they go outside.'

'Good.' He nodded, raking his fingers through his hair. 'They're always hanging about over there, trying to spot otters and seals.'

'They don't go near the bank, Duncan. I've told them clearly that it's not safe.'

'Aye, but do they listen?'

Wanting to divert the conversation away from yet another argument over his belief that she allowed their daughters to run feral, at times, Catriona smiled at him. 'Want a sandwich, McGrumpy? I'm making one for the girls anyway.' She pulled some cheese and a tomato from the fridge and set them on the wooden-topped island that separated the kitchen from the dining area. Above her head, her prized collection of copper pots hung from an antique laundry rack that Duncan had installed, and fragrant bunches of lavender and herbs from the garden were drying between the gleaming pots.

'Yes, please.' Suppressing a smile at the name she'd called him, Duncan rounded the island.

'How's work going, love?' Catriona sliced some of the nutty-flavoured Orkney cheddar he loved. 'Getting much done?' She stroked his arm as she slipped past him.

'Yeah, it's fine. I've got to get the plans for the new bridge through to the architect by the end of the day. Shouldn't be a problem.' He shrugged.

His work as a civil engineer had always fascinated Catriona, and when they'd met at university in Glasgow – he in his final year and she in her first, studying languages – their connection had grown slowly from friendship to something more. There had been an instant physical attraction, but Catriona had found him moody, apt to leave her unsure of which version of Duncan she'd be meeting that day. As they had got to know each other better, she had rationalised his behaviour as a symptom of his singular focus and profound intelligence, and before long it had become part of them, as a couple, as much as the love they shared for one another.

He walked over to the long farmhouse table – where they ate dinner as a family, every evening when he was home – pulled out a chair and sat down, dragging the local newspaper in front of him. 'If I get really stuck in, I might have the boat ready for the regatta this year.' He flipped the page.

The village of Plockton, with its picturesque harbour and pretty, stone terraced houses and high street, held an annual regatta for the members of the sailing club. Twelve days of races, concerts and special events culminated in a huge street party, followed by singing and dancing in Harbour Street, as local bands entertained the crowd with traditional music. Duncan had never participated in the races before, but he was a keen novice sailor, and after spending more than a year restoring the old boat, he'd told her he intended on joining the sailing club as soon as it was finished.

'That'd be great.' She nodded, slicing through the sandwich, and putting it on a plate. 'When do you leave for Singapore?' She walked over and set the plate in front of him.

Duncan's frequent business travel had often caused tension between them, especially when the girls were younger, but now they had all grown into the pattern of their lives, accustomed to his absences, and Catriona reasoned that it had helped them appreciate their time together more. The girls would enjoy the additional freedom Catriona allowed them when he was away, while they counted off the days until he came home, anticipating the exciting gifts he'd bring them from India, Dubai, or Rome.

'In ten days.'

'Oh, good. You'll be here for the girls' birthdays, then.' She smiled.

'Yep. I'll be meeting the development group out there, about the marina project.' He took a bite of the sandwich, his elbows propped on the table. 'They seem like a decent lot.' He nodded to himself. 'Anything coming up for the girls while I'm away?' He looked over at the window.

Catriona assembled another two sandwiches. 'Not much. They've got a school outing to Dunvegan Castle, and there's Brownies, of course.' She smiled. 'There are badges coming up for something or other. I forget what.'

'You're mother-of-the-year, right enough.' Duncan laughed, stuffing the remainder of half of his sandwich into his mouth.

'Hey, watch it.' Her eyebrows jumped. 'Who's the one who disappears all the time and leaves good old mother-of-the-year to deal with everything?' She widened her eyes as he grinned and held his hands up in submission. 'Yeah, I thought so.' She laughed softly as she turned and walked to the back door.

Outside, the wind was brisk, carrying the tang of the loch, mixed with the heady fragrance of the rosemary bushes she had planted at the start of the path that led to the edge of the water. Catriona pulled her cardigan closer round her slender frame and scanned the garden, looking for the girls. Hearing April shouting, she turned left and followed the slate path to the lawn at the side of the house.

The girls were crouched down, heads close together, looking at something on the grass.

Curious, Catriona crossed the lawn and leaned over them. 'What've you got there?' She gathered the hair that had blown across her face, tying it up into a ponytail with the band that permanently resided around her wrist, then laid her palm on Hope's back.

'It's an egg.' Hope looked up at her, the sky-blue eyes, identical to Catriona's, full of concern. 'How did it get here, in the middle of the grass?' She held her palm up.

April had knelt down and was reaching out to touch the little blue egg, when Hope spotted the movement. 'Don't touch it, April. If you touch it, the mother won't want it.' She huffed.

Catriona marvelled at the nugget of knowledge, wondering where Hope had picked it up, but Catriona also felt the sting that Hope's rebuke had caused in April, who snatched her hand back and dropped her head. 'It's all right, sweetheart.' Catriona put her finger under April's chin and lifted it, seeking the soulful turquoise eyes. 'If it was in a nest, it'd be best not to touch it, but I don't think this wee egg is going to make it now, anyway.' She turned to Hope who was frowning.

'Why not?'

'Because it's likely that another bird stole it from the nest and then dropped it. I think that would have damaged it. Plus, we don't know how long it's been here, in the cold.' She tucked a strand of hair behind Hope's ear. 'Come inside now, your lunch is ready.'

'But it's not even broken.' Hope hunkered closer to the egg, her wellingtons like two yellow chevrons against the lush green lawn.

April stood up, the wind lifting her hair in a veil behind her. 'Can we save it, Mummy? Maybe put it in a box and see if it hatches?' She eyed Catriona hopefully.

'Yeah, we could have it our room, then we can take care of it,' Hope chimed in, standing up, moving over next to her sister, then gently taking April's hand.

Smiling again, April gazed at Hope with such adoration that Catriona's throat narrowed.

'It won't hatch, my loves. I'm sorry.' She held her hands out to them both. 'But, if you like, we can put it in a little box and leave it in the conservatory for a while.'

The girls looked at one another, their eyes locked, and, as often happened, Catriona sensed that they were communicating without the need for words.

Then, Hope turned to her and nodded. 'OK, but promise we can keep it?'

Catriona nodded. 'Yes, you may. Now come inside and have your lunch. Maybe you can sit with your dad for a bit before he starts working again.'

The girls each slipped a chilly hand into hers and they crossed the lawn together. Then, lining up, one behind the other, they played hopscotch along the path to the back door.

Inside, enjoying the wave of warmth that greeted them, Catriona hung the girls' anoraks on the wooden hooks behind the back door and ushered them to the kitchen table.

Duncan had set his plate in the sink and was already back at his desk, the conservatory door firmly shut.

Sighing, Catriona put a sandwich in front of each child and filled two glasses with milk. 'Eat up and maybe we'll go into the village later.' She nodded towards the window. 'If the rain holds off.'

'What about the egg?' Hope spoke around a mouthful of bread. 'We need to rescue it.' Her earnest tone touched Catriona. When Hope was passionate about something, it absorbed her entirely, a quality that Catriona admired in her daughter.

'Right. I'll go and get it now.' She pulled her jacket from the hook. 'Stay here and eat, and keep the noise down, OK?'

Hope took only a moment to register, then grinned, her milky moustache turning up at the corners. 'You mean, keep the noise down, *April*.' She turned to her sister, who had just taken a giant bite of her sandwich.

'Hey. You're loud too,' April pouted, then stuck her tongue out, exposing a messy mush of bread and cheese.

'Ewww, you're so gross.' Hope giggled as April leaned closer to her, the sloppy mouthful balanced precariously on her tongue.

'That's enough, you horrible creatures.' Catriona fought a smile as she shook her head at them. 'Seriously, April, enough.'

The tiny robin's egg lay nestled on a bed of cotton wool inside an old soap carton they'd torn the top off, and Catriona had placed it on a bookshelf, close to the window in the conservatory. Having had their bath, she'd let the girls come downstairs for a while to check on their treasure before they went to bed, and in their bumblebee pyjamas and fluffy slippers, each with their hair in a tidy plait, they were now hovering over the egg, whispering to one another.

Duncan was in the conservatory with them, but hung back, standing close to the door, his eyes glued to the dim glow of the monitor on his desk across the room.

In the kitchen, Catriona's back was aching from lugging a pile of logs in and stacking them by the fire in the living room, and she was looking forward to a long soak in the bath. She and Duncan had enjoyed making some changes to the cottage when they'd moved in, a kitchen renovation being their first priority. They'd taken down a wall between two small rooms to create the airy kitchen/dining-room and had chosen stainless-steel appliances and ivory-coloured cabinets to complement the existing flagstone floor. Duncan had suggested adding a wider window, above the sink, to maximise on the view and add to the brightness of the space, and Catriona loved to see the morning light spear through the glass, dancing off the surfaces, as she started her day.

Behind the kitchen, the living room spanned the length of the cottage, with two sofas at one end, flanking the fire. The front hall split the room neatly in two and, at the opposite end, the old piano that Catriona's parents, Iris and Will, had given them when they'd moved in stood against the wall. It badly needed tuning and had rarely been played in all the time they'd lived here, but when Duncan suggested they get rid of it, Catriona had insisted they hold on to it in case one of the girls, or maybe even she, took lessons someday. Duncan could play three or four tunes badly, and when he was in the right mood, he'd sit on the cracked leather stool, with Hope and April either side of him, and make them laugh as he pretended to be a concert pianist, exaggerating his movements, flicking his hair theatrically as he banged out 'Chopsticks' or 'Three Blind Mice'.

Upstairs, the master bedroom – a bright room with two dormer windows overlooking the loch – had a compact en-suite bathroom that they'd designed around the clawfoot tub that Catriona had always dreamed of.

Opposite the master on the left, and next to the small bedroom that had been the nursery, was the girls' bedroom, overlooking the side of the house, with a view of the river. They slept in a set of bunk beds, under a gossamer, tent-like drape that was covered in tiny fluorescent sequins that glowed when the lights went out. They would take turns sleeping on the top bunk, until they turned six, when Hope had volubly decided that she would stay up there now, as she didn't want April to fall out, despite the safety bar that Duncan had installed. Catriona had asked April if she minded, and she had smiled shyly and said, 'No. Hope can have it.'

April's devotion to Hope was such that she'd have given up anything, and gladly, if it made her sister happy. While Catriona loved her for that, she sometimes worried that April gave in too easily to the more forceful Hope. This dynamic had begun when they were small children, in nursery school, when Hope had assumed the role of protector of her quiet and sometimes fearful sister, one day telling a bossy child that he needed to leave April alone or she'd wallop him.

Catriona would observe her daughters, and how they interacted, marvelling at Hope's obvious sense that April needed looking after. April did, in truth, hang back in company, keep herself to herself and defer to Hope, most of the time, but April was a happy child, seemingly content to be the wing-person to her heroine.

Snapping her out of her reverie, Duncan walked into the kitchen, his long arms stretching above his head. His shirt rose above the waist of his jeans, revealing a strip of smooth skin. 'I'm done in. Aren't they going to bed?'

Catriona skirted the island and switched off the overhead light, leaving only the moonlight, bouncing off the loch, illuminating the room. 'How about you put them to bed, tonight? They'd love it.' She eyed him in the dim light, waiting for him to find a reason why it would be better if *she* did bedtime duty, as he usually did.

'Why don't you do it, and I'll pour us a drink?' He took her hand and pulled her close to his chest. 'Shall we light the fire?'

Catriona leaned into him, the faint scent of soap mixing

with his warm breath as she wrapped her arms around his middle. The familiar tinge of disappointment filtered through her at him hovering on the outside of the girls' routine, like a visitor, or a beloved uncle, rather than a fully engaged father. She looked up at him. 'You should spend more time with them when you're home. These moments are precious, Duncan. Soon they won't care if we put them to bed or play a game with them.' She looked up at him. 'But for now, it means everything.'

He met her gaze, a familiar reticence lurking behind his eyes. 'I will. I'm just tired tonight.' He kissed her lightly on the forehead and moved away, leaving her feeling disappointingly alone.

2

Catriona and Duncan sat side by side, in the living room, their feet mingling on the low, cherry-wood coffee table, and two glasses of amber-coloured cognac glinting in the fire-light. The girls were up in their beds, Catriona having read them a story, and now Jonny Lang's gritty voice filled the silence around them as they stared into the flames, together and yet separated by their thoughts.

With the weekend almost over, and thinking through the busy week ahead, Catriona lifted her glass and sipped the smoky cognac, relishing the slow burn of the swallow. Reluctant to crack the comfortable veneer of the evening, she rolled her shoulders back and sighed.

'What's up?' Duncan reached for his glass. 'I know that sound.' He slumped back against the cushion and took her free hand in his.

Catriona took a moment to edit her thoughts. Duncan was an intelligent, hard-working man, who loved her, and his daughters, but there was something lacking in his ability to sense a mood, read a room, the way Catriona did. He would lose himself in whatever he was interested in to such an extent that everything else was considered a distraction, or simply an annoyance. It could be his work, that had become all-consuming of late, or even working on the boat, and this pattern had become a familiar bone of contention between them.

As Catriona mulled it over, not for the first time, she recognised parallel behaviour developing in Hope. With her daughter, she put it down to her being bright and passionate, but in her husband, she saw it as an emotional failing, and the realisation was uncomfortable. 'I just wish you could appreciate the girls while they're young. They adore you – worship you, actually – and I feel that sometimes you don't make enough room for them in your life.' She tucked one leg under her and turned to face him. 'We fought so hard to have them, to make a family, I just don't want you to wake up one day and find that they've left you behind. You'll regret it, Duncan.'

He slumped lower in the seat, releasing her hand. His profile was sullen as he stared ahead, his thick hair feathering over his ear and his jaw twitching as if he was chewing on his next statement, softening it enough to share it. 'I'm not you, Cat. I've never been that way with them.' He blinked, lifting his glass up under his nose. 'I try, but it doesn't come as naturally to me, especially with April.' He paused, as Catriona's heart contracted. To hear him say it out loud, give voice to her mounting observations over the years, was painful. 'She's so timid and hard to get sometimes. Hope is just Hope. In your face, and full of life.' He turned to her, his brow creasing. 'Maybe it's just down to genetics, or chemistry, plain and simple?'

Catriona leaned forward and set her glass on the table, her face flushed and her pulse quickening. She knew he wasn't callous, or uncaring, but his last statement left her raw inside. 'We can't pick and choose when we want to parent them, Duncan. We *are* their parents, through thick and thin, regardless of the circumstances of their birth. If you choose not to be part of that, all the time, with *both* of them, I don't know what's ahead for us.' She pushed herself up from the sofa and stood in front of the fire, suddenly needing to feel the warmth of the flames, grounding her in this increasingly unsettling conversation.

Duncan sat upright, as if her words had sent a spark through him. 'What does that mean?' He frowned.

She raked her hair away from her face and focused on his dark eyes. 'Honestly? Sometimes I feel alone in bringing them up.' She forced a swallow, her eyes prickling. 'Even when you're here, you're not fully here.' She paused. 'This is what we both wanted and yet ever since we brought them home, you've gradually stepped back, like you're easing yourself out of this family.' A tear forced its way over her lower lid, and she swiped it away. 'I didn't ever think I'd be saying this to you, but are we what you want?' She pointed at the ceiling, her eyes stinging as a large log shifted in the pile of embers and a tiny twist of smoke filtered up the chimney.

Duncan's eyes widened and he stood up, his glass dangling at his side and some cognac sloshing onto the rug. 'Of course you are.' He walked towards her. 'How can you ask me that?'

Catriona held her palm up, not wanting his touch to dissolve her determination to have this out, once and for all. 'Because sometimes you make me feel, *us* feel, that we're getting in the way of something more important.' She scanned his face. 'Are we, Duncan?'

He set his glass on the broad mantel and, before she could resist again, he drew her into his chest. His arms were around her, his hands firm on the small of her back, and his face dipped into the curve of her neck. 'Of course you're not getting in the way. I'm sorry if I made you feel that way.' He paused. 'I'll be more present, and I'll try harder with April.' His breath was warm on her collarbone. 'I don't know what's wrong with me. They're great kids, and I love them both.'

At this, Catriona gently pushed back from him. 'Yes, they are, and you need to make sure they *both* know that you feel that way. Don't forget, they still don't know there's any difference between them, and the way you treat them needs to reflect that.' She laid her palm on his chest. 'Promise me, Duncan. This is serious.'

He covered her hand with his own, his eyes glistening in the firelight. 'I promise.'

When the girls had turned seven, the subject of April's adoption had come up again, as Catriona and Duncan were consistently on different pages about when to tell the girls the truth. Catriona had thought it was important to wait until they were at least eight or nine, before they tried to explain the magical way that April had come to be their daughter. Duncan, on the other hand, had felt that the sooner they told her the better, as it would then become less of an issue. They'd argued numerous times, but Catriona had persuaded him to wait, and while dubious about the decision, Duncan had agreed.

Now, as she felt her husband's steady heartbeat through his shirt, Catriona questioned her decision – her having made them hold back perhaps contributing in some way to Duncan, in turn, holding back from April.

Shoving down the self-doubt, she stepped forward and circled his neck with her arms, letting her cheek settle on his chest. 'I love you, Duncan. I know you have a lot on your plate, with work and all the travel, but this is our family.' She closed her eyes. 'We'll both make mistakes, that's guaranteed, but as long as we're in it together, we'll be OK.'

He hugged her tightly. 'I know, Cat. I'm here. I'm right here.'

Three days later, back into the routine of the week, the girls had gulped down their breakfast and got their school bags ready, while Catriona took one last sip of hot coffee, before bundling them into the Land Rover.

The spring morning was bright and clear, and the smell of seaweed lingered on the dewy breeze. The sky was a vivid blue over the loch, with a few straggly clouds stretching away across the water, a thicker collar shrouding the distant peaks of the Cuillins.

Catriona planned on dropping the girls at school, heading to the village hall for her tai chi class, then home via the shop. As it was Wednesday, the butcher's van would be in the village, so she could pick up a leg of local lamb – Duncan's favourite – for their dinner. She also wanted to go to the pier and buy some fresh fish for the weekend. The boats came in around 3 p.m., so once she'd picked up the girls from school, she would take them with her.

Her friend Mungo had promised to save her some fresh haddock from his catch, and Catriona looked forward to seeing the old duffer each week. He was an archetypal, salty seadog with his own tankard lodged behind the bar in the Harbour Arms and a laugh that could strip wallpaper, as Catriona's mother would say. Mungo's face was deeply tanned, and he had bright blue eyes, a bulbous nose, a mass of silver hair and one missing pinkie that, more than once, he'd told the girls was taken from him by a shark. Catriona knew that, in fact, he'd lost it to a stray wire on a lobster boat when he was a novice, but she'd never spoiled his fun by telling the girls the truth, their wide eyes and rapt expressions enough of a reward for keeping Mungo's secret safe.

Catriona also had one tutoring session booked for 5 p.m. that evening, with a local boy who was struggling with his French Higher. Duncan had gone into the Fort William office to work and wouldn't be back until around 6.30 p.m., so she'd have plenty of time to get everything done before they could all sit together at the table and enjoy some family time.

Behind her, in their car seats, Hope and April were murdering 'Let It Go', from *Frozen*. Their forced drama and the exaggerated hand gestures that Catriona caught flashes of in the rear-view mirror were hilarious. 'You two should be on the stage.' She laughed at their flushed faces, as she turned the car onto Innes Road.

The primary school stood ahead of them, a pretty sandstone building with a peaked porch over the front door, a gabled slate roof and stone arches over a line of curved windows, like a row of honey-coloured eyebrows above the glistening glass. The tall chimney on one side always made Catriona smile, as she pictured a group of Dickensian children gathered around a crackling fire, while their teacher read to them by candlelight.

She pulled up in front of the building. 'Right, you two. Are you ready?'

Hope unclipped her seat belt, then, before her sister could do it herself, reached over and undid April's. 'Yep.' She beamed. 'It's Gaelic today.' She shouldered the door open as Catriona rounded the car and helped them both out. Hope's enjoyment of learning another language was a joy – the reflection of Catriona's own talent a gift in itself, and a reminder of their connectedness.

'Good. You can teach me what you learn when you get home.' Catriona adjusted April's backpack, gently loosening the hair that was trapped under the straps on her shoulders.

'Can we have macaroni and cheese for tea?' April smiled up at her, her cheeks pinking in the chilly breeze.

'I'm making Dad's favourite tonight, roast lamb, but we can have mac and cheese tomorrow, love, OK?'

April pouted theatrically. 'OK.'

Hope grunted behind her. 'I don't want to eat a baby lamb.' She grimaced.

Taken aback, Catriona's eyebrows jumped. 'We have it all the time, sweetheart. Don't you like it anymore?'

Hope shook her head violently. 'No, because it's cruel.'

This new objection caught Catriona off guard. While she didn't want to quash her daughter's sensibilities or suggest she shouldn't have a conscience or an opinion about eating meat, the thought of trying to accommodate a vegetarian eight-year-old was daunting.

She pulled Hope's anorak closer around her front and smiled down at her daughter. 'We can talk about it later, all right?'

Hope looked dubious, her cheeks puffing out as she eyed her mother. 'OK.'

Next to her, April had slipped her hand into Hope's. 'I don't want to eat lambs either.' She stuck her narrow chin out, her eyes on Hope's profile. 'It's cruel.'

Catriona lifted her eyes to the sky, took a breath and then gently turned her daughters around, to face the school gate. 'Off you both go. Have a lovely day, and I'll see you this afternoon.'

The girls waved over their shoulders as they walked into

the playground, hands still linked, and their heads tipped towards each other. Smiling, Catriona jumped back into the car.

She loved their village, with its breathtaking views of Loch Carron, the small but lively centre, with rows of sandstone cottages and characterful stores she frequented almost daily. She particularly loved the gentle curve of Harbour Street, lined with pretty, terraced homes overlooking the water. Each had a compact but lush garden across the road, sitting between the street and the sea wall, and the patchwork of bright lawns cast a perfect contrast to the deep blue of the water beyond.

Thanks to the North Atlantic Drift flowing into Loch Carron, Plockton's climate was relatively mild, and the sheltered bay created a perfect environment for the New Zealand cabbage palm trees that grew around the harbour. As they stood, comfortably surrounded by waxy rhododendrons, pink magnolias and clematis vines, rows of dense green hostas and banks of fragrant roses and camellias, the combination gave Plockton a subtropical appearance that drew a good number of visitors in the warmer weather. The community that had once relied on fishing and crofting now had a healthy flow of tourists, and the bay had become a haven for visiting yachts in the summer, the regatta being a major attraction.

As she drove along Harbour Street, stopping to let an elderly lady cross and go into the local shop, ahead of her Catriona spotted the village hall, a handful of cars filling the compact car park. Her weekly tai chi class had become a ritual that she rarely missed, and she would breathe away her over-occupied mind as she enjoyed the gentle combination of movements.

As she parked next to a battered old bicycle, its front

tyre wedged in the metal bike-stand, Catriona's phone rang. Dragging it from her bag, she saw Duncan's name on the screen. He rarely called her during the day, so, frowning, she put the phone to her ear. 'Hey, what's wrong?'

Duncan made a huffing sound. 'Does there have to be something wrong?'

'Well, you never call me in the day unless your hair is on fire, so...' She halted. 'What's going on?'

'I've had a call from Singapore. They want to bring the meeting forward.' He paused. 'I need to leave on Friday.'

Catriona felt the familiar suck of loss that always accompanied his imminent departure on a business trip. 'Oh, right.' She watched two tracksuit-clad women walk across the car park, heading for the door of the village hall. One tall, the other shorter, their shoulders bumped as they both laughed, the joyful sound carrying towards her on the quickening breeze. 'So, you'll miss both the girls' birthdays?' She frowned.

'Yes, sorry. There's nothing I can do, love. Stewart is rebooking our tickets as we speak.'

Stewart Dunn was a friend and colleague of Duncan's. A soft-spoken, gentle giant of a man whom Duncan had known since university.

'Well, we'll just have to celebrate without you.' Catriona sighed as she twisted the rear-view mirror towards her and dragged her hair back into a ponytail. She wound the ever-present elastic band from her wrist around the fistful of hair, this one having once held a bag of new potatoes closed.

'Sorry, I know you hate when plans change,' he said. 'But the sooner I go, the sooner I'll be back.'

She shook her head at his customary platitude, lifting her bag from the passenger seat. 'True enough.' She opened the door. 'I've got to go, Duncan. Class starts in a minute.'

She slid out of the car, noticing the newly installed layer of tarmac and crisp white lines delineating the parking spaces.

'Cat, are you OK?' He sounded concerned.

Pushing down her rising frustration, Catriona locked the car and walked towards the hall. Their lives revolved around Duncan's work. It was the way it was, and the way it had always been, but as the years went by, and she felt increasingly abandoned, Catriona was becoming less inclined to wave it off as an unfortunate necessity. Just once, she'd have liked him to say no to an unreasonable request, or a last-minute change that left her juggling all her own commitments in order to cope with everything at home, by herself. 'I'm fine. I'm just going to be late for class. Let's talk about it tonight.' She rested her hand on the wooden door, seeing the group of students gathering at the back of the hall, near the raised stage.

'OK, fine then,' he huffed. 'See you later.'

'Bye.' Catriona slipped her phone into her bag and pushed through the door, where the other women had already begun taking their places.

Tightening her ponytail, Catriona re-ran the conversation with Duncan. That he had to leave sooner was frustrating, but more than that, she was annoyed at herself for simply complying, without so much as a complaint. Even as she tried to rationalise it, each time he chose work over family, the tiny crack that was forming between them grew a little wider, and Catriona was afraid to lean in or look too closely into the empty space that it was creating in her marriage.

3

The following morning, as Catriona and Duncan lay in their bed, the light beginning to seep in from behind the blinds, Hope tiptoed into the room. Registering her presence, but still half-asleep, Catriona lifted the duvet and opened her arms. Hope climbed in, rolled in to face her mother and draped her arm across Catriona's chest. 'Mum, I don't feel well,' she whispered. 'My tummy hurts.'

Catriona rubbed her eyes, adjusting to the dim light. 'What kind of hurt, love?'

'Grumbly, down here.' Hope shifted, laying her palm across her lower abdomen.

'Are you feeling sick?' As Catriona lightly pressed her palm to Hope's forehead, she suddenly registered what was happening. Having brought his departure forward, Duncan was planning on working from home today, then leaving for the airport first thing the following morning. Hope knew of this plan, and as Catriona felt the cool skin under her fingertips, she was certain that Hope was angling to stay home today, too. Catriona understood, wanting to cancel her own busy day to stay close by and grab a few moments here and there with her husband before he disappeared again. However, Hope had a test at school, and then Brownies that evening, when she and April would be qualifying for their badge in Zero Waste, something Catriona knew Hope was proud of. Shifting to face her daughter, Catriona tucked a long strand of hair behind Hope's ear. 'Are you sure it's not just because you want to stay at home, with Dad?' she whispered, scanning her daughter's face. 'Hope?'

'No.' Hope lowered her eyes and squirmed, her feet tangling in the duvet enough to tug it away from Duncan's shoulder, waking him up.

'Hey, what're you doing in here?' He smiled sleepily as Hope climbed over Catriona and wriggled in between them.

'I'm not very well,' she sighed, as Catriona, flipping over, caught Duncan's eye and shook her head slightly.

Catching on, Duncan nodded. 'Right, well we'd better take you to see the doctor, then.' He made to get up, but Hope grabbed his arm.

'No, Dad, I'm not that ill. Just a little sore, in my tummy.' She sat up and cupped her stomach. 'Can I be off school today?' Her eyes were wide, her lower lip protruding as her pyjamas stretched across her narrow middle, a jumble of bumblebees and dandelions lying under the curtain of auburn hair that had split over her shoulder.

'Hmm, I don't know. What do you think, Mum?' Duncan looked over at Catriona, a smile tugging at his mouth as he raked the mess of hair away from his forehead.

Catriona pushed herself up and rested her back against the padded headboard. 'I think you need to go to school, sweetheart. You've got a spelling test, and you don't want to miss Brownies, do you?' She took Hope's hand, feeling the softness of her daughter's skin under her fingertips.

'But my tummy hurts,' Hope whined. 'Honest it does.'

Duncan sought Catriona's eyes, his mouth dipping in a mock pout. 'What do you say, Mummy?'

Irritated at potentially being made the bad guy in this scenario, she frowned. 'If you're really not well, Hope, you need to stay in bed. No running around the house or playing outside. Do you understand?'

Hope nodded, her face brightening. 'I'll stay in bed.' She nodded again. 'Quiet as a mouse.'

At this, Duncan laughed, then straightened his face as soon as he saw Catriona's expression.

'It's not funny, Duncan.' She pushed the duvet away and stood up, the carpet soft between her toes. 'I have a full day today. I need to shop, and I have a dental appointment at eleven. Then I have two tutoring sessions this afternoon. Even if she stays here, I still have to take April to school and then Brownies, so I can't watch Hope.' She nodded at Hope, who had curled into Duncan's side, her small hand possessively gripping his forearm.

'I'll keep an eye on her.' He shrugged. 'She can sit in with me if she's quiet.' He looked down at his daughter, who was now grinning up at him, adoringly. 'You'll behave, right, Hopeful Mactiggiwinkle?' He hugged her close, making her giggle by using his pet name for her.

'I promise.'

Catriona pulled on her robe and shoved her feet into her slippers. 'Right, well, off back to bed, missy.' She pointed at the door. 'I'll bring you a drink and some milk of magnesia in a bit.'

At this, Hope's smile dimmed. 'Do I have to have that stuff?' She spoke to Duncan, who had also got up and was walking into the bathroom.

'It's up to Mum.' He turned to look at Catriona.

'Yes, you do. And I think as Dad is so keen to keep you here today that he should have a dose too. In case he catches what you've got.' She caught Hope's eye and winked. 'What do you think?'

Hope's face split into a mischievous grin. 'Yes, he should.'

Duncan turned and met Catriona's gaze, his dark eyes glittering. 'If Mum says so.'

'She does.' Catriona gave a single nod, then turned and walked into the hall, to find April padding towards her, her hair tousled and one fist grinding her eye.

'Where's Hope? I woke up and she wasn't there.'

Catriona bent and swept April up onto her hip, noting how much heavier she was of late, her legs feeling impossibly long, and her feet now almost reaching below Catriona's knee. 'She's got a tummy ache, darling. She's going to stay at home today.'

April circled Catriona's neck with her arms, her head nestling against Catriona's collarbone. 'Can I, too?'

Catriona carefully made her way down the stairs. 'No, love. You need to go to school.' In the kitchen, she sat April on her favourite chair at the table, then set about making breakfast.

'But if Hope is ill, maybe I should stay here to look after her?' April leaned forward and dropped her chin onto her forearms, her eyes following Catriona around the room.

Smiling, Catriona set a glass of orange juice in front of her daughter. 'Daddy and I will be here. Hope will be fine, sweetie.' She lifted both the Rice Krispies and Frosties boxes and shook them, wiggling her eyebrows. April pointed to the Rice Krispies, so Catriona filled a bowl for her, then sliced some banana on top. 'You can do your own milk. OK?'

She pushed the carton towards April, who sat up and nodded, and painstakingly poured some milk into the bowl, her rosy tongue clamped between her front teeth. The look of concentration was so sweet, so utterly endearing, that Catriona's heart flip-flopped. This child had such a gentle nature that it brought forth a fierce sense of protectiveness in Catriona, and seeing that same quality in Hope, and how she treated April, was wonderful to witness.

She pulled out a chair and sat next to April. 'You're such a good girl.' She ran her hand down the slender back, her fingers feeling the tiny bumps of the vertebrae, and for a split second, she forgot that she'd had no part in their formation. That April was not her birth child rarely surfaced in her mind, as, for Catriona, she was every inch as precious as Hope. 'I love you, sweetheart.'

April turned to look at her, her cheeks pulsing as she chewed. 'Love you too, Mummy.'

Overcome with gratitude at the glorious children she'd been gifted, Catriona's eyes began to burn, and not wanting April to notice, she grabbed yesterday's newspaper and began scanning the pages.

An hour later, Catriona had dropped April at school with her Brownie gear in her backpack. On the way to the shop, Catriona had called Karen, the Brownie unit leader whose daughter Sophie was in Hope and April's class at school, and who lived just along the road from them. She'd asked Karen if she could possibly take April to Brownies at the village hall after school, then drop her home, and Karen had been happy to help.

'Of course, Catriona. No problem at all. I'll drop her back around five, if that's OK? I have to pick up some bits and pieces of shopping on the way home, but it shouldn't delay us too much.'

'Thanks a million, Karen. My day is pretty hectic, with the usual stuff, and some tutoring this afternoon. It'd be a big help if I didn't have to go out again, as I have Hope off school today.' She'd pictured Hope as she'd left her, tucked up in bed with a book and a cup of weak tea.

'Oh, I hope she's OK?' Karen had sounded concerned.

'She's fine.' Catriona had tutted. 'A case of just wanting some extra Dad time, I think.'

Karen had laughed. 'Oh, right. Well, that happens, I suppose.'

Over the next three hours, Catriona had rushed about, shopped, dropped a stack of books back at the library, seen the dentist and dashed home to make lunch for Hope. When she walked into the kitchen, around noon, Hope was at the table eating a sandwich. 'So, you're feeling better then?' Catriona dumped the bags on the table and lifted her eyebrows at Hope, who blushed.

'Yes. Daddy made me some lunch and I'm going to sit in his office after and read a book.' She let her palm settle on an illustrated copy of *Alice in Wonderland* that Catriona's mother had given them as a gift, after they'd brought Hope home from the hospital. It had become a favourite of both the girls and, seeing the pretty cover, Catriona pictured the routine of her snuggling down, with one daughter under each arm, and reading to them in the bottom bunk.

'Right, well, that's good, my love.' She nodded. 'I'll make you a hot drink in a minute.'

Catriona began unpacking the bags and putting the shopping away. When she'd finished, a few moments later, she turned back to the table to see an empty plate, and Hope gone.

Glancing into the conservatory, she saw that Duncan was at his computer, his phone wedged under his jaw. Hope was curled up on the wicker sofa, the book in her lap and a blanket around her shoulders. Duncan's back was to her, but Catriona could see her daughter raise her head every few moments, as if making sure that he was still there.

Catriona made herself a coffee, then threw a load of laundry into the washing machine. Having little appetite, she skipped lunch and began preparing for her first student.

A young man named Mike, who needed help with his German course at college, had arrived on time, at 3 p.m. Duncan was taking a break for a while to give her the room and had walked down to the boathouse to check on his restoration project. He had taken Hope with him, despite Catriona saying that she really needed to stay indoors, but one pleading look from her daughter, and a disarmingly crooked smile from her husband, and she'd buckled, as always, allowing Hope to go if she put on her coat and wellingtons. 'She'll be fine, Cat.' He'd patted her arm. 'I'll keep an eye on her.'

'You'd better,' she'd warned. 'And, Hope, you stay close to your dad, OK? No wandering off.'

Hope had nodded, her face flushed as she'd slipped her hand into Duncan's as they'd headed for the door.

Now Mike had finished his lesson and was gathering his books, shoving them into a tattered backpack. 'Thanks, Mrs Anderson. You make it so much clearer than my teacher.' He nudged his dark-rimmed glasses further up his nose. His pilled Arran sweater had seen better days, and his dark jeans and walking boots looked as if he'd recently been mud-wrestling in them.

Catriona suppressed a smile as she put her notebooks back on the shelf she used in the conservatory, then followed him through the kitchen to the front door. 'You're really getting the hang of the conjugations, Mike. It's just a case of being consistent with your revision and making sure to memorise the exceptions.' She held the door open for him, waving to his mother who sat in her Golf, parked out on the road. 'See you next week?'

'Yeah, see you then.' Mike slung his backpack over his shoulder, shoved his lank blond hair from his forehead and trudged up the drive towards the car.

Back in the kitchen, Catriona checked the time. She had ten minutes before her next student, Olivia, arrived at 4.15 p.m. Olivia was a shy, lanky teenager with more piercings than Catriona would have been comfortable with for her own daughters. The child of one of Catriona's tai chi class cohorts, Olivia struggled with several of her high-school classes, and Catriona had been helping her with French. Olivia had an ear for the language, and Catriona had been encouraging her to read all her coursework and test questions out loud, which seemed to be helping.

Catriona calculated that there was still time to throw some chicken and vegetables into a pot. She was determined they would have a last family dinner before Duncan left on his trip, especially as he'd be missing the girls' birthdays the following week.

April was due back at 5 p.m., and as Catriona realised how little time she'd have alone with Duncan, after the girls had gone to bed, she felt the familiar tug at her core – the knowledge that she'd soon be looking over at an empty pillow, again. Sighing, she opened the fridge and began taking out the dinner ingredients.

. . .

Having waved Olivia off on her bike, Catriona walked back into the kitchen. The clock on the cooker said 5.15 p.m. and there was still no sign of Duncan and Hope coming back inside. Hope was still in her pyjamas under her coat, and annoyed that Duncan wouldn't have thought to bring her in already, Catriona turned towards the back door. Just as she was about to pull her jacket off the hook, a flash of a yellow wellington caught her eye, she presumed belonging to Hope, finally hightailing it inside. Relieved, Catriona turned back to the stove, and lifting the heavy lid off the pot, stirred the stew.

Next to her, her phone rang, so she dropped the spoon in the rest and answered it.

'Hi, Catriona, it's Karen. I just dropped April off and watched her run down the drive, but I wanted to make sure she got inside before I left.'

Catriona glanced at the window, realising that the flash of yellow she'd seen must've been April, after all. 'Oh, yes. I saw her in the garden, probably looking for her dad.' Catriona nodded to herself. 'Thanks for checking, Karen, and thanks again for dropping her off.'

'Pleasure. Chat soon, then.'

A few minutes later, puzzled as to why April hadn't come in to see her yet, and increasingly concerned that Hope and Duncan still hadn't come back inside, Catriona walked out to the conservatory. The light was dimming, the view of the loch fading into the soft purple of the gloaming, Catriona's favourite time of the evening. Shivering, she hugged herself as she scanned the garden, wondering where her family was, when a piercing scream tore through the twilight. It was a sound she would never forget. A sound that would haunt her for the rest of her days.

4

Catriona threw the French doors open and ran along the path to the damp lawn, feeling the moisture instantly permeate her thick socks. She squinted into the gloom, her pulse racing as she tried to locate the source of the series of frightening wails that were now coming consistently from her left. As she began running towards the river, she recognised April's voice, high-pitched and desperate. 'Hope. No. Come back. Hooooooope.'

Catriona's skin was instantly clammy, her breaths coming in sharp spurts as she raced across the grass to the side fence. As she reached the broken section, on the other side, she saw, to her horror, that April had slid down the bank and was wading into the river, her hair flying wildly behind her in the breeze as she screamed her sister's name, over and over.

On the bank, where the land had been crumbling away into the water, lay a single yellow wellington, wedged in the mud. Seeing it, Catriona felt as if the ground had given way underneath her. With her stomach heaving, she squeezed through the gap in the fence and bolted towards the river. Wading through the frigid, churning water, she reached for April, who was a foot or so away from her. Shouting April's name, Catriona's feet slid dangerously on the slick stones in the shallows. 'Come back, April. Come back here.' She screamed so loudly that the sound tore at the flesh of her throat.

Within moments, Duncan was sprinting towards them, the headphones that he wore when using the electric sander slung around his neck, and his hair ruffled by the quickening wind. 'Get her out, Cat,' he yelled, pointing at April, just as Catriona finally reached her daughter and clamped her hand around April's wrist.

As she began pulling April back to the bank, Duncan yanked off his boots and dived head first into the water. Shocked and confused, Catriona struggled to get April back on dry land, watching as her husband swam away from her, with the current. Suddenly, the broken pieces of the scene before her began to gather, forming a picture that was nothing less than a freakish nightmare. Duncan was swimming towards something, a dark shape bobbing in the water as it flowed quickly away from the house and out towards the loch.

As Catriona held a struggling April against her chest, the muddy bank sliding away under her feet, in the distance she saw an arm go up, a slender arm, a child's arm. Hope's arm.

'Nooooooo,' she screamed. 'Hooope.' Overcome by nausea, Catriona was beginning to lose her grip on the still struggling April. Mustering all her strength, she gave one final tug, landing them both in a heap on the drier, safer part of the bank.

April was wailing, a guttural keening that curdled

Catriona's blood. 'Let me go, Mummy. I can help her. Let me gooooo. Hoooooooope.'

Tears were coursing down April's cheeks, and Catriona began to tremble as she held her close. Locked together, they both stared out across the water, seeing Duncan's head bobbing up and down as he made progress towards Hope. As Catriona watched, the dark shape of her child went under the surface for a few, agonising seconds, then appeared again, the swift-moving water carrying her further away from her father.

Catriona held April tighter and rocked her in time with their breaths, their racing hearts close together under their sopping-wet clothes.

'Let me go.' April jerked away from her arms as, once again, to Catriona's horror, Hope's head went under the water. As she eventually surfaced again, Duncan seemed to be getting further away from her, despite his desperate strokes.

April's wails were now fading to white noise as, gripping her tightly, Catriona watched the ghastly scene in front of her unfold, her mouth open in a silent scream. Hope slid beneath the surface for a third time, the water closing over her head like a set of curtains hiding the players on a stage. 'Hoooope,' Catriona screamed as Duncan's hips came up above the surface and he dived under the water.

What seemed like minutes later, but was probably only a handful of seconds, he resurfaced, shook his head like a dog, then dived again. By this time, the pull of the current had carried him well out into the loch, the frothy river twisting into the stiller water that lay ahead of the house, the serene slice of nature that they all treasured so much now taking on a sinister pall.

Catriona couldn't breathe, her lungs collapsing in on

themselves as she continued to grasp April to her chest, the twosome rocking as their tears flowed, the wind chilling their damp cheeks. The light was almost gone as, finally, Catriona saw Duncan's head bobbing back towards the bank, a second dark head close to his jaw as he struggled against the current.

Her heart clattering in her chest, Catriona released her grip on April. 'You stay here, do you hear me?' She held April's shoulders as the child nodded. 'I'm going to help Daddy.' April's eyes were huge, her chin quivering as tears coated her ashen cheeks.

Catriona turned back to the river and ran to the edge, seeing Duncan drag Hope onto the mud and then collapse next to her. The bank was treacherous, giving way under Catriona as she tried to reach them, providing no purchase as she slid and then fell onto her side.

A few feet away from her, Duncan rolled onto his back, his chest heaving under his sweater. Hope lay next to him, her arm above her head, her face tipped towards the ground, her long hair matted and covering her pallid cheek like an eery doily. Panting, Catriona pulled herself to her knees and crawled towards her daughter.

Meanwhile, Duncan heaved himself up and immediately rolled Hope onto her back, moving the hair from her face with his muddy hand, leaving ugly streaks on the perfect skin of her cheek. As Catriona reached them, Duncan had his fingers in Hope's mouth, then he clamped his mouth over hers, and pinched her nose, forcing his breath into her. Catriona, on a reflex, began counting out loud as he then sat back and pumped Hope's little chest with the heels of his hands. 'One, two, three, four...'

'Check her pulse,' Duncan shouted at Catriona, whose

fingers were already searching for movement at Hope's slender wrist, and then her throat.

Feeling nothing, she shook her head. 'Oh, God. I can't find it.'

Duncan leaned forward and tried again. His broad back was arched over their daughter, her one bare foot lying motionless next to the other one, still in the remaining wellington, her pyjama bottoms tucked neatly inside it.

The last strand of control suddenly snapped inside Catriona, and she howled, 'Duncan, turn her on her side. Thump her back. For Christ's sake, do something.' She swiped at her eyes, getting mud in them as she grabbed Hope's coat and yanked at her.

'Not yet.' Duncan shoved her off, sending her back onto her bottom in the mud. 'She needs air.' He closed his mouth over Hope's once more and breathed into her lifeless form.

Unable to move, Catriona heard a ghastly sound, a disembodied wail. Behind her, April was curled into a ball on the bank, her mouth gaping into a horrific, distorted oval. Torn by the need to stay put, bring her beloved Hope back to life, and to go and gather April into her arms and comfort her, a creeping paralysis held Catriona to the spot.

The light was all but gone now. The glitter of a boat flickered far out in the distance, and the sounds of the encroaching night, and of a seabird's call, floated in across the loch, but all Catriona could hear was the huff of Duncan's breaths, leaving his body and entering her daughter's.

As her limbs began to shake uncontrollably, Duncan was pumping Hope's chest again, his fingers laced through each other. Seeing her daughter's ribs buckling under the pressure, Catriona grabbed Duncan's sweater and pulled him back to his heels. 'Stop, Duncan. You're hurting her.'

Her voice was rough, the words tasting like poison as she pressed her fingers into the clammy skin of Hope's neck. No matter how long she waited, or where she sought the pulse of life, nothing came. A pain that had no words adequate to describe it built in her chest, and Catriona knew, sickeningly, assuredly, that one of the brightest lights of her life, and her reasons for being, her beloved Hope, was gone.

The ambulance had taken Hope's body away, along with a stricken Duncan. He'd been speechless, wrapped in a silvery blanket and shaking, as the paramedic had helped him into the back. Two police cars still sat out on the road, their bright lights revolving silently above them, scarring the night sky with blood-red beams.

Catriona sat at the kitchen table, an untouched cup of sweet tea in front of her that one of the police officers had made. April, who'd finally cried herself to sleep, was wrapped in a blanket in her arms. Catriona's matted ponytail was plastered to her back and her jeans stuck to her thighs, thick clumps of mud having swamped her as she'd sat on the bank and cradled Hope to her chest, while Duncan called for help.

Now, as she stared at the dark rectangle of the kitchen window, it hurt to breathe, to blink or swallow, every reflex and sensation a reminder of things her sweet Hope would never feel again. Each sinew, tendon, muscle, and cell that worked to keep Catriona upright was screaming at her to move, to let go of April and allow the blood to flow back into her numb limbs, but she was afraid to. If she let go, she might never find her footing again.

. . .

Two hours later, Catriona saw headlights flash across the side lawn as a car pulled into the driveway. The thump of the door shook her from her drugged-like state, her arms now totally numb as she held her daughter, the two of them frozen in place. As she shifted painfully on the hard chair, April stirred, her eyelids lifting slightly, then, as Catriona held her breath, closing again and her breathing returning to the steady rhythm that spoke of sleep, of shelter from the pain that waking would bring.

Keys rattled in the door and then Duncan walked into the kitchen, his face pale and his jacket hanging off one shoulder. The wind that came in with him carried the musk of rosemary, the loch and something else Catriona couldn't place – something acrid. He dropped the keys on the table, shrugged off his jacket, dragged a chair out opposite her and sat down. 'Cat.' His face was ravaged, his eyes heavily hooded and his mouth drooping.

Unable to find her voice, or meet his gaze, Catriona simply nodded.

'Have you eaten anything?' He ran a hand through his tousled hair, his eyes flicking to the pot that stood on the stovetop.

Repulsion pulsed through Catriona, so cold and dangerous that it stole her breath from her. How could he possibly think about food? Her daughter was dead. Her sweet face bloated, her glorious hair a mass of twigs and slimy algae, her one bare foot...

Catriona closed her eyes. It was too much. She couldn't do this. Not again.

'Cat?' He stood up, the chair scraping loudly on the stone floor.

Catriona's face ached from hours of clenching her jaw, the pressure on her teeth the only thing preventing her mouth from gaping, keeping the wrenching wails that roiled inside her from filling the silent room.

Duncan crossed the kitchen and lifted the lid on the pot, the smell of rich chicken stew making Catriona's lip curl as she closed her eyes. The sight, or even the notion, of anything as normal as food was incomprehensible. When she opened her eyes, he was standing in front of her. 'Cat, I...' He crouched down, his face only inches from hers. 'I'm so...' His eyes filled as Catriona's arms finally gave way and April began to slip from her grasp.

'Take her, please.' She croaked. 'I can't hold her...'

Duncan stood up and gently lifted April from her arms, his eyes drilling into hers.

'Put her to bed, please.' Catriona stood up, her legs threatening to give way as she steadied herself against the table, blood coursing down towards her ice-cold toes.

Duncan nodded, hesitated for a moment, then turned towards the stairs.

Catriona walked to the sink, took an empty mug from the draining board and filled it with water, the cold mass that had been forming in her middle growing as she drank. She closed her eyes but, flooded with horrific images that tore the breath from her once again, she dropped her chin to her chest.

A few minutes later, Duncan came back into the room. As she turned to face him, Catriona felt the air around her thicken, as if she could not draw it in. She focused on his hooded eyes and forced her voice to work. 'Where were you, Duncan?' she whispered. 'What happened?'

'Cat, I...' Seeing her expression, he halted his progress towards her, his features seeming to crumble. 'I was working on the boat, with my headphones on. She was mucking about inside the boathouse, putting my tools back on the wall rack. Then she got bored and asked me to take her down to the river to look for seals.' His voice caught as Catriona felt her cheeks burning, even the sound of his voice making her skin prickle. 'I told her to wait a few more minutes, just until I was finished sanding.' He paused, his face contorting, his pain something that Catriona could muster no sympathy for. 'Then, when I turned around, she'd gone.' He dropped his chin, his mouth gaping as his hands went to the back of his head.

As the room began to spin, his voice fading, then booming inside her head as he got closer, she gripped the counter, then, as he reached for her, Catriona slipped into blissful darkness.

She felt his hands on her back as he carried her to the bed, and the sag of the mattress as he lowered her onto it. He dragged the chenille throw from the end of the bed and draped it over her. She began to shiver, mildly at first, and then violently, her face tacky with sweat as her fingers went numb, their tips growing icy.

'Catriona love, you need to breathe.'

His eyes were wide as she took in his face, the strained expression, the prominent jaw, the long nose, the heavy brows, and matted hair. All these elements made up the man she'd loved for nearly nineteen years, and yet now, something had shifted inside her. As she tried to decide what it was, cold realisation ripped the air from her. It wasn't that he had changed, it was that how she felt about him had. As she forced herself to breathe between the pulses of pain that were crushing her heart, she couldn't look at him anymore.

Rolling onto her side, she turned her back to him, trying

to banish his face and everything it signified from her mind. He had let her precious girl drown. He had taken his eyes off her. He had let this happen.

Seconds later, she sensed him rounding the bed. He sat on the edge and tentatively touched her hand. Her eyes shot open, and she held her palm up. 'Don't, Duncan.'

'What?' He looked stricken.

'I can't.' Her eyes filled once more, his features blurring. 'Just go, please.' She pulled her knees protectively up to her middle. 'I need to sleep.'

Duncan lingered on the edge of the bed, his breathing ragged, as she willed herself to slip into the darkness again, a place where she could not see, hear, or feel. The place where Hope now lingered, devoid of light, sensation, and of pain.

5

A week had passed since Hope's death and Catriona was operating in a fog. Nothing felt real as she circled the cottage, counting the hours until she could go back to bed. After another fitful sleep, she would wake in the morning, and it would take a few seconds for her to register that the nightmare was a reality. She'd curl up under the covers and stifle her sobs in her palm, while Duncan showered and thumped around in the bathroom.

He had been hovering around her, working solely from the house, his Singapore trip cancelled. He had managed all the formalities surrounding the police, the inquest, and the funeral arrangements. Catriona had let him, unable to absorb the sickening truth of what was going on.

The more present he was, the more Catriona retreated. She would sit out in the garden, take April walking in the hills around the house, or along the sea wall on Harbour Street. Mother and daughter would often end up out at the end of the old pier, letting the salty wind pluck at their coats as they huddled together, silently staring out at the choppy water and the majestic hills beyond.

Catriona and Duncan had barely been speaking to one another, as she was afraid that if she were to crack open, what might spill out could permanently damage them. Instead, she had focused her attention on April, who was in such visible pain that Catriona had begun sleeping on the top bunk, afraid to leave her alone at night.

April was having night terrors, waking up, eyes wide, and shouting for Hope. Catriona would cradle her, singing softly to her. As soon as she fell back to sleep, Catriona would climb up the narrow stepladder, adjust the pillow and curl up under the pony-printed duvet that still smelled of Hope. She would turn her face into the soft feathers and breathe slowly, in and out, each breath a reminder of everything she had lost.

Duncan would inevitably come in and check on them in the night, but Catriona could only hold her breath and feign sleep, waiting until he'd left the room to exhale and let the tears that were permanently waiting, come.

He still hadn't said he was sorry, and while he'd approached her several times, the words seeming to hang on the tip of his tongue, he'd never voiced it. Alongside her pain, anger was simmering inside her, constant and barely concealed. While it would fix nothing, change nothing, she wanted to hear the words – hear him admit that he'd done what he always did; let something else draw his focus, become more important than his daughter, his family. This time, the consequences had been more than bruised feelings, they had been life-changing and catastrophic, and perhaps, Catriona was afraid, unforgivable.

This morning – the eighth day without Hope – Catriona was making toast for April, who was in the living room watching Animal Planet on TV. She'd been eating like a bird, picking at whatever Catriona put in front of her, then pushing her plate away, her small frame seeming to be shrinking in front of Catriona's eyes.

As she spread some butter on the warm toast, Duncan came into the kitchen, his jacket on and a laptop case dangling from his hand. 'I've got to go into the office, today.' He stood still as she stared down at the buttery knife. 'Cat, did you hear me?' His voice had an edge to it that surprised her.

Her head snapping up, she met his gaze. 'I heard you.' Her eyes flashed.

His shoulders seemed to droop under the dark suede of his jacket, his hair hanging lankly over the back of the tipped-up collar. 'Just thought you'd want to know.' He glanced at the toast on the chopping board. For a second, Catriona wanted to offer it to him, knowing he had not had breakfast, but she didn't, her ability to be knowingly unkind to him new, and shocking.

As she let the sensation float up inside her, sympathy entered the mix, and as she watched him skirt the island, heading for the hall, she cleared her throat. 'Duncan.' He turned, a hopeful expression lighting his eyes. 'Take some fruit.' She pointed at the bowl, then went back to buttering the toast, watching him out of the corner of her eye. His face fell as he reached for an apple, his big hand seeming to dwarf the waxy green sphere.

'I'll be back around seven, so don't wait for me for dinner.' He shoved the apple into his pocket and took his keys from the metal hook at the back door.

Seeing his shoulders slumped, his head drooping forward, Catriona sighed. Lifting a banana from the bowl, she took a packet of crisps from the cupboard, tucked them into a brown paper bag and handed them to him. 'Here.'

His sagging eyes lifted at the edges as he accepted the

bag. 'Thanks, love.' He leaned in as if to kiss her, but Catriona moved back, just as April walked into the kitchen. She had been all but silent these past few days, sitting at the table with her mouth pressed tight and simply nodding or shaking her head if they asked her something. Catriona had been trying to coax her to talk about how she was feeling, but with no success.

'Where are you going, Dad?' Her feet were in her fluffy slippers, and her bumblebee pyjamas brought with them such a vivid picture of Hope, lying on the muddy bank, that Catriona's heart faltered.

'To work, April Mactiggiwinkle.' Duncan used her pet name, and hearing it, April smiled, an even rarer occurrence now than her speaking.

'Will you be home for tea?' She padded across the floor and held her arms up to him.

Catriona willed him to bend down, lift April up into his arms as he would have Hope. As Catriona watched, her chest tight, he hesitated, then reached out and cupped April's chin. 'I've got to go. See you tonight, though.' He bent down and kissed the top of her head. 'Be good for Mummy, OK?'

Disappointment flooding her, Catriona walked over and swung April up onto her hip. 'Don't forget Mum and Dad are arriving tonight.' She met his eyes, waiting for any sign of dissent.

'Right, I know.' He nodded. 'I'll see you later.' He gave her a sad smile and walked out the back door.

Catriona hitched April higher up on her hip, taking in the scent of the baby shampoo she still favoured. April had not been back to school since the accident, her ability to stop her tears lasting only as long as nothing reminded her of her sister. Catriona had called the school, explained what had happened and said she'd bring April back when she was ready. The head teacher had been shocked. 'Mrs Anderson, I am speechless. I'm so, so sorry that this happened, that you're all going through this. We will all miss Hope so much.' Mrs Brighton had sounded breathless. 'Is there anything at all that we can do?'

Catriona had thanked her but said, no, there was nothing they needed, picturing the steady stream of people that had started coming by since the day after Hope's death: neighbours from the village, her tai chi friends, the local vicar, even old Mungo, each delivering packages of fresh fish, casseroles, pies, loaves of home-baked bread, tins of biscuits and baskets of fruit. Now, her pantry, fridge and every available space in the kitchen was full of food that none of them had any appetite for.

The only people Catriona wanted to talk to, never mind see, were her parents. As soon as she'd called them, the morning after the accident, a devastated Iris had done exactly what Catriona had known she would do. 'We'll throw some stuff in the car and be there tonight, sweetheart. Just hang on.'

Despite her positive message, her mother's voice had been clogged with pain, making Catriona cover her eyes and push out a slow breath. Unable to contemplate speaking about what had happened yet, she had suggested they wait a few days and come just in time for the funeral service.

Iris has sounded dubious. 'You'll need us there for support, Catriona, surely? And I can help with April. We'll not be in the way, or make things difficult, at all.'

'It's not that, Mum.' Catriona had swiped the fresh tears from her cheeks. 'I think we just need a few more days to be by ourselves, before we can cope with anyone else being here, in the house.'

'If you're sure,' Iris had said. 'Whatever you want we will do, love.'

Her parents had moved to Cornwall five years earlier, buying a picture-perfect cottage right on the sea, in Mousehole. It had been a dream of theirs ever since they'd honeymooned in the quaint town, forty-five years earlier. When her father had retired from the navy, they'd sold the family home near Loch Lomond and found the perfect house, and with a mixture of excitement and sadness at being further away from Catriona, Duncan, and the girls, they'd gone south.

Catriona knew that the distance was already somewhat painful for her parents but that they'd begun to feel isolated, sad to be missing their grandchildren growing up. The previous year, they'd talked about moving back to Scotland, but Duncan and Catriona had persuaded them that they shouldn't give up their stunning cottage, at least for now.

Knowing that they were arriving that evening, Catriona was nervous, but also relieved that she'd have a distraction and company she could rely on to allow her to be wherever she needed to, emotionally. Her parents were her safe place, and Catriona couldn't wait to hold them close, let them comfort her and remind her of who she was before her life had imploded.

Her father, Will, was a mild man. A gentle giant with clear blue eyes, a head of thick, silver hair and a rumbling voice that still carried the subtle twang of Aberdeen, where he'd grown up. A devoted father, he adored her and her mother, and seeing her parents together, sneaking off to the kitchen to hold each other and kiss, after almost five decades, never failed to make Catriona feel grateful.

Iris was a petite blonde, with eyes the colour of toffee and tiny pearls of teeth that were so perfectly straight they almost looked fake. Despite her diminutive size, she had a presence that drew focus, and her manner was warm and inclusive, no matter who she was around. She was everything Catriona aspired to be: intelligent, humble, devoted to her family, calm in a crisis, logical, gentle with her sage advice and, most of all, endlessly patient with the children.

Children. The word, by definition, meant more than one, and as Catriona felt Hope's excruciating loss all over again, she held April tighter to her side.

The little girl wriggled on her hip. 'Mummy, too tight.' She eased herself back, her turquoise eyes scanning Catriona's face. 'You're so sad, now.' She put her fingertips gently onto Catriona's cheek. 'I'm sad, too.' She leaned in, her forehead touching Catriona's. 'I love you, Mummy.'

'I love you too, little one,' Catriona whispered, her eyes stinging at April's touching empathy, holding still, and soaking it in for a few seconds. Eventually, Catriona lifted her chin. 'Let's get the bed ready for Nana and Gramps, shall we? They'll be here in time for tea.' She set April down and tucked a long hank of hair behind her ear. 'You can help me with the pillowcases, OK?'

April nodded, then yawned widely. 'I'm so sleepy.'

Catriona smiled at her daughter, the flushed cheeks and earnest eyes tugging at her middle. April still wasn't sleeping well and it seemed to be catching up with her. 'Maybe you can have a wee nap after lunch, in our bed?'

April pouted, her lips forming a rosy crescent. 'OK.'

Upstairs, the room that had been the nursery now had a double bed in it, with a small bedside table each side and an antique chair in the corner, covered in the warm cream and soft purple of the Clan Anderson, Arisaid tartan. The ivory-coloured curtains skimmed the pale carpet, the double window overlooking the drive and the sliver of garden at the front of the house.

Catriona had redecorated when the girls had moved into the bigger room next door, and other than her and Duncan sleeping in here occasionally, if one of them were ill, the room sat empty.

As she pulled clean linen from her grandmother's old bow-fronted wardrobe in the corner, a flashback to her parents' last visit for the girls' birthdays the previous year brought her to a standstill. Iris had baked a triple-layered chocolate cake, with raspberry filling, and Hope had eaten two huge slices, her mouth rimmed with shiny chocolate as she'd talked constantly about her Brownie baking badge that she'd got the day before. Catriona had sat back, watching her girls, a glow of pride warming her, as April, while daintily eating her small slice of cake, had reached over and patted Hope's back when she swallowed some milk wrong. Seeing it too, Iris had caught Catriona's eye and pressed her palm to her chest, and mother and daughter had shared a moment of understanding. April's love for Hope was so apparent that it shone through her every interaction with her sister.

Snapping Catriona back to the moment, April sniffed as she lifted a clean pillowcase and began awkwardly stuffing a pillow inside. 'This is hard,' she huffed, the tip of her tongue protruding from between her teeth. 'I can't do it.' She quickly dropped the pillow and cover onto the bed and her chin began to quiver.

Wanting to keep her focused on something practical, Catriona lifted the cover and held it out to her daughter. 'Come on, sweetheart. You can do it. Remember to just get the first two corners in, then—'

April's face crumpled, and a tear began to track down

her cheek. 'I can't. Hope always did it.' She gulped, her little hands clenching at her sides. 'I'm no good at it.'

Catriona sat heavily on the edge of the bed and drew April onto her knee. It was true that Hope, the more confident of the sisters, had usually taken on this task, as she had many similar things, but Catriona had never considered that, as a result, April had just given up trying. The realisation made Catriona feel remiss, in not paying closer attention to what had been going on.

'You can do more than you think, April.' She pressed her cheek to April's damp one. 'You just have to keep trying and you'll get it.'

April shook her head, a tear dropping and spreading into a dark oval on Catriona's jeans. 'I need Hope. She fixes things. She helps me.' April's voice shook with a mixture of sadness and anger, making the hairs on Catriona's arms stand to attention. She hadn't allowed her own anger to surface, keeping it squashed inside until sometimes she could virtually taste it, so hearing her little girl letting hers show shook her. April was braver than she was, and the lesson was unsettling.

Suddenly, Catriona knew what she needed to do, so she wiped April's cheeks with her thumb, pulled her shoulders back and blinked her vision clear. 'Sometimes when we're really sad, it turns to feeling cross and that's OK.' She focused on April's watery eyes, the thick lashes clogged with tears. 'If we let it out, it can take some of the hurt away and make us feel better.' A tiny frown cut across April's forehead. 'Do you want to try it?'

April took a few moments to consider, then nodded, her chin dropping to her chest.

Catriona smiled at her and then, gently moving April

off her knee, stood up. 'Right. See that pillow?' She pointed at the bed. 'Give it a good thump.'

April's head came up, her eyes questioning. 'Really?'

'Yep. A good thump, right in the middle.' Catriona mimed the action.

April's frown deepened. 'Why?'

'Just trust me.' Moving behind her daughter, Catriona put her hands on April's shoulders. 'It'll feel good.'

April shifted her feet, the fluffy slippers opening to a ten-to-two position on the carpet.

Feeling the narrow shoulders tensing under her palms, Catriona dropped her hands to her sides. 'Want me to go first?' She moved to April's side.

'Uh-huh.' April nodded, biting her bottom lip.

'All right, stand back.' Catriona gave April a smile. 'Here I go.' She made a fist with her right hand and leaned over, punching the pillow, the feathers yielding to her knuckles in a satisfying way.

April laughed, the sound such a rarity now that it brought fresh tears to Catriona's eyes.

Next, she made two fists and began beating the pillow, again and again, until feathers started to float up from the bed and a powdery smell filled the air around her. As she continued to punch, suddenly April's little fists were there, next to Catriona's, April's blows coming fast and causing more feathers to work loose from the damaged pillow. 'Go for it, April. Give it all you've got.' Catriona slowed her punches, letting the little girl move in front of her, rivulets of chestnut hair covering her back as she leaned into the task.

Without prompting, April began to growl something under her breath, in time with the blows, making Catriona hold still, straining to make out what she was saying. Then, the words began to clarify themselves as April's thumping gradually slowed. 'I. Want. My. Sister. I. Want. Hope. Hope. Hope. I. Want. Hope.'

Catriona stepped back, her hand covering her mouth, and turning towards the door, she whispered into her palm, 'Oh, my God. So do I.'

6

Iris stirred a giant pot of soup, the tang of the fresh orange zest she'd just added to the simmering carrot mixture filtering across the room to Catriona, who sat at the table, wrapped in a soft shawl nursing a mug of tea. The traumatic events of the day, getting through the funeral and the small reception afterward, being among people, breathing in and out as she shook hands, and accepted unwanted hugs, had left her feeling bruised. Now her entire body was sore and her head pounding.

Her parents had been with them for three days. At the first, emotionally wrought meeting, Iris and Catriona had gripped one another and sobbed, with April squashed between their waists, while Will hung back, his nose red and his eyes full.

Gradually, the days had begun to ease into each other. Iris and Will had taken over the day-to-day chores – shopping, cleaning, intercepting the well-meaning visitors and the stream of food still being delivered, relieving Catriona of the challenge of greeting people and thanking them for their thoughtfulness. 'You have some good friends here, darling.'

Iris had methodically stacked away the offerings in the freezer, her face flushed as she stoically fought her own tears. 'Your family means a lot to this community.'

Catriona had nodded, both recognising and feeling grateful for the truth in her mother's words, but their message felt useless in the face of the cavernous hole that she was breathing around each and every second.

The house had become mostly quiet, Catriona cancelling all her tutoring sessions, going on long walks in the hills outside the village and still sleeping in the girls' room. Duncan had been isolating himself in the conservatory, engulfed in work, and April had become more withdrawn and tearful as the funeral had approached. Now, with the dreaded event finally behind them, Will and Duncan had taken her for a walk on the pier, and Catriona was soaking in her mother's comforting presence.

'Where are your bay leaves, love?' Iris opened the upper cabinet next to the stove, rising onto tiptoe to scan the jumble of herb jars.

Catriona swallowed over the ever-present lump in her throat and leaned back in the chair, the wooden struts digging into her back. 'Middle shelf, on the left, I think.' She sipped some tea, noticing the slight tremble in her hand as she lowered the mug back to the table. 'Thanks, Mum.' She smiled at her mother's back, the familiar angle of her shoulders and the shiny cap of silvery-blonde hair a soothing sight for Catriona's raw eyes.

'Of course, love.' Iris turned to face her. 'I just wish we could do more.' Her eyes filled. 'It's just so hard to believe that wee Hope is gone.' She sniffed, returning deliberately to the pot that was now steaming on the stove. 'I keep expecting her to run in, chattering like a budgie.'

An image of the coffin, so small and sleek, the white

lilies quivering on its top as the pall-bearers carried her darling daughter to her resting place, brought Catriona's eyes closed. Hope's grave was at the top of the cemetery, on the misty hillside overlooking the loch. Nothing could have prepared Catriona for seeing her baby girl being lowered into the ground. No parent should ever have to witness, or experience that kind of crippling loss. Yet now, Catriona was expected to survive it for a second time.

Not only had the funeral itself been unimaginably hard, but the night before, she and Duncan had argued. He'd walked into the bedroom as she was getting ready for bed, his expression sullen.

'What'll we do with April tomorrow?' He'd sunk onto the low chair in the corner, near the window, his hands linking between his long thighs as he leaned back and scanned the ceiling.

'What do you mean?' Catriona had frowned as she pulled her robe on and tied it around her narrowing waist.

'Who'll watch her while we're at the funeral?' He'd sat upright, his eyes boring into hers.

Catriona had lowered herself onto the end of the bed, digesting what he was saying, and unable to believe that he meant what she thought he meant. 'We won't need anyone to watch her. She'll be with us.' She'd frowned.

Duncan's face had darkened as if the light hanging above him had snuffed itself out. 'No way, Cat. She's not going to go through that.' He shook his head. 'She's far too young to understand.'

A wave of fury had risen up inside Catriona, and she'd fought to corral it. 'Duncan, are you kidding? She saw her sister, her best friend, the other half of her heart, die. She needs to go. To say goodbye. If she doesn't, she might never get over this.' Determined not to cry again, she'd stood up and turned towards the door.

'Cat, don't walk away. We're not finished talking about this.' His voice had had an edge to it that had stopped her in her tracks.

She had turned to face him. 'She's going, Duncan. I'm sorry, but I'm not discussing it anymore.'

As she'd walked out into the hall, she'd heard him grunt something, then say her name, so she'd swung around to see him pacing towards her.

'What, Duncan?' She'd stood her ground. 'What is it?'

He'd stopped in front of her, his big hands clamping around her shoulders, his warm breath floating across her face, making her blink. 'How long is this going to go on?' He'd looked broken, as if the sharp lines of his face had changed into the time-worn ones of his father. 'We need to get through this, together. When are you going to stop freezing me out?'

As she'd taken in his watery eyes, the tortured line of his mouth, Catriona had struggled with the building anger that she'd been dealing with daily, since her precious girl had been torn away. Catriona had taken a steady breath and looked him in the eye, and the words she'd been holding at bay had gushed out, raw, perhaps cruel, but needing to be said. 'You should have been watching her, Duncan. Why did you let her out of your sight?' Her voice had cracked, but she'd held his gaze.

'I know. Don't you think I know that? That I don't think about it every second of every day?' He'd taken a ragged breath. 'What do you want, Cat? Tell me, for God's sake.'

'What do I want?' She'd pushed out a breath and whispered, 'I want my daughter back.'

He'd dropped his chin and shaken his head, then, after a

few moments, he'd looked up and sought her eyes. 'What can I do?'

Before she could edit herself, Catriona had whispered, 'What you can do now is nothing. It's what you should have done when you had the chance, but didn't.' Her voice had given way and her eyes had flooded with tears, any regret at causing him pain lost inside her own.

He'd gasped. 'I swear to God, Cat. It was no more than five minutes. I looked away for five minutes.'

She'd looked up at him and gulped down a sob. 'That was all it took, Duncan.'

Now, a chill running down her back, Catriona shoved the half-empty mug away from her. 'Do you think I did the right thing, Mum? Taking April with us today?'

Iris took a few moments to respond, just enough time to make Catriona second-guess herself, then her mother turned to face her. 'Darling girl, there's no right or wrong here. You followed your instincts, and as far as April goes, you know her best.' She gave a sad smile. 'Eight is young, right enough, to have to deal with all this pain, this kind of loss.' She shook her head, her hair forming a ghostly halo as the light of the gloaming streamed in the window behind her. 'But she saw far worse on that night.' Iris wiped a tear from her cheek. 'Let's hope there will be some healing from her having the chance to say goodbye.'

Catriona nodded, relief flooding through her. 'Right, that's what I told Duncan.' She straightened the tartan place mat in front of her, flicking some crumbs off onto the floor. 'He just doesn't...'

Iris tipped her head to the side. 'Doesn't what, love?'

Catriona sifted through everything she wanted to say. All the frustrations she'd been bottling up over the years bubbling to the surface; the hurtful slights, his long absences, him hovering on the periphery of their family. She was afraid that if she opened that door, she'd sound like an ungrateful, wicked harridan, so, letting her breath out slowly, she said, 'Nothing. It doesn't matter, Mum.'

Iris frowned, crossing the room, and sitting in the chair next to her. 'Catriona, you've both been through so much. This is unthinkably unfair. But you and Duncan are both strong, and even stronger together. You'll get through this, my love.' She reached out and took Catriona's chilled hand in her warm one. 'You are the bravest person I know. You just have to give it time.' Iris tucked a long twist of hair behind Catriona's ear, the comforting sensation of her mother's fingers, gently putting things back into their rightful place, transporting her back to her childhood.

'Oh, Mum.' She dropped her head onto her forearms, the weight of what she carried inside crushing her. 'I just wish it was that straightforward.'

It was eight days since the funeral and Duncan still hadn't cried, at least as far as Catriona knew. He had been going back into the Fort William office for the past three days and, whenever he was home, he was embedded in the conservatory, or down in the boathouse until after dark. Then he'd come back in, eat whatever Catriona had left for him and watch TV in the living room until the wee hours.

The previous day, he'd mentioned something about the Singapore trip being back on, and Catriona found that she was hoping it was soon.

She was wrung out, her insides ragged and her throat raw, the tears seeming to be endless. She'd tried to stem them until she was alone, for April's sake, as the little girl had retreated even further into her shell. Catriona had tried coaxing her with her favourite foods, letting her stay up a little later than usual, taking her to the cinema to see the new Disney release. While April went along with all the enticements, it was half-heartedly, her little mouth tightly set, and her eyes, so full of pain, seeming to take over her young face.

Iris and Will were due to leave after lunch, and Catriona was dreading being left with no buffer between her and Duncan, the atmosphere thick and their conversations stilted and sporadic. Now, as she stood at the sink rinsing the breakfast dishes, her father came into the kitchen. Rather than sit at the table and draw the newspaper towards him, as was his habit, he walked over to her side and slung his arm around her shoulders. 'Hello, daughter of mine.' He pulled her gently into his side as Catriona dried her hands on a towel and slipped her arms around his waist.

'Hello, father of mine.' She could smell toothpaste and the spice of his aftershave. The endearingly old-fashioned habit he had of patting his face with it, just like in the ads, always made Catriona smile.

'So, we're off in a few hours.' He stared ahead, taking in the view, the bright April morning crystal clear, as was the outline of the Cuillins crouched in the distance, wearing their misty collars.

'I know.' She sniffed. 'I wish you could stay longer.'

Will gave her a tight squeeze, then released her, stepping back to scan her face. 'Will you take a walk with your old man?' His brow lifted in question as the tanned skin of his forehead folded above his silvery brows. 'Looks like a good day for a wee jaunt.'

The idea of spending some time alone with her father was like accepting a warm blanket on a cold day. 'I'd love that.' She turned to look across the hall, towards the living room, where Iris and April were doing a *Jungle Book* puzzle at the coffee table. 'But I can't leave April.' She shook her head.

'She's fine with your mum. Come on, love. Let's take a flask and go down to the loch. I haven't had a chance to do my usual route yet, and you know how I love...' He stopped himself, his face colouring slightly.

'What is it, Dad?' Catriona put her hand on his arm.

'I'm an oaf.' He frowned. 'You don't want to be going down there.' He nodded towards the water. 'I'm sorry.'

His obvious discomfort affected her so deeply that her heart faltered. 'Dad, it's OK. I have to, sometime. I can't exactly ignore it.' She turned to face the window just as a flock of starlings swooped across the sky, floating in a giant cluster of dots, synchronised in every twist, turn, and ride on an updraught. 'If I'm going to go down there, I can't imagine going with anyone else.'

He turned to face her, his eyes glittering. 'Catriona, I just don't know what to say, love.' He shook his head sadly. 'I've never been one for words, well, not many of them.' He shrugged, as Catriona gave a soft laugh. 'If I could just fix this for you. Change things. You know I'd give everything...' He pulled a hanky from his pocket and wiped his nose.

'Dad, I know.' Catriona moved closer and hugged his arm. 'You're the best dad anyone could have,' she said. 'Stick the kettle back on. I'll make some tea and then we'll go.'

He laid his palm on the top of her head. 'Are you sure?'

'Yes, I'm sure.'

Having checked on April and Iris, leaving a plate of ginger biscuits on the coffee table, and hugging them both,

Catriona pulled on her jacket and followed her father out into the back garden.

He carried the flask of tea she'd made and smiled at her, encouragingly. 'Come on, Catkin,' he beckoned to her. 'The sun's out to greet us.'

As she closed the door behind her and stepped onto the flagstone path, her pulse began to quicken, as she hadn't been out here since that night. Now, as the row of rosemary on either side of her scented the breeze, an image of her woollen socks, slapping down on the stones as she darted towards the lawn, brought her to a standstill. Flooded with the memory of following the blood-curdling screams, and squinting into the dim light of the evening that would change things forever, she pressed her eyes closed and curled her hands into fists at her sides.

'Catriona?' Her dad was by her side. 'Are you OK, love?' He looped his free arm through hers. 'We don't have to do this.'

Her breaths were coming fast and shallow and she tried to count them, summoning her relaxation technique of four counts in, seven held and eight counts exhaled. Gradually, her heart settled, and she opened her eyes.

Her father was staring down at her, his jaw twitching. 'We really don't have to.'

She pushed her shoulders back and filled her lungs, tasting the brine of the loch and feeling the slight moisture in the air coating her windpipe. 'No, it's OK, Dad. I need to.'

The short walk took them through the wooden gate beyond the boathouse, across the unkempt back lawn of the cottage next door, that had lain empty for the better part of a year, and then down a narrow path where long grasses brushed their shins. The path skirted the edge of the loch until they reached a break in the grasses, leading to five large boulders that served as stepping stones. Beyond them, the narrow strip of the shore, dotted with glistening pebbles, stretched away towards the village.

Will was ahead of her, carefully finding his footing, and glancing over his shoulder every few steps, as if she might have changed her mind and turned back to the house. His protective concern was touchingly predictable, and as Catriona followed him, keeping her eyes on the back of his wax jacket, rather than the shimmering water to her left that had claimed her baby girl, the gentle rhythm of their progress began to soothe her.

Fifteen minutes later, Will turned inland, heading for the small hill that would lift them above the shore and give them a clear view of Loch Kishorn and the impressive slopes of Beinn Bhàn, her father's favourite spot to picnic. Among the golden gorse was a patch of scrubby grass, sheltered from the breeze by the hillside rising behind it, where they settled themselves.

He handed her the flask. 'Will you be mother?' He smiled at her as she took it from him and removed the top.

Pouring carefully, Catriona handed him a cup and lifted her own to tap it. 'Cheers, Dad.' She found a smile. 'Thanks for coming, for everything you and Mum...' She watched as he sipped the hot liquid, his free hand swatting the air.

'Don't thank us. We'll always be here, Catriona. Always. You know that.' The cup hovered under his chin as a tendril of steam rose from the surface of the tea and was carried away by the breeze.

'I do know. But still. Thank you.'

Will nodded, looking out at the view. 'It never gets old, does it?' He sighed. 'Will you ever look at it the same way?'

The question caught her off guard, as in all the years

she'd known him, her father had tended to veer away from uncomfortable subject matter. She'd put it down to his military career, the slightly removed, almost dispassionate way he dealt with problems, so this delving into emotionally charged territory was unexpected.

She took a few moments to gather herself, then shook her head. 'It wasn't the loch's fault, Dad.' She set her cup on the grass next to her. 'It was...'

Will turned to look at her, his eyes full of concern. 'It was what?'

Catriona looked away, swimming through the waves of bone-deep sadness and anger her truncated statement had released.

'It was what?' he asked again, this time a slight lift to his brow making her cheeks warm.

'Nothing.' She dropped her gaze, picking some invisible fluff from her jacket.

'What were you going to say?' Will shifted on the ground, turning to face her. 'Spit it out, love.'

She took in the open face, the kind eyes that had witnessed her entire life thus far; all her childhood successes, and failures, her first love, first broken heart, leaving home for university, her graduation, her wedding, her struggles with infertility, all the while steadfast, loving and filled with the certain knowledge that she, his daughter, would never let him down. Right at this moment, she felt like a total failure, as both a mother and a daughter, and that was more than she could bear. She wanted to scream what was in her heart, but the words were hard to say out loud, never mind share. And yet, the longer he looked at her, calmly, expectantly, the more they pushed up inside her until she couldn't contain them any longer. 'It was Duncan's fault.' Her voice caught, cracking his name in two. She couldn't continue, her throat clamping shut as she pressed her eyes closed, more tears rising from the bottomless well inside her, as she fought to keep them down.

'Whoa there, daughter.' His voice was carried off by the brisk wind, but she didn't miss the shock it contained. 'You can't mean that?'

She opened her eyes, swallowing hard. 'I do.' She met his wide-eyed gaze, his frown deepening as he curled his legs under him and shunted closer to her. 'He was too caught up in his bloody boat. If it's not that, or work, then it's something else.' She gulped. 'I'm sorry, Dad, but it's true.'

Will took her hand in his, the long fingers trapping hers. 'Catriona, love, you're speaking out of grief.' He squeezed her frigid fingers. 'I know Duncan is away a lot for work, but he would never let anything come between the two of you, and the girls.'

Catriona swiped her damp cheeks. 'I know how hard he works, Dad. Believe me, I've lived with it for nearly seventeen years.' She took a breath. 'He took his eyes off her. He always does.' She gulped. 'And I'm so angry, I can hardly look at him.'

Will's eyes softened, as he released her hand. 'Catkin, you're in pain. Things will look different in time.' He halted as her eyes flashed.

'No, Dad. I'm not making excuses for him.' She swallowed hard. 'Not anymore.'

7

Seeing her parents' car pull away had left Catriona emotional and conflicted. While she was sad to see them leave, she knew that she, Duncan, and April needed to start navigating the new landscape of their lives without anyone else around to dilute the stark reality of it all.

Duncan had left for Fort William right after breakfast, so had said his goodbyes then, and when it was finally time for her parents to leave, Catriona's mother had tearfully clung to her in the driveway. 'Just call. We'll come back whenever you need us, love.' She'd cupped Catrina's cheek. 'You can do this, Catkin.'

'I love you, Mum. Drive safe and call me from the road.' Catriona had kissed her mother's soft cheek, the scent of her face powder and the fresh loaves she'd insisted on baking before she left lingering on her skin. 'Thanks a million. You and Dad are lifesavers.'

As Catriona had hugged her father, April had hovered behind her with her fingers in her mouth. Eventually, she'd waved at the car, her other hand gripping the back pocket of Catriona's jeans. While this was something new, Catriona felt the welcome contact like a safety chain, keeping her and April connected.

Now they were in the living room finishing April's favourite jigsaw puzzle of the Loch Ness monster. 'Here's a piece of sky.' Catriona handed the piece to April, who turned it this way and that, then leaned over the coffee table and popped it into place. 'Well done.' Catriona smiled at her daughter as April stared at the remaining puzzle pieces on the table, her jaw slack, and her eyes worryingly vacant. Afraid that April would slip further into the shadowy place she occupied these days, Catriona employed her distraction technique. 'What do you want for dinner? Anything goes.' She stood up and walked to the window. 'April?'

Getting no reply, Catriona turned and looked out at the driveway. The mid-afternoon light was casting a golden film across the gravel, as the time for her first tutoring session since Hope's death approached. Feeling oddly nervous about it, she checked her watch and, turning around, was surprised to see that April had left the room. Frowning, Catriona walked across the hall and into the kitchen, but seeing it empty, she went and checked the conservatory. There was no sign of April anywhere.

As anxiety began to pluck at Catriona's chest, for a second, she started to relive the events of that hideous night, but then, she consciously reeled herself in and, running through several potential scenarios, sprinted up the stairs, two at a time. 'April? Are you up here, love?'

She walked along the hall and opened the girls' bedroom door to see April curled up on the top bunk, her face turned into the pillow, the exact same position Catriona took up each night.

She still hadn't changed the sheets on Hope's bed, afraid to erase the lingering scent of her sweet girl, and seeing April wrapped in the wrinkled duvet made Catriona stop short. 'April?' She walked slowly to the bunk bed, her heart now racing. 'Sweetheart, what are you doing up here?'

April slowly turned her face away from Catriona, towards the wall. Her eyes were closed, but the lids flickered with the obvious effort of her keeping them shut.

Puzzled, but overcome with relief that April was all right, Catriona carefully drew the duvet up around her shoulders. 'If you want to have a nap, that's OK,' she whispered, tucking the covers in close along her daughter's sides, something she knew she liked. Then Catriona swept a strand of hair from April's cheek and, stepping up onto the side of the lower bunk, leaned over and kissed the ivory temple. 'I've got a student coming in a few minutes, but I'll come and check on you in a wee bit.' Seeing no response other than April's eyelids puckering, Catriona lowered herself to the floor, hesitated for a moment, then walked quietly into the hall.

April taking herself off to bed in the daytime was another new development, worrying behaviour that Catriona knew she'd have to monitor. A part of her understood it completely, wanting nothing more than to hide under the covers herself most mornings, rather than face another day without Hope. However, April's deliberate retreat from company, rather than seeking comfort with herself, or Duncan when he was home, sent Catriona's heightening concern into overdrive.

April had been growing quieter and more withdrawn as the days passed and knowing that she was helplessly watching her little girl struggle with the same destructive, buried feelings that she, Catriona, was having, tore at her like a set of cruel claws. The only thing she could hope to salvage out of all of this tragedy was to protect April from any more hurt, but it seemed she was failing on that score, too.

Heartsore, and suddenly drained of energy, she went quietly down the stairs and into the conservatory. As she stacked the appropriate textbooks on the desk, preparing for Olivia's lesson, an image of April's face, now devoid of joy and as closed off as her eyelids had just been, flickered behind Catriona's eyes. Blinking the sad picture away, she resolved to ask her doctor if he could arrange for April to have some grief counselling. Even as she considered it, the thought that April might not be the only one in the family needing a little help at the moment loomed large.

As she turned away from the desk, the soapbox on the windowsill caught her eye. It had been there since the girls had rescued the tiny egg and now, Catriona lifted it carefully, balancing it in her palm. Inside, the perfect blue oval lay nestled in a cotton-wool bed, and the sight of it set off a cascade of memories; the sisters chasing each other, four bright yellow wellingtons against the lush grass, them shouting into the wind as their hair flew wildly around their flushed faces, their mingled voices, high-pitched and full of joy, ringing across the garden. Lingering in Catriona's mind's eye was April's smile, as she watched her sister, taking her cues, as always, from Hope. The pictures kept coming and as Catriona blinked, trying to focus on the robin's egg, an idea began to form, something that might help her coax April from her self-imposed isolation.

Duncan sat at the kitchen table, his empty plate in front of him. He'd been late home from the office and had missed April's bedtime, so he and Catriona were now speaking in hushed tones as she sat opposite him, nursing the remains of a glass of wine. The idea she'd had earlier had grown roots, and she wanted to talk to him about it before he left for Singapore.

'So, when are you leaving again?' She swirled the wine around, the rich Burgundy leaving long, watery legs inside the glass.

'Day after tomorrow.' Duncan stood up, lifted his plate and walked to the sink. 'I'll be away eight days.' He slid the plate and cutlery into the dishwasher and lifted the wine bottle from the counter.

'Right, I know.' Catriona sipped some wine, then shook her head as he offered her more. 'Is Stewart going too?'

'Uh-huh.' Duncan tipped the remainder of the wine into his glass and sat down. He lifted it up, staring at the deep-red liquid, his eyelids flickering as if he were looking at a bright light.

Catriona loved the small wrinkles that had recently appeared at the edges of his magnetic eyes, a testament to the length of time they'd spent together, but seeing the new sag to his mouth, and the way his cheeks had become concave, much like her own, sent a ripple of sadness through her. This whole situation was brutal and while she wanted to rail at him, pound his chest with her fists and cause him physical pain, the only thing holding her back was the shadow of her deeply buried love for this man.

The chasm between them was growing wider and deeper by the day, and the truth of that hurt her profoundly, but she couldn't seem to banish her anger towards him. Everyone made mistakes, she knew that, but this was more than that. He hadn't put Hope first, then he'd let her sneak away.

Draining her glass, Catriona pushed it away and waited for him to look at her. As she waited, counting her breaths, finally, he lifted his chin and met her gaze. 'Duncan, I've had an idea.'

He nodded, setting his glass down.

'I was thinking it might be good to get April a pet. Some kind of little friend she can care for.' She paused as his eyebrows lifted. 'You know how she loves animals.'

Duncan frowned. 'Hope loved animals.' His voice was rough. 'I think April just went along with her sister on that.'

Catriona clenched her teeth. Why could he never give April credit for having a personality, likes and dislikes of her own? 'It wasn't just because of that.' She shook her head. 'She's always loved them. Remember when we looked after her school friend's rabbit for a few weeks last year, while they were away in South Africa? It was April who fed her, changed the straw, and sat on the grass with her for hours feeding her lettuce leaves. And remember Billy? She cried for three days solid when that silly budgie died.' Frustrated, Catriona stood up and put her empty glass in the sink. The inky night-sky was framed by the window and sprinkled with stars that glittered through the thin blanket of cloud huddled over the loch.

'Oh, right.' Duncan cleared his throat as she turned to face him.

'So, what do you think? It might bring her out of herself a bit, if she has to be responsible for another living thing.' The word *living* made Catriona flinch, the harsh reminder that this was a state no longer applicable to her darling Hope darting through her body like an electric shock.

Duncan was watching her, as if he felt the volts ricocheting between her bones. 'I suppose it might be an idea.' He shrugged, then seeing her expression, he nodded. 'I dunno, Cat. You decide.'

A flash of irritation made her blink several times as she

fought to edit her reply. Did he not always leave everything to do with the girls up to her, anyway? 'Duncan, I'm asking what you think.' She held his gaze. 'For once, can you please just—'

'Mummy?' April appeared in the doorway, her hair matted at the back of her head and her cheeks flushed, as she ground her left eye with a fist. Her pyjama top had ridden up her back and her feet were bare.

Catriona quickly circled the table. 'What is it, darling?' She bent down and scooped April up into her arms, catching the faint scent of something she couldn't place. As April wrapped her arms around her neck, Catriona immediately felt the dampness of April's pyjama bottoms. Catriona's surprise was overtaken by a surge of sympathetic understanding, as she leaned in, and whispered in April's ear, 'Have you had an accident, sweetheart?' She gently set April down and met Duncan's questioning eyes. He was frowning as he shoved the chair back from the table and then made to come towards them.

Catriona shook her head, almost imperceptibly, as April began to cry softly, her head drooping forward, and her face obscured by curtains of hair.

'The bed is wet.' She sniffed, her shoulders quivering as she hiccupped. 'I didn't do it on purpose.'

Catriona's heart faltered. 'Of course you didn't, darling.' She tidied the hair behind April's ears revealing the prominent widow's peak, and the turquoise eyes, miserable and full. 'Come on. Let's go and fix it, shall we?' Catriona took her hand. 'Say goodnight to Daddy, before we go up.'

Duncan was hovering at the end of the table, his hands in his pockets. 'Give me a kiss then, April Mactiggiwinkle.' He leaned down and stuck his jaw out, his hands still in his pockets.

Seeing him ready to receive a kiss, but not reaching for his daughter to hold her and comfort her, Catriona's anger heightened.

April walked to Duncan and kissed his cheek, her palms going to either side of his face. 'Night, Daddy.' Her hands lingered on his cheeks, then dropped back to her sides.

'Night, little one.' Duncan's voice was gentle as he widened his eyes at Catriona, but she just shook her head at him, then silently led April out into the hall.

With clean pyjamas on, April now lay fast asleep in the middle of Catriona and Duncan's bed. 'Shall I put her back?' he whispered.

'No. Leave her. She's fine for tonight.' Catriona looked down at her daughter, the now ever-present frown gone from the narrow forehead, and one hand curled under her jaw like a tiny paw. 'She looks too relaxed to move.' Not waiting for him to protest, him having been adamant that the girls shouldn't sleep in their bed with them after they were a few months old, Catriona carefully slipped her feet into her slippers and tiptoed into the bathroom.

When she came out – ten minutes later – Duncan was reading in bed, wearing an old, faded T-shirt with the Glasgow university logo stretched across his chest. April was curled up on her side facing him, her hair splayed across Catriona's pillow.

'Did she wake up?' Catriona slipped her robe off and gently pulled back the duvet on her side, suddenly nervous about being back in the same bed as Duncan for the first time in weeks.

'No. She was a bit restless for a few minutes, then she

settled again.' He smiled tentatively at Catriona. 'Glad you're back. I've missed you.'

Unable to echo the sentiment, she simply nodded, slipped into bed and carefully moved April's mane from her pillow. Then, settling herself, she lifted the French novel she was reading from the bedside table. She was aware that he was still looking at her, but she couldn't meet his eyes, see the question there, or perhaps the hurt. She didn't know what she might do if he asked her again, how long this would go on, because she had absolutely no idea.

8

Two days later, Duncan had left at dawn, tossing his small suitcase and laptop bag into the back of the taxi as Catriona stood shivering in the open front door, her long cardigan wrapped over her pyjamas and her feet in thick socks.

She'd seen her breath, smoking into the May morning, as she'd watched the taillights on the cab flicker momentarily. It had caused a tiny lift of hope at her core as, surprised that she cared, she'd wondered if perhaps Duncan was having doubts about leaving, perhaps realising that he needed to stay. To fix this. Then, the car had crunched away over the gravel, taking her momentary hope with it.

As the lights had disappeared around the corner, she'd been struck that this was the first time ever that Duncan had left for any length of time without kissing her properly. While things were strained between them, a mixture of sadness and fear at the dismissive peck he'd planted on her cheek had curdled inside her, sending her back to bed with a deep sense of foreboding that she could not shake.

Now, she had another hurdle to clear. Today was the day that she'd decided April should go back to school, and

Catriona knew that it wasn't going to be easy. The little girl had become all but monosyllabic, her voice – whenever she did speak – little more than an echo of what it had been. There was no laughter behind it, no mischief, no sense of joy anymore, and it broke Catriona's heart all over again each time she tried to coax a response from her formerly happy child.

April had slept in beside them for the past two nights, and now, having lain next to her daughter for half an hour, watching the rhythmic rise and fall of her little chest, Catriona rolled onto her side and gently patted April's back to rouse her. 'Wakey wakey, sleepy Mactiggiwinkle,' she whispered, the light creeping in under the curtains turning the room a silvery white. 'Time to get up.'

April yawned, her arms stretching above her head, then she opened her eyes sleepily and assessed Catriona.

'We have to get you ready for school. You're going back today.'

April's serene expression disintegrated, her lower lip protruding. 'No.' She shook her head, her eyes darting to the door as if looking for an escape.

'Sweetheart, you need to go back. You've missed over two weeks now, and your friends are missing you, too.' She smiled at the flushed cheeks and the mass of lush hair, soft under her fingertips as she gathered it into a loose twist at April's shoulder. 'Come on. We'll have a nice breakfast, then I'll take you to school, and then, this afternoon, when I come to get you, we can go to the harbour and see Mungo, if you like?'

April rubbed her eyes and sat up, her fingers then plucking at the duvet as she glanced around the room.

'Come on, let's get up.' Catriona held her daughter's chin. 'You can have toaster-waffles if you like.' A treat that

Catriona rarely allowed the girls to have, due to the giant dose of sugar they contained, she hoped this offering would elicit a response, however small. Instead, April shook her head.

'Not hungry.' She pushed the duvet away and shuffled to the edge of the bed, her bare feet dangling above the bedside rug in such a childlike, uncomplicated way that a knot formed in Catriona's chest.

'You have to eat something, April.' Catriona held her hands out and helped her daughter stand, noticing the way her pyjama bottoms hung around her hips, and how the top now seemed to swamp her delicate frame. Having seen the same signs in herself the day before, her jeans slipping lower around her waist and her wedding ring spinning loosely on her finger, Catriona resolved that today they would start eating properly again, even if that was all they achieved.

Leaving April at school had been brutal. While she hadn't cried, her eyes had been brimming and her chin wobbling as, at the gate, Catriona had adjusted the straps on her back-pack. 'Have a good day, sweetheart.' She'd bent to kiss April, only to have her pull away, sending a shard of hurt through Catriona as sharp as any blade. 'Bye, then.' She'd waved as April had trudged up the steps towards the waiting Mrs Brighton, who'd opened her wool-clad arms and hugged the child into her waist.

Catriona had called the previous morning to tell Mrs Brighton that April would be coming back in the following day, and the head teacher had assured her that she would personally keep an eye on April until she had settled. It had been heartening to see that the kindly woman cared enough to greet April at the door, and the surge of gratitude that filled Catriona had made her eyes prickle.

Seeing Catriona hovering at the gate, Mrs Brighton had waved and nodded, mouthing, 'She's fine,' as April had deftly wriggled out of the hug and walked into the school.

Now, with her first day back behind her, April was quiet in the back of the car as Catriona parked as close to the harbour as she could. While it was a mild afternoon, with just a thin belt of cloud splitting the bright blue sky over the loch, Catriona was still feeling chilled. It was a symptom she recognised from when she'd come home from the hospital, after the twins were born. Knowing it went hand in hand with her lack of appetite and – having found April's sandwiches untouched in her backpack when she'd picked her up – she was even more determined to make them both a wholesome dinner.

Checking her watch, she got out of the car and opened the back door. 'Let's get that off you.' She reached in to unbuckle April's seat belt when the little girl batted her hands away.

'I can do it.' She looked sullenly up at Catriona, who took a step back, once again reeling from another, unexpected rejection.

Taking a second or two to rally, Catriona reached over and grabbed her bag from the back seat, her heart ticking alarmingly under her sweater. What was going on? Why was April pushing her away? 'Come on, slowcoach. Mungo's boat will be in, and we'll miss all the good fish.' She found a smile for April, who had shed her jacket and was standing next to the car, nibbling the skin around her thumb. 'Better take your jacket, love. The wind out at the boats can be chilly.' Catriona pointed to the red jacket crumpled on the floor behind the driver's seat.

'Not cold,' April huffed, her flushed cheeks puffing out as she pouted.

A spark of irritation made Catriona press her lips together as she took in the little face she loved, so much, distorted by what clearly looked like anger. 'April, bring your jacket, please.' She pointed again. 'It's not a negotiation.'

April folded her arms across her chest and met Catriona's eyes, the turquoise pools sparkling with something Catriona had never seen before. If she'd had to put a name to it, she'd have called it dislike, and seeing it sent a ripple of shock coursing through her.

Catriona negotiated her way around the small crowd of locals gathered in the harbour. Mungo's old fishing boat was anchored in the usual spot, halfway along the long pontoon, behind a large crab boat. Catriona waved at the old man, who was standing on the deck, handing heavy baskets down to his grandson, Harry, who was stacking them on the dock.

The boat had seen better days. The royal-blue paint on the hull was badly faded and the remains of the crimson stripe along the upper rail, and on the wooden frame of the small cabin, chipped and patchy. The name, *Sally-Anne*, had once been glossy black but was now a silvery grey, the 'A' in Anne all but invisible, and the battered tyres that dangled from the side on fraying ropes, to act as bumpers, were bleached to off-white by their exposure to years of water and sun.

Seeing the curved back and wizened face of her old friend, the shock of silver hair above the bright eyes and the leathery skin around them folding in pleasure, Catriona blinked repeatedly as she gripped April's hand. This was the first time she'd been here since Hope's death and, suddenly, having one screamingly empty hand rocked her, the sense that she was falling through space making her sway momentarily. As she hesitated a few feet from the boat, Mungo seemed to register what was going on and beckoned to Harry, who leaped back onto the deck like a cat and leaned in as his grandfather spoke close to his ear.

As Catriona watched, Harry jumped back down onto the pontoon and began raking through a large cool-box full of fish, his back towards her and his oiled dungarees so baggy around his lean form that they resembled clown trousers.

Taking a deep breath, letting the musty fish smell fill her lungs and coat the back of her tongue, Catriona tightened her grip on April's hand and walked up to the boat. 'Hello, the boat,' she called as Mungo raised a big paw.

'Hello, the shore.' He grinned, revealing the gap in his front teeth that, when he stuck the tip of his tongue through the hole, to make them laugh, had always sent the girls into a fit of giggles. 'Coming aboard th'day?' He looked down at April, who was lingering behind Catriona, her fingers twitching in Catriona's grip as she shook her head.

'Not today, Mungo.' Catriona lowered her chin, her eyes saying everything.

Behind her, the sounds of the harbour melded together like a musical score; shoppers calling to one another, the snap of metal lines hitting the masts of the row of boats tied up along the pontoon, fishermen touting their wares, the slap of fish being piled up on big sheets of paper, ready to go into open shopping bags. Catriona tried to let it wash over her, perhaps carry her away, but drowning it all out was the thump of her own pulse.

Mungo nodded, patting the air. 'Nae problem. I'll come

tae you.' He then heaved himself over the side of the boat, his lumpy boots landing solidly on the pontoon, next to Harry. 'So, how's things? I'm awfy sorry about wee Hope, Catriona.' He wiped his hands on a filthy cloth that was dangling from his pocket and, to her surprise, she saw his eyes fill. 'It was a lovely service, though.' He held her gaze and, without any more words, told her that he felt her pain.

'Thanks, Mungo.' Once again battling the tears that overtook her any time she was shown kindness at the moment, Catriona found a smile and patted his thick, scarred forearm. 'We've missed you.'

'You too, lass. And you, wee one.' He tipped his head to the side, trying to catch April's eye. 'Are you here straight from the school?' He spoke to Catriona now, and she nodded.

'Yep, first day back today.' She grimaced. 'Now, we're looking for some haddock so we can make April's favourite fisherman's pie for tea.'

Behind Mungo, Harry was filling a bag with fish. 'Hi, Mrs Anderson.' He smiled at her, the piercing blue eyes, mirrors of his grandfather's, glittered beneath the matted blond hair. It stuck up from his head as if he'd used designer products rather than gusts of salty wind to shape it. 'I've put four beauties in here for you.' He held the bag out to her. 'Grampa says no charge th'day.'

'No, I can't. Please let me pay you.' She turned to Mungo, who was shaking his head.

'Not at all. Next time.' He grinned. 'I'll charge you double.'

Catriona laughed, aware of the trickle of relief it gave her. 'Thanks, you old sod.' She accepted the bag from Harry. 'You two need to come and eat with us again some-time. It's been too long.'

Mungo had turned to rummage in the cool box, his thick arms wrestling with a mixture of silvery fish and crushed ice. 'Wait a sec. I've a couple of braw herring in here you can take, for Duncan.'

Catriona reached over and patted his shoulder. 'Don't worry, Mungo. He's away again.'

Mungo swung around, his brow deeply folded. 'Away?' Catriona sensed the unsaid half of his question as being 'at a time like this?' but she simply nodded.

'Yep, no rest for the wicked.' She shrugged. 'He'll be back next week, so I'll come and get some then.'

Mungo nodded, once again scrubbing his hands with the dirty cloth. 'Aye, OK then.'

Catriona shifted the heavy plastic bag up her arm. 'Thanks a million for the haddock. We'll enjoy this, won't we, April?'

April was looking out at the water, her cheeks pinking up in the breeze that was making her long plait bounce behind her shoulders. In profile, she looked sullen, her mouth firmly closed and her chin slack, this new aspect to her daughter's countenance sending a twist of sadness through Catriona.

'Right, we better be off. Time and tide...' She smiled at Mungo, who was nodding sadly.

'Aye, we'll see you next time.' He lifted a hand in good-bye, then took a step towards them. 'Catriona, if you need anything... I mean, I know you've family and all that...' His leathery face darkened. 'Just say the word, lass. A'right?' He eyed her. 'A'right?'

Catriona simply nodded, her tongue pressed hard against the roof of her mouth to keep her from flinging her arms around his craggy neck and sobbing into his salty shirt.

9

April had eaten about half the portion of fisherman's pie that Catriona had given her, and then had nibbled on some shortbread, so Catriona was content that she'd had enough to let her leave the table. April now sat in the living room watching her favourite programme, *All Creatures Great and Small*, while Catriona did some laundry.

April had said perhaps five words since they'd got home from the village, and the quieter she became, the more Catriona craved her voice, hovering around her, afraid that should April say something, she might miss it.

By the time Catriona had folded the clean clothes and put them all away, April was lying on the sofa, her feet under a cushion and her eyelids drooping. She looked relaxed until Catriona said her name, when her face closed again, her eyes becoming glassy and her mouth dipping. 'Time for bed, love.' Catriona held a hand out to her. 'Up you get.'

April swung her legs around, lifted the remote and turned off the TV, then pushed herself up from the sofa. 'I can sleep in my own bed tonight.' She shoved her feet into her slippers as Catriona caught her breath.

'Are you sure? I thought since Daddy was away, we could snuggle in my bed.' Her empty hand lingered in the air, as April shrugged.

'I'm a big girl. I can be in my own room.' She eyed Catriona, her tiny white teeth clamping over her lower lip.

'I know you're a big girl, darling.' Catriona let her hand drop. 'If you want to sleep in your own bed again, that's wonderful.'

April nodded, then for a second, Catriona thought she saw a flicker of doubt behind her eyes, but then it was gone. 'I want to.'

Catriona followed April upstairs, handed over her pyjamas, watched her clean her teeth, then tucked her into bed. Overcome with relief when she said she wanted a story, Catriona read from the tattered, hardbacked copy of *Mulan* that Iris had given her on her sixth birthday, and that had been one of Hope and April's favourites. Now, as she softly closed the book, April's breathing was slow and rhythmic, and her eyes were closed, this time the lids completely still.

Sliding from the bed and tiptoeing across the room, Catriona turned the light off and hesitated in the doorway for a few moments, taking in this more familiar form of her daughter, the gently curved cheek, the hint of a smile at the corner of the full mouth, the little hand wound around the tail of her toy monkey, Hamish. Reluctant to let this serene moment go, Catriona leaned against the door frame, the gentle tick of the Mickey Mouse clock on the bedside table the only sound in the room. The night sky was still glowing behind the curtain and just as she considered climbing up onto the top bunk for a few moments, her phone buzzed in her pocket.

Stepping out into the hall, Catriona pulled the door almost closed, then took her phone out. Her mother had texted her.

Are you OK? Please call me.

Catriona scanned the message a couple of times, then typed her reply.

I'm OK. Can you chat tonight?

Within seconds, a reply bloomed on the screen.

What time?

Catriona smiled as she replied.

I'll call you in a while?

Mother and daughter had settled themselves in front of their respective laptops, to video-chat, Catriona in front of the fire in the living room. They'd talked about their days, until the conversation had eventually turned to Duncan.

'So, when's he back?' Iris frowned.

'A week or so.' Catriona sipped some wine, letting the rich Bordeaux sit on her tongue for a few seconds.

'But are you feeling all right about him being away again, so soon?' Iris tipped her head to the side, her gentle eyes questioning.

Catriona smiled at her mother. 'He's got to work, Mum.

This was an important meeting that got postponed when...'
Catriona blinked, then stared into the fireplace as a solitary
flame licked up the side of the remaining chunk of log.

'I know, Catkin, but what I mean is, are you OK being
on your own?' Iris's face gave away her concern.

'I'm fine. April and I are OK.' Catriona hesitated,
wanting to tell someone about the disturbing changes she
was seeing in her little girl, but something held her back.
'We're fine.'

Iris scanned her face, then frowned. 'If you say so. But
you know your dad and I are here. He's worried about you
all.'

'Thanks, Mum. I appreciate that.' Catriona sipped some
more wine. 'I just need to get through a day at a time. Some
days it's doable, then others it's all I can do to get out of bed.'
She stared at her glass, her breathing ragged. 'If it wasn't for
April, I'd be totally screwed,' she croaked.

Iris nodded. 'I know. How is she coping? It must be so
hard for her, poor wee mite.'

An image of April, arms folded stubbornly across her
chest, and her chin set in its new, defiant way, made
Catriona blink. 'It is. She's dealing with it as best she can,
but I'm thinking she might need some counselling. She's
crushed, and very angry, Mum.' Having let this worrying
nugget of information slip out, she bit down on her lower
lip. 'Anyway, we'll figure it out.'

Iris was looking at her intently. 'How's Duncan dealing
with it all?'

Catriona swirled the wine in her glass, scanning her
mother's open face, battling with the need to confide in
someone. She set her glass on the coffee table, then met
Iris's eyes. 'He's doing what he usually does. Hiding behind

work.' She paused, the statement crouched between them like a wick waiting for a flame. Unable to hold back any longer, she blurted, 'I'm finding it hard to be around him, and it's eating away at us.' Catriona felt the familiar burn of tears behind her eyes and raked her hair into a rough pony-tail, snapping the band from her wrist around it.

'Your dad told me what you said to him.' Iris frowned again. 'But it was an accident, Catriona.'

Catriona took in the clear toffee-coloured eyes, the full mouth, and suddenly all she wanted to do was spill her guts, share everything that was churning inside her. Instead, she just shook her head.

Iris's eyes widened as her hand went nervously to her mouth, and Catriona knew that her lack of response had shocked her mother, but for now, it was the best she could do.

After telling her mother that she couldn't talk about it anymore – and saying goodbye to an emotional Iris – Catriona had gone into the bathroom and let angry tears wash her face as she stared at herself in the mirror, every ragged breath in and out like a series of claws slashing at her lungs. When she was cried out, her eyes swollen and her sides aching from the effort of controlling her sobs, Catriona had rinsed her face, swept her hair back up into a band, then crept in and checked on April.

She had been sleeping peacefully, Hamish's tail still wound around her fingers and her second favourite toy, Harvey, a ratty, velvet rabbit with one ear missing, tucked under her other arm. Catriona had added a light blanket on top of the duvet, as she herself was still shivery, and she didn't want April to wake up cold. Then, she'd leaned in carefully and dropped a kiss on April's forehead before tiptoeing out into the hallway.

Having had a long soak in the bath, a towel bundled up behind her head, and a second glass of wine balanced on the bath caddy, Catriona had emerged from the soapy water. The chill of the bathroom against her glowing skin had made her shiver. She'd stared in the mirror, taking in the new angles to her face, the more prominent cheekbones, the matching dark crescents under her blue eyes, and the tiny wrinkles that had appeared around her mouth over the past couple of weeks. Her face was a roadmap to her emotions and every line, dip and furrow a sign of what was going on under the surface, beneath her breastbone and deep inside the muscle of her heart. Sighing, she'd combed out her long hair, plaited it loosely, pulled on her pyjama bottoms and an old sweatshirt. Then she walked into the bedroom and crawled under the duvet, intending on reading.

The book she was halfway through was about a group of French Resistance fighters during World War Two and while she had been enjoying it a matter of a few weeks earlier, now, whenever she picked it up, she found she was reading the same paragraph repeatedly, until she'd close the book and dump it back on her bedside table. Tonight, however, she was determined to persevere, hoping that if she could just get through this chapter, she'd get back into the flow of the story.

As she lay under the covers, rubbing her feet against each other, she was struck by the sad metaphor that seemed to reflect her life. If she could just get through this chapter, perhaps she had a chance of getting back into the flow of living, but each time she took a step forward, she would find a sock of Hope's in the laundry basket, see the matching red jackets hanging on the coat hook, hear footsteps behind her and turn expecting to see those bright blue eyes, the button nose, the lustrous auburn hair, and suddenly she'd feel that she'd slipped backwards so far that she might never regain that ground again.

Swallowing a sob, she turned on her side and was about to reach for her book when her phone buzzed on the bedside table. Lifting it, she saw a text from Duncan.

Landed safely. All OK. Don't forget to lock the back door.
D x

As she read it, she marvelled at him reminding her of something so mundane, rather than ask how she and April were, when their whole world was tipped on its axis. Yet she immediately realised that she had indeed forgotten to lock the back door, as she frequently did. That he knew her so well brought a lump to her throat. How easily they had let things get in the way, peel them apart one tiny disagreement at a time, until now, when she felt as far from him as she ever had in their life together.

As she sat up and threw the duvet off, she pictured Duncan sitting in an ultra-sleek hotel room in Singapore, a spray of city lights glittering all around the skyscraper, a cold beer next to him and his laptop balanced on his knees. The thousands of miles that now separated them felt oppressive, adding a physicality to the emotional distance she'd been feeling ever since the accident. The combination was overwhelming, and her breaths became shallow as she longed for the time when they'd been inseparable, even by geography. When he'd video-chat with her from far-flung corners of the world, at all hours, staying on camera until she fell asleep, cracking bad jokes and reminding her of how many days it was until he would be home. She missed that closeness so much that it gaped inside her, like an open wound. She missed the sense of them pulling in the same direction, instead of away from one another, and as she stared down at her phone, wanting to open a tiny window that he could crawl through, she typed through blurry eyes.

Going to lock up now. X

10

A week later, after only one disturbed night in her own bed, April had consistently been sleeping in beside Catriona again. April always started off in the bottom bunk then, around ten o'clock, would tiptoe into her parents' room carrying Hamish and Harvey, wordlessly slip under the covers and turn her back to Catriona and go to sleep. Initially, Catriona had talked to her, asked if she wanted a drink, or a story, but April would only whisper 'No', until eventually Catriona simply greeted her with a smile, pulling back the duvet and tucking her in.

After the sixth night of this happening, Catriona had begun to worry that she'd have to wean April off the practice before Duncan got home, knowing his feelings on it. For now, though, she found her daughter's presence comforting. As Catriona lay in the dark, often sleepless, an ache so deep inside her that it seemed to have become part of her DNA, she would wipe away silent tears – tears for her lost children, for her little girl who was now in so much pain, for herself and for her ailing marriage.

Duncan had been texting her each evening, and they'd

had two brief video calls. Both times he'd appeared rushed, checking his watch, and moving the laptop around the hotel room, making Catriona feel seasick. The last call they'd had had been the previous night, when he'd seemed more relaxed, sitting out on the balcony of his room and talking about coming home.

Catriona had dug deep, trying to muster some enthusiasm in her voice. In truth, she was nervous to have him home, after the prickly way they'd parted and the somewhat perfunctory messages they'd exchanged over the time he'd been away.

Now it was Saturday afternoon, and he was due back that evening. For April's sake, Catriona was determined to make a proper family meal, so she had finished her one tutorial with Olivia, dashed to the village for some shopping and cooked a rich casserole. The table was laid in the kitchen, and she'd bought a bunch of pale pink hydrangeas that she'd arranged in a butter-coloured vase and sat in the centre. Satisfied with her efforts, lastly, she'd added a single silver candlestick with a long beeswax candle, carved like honeycomb, and the crystal water goblets Duncan's twin brother, Ian, a lawyer who lived in St Andrews, had given them the previous Christmas. She'd even set a goblet at April's place, desperately wanting the child, whom she was afraid was slowly retreating from her, to know that she belonged not only at this table, but firmly in their lives.

April had smiled wanly when, after breakfast, Catriona had told her that her daddy would be home that evening. Catriona had then watched her slip out of the back door and walk across the grass, Hamish and Harvey both dangling from her hand as she looked down at her feet rather than out at the view.

Having hovered at the kitchen window for a few

minutes, afraid to take her eyes off April's outline, somehow newly small and fragile against the magnificence of the landscape that was framing her, Catriona could take it no longer. She'd followed her daughter outside and, taking her hand, they'd walked left together, to the river side of the garden. The fence, now repaired, separated them from where they'd lost Hope.

Catriona had knelt on the dewy grass as the breeze had tugged at the water's surface, making it gurgle. The smell of clover and sea salt had hung heavy in the air, as she'd drawn April onto her knee. 'Sweetheart, you know you can tell me when you're feeling sad and missing Hope, right?' She'd swept April's long hair over her shoulder and waited.

April had simply nodded, leaning slightly away from Catriona, the tension against her forearm another hurtful sign of April's wish to separate herself, not only emotionally but physically.

Catriona had sighed, released her daughter and stood up. 'Right, let's go to the village.' She'd held a hand out to April, who, after a few agonising moments, had slid her cool fingers into Catriona's, sending a spark of hope through her that maybe, just maybe, they would get through this and back to where they'd been before the night that had changed everything. Damaged everything.

Now April was watching a nature programme, and as Catriona checked the clock on the cooker, she calculated that Duncan would be back in approximately two hours, leaving her plenty time to take a bath and talk to her mum. Just as she was reaching for her phone on the kitchen counter, it rang. Seeing her mother's number, Catriona smiled as she answered it. 'Hi, Mum. How are you?' She circled the table and stood at the sink, taking in the view. The loch was glittering like a broad, diamond-studded ribbon in the late-afternoon light. Two small boats were bobbing out in the distance, their sails billowing as they followed one another across the horizon, their thin masts pointing purposefully skyward into the bright blue above. 'I was just going to call you.'

'Hi, love. Great minds, eh?' Iris laughed softly. 'We're fine. How are you?'

Catriona gave a half-smile. 'Yeah, you know. We're still here.' She shrugged. 'Coping.'

Iris sighed. 'I know. It's such a vapid question, but it's so hard to know what's right.' She hesitated. 'I know you're struggling, every single moment. I just want you to know that I'm right there with you. You're all always in our thoughts, and in our hearts, Catkin.' Her voice cracked, bringing Catriona's eyes closed.

'It's OK, Mum. I know that. Please don't cry.' Still unable to accept too much kindness without falling apart, Catriona swallowed hard. 'What's Dad up to this weekend?'

After a few minutes of small talk, Iris filling her in on Will's latest project building a kit model of an aircraft carrier that was driving her mad, tiny bits of balsa wood and sticky brushes having taken over her kitchen table, Iris turned the conversation to Duncan. 'So, he's home tonight?'

Catriona walked into the hall to check on April, who was snuggled under a blanket with her head on Hamish, as she stared at the TV, where a pride of lions was pacing across a dry-looking African plain. 'Yes, in a couple of hours, actually.' She checked her watch again, a ripple of nerves worming up her insides. 'I'm a bit anxious about it, to be honest.' The words out, she bit down on her bottom lip, as oversharing had not been her intention.

'Why, love?'

Catriona went back into the kitchen, then through into the conservatory. Switching on a table lamp, she sat on the wicker sofa and, shivering, tucked her legs under her and hugged a soft cushion to her front. 'Things were pretty strained when he left.' She paused. 'Well, for a while now.' Once again giving away too much, she pressed her eyes closed, trying to picture the frown that would inevitably be creasing her mother's forehead.

'I know you were struggling, but I thought with a little time, and him being away for a while, that you'd be able to sort things out.' She covered the phone and mumbled something, then, hearing the muffled rumble of her father's voice in the background, Catriona wished she could take back what she'd said. And yet, the need to tell someone was overwhelming.

'It's just that we don't seem to know what to say to one another at the moment.' Catriona shook her head. 'But don't worry. We'll get through it.' As she said the words, they instantly floated away from her, like they were being carried on a breeze, their weight and significance stark against the glowing light of the afternoon.

'Just give it time, Catriona. You've been through hell, the pair of you. It's only natural that this amount of pain will get between you, for a while.'

Catriona nodded, the wisdom behind her mother's words not lost on her. 'I know. Thanks, Mum.' Getting up from the sofa, Catriona caught a movement in the corner of her eye. As she turned around, she saw April hovering in the doorway with her fingers in her mouth and her sweater sleeve hanging loosely around her narrow wrist. This emerging pattern of leaving the room, then reappearing silently, took Catriona by surprise, as she extended her hand to her daughter. 'Come and say hello to Nana.' She smiled at April, who dropped her hand to her side and walked towards her, each step seeming to drain all the energy from her small body.

Duncan's suitcase stood at the bottom of the stairs. No matter how many times he travelled, the pattern was always the same when he got home. He'd come through the door, kick off his shoes, dump his bags and coat and kiss Catriona, before heading into the living room and pouring himself a healthy whisky. Then he'd come back into the kitchen, drag his case to the stairs and ask where the girls were.

Catriona would wind her arms around his neck, pull him close and kiss him again, tasting the smoke of the whisky and catching the mustiness of travel lingering in his hair. Then she'd call the girls, whether they were out in the garden or upstairs, engrossed in some game in their room. They'd thunder into the kitchen, arms and legs flying as they launched themselves at Duncan, their eyes trained like birds of prey on the suitcase out in the hall – the promise of a present making their faces flush.

Duncan would sometimes torture them, winking at Catriona as he asked them about school, Brownies, who had perhaps seen an otter or a seal on the riverbank, or who'd been the best behaved for their mum. The girls would begin to hop excitedly from foot to foot, their staccato answers punctuated by much huffing and clasping of hands until he'd finally say, 'All right then. Let's see what's in the case for you,' at which point Hope would dart into the hall and dive on the bag, yanking at the zip until he'd laughingly ease it open for her. He'd stand back, his arm going around Catriona's shoulder, and they'd lean in towards one another, soaking in the excitement that was pulsing from the girls' backs, as they crouched over the messy contents of the case, their little hands digging around in Duncan's clothes.

It was a precious ritual that Catriona looked forward to, at the end of every trip, but so far, this homecoming had been quite different. Duncan had hugged her rather than kissing her and now was in the living room. As she worked through the mixture of emotions his chilly greeting had created, a conflicting cocktail of hurt and, oddly, relief at not being kissed swirled inside her as she heard the clink of the whisky decanter. Shaking it off, she walked into the hall as he emerged from the living room, his shirt wrinkled around his middle and his glass dangling at his thigh.

'So, how was the trip?' she asked, taking in the lines that were now etched around his mouth, like a set of brackets. 'Good meetings?'

He nodded, running a hand through his hair. 'Yeah, we got sign-off, which is great.' He edged past her and walked back into the kitchen. Catriona's skin prickled as she took a breath, and then followed him.

'How was Stewart?' She walked to the counter by the stove and poured herself a glass of wine. 'Happy with the results?' She turned to see Duncan pull out a chair and flop down at the table, his eyes flicking around the room.

'Yes, we both were.' He nodded. 'We got the start date we wanted, too. The planning application has gone in and, all being well, we're aiming to break ground in three months.' He took a large swig of whisky, then, frowning, lowered the glass to the table. As he looked down, he noticed the flowers and gave a half-smile. 'Those are nice.' He looked up at her. 'How have you been?' His face softened, sending a flicker of recognition through her, so she nodded.

'You know.' She shrugged, grappling for something that

would sound remotely positive. 'Day by day.'

His expression seemed to close again, his eyes becoming hooded. 'Yeah.' He blinked several times. 'Same.'

Catriona took a deep breath, the effort of having to edit her thoughts around him already making her weary. 'April's upstairs. Let me call her.' Before he could respond, she set her glass down and walked into the hall. 'April. Daddy's home. Are you coming down?' She gripped the bannister, straining to hear whether April had left her room. Just as she was about to call again, she heard the floorboards creak in the upper hall and then April appeared at the top of the stairs. She'd put on her pyjamas and was wearing Hope's lilac dressing gown, rather than her own lemon one. Seeing it, Catriona caught her breath, her eyes suddenly burning and her mouth becoming slack. She stammered, 'Um, are you coming down, sweetheart?'

April hesitated at the top of the stairs, then began walking down, her fluffy slippers seeming to dwarf her little feet. 'I got ready for bed.' She slid one hand down the bannister and kept her eyes on the stairs in front of her, Hamish and Harvey both dangling from her free hand.

'I see that.' Catriona waited for her to get to the bottom, then took her hand. 'It's quite early, sweetheart, but that's OK.' She kept her voice light. 'Jammies are always comfy.'

In the kitchen, Duncan was gone, and his empty glass sat on the table. Surprised, Catriona swung around and looked into the conservatory. His profile was sharp against the window as he stood at the desk, his head bent as he scanned the laptop screen. His back formed an inverted question mark as he stroked the trackpad, then he straightened up, his other hand pinching the base of his neck.

A flash of disappointment, tainted with anger, warmed Catriona's face as she held April's hand a little tighter. Did he not realise that he still had a daughter – still wanting her father's attention and love – scared, lonely and missing her sister more than she could express? Just as she was about to lead April into the conservatory, Duncan seemed to sense that she was looking at him, so he turned, then walked towards them, a strained smile curved around his lips.

'Hey, April Mactiggiwinkle. PJs already?' He held his hands out to April, who let go of Catriona's hand and trotted over to him. As Duncan leaned down to her, she hugged his neck, her little eyes closing as she held on, the poignant scene making Catriona blink against the prickling in her eyes.

'I was tired.' April stepped back from Duncan, her lower lip protruding. 'These are cosy.' She patted her thigh, the bumblebee fabric of her pyjama bottoms flapping around her skinny leg.

'Good call.' Duncan nodded. 'I might put mine on, too.' He looked over at Catriona and stuck his bottom lip out. 'What do you say, Mum?'

Catriona shook her head. 'You two are a daft pair.' She made an exaggerated tutting sound, then turned back towards the kitchen. 'Dinner will be ready soon.'

As she reached the stove, April appeared behind her, her hand grabbing the pocket of Catriona's jeans. 'Mummy?' Her voice was little more than a whisper.

'What is it, love?' Catriona turned and let her hands settle on April's shoulders. Her eyes were glittering and her chin was quivering.

'Is it OK to get a present, without Hope?'

Catriona felt a stab of pain high up under her ribs as her eyes instantly filled again. 'Oh, April. Of course it is, my love.' She pulled her close, the little girl's head pressing into her middle. 'Let's go and see what's in the case for you.'

11

Catriona lay in the bed, waiting for Duncan to come back. He'd let April stay with them for around half an hour, but as soon as her eyelids had grown heavy and her breathing had slowed, he'd gently lifted her out of the bed. Catriona had told him to leave her be, but he'd just shaken his head. 'She needs to get used to her own bed again, Cat. This isn't good for her.' He'd stood at the bottom of the bed, April in his arms, his T-shirt clinging to his chest in a way that made Catriona swallow.

Part of her wanted him to take April to her own room, then come back and pull her, Catriona, to him and kiss her like he'd truly missed her, the way he used to, while another part of her wasn't certain she wanted to be that close to him again. Overcome by a slew of conflicting emotions, roiling inside her like an angry sea, she'd closed her eyes, counting her breaths until eventually he'd come back into the room.

Now, her heart rate picked up as he got back into bed and switched off his bedside light, leaving only the gentle glow of the night light in the bathroom illuminating the room. As she lay still, bracing herself for his hand to reach for hers, instead he whispered, 'Cat, what's going on?'

Frowning, she turned to face him. 'What do you mean?' His minty breath brushed her cheek.

He sighed. 'Was April like this all the time I was away?'

Catriona took a breath, needing a moment to formulate her reply, then pushed herself up and turned her light back on.

Duncan sat up too, his forehead deeply furrowed. 'What now?'

She pressed her eyes closed, a tickertape of things she wanted to say rushing through her mind. Was he just noticing now that their daughter had become a shadow of her former self? A timid, monosyllabic slip of humanity, uncomfortable in her own skin and unsure how to function in a world without her best friend, her beloved sister.

Catriona pushed out a shaky breath, opened her eyes and turned to Duncan, who was staring at her, his mouth slightly open. 'I've been telling you, for so long, that she needs your attention. And she needs to feel loved, now more than ever. She needs to understand that it's OK for her to still be here, without Hope.' Catriona's forced whisper grabbed at the back of her throat, and she paused, determined to hold back the tears that were pressing in. 'You promised me, even before...' Her voice faltered. 'You said you'd make more of an effort to connect with her, spend time with her. You said you'd try.' She wanted to grab his giant shoulders and shake her message into him. 'She is a child, and she is grieving, just like we are, but she's not able to express how she feels. She's nine, Duncan. Nine. We are the bloody adults here, and we need to help her in any way we can by going to her, not waiting for her to come to us. Don't you understand that?'

The urge to jump up from the bed and run out into the hallway, to put physical distance between them again, was overwhelming.

His molten eyes were wide, his lips pulsing as if he was biting his own tongue.

'She is withdrawing more and more by the day. I feel like I'm losing her, too, and I just can't bear it.' Catriona's brittle voice gave way to a sob, and she clamped her hand over her mouth, panting into her palm. As he made to touch her shoulder, she leaned away from him. 'You have to try to understand her and be her damn father, Duncan. She needs you to step up and put her first, for once in your life.' Catriona took in his shocked expression, tears now freely trickling down her face. 'If you want any kind of relationship with your daughter, now is the time, Duncan. This is it.' She held her hands out, palms up, her fingers quivering. 'It's up to you.'

His frown deepened as he shoved the duvet off and got out of bed. Catriona watched as he paced across the room, massaging the back of his neck. Then he turned to face her, hands on his hips and his cheeks highly coloured. 'You know, it was always you and the girls. The three of you in your little clique. You'd let them run riot around here, and then Daddy would come home from a trip and, all of a sudden, I'd feel like I was gatecrashing a party that'd been going on for ages without me.' He swung his arms out at his sides. 'I know the girls resented me for being away. And so did you.' His voice rumbled as Catriona looked at him, her eyes flashing as she ran through myriad situations, still trying to look at it from his perspective, give him the benefit of the doubt, despite everything. But she only saw his back as he'd leave a room, his shoulders hunched over his laptop as the girls tried to get his attention, or him occasionally barking at them to be quiet when he was trying to work. Then, before she could stop them, the words spilled out.

'You can't be serious, Duncan. It was never like that. They've always adored you, but you were the one who stepped back, distanced yourself. We were always right here, wanting you to be here *with* us.' She pressed her palm into the mattress. 'Didn't you get that?'

He stared at her, his fingers making deep furrows in his hair. 'I tried. I really did.' He shook his head. 'It was easy and more natural with Hope, and she was my bridge to April.' He shrugged. 'I'm ashamed to say it, but it's always been harder with her. She's never responded to me the way Hope did, and I can't connect with April the same way you do.' His voice caught, his tortured expression leaving him raw and vulnerable. 'Now Hope's gone, I don't know how to *be* with April.' He nodded towards the door. 'I don't know what to do, Cat.' He paused, his eyes flicking around as if searching for something solid to land on. 'Perhaps...' He paused. 'Perhaps if she was really mine, I mean, my flesh and blood?' He held his palms up, his eyes searching her face for something she could not give.

'Shhh, Duncan. For God's sake.' She glanced at the half-open door.

Duncan was ashen now, his hands hanging at his sides. 'Look, I didn't mean that I don't...' He halted, then gradually his face darkened. 'You know, we should've told her bloody years ago about being adopted, but you were so sure we shouldn't,' he said, his voice rough and low.

Catriona recalled a conversation when April had been six and she'd asked Catriona why her hair and eyes were a different colour to Hope's. There had been a deeper question in April's eyes that Catriona had chosen to ignore, placating her by saying that lots of sisters had different features.

A wave of nausea forced Catriona out of the bed, and just as she leaned down to grab her robe from the chair, a shadow flicked past the door. Time slowed down as Catriona took only seconds to figure out that April must have been in the hall, perhaps on her way back to their room, and had heard what Duncan said.

Catriona's stomach lurched, her mouth going dry as she clasped her forehead, fear making her sway. She knew that April would have interpreted the full meaning of what he'd said, and now, there was no way to take it back. 'She heard you,' she sputtered. 'She just heard you.' She pointed at the door, her hand shaking. 'Oh my God, Duncan. She was outside the door.'

Fumbling with her robe, Catriona turned her back on him and rushed out of the room.

April was on the sofa in the conservatory, her back curled towards the room and her face buried in the cushion Catriona had left there earlier. Hamish lay on the floor, his tail in a perfect coil, as April hiccupped, her body juddering with the effort of breathing between sobs.

Catriona flipped the lamp on and, sitting beside her, pulled April's stiff little body onto her lap, moving the hair from April's face and wiping her cheeks with her thumb. 'Come here, sweetheart,' she crooned. 'Come to Mummy.'

April resisted for a few moments, then she folded forward and buried her face in Catriona's neck. As Catriona tried to comfort her, the scariest part of this whole scenario was that April wasn't crying in a normal way. Her body was quaking, tears soaking Catriona's skin, but not a sound was escaping the little girl.

Afraid she might choke, Catriona eased April away from her and locked on her eyes. 'Sweetheart, you need to breathe. Can you take a big breath for Mummy, then blow it out, like this?' She mimed the action, her mouth twitching as she tried to keep April's focus. 'April, love. Please just take a breath for me.'

After a few, interminable seconds, April shakily sucked in air, tears continuing to pool in her eyes and spill down her ashen cheeks, then she blew it out. Her hands were now twisted in the cushion, the small fingers working themselves into knots, and her bare feet were fully flexed, the tension visible as it coursed through her body.

Catriona's throat knotted tighter as she tried to stay calm. 'Good girl. Now do another one for me.' She nodded, once again showing April what she wanted her to do.

The little girl hesitated for a moment, then repeated the deep breath, a little colour returning to her face. Relieved, Catriona stroked her back, feeling the course of the silent sobs rippling through her daughter.

Behind them, Duncan appeared in the doorway, his face pale and his eyes full of concern. 'Is she OK?'

Catriona hugged April closer and spoke quietly, his rebuke of moments ago still ringing in her ears. While all she wanted was to comfort her daughter, find the words to take her pain away, all she could think was that she had contributed to this mess. Her insistence that they not tell April about her adoption had put them in this position, and she had to face the truth of that. 'I think we need to have a family talk.' She glanced over at Duncan, who crossed the room and pulled the chair out from the desk. 'It's time.'

'Right. OK.' He sat down, leaned forward and linked his long fingers between his knees. 'Let's talk.'

Telling April about how she became their daughter was less traumatic than Catriona had anticipated. Once she began to talk, she found that the words came easily, an organic flow of truths that built the picture of a beautiful life, begun in one scenario, then transplanted to another in order to grow. She spoke slowly and quietly, stopping now and then to ask April if she understood, but receiving no reply, she continued. Eventually, she finished by telling April that there was no more precious a gift than a child like her, and that her birth mother had given them that gift to treasure, forever.

All the while, April sat on a low stool, between Duncan and Catriona. The lamp behind her was casting a golden glow around the conservatory and her eyes were glittering, although the tears had finally stopped. Now, she looked at Catriona, a tiny frown pulling at her forehead, then over at Duncan, then back to Catriona, as if waiting for one of them to stand up, throw their arms wide and tell her this was all a joke, but as Catriona finally stopped talking and held her arms out to April, the most startling thing happened.

April sat up straighter, shoved the hair away from her shoulders and tugged her pyjama top down at the back. Her face seemed to clear of all emotion, and she licked her lips, as if preparing to speak, but rather than talk she simply stood up, walked across the room, picked Hamish up from the floor and headed into the hall.

Taken aback, Catriona turned to Duncan, who stared at the door, watching April disappear into the hall and then turn towards the stairs. 'What the hell?' He met Catriona's gaze. 'Should we go after her?'

Catriona was already up. 'Of course we should,' she snapped. 'Are you coming?'

Duncan stood up and straightened his twisted pyjama bottoms, his bare feet looking huge and ungainly against the pattern of the brick floor. 'Yeah, I'm coming.' He crossed the room, and just as Catriona was about to walk into the hall, he grabbed her hand. 'Cat?'

'What?' She swung around to face him.

'I...' He searched her face. 'I'm sorry for what I said up there about you...' He jerked his thumb towards the ceiling.

He took her hand in his, but she pulled it away. 'It's not important now, Duncan. We need to go to April.' She closed her eyes momentarily, then opened them to see him staring down at her. 'Before it's too late.'

Nothing that Catriona said could elicit a response in April. She lay on the bottom bunk, her back to the room, Hamish and Harvey both tucked under her chin and Hope's robe now tossed onto the floor. Catriona had lain next to her, curled behind her stiff little form, but no matter how she coaxed or cajoled, her daughter refused to turn to face her.

Duncan had sat on the floor, then perched awkwardly on the end of the bunk, his big hands clenching and releasing as he observed Catriona's efforts. He left the room twice and came back in, and, each time, Catriona hoped that he might have come up with some small enticement, an idea of how to reach April, who seemed to have stepped into a place where they were denied entrance.

The silence was terrifying, and Catriona looked over at Duncan, wide-eyed, mouthing, 'What shall I do?'

His mouth dipped at the corners. 'I don't know,' he whispered back, his shoulders bouncing.

. . .

After an hour of persevering, and April's breathing finally settling into a steady rhythm, Catriona carefully slid away from her and stood up.

Duncan was sitting on the floor again, his legs crossed and his hands gripping his knees. 'Is she asleep?' he whispered.

Catriona tucked her tousled hair behind her ears, her insides aching as if she'd been punched.

'Yes, I think so,' she replied, then pointed at the door.

Duncan followed her into their bedroom and carefully closed the door behind them. Catriona sat on the bed, her legs shaking. She pressed her palms onto her thighs to try to stop the movement, but the more she tried, the worse it seemed to get, until she was shivering uncontrollably.

Seeing what was happening, Duncan grabbed a soft blanket from the chest under the window and wrapped it around her shoulders, gently easing her back into bed, then pulling the duvet up around her. 'Cat, try to relax.'

His voice was fading as she looked at his face, the face she knew so well that she could have drawn it, blindfolded. His soulful eyes were darkly shadowed, the lines around his mouth seeming to have deepened even more since earlier that evening. He circled the bed and climbed in on his side, then reached for her.

Catriona felt as if she had left her body, as if she was floating above the bed, watching herself leaning into him, her head finding his shoulder and her hands being covered by his. Right now, all she wanted was to release the pain that was racking her limbs, spiralling inside her head and making the back of her throat burn.

As she gradually felt herself settle back into her skin,

the shivering beginning to stop, she closed her eyes, unable to look at the anguish on her husband's face. She wanted to comfort him, to tell him that this unholy mess was not entirely his fault, but even as she finally felt the moisture returning to her mouth, she was unable to form the words.

She was unsure how long they'd stayed like this, linked together and yet more divided than ever, so when Duncan moved, slipping his arm from behind her back, the break in contact was like a snap of static electricity, bringing her bolt upright. She watched as he stood up, the dim light coming in from behind the curtains outlining his shape against the wall. He looked like a stranger. His broad shoulders newly rounded, his head hanging forward sightly, as in defeat, and he was thinner than she'd ever seen him. His stomach was concave now, rather than having the gentle, well-fed curve it once had, and seeing the changes in him, Catriona was momentarily filled with regret. She'd been so hard on him, so cold and unwilling to forgive, that now she was afraid that even if she could, it might be too late.

As if he'd read her mind, Duncan walked around to her side of the bed and sat on the edge, taking her icy fingers in his. 'Cat, I need to say something.' He sought her eyes. 'Just hear me out, OK?'

Unsure of what was coming, she simply nodded.

'I did this. I broke us.' His voice caught. 'I am to blame, for everything, and I think it'd be best if I go for a while.' He dropped his gaze to the floor. 'Just to give us all some time, and space.'

Catriona felt as if the mattress was melting underneath her. 'Go where?' she croaked.

'Fort William. I can stay in the company flat, just until things settle down a bit. I think the distance will do us all good.'

Everything was slipping away from her. Her sweet girl was gone, her other daughter had retreated into an impenetrable shell and now her husband, the man she'd spent nineteen years with, the man she'd loved, married, and built a family with, was going to go, too. Unsure why she was surprised, Catriona's mouth clamped shut. This was his MO. He withdrew when things got tough, disappeared back inside his work, exercising a form of denial that, while she resented it, she had learned to live with over the years. After Faith died, when they'd brought Hope home, he'd been physically present most of the first few months, but he'd begun to hide from rather than face his emotions. He had stepped back then, and he was stepping back again now, just when she needed him the most.

As Catriona took a shaky breath, she pulled her hand away from his fingers. 'Don't you think we need to find a way through this, together?'

He shook his head, turning to look at the window. 'I seem to do nothing but make things worse. Injure both of you.' He nodded at the door. 'It's for the best, Cat.'

She looked at him, afraid that if he walked away, she'd be unable to stop this dangerous momentum, her entire life becoming like quicksand under her feet. As she stared at his profile, wishing for a solution, he turned back to face her, his eyes scanning her features, each in turn, as if he was committing them to memory.

As she shifted up in the bed, she whispered, 'Don't do this again, Duncan.'

He stood up, hesitating for a few seconds before walking back around to his own side of the bed. Pulling back the duvet, he got in and turned to face the window. 'I'll go tomorrow.'

12

A week after Duncan left for Fort William, April had still not spoken a word. Catriona was doing her best to give her space and not pressure her, but as each day passed without the sound of her daughter's voice, so Catriona's anxiety over April's state of mind was building, to a dangerous crescendo.

Duncan was calling or texting each night, and Catriona had started watching her phone, around 8 p.m. Their conversations were short, and subdued, and primarily about April and her sustained silence, but they were still welcome within the new quiet of the house, and the empty space that Duncan had left in her heart.

Catriona had called the school to let Mrs Brighton know what was happening with April, and to tell her that if it continued much longer, she was going to look for a counsellor. Typically, the head teacher had been warm and sympathetic. 'Mrs Anderson, as I'm sure you know, children often internalise trauma. It's a self-preservation thing.' She'd sighed. 'We'll keep a close eye on her here at school, but please let me know if you decide to explore some coun-selling. I think it might be wise.'

Now, having had a restless night, and another wet bed to deal with in the girls' room, where April was now staying, Catriona woke to the sound of beeping. For a moment, she thought it was an alarm of some kind, then she recognised the warning signal of a vehicle reversing. Rolling onto her side, she checked the clock, the display showing 7.49 a.m., and as she sat up, the beeping stopped.

Curious, she walked to the window, pulled the curtains, and stretched her arms above her head. Unable to see the drive-way, or street, from her window, she shifted her focus towards the house next door, and then the beeping started up again. Frowning, she pulled on her robe and went down the stairs, following the sound through the kitchen and into the living room. As she opened the curtains and looked out at the drive, on her left a large lorry was backing up the drive of the neigh-bouring cottage, the little double-gabled house with the leaded-light windows that had been empty for more than a year.

The previous owners had been an elderly couple, called Sheila and Ken Mackenzie, who'd been keen birdwatchers and sailors. They'd lived in the house for fifty years until the garden and general upkeep had become too much for them and then they'd moved into an assisted-living facility near their daughter, on the Isle of Skye. Catriona and Duncan had missed the sweet couple when they'd gone, Ken being the one who'd got Duncan interested in restoring the old boat and Sheila, a wonderful seamstress, forever leaving personalised, embroidered pillowcases, intricately stitched bookmarks and hairbands for the girls on their back step.

They'd told Catriona that they weren't selling yet but would see how it went on Skye before they made any final decisions about the house, so noting the bright blue AG Movers logo on the side of the van, Catriona sighed. Obviously, Skye had worked out, and, sadly, their old friends would not be back.

Going into the kitchen, she filled the kettle and set it to boil. The June morning sky was bright, a breeze ruffling through the row of gorse at the left of the lawn. Catriona had not been back to that side of the garden since sitting out there with April a week or so earlier, the unpredictable river lurking beyond the fence still harbouring painful memories that were hard to face.

As Catriona opened the back door and went out onto the step, she heard voices filtering over from the next-door garden. Her curiosity piquing, she walked along the flagstone path, stopping where the rosemary bushes ended in a small rockery and the lawn stretched away towards the loch. As she bent down and picked some deadheads from a patch of pansies that she'd been neglecting recently, a young, fair-haired boy – she guessed to be around ten or eleven – walked along behind the fence to her right that separated the Mackenzies' garden from theirs. Catriona was careful to look busy, in case he turned and saw her, but the boy was focused on the loch, his face rapt as he crossed the unkempt lawn, eventually disappearing behind the outline of their boathouse – another place Catriona had not ventured since that night.

After a few minutes, she took a deep, cleansing breath, the rich scent of rosemary filling her head, then tossed the little pile of pansy heads behind one of the larger stones in the rockery and turned back towards the house. Just as she reached the back door, she heard the boy calling to someone.

'Look, it's a seal.' His voice was bubbling with excitement. 'Look, Pops.'

Catriona turned to see him running across the lawn, followed by a tall man with thinning grey hair and a walking stick and then a slender woman wearing a long floral skirt, a white, short-sleeved shirt, and a floppy straw hat.

'Wheesht, Graham. You'll wake the neighbours,' the man said, laughter bubbling beneath the warning. 'We're coming.'

Half hiding in the doorway, Catriona watched the threesome walk to the edge of the water, then the boy lifted a stone and skimmed it across the surface, it bouncing three times before it sank into the murky depths. 'Whoa, a triple,' he shouted, as the woman pressed her finger to her lips. 'Sorry.' He raised his palms in apology. 'I forgot.'

Seeing the unbridled joy in the young face, something she missed like a flower misses the sun, Catriona swallowed hard, went back inside and quietly closed the door. There were reminders everywhere of the vibrant life that had once pulsed from their home and their little family, before they'd lost Hope, but that simple smile had knocked the wind from her.

Taking a few moments to compose herself, she scanned the tidy kitchen, the bunches of fragrant herbs hanging from the laundry rack and the glimmering copper pans seeming dull and lifeless now. The smell of coffee still lingered from the previous evening, and taking it all in, Catriona knew she needed a project. Something to stop her from losing her mind.

Seeing the tin that stood on the counter, usually filled with Duncan's favourite biscuits, she nodded to herself.

Perhaps she'd dig out her baking trays and get April to help her make something to welcome their new neighbours. It would be nice to have the old cottage occupied again, and she hoped that the new family would be pleasant to have around.

After lunch, with April still sitting silently at the kitchen table, Catriona pulled the flour and other ingredients out and set them on the counter. 'Are you going to help me make shortbread, sweetheart?' She looked at April's pensive profile, as she stared blankly out of the window. 'April?'

April turned to face her, her hair clinging to her cheek as if it were damp. She met Catriona's eyes for a few moments, then shrugged, her bottom lip protruding.

'Come on, it'll be fun. We'll make a double batch, then take some over to the new neighbours. They have a boy, perhaps a wee bit older than you.' Catriona took the large glass mixing bowl from the cupboard under the stove. 'I'll measure and you can stir.' She set the bowl down and waited, seeing April's eyelids fluttering as if she was considering the value of getting involved in this seemingly frivolous activity.

As Catriona sifted through her own feelings, baking – when her husband had literally just left her, and her daughter was now shutting her out completely – did seem strange. However, Catriona knew that if she cut into the butter, sifted the flour, added just the right amount of sugar, lightly massaged the crumbling dough between her fingertips and pressed it into the baking tray, it would turn out fine. Right now, there was little else in her life that she could control this way, and the more she thought about it, the more she needed to have just one thing turn out right.

'April, please. Come and help me.'

She watched April blink several times, then shake the hair from her face. Eventually, she stood up. Her jeans were baggy around her thighs and the giant fluffy slippers looked bizarre at the end of the birdlike shins as she lifted Hamish from the table and made her way slowly to where Catriona stood.

Relieved, Catriona pulled two aprons from the drawer. 'Which one do you want? Tulips or tartan?' She held them both up, knowing that, in the past, the girls had fought over the one with the tulips on the front.

April glanced from one to the other, then took the tartan apron from Catriona's hand.

Surprised, but scrabbling to keep April engaged to whatever degree she could, Catriona spoke brightly. 'Right. Turn round and I'll tie it for you.' She drew a circle in the air with her index finger.

April turned her back on her mother, lifting her arms slightly to allow Catriona to circle her waist and secure the apron. Turning back around, with Hamish dangling at her side, April looked down at her front, as a single tear oozed over her bottom lid. The sight of the glossy bubble sent a shot of pain directly into Catriona's heart as she let her palms settle on April's bony shoulders.

'April, please speak to me, love. Tell me what's happening in here.' She gently tapped April's chest. 'Let it out.'

April eyed her, her mouth now pursed, as if words, wave after wave of them, were trying to get out, but she was holding them prisoner.

Catriona stood on the doorstep of the old Mackenzie house, a flutter of nerves making her question the wisdom of this impromptu visit. She used to enjoy when her tai chi friends dropped in without phoning first, but it was risky to simply turn up uninvited when she didn't know these people. And yet, the idea of simply speaking to someone who knew nothing of her story was liberating. Convincing herself that all would be well, she forced her shoulders back.

Before leaving home, she'd gone into the bathroom to brush her hair. Shocked at how drawn she looked, her blue eyes cupped by dark shadows and her lips fading into the creamy wash of her skin, she'd dug out an old lipstick, swiped some on and then dusted a little rouge over her cheeks. Satisfied that she didn't look quite so ghostlike, she'd switched off the light and gone to find April.

April had been reading in bed and reluctant to come, but Catriona had insisted, and now, April was at her side, her eyes dull and her face pinched. 'Want to ring the bell?' Catriona nodded at the old-fashioned, wrought-iron pull. 'You just pull that down.' She waved the plate of shortbread at the handle.

April flicked a glance over her shoulder, then reached up and pulled the bell.

Within moments, the heavy wooden door swung open, and the woman Catriona had seen in the garden earlier stood in the narrow hallway. 'Come in, come in. The kettle's already on.' She grinned, her suntanned cheeks folding into a smile with such warmth that Catriona was surprised to feel her eyes fill. The woman pointed at the plate in Catriona's hand. 'Shortbread's our favourite.'

Catriona hesitated, unsure how she knew what was under the tinfoil. 'Um, right. Yes, we love it too.' She smiled at the woman who had stepped back to make room for them. 'We just wanted to welcome you to the village.'

The woman's long floral skirt tipped the tops of her

leather clogs. Her white shirt was softly wrinkled, showing off her bronzed forearms and throat, and her hair, a fantastic river of silver and grey waves, was longer than Catriona's, grazing her waistband at the back. As Catriona took her in, her new neighbour opened her arms wide and beckoned to them. 'Come away in, then.' She reached for the plate, so Catriona gave it to her, then took April's hand.

'I'm Catriona Anderson, from next door, and this is my daughter, April.'

'Hello, Catriona, and April.' The woman smiled down at April, who smiled back shyly. 'What a lovely name you have. I'm Peg.' She pressed her free palm to her chest. 'Just like a clothes peg.' The name seemed to fit the vibrant woman perfectly, a snappy moniker that made you smile, even as you said it.

They followed Peg along the hall, a waft of lavender hanging in her wake, and into the warm kitchen, where Catriona had sat many times with her old friends the Mackenzies, sipping tea and putting the world to rights.

The room was surprisingly different, and Catriona took a moment or two to take in the changes. It wasn't that the bones of the space had changed, the oak cabinets and butcher-block counters still there, the double-wide window at the sink overlooking the loch, the ceramic-tile floor and glass-paned door leading to the back garden, it was more the atmosphere that was vastly different.

Gone were Sheila Mackenzie's fussy, flounced table-cloth, clamped over the rickety melamine table, the plastic chairs, and the crocheted trim that she'd tacked along the top of the curtain pelmet. In their place, a stunning wooden table the colour of amber, with rough-hewn edges, domi-nated the room. A series of mismatched wooden chairs, each looking custom-made, hugged the table, and where

Sheila had had plastic containers stacked on the open shelving, either side of the stove, now stood a series of pot-bellied
pottery jars, some with a thick cork stopper in the neck and
others open. They were labelled with chalk – Marjoram,
Sage, Comfrey, Willow, Valerian – a veritable pharmacy of
herbs that filled the room with an almost overwhelming fog
of perfume.

Catriona's eyebrows lifted. 'Wow, it looks great in here.'
She smiled at Peg, who was pouring steaming water into a
large teapot, next to which sat a tray with five earthenware
mugs, ready and waiting. 'That table is incredible.' Catriona
hovered near the door, April hanging back behind her.

'Aye, it's a pretty one. One of Bruce's better efforts. He's
my other half.' Peg put the lid on the teapot and then lifted
the tray. 'It's nice out. Shall we sit in the garden?'

Catriona suddenly craved the fresh air, the idea of
sitting outside seeming like the only thing she wanted to do.
'That'd be lovely.' She nodded. 'Shall I bring the
shortbread?'

'Smashing.' Peg smiled. 'Now come and meet Bruce and
our grandson, Graham.'

Outside, on the little circle of slate that Ken Mackenzie
had installed years ago, a wrought-iron table and four chairs
sat, surrounded by several large terracotta pots filled with
trailing ivy and bright crimson geraniums, giving the spot a
distinctly Mediterranean feel. Catriona set the plate on the
table and pulled out a chair, the serenity of the scene
seeping into her ragged heart. 'Gosh, it looks like you've
been here forever.' She nodded at the colourful pot next to
her. 'How do you get them to flower so beautifully?'

Peg put the tray down, then dragged a chair back and
sat. 'Tea. They love the dregs.' She tapped the pot. 'Let it
cool, mind, then pour it in, right at the base of the plant.'

Catriona nodded, helping April onto the chair next to her. April had Hamish and Harvey in her hand, so Catriona pulled April's chair in closer to the table and tucked the mangy monkey and threadbare rabbit in behind her daughter's hips. 'I'll try that.' She met the older woman's kind eyes, the colour of cornflowers. 'Thanks for the tip.'

As Peg began to pour the tea, behind her the young boy who'd been skipping stones earlier darted across the lawn towards them. His thick hair was blonder than Catriona remembered, cut short around his long face, and his eyes, an electric blue, were glittering as he smiled. 'Hi, Nan. Pops says is the tea ready.' He stopped at the table, panting slightly as he dragged his hand over the crown of his head, and then, catching Peg's eye, he turned to look at Catriona. 'Sorry, I didn't know we had visitors.' He grinned, his two front teeth ever so slightly overlapping, giving him an impish appearance that sent a wave of instant affection through Catriona.

'Graham, this is Mrs Anderson, and young April, from next door. They've brought shortbread.' Peg nodded at the tray. 'Get yourself a cup and sit for a bit.' She gestured towards the chair next to April.

Graham lifted a mug, slopped some milk into it, then flopped down next to April. 'I want to go and see Guinevere in a minute. The puppies are climbing all over her and she just lies here, like whatever.' He laughed, a deep chortle that seemed too mature for his youthful body.

Peg tutted. 'Pass the milk to Catriona, please.' She rolled her eyes at Catriona. 'Honestly.'

Graham coloured slightly as he leaned forward and pushed the jug towards Catriona. 'Sorry.' He grimaced. 'I'm in trouble again.'

Catriona shook her head. 'It's fine. We'll survive, won't

we, April?' She turned to her daughter, who was watching Graham intently. 'So, you have a dog?' Catriona asked Graham.

'Two. Guinevere and Lancelot. They're German Shepherds.' He smiled. 'Guin had six puppies last month, four boys and two girls.' He sipped some tea. 'They're really cute.'

Catriona smiled at the bright, open face, then turned to Peg. 'Guinevere and Lancelot? Shouldn't it be Arthur?'

Peg gave a devilish grin. 'Well, it was Lancelot who put the twinkle in her eye, wasn't it?'

At this, Catriona laughed, the reaction that had once come so easily now feeling foreign, and yet natural at the same time.

As she let the freeing feeling course through her, Graham looked over his shoulder at April, who was now staring at the shortbread, her chin dipped to her chest. 'Want a biscuit?' He lifted the plate and held it out to her. 'Better be quick before my Pops gets here. He'll scoff the lot before you get any.'

Once again, the deep laugh made Catriona smile. There was something very grounded and gentle about this young boy that drew her in.

Peg chuckled. 'He's not wrong, April. It's the land of the quick and the hungry, in this house.' She pointed at the plate. 'Take some, pet.'

April looked up at Graham and it seemed to Catriona that for the first time in weeks there was a light behind her daughter's eyes. A sign of engagement that gave her hope that April, her sweet, amenable child, was still in there beneath the sullen, silent creature that had inhabited her daughter's body. Then, to Catriona's delight, April smiled, her hand going out to the buttery shortbread.

Peg nodded approvingly. 'That's my girl.'

Reluctant to let go of the sense of calm that these new neighbours had unwittingly given her, but suddenly anxious not to outstay their welcome, Catriona leaned back in the chair. 'We won't stay too long. It's so lovely to meet you, but we don't want to take up too much of your afternoon.'

'Och, you can't go yet. You've just got here, and you've still to meet Bruce. And Graham wanted to take April to meet the dogs, didn't you, Graham?' Peg looked at the boy, who nodded enthusiastically.

'Yeah. Do you want to, April?' He spoke gently, as if he sensed her fragility, and Catriona's heart folded over at his unexpected empathy. 'They're inside, in the airing cupboard, cos it's so cosy in there.' He grinned.

April looked over at Catriona, her eyes asking for permission, and Catriona found herself nodding before she could decide whether they should leave or not.

'Grand. Off you two go.' Peg slapped the table. 'And please go and tell your granddad to come and get his tea before it gets cold.' She tutted. 'Once he gets out in that garden, a blasted bomb could drop and he'd not notice.' She laughed softly. 'Silly old bugger.'

Catriona smiled at the fondness in Peg's voice, instantly missing that warm feeling of talking about the one you love with such ease and comfort.

As they drank their tea, Peg told Catriona about their recent move from Perth and their decision to rent for a year until they figured out where they wanted to retire, permanently. The whereabouts of Graham's parents didn't come up, and sensing that it was a sensitive subject, Catriona didn't prod.

Peg's voice bubbled like warm liquid as she told her

that Bruce was a carpenter who'd sold his business after having a stroke a year earlier. Finally, at sixty-eight, he was ready to put down his tools, other than for the wood-carving and furniture making that he did for fun. 'He's great at carving birds.' Peg bit into a slice of shortbread. 'He gets the details, the wee things that you wouldn't notice, like the exact way the feathers lie, their tiny feet.' She made a claw with her hand. 'He's really good.' She smiled proudly.

'That's wonderful. I'd love to see some more of his work.' Catriona looked out at the loch, the afternoon breeze beginning to chill her as she breathed in the salty perfume of the water. Above them, a seagull screeched as it circled the end of the garden, its wings curving upwards with the quickening wind, and Catriona shivered involuntarily.

'Are you all right?' Peg sounded concerned. 'You're a wee bit pale.' Her eyes were full of sympathy. 'I'll not beat about the bush, Catriona. I heard what happened to you. This is a small village, after all.' She shook her head sadly. 'It's diabolical, so it is. No one should have to go through that.'

Taken aback, Catriona blinked as a slew of different feelings crashed in on one another – pain, fear, loss, and sadness so thick and all-consuming that there seemed no way through it. Then came a sliver of disappointment that Peg knew their history, making Catriona sad that her new haven had been contaminated already. As she rode the wave of emotions, she gradually released her breath.

Without knowing why, she was suddenly sure that short of her mother, Peg was the only person she could possibly talk to about what she'd been through. Even as she felt it, it made no sense, as this woman, however kind, was a total stranger. Catriona leaned back in her chair and scanned the horizon. 'April's dad is away at the moment, too. It's difficult to explain.' She felt her cheeks warming.

'Hmm, it often is.' Peg nodded, swirling the tea inside her mug.

Sensing Peg's assumption that Duncan was less than the man he was, on a reflex, Catriona came to his defence. 'He's a good man, Peg. Things are just so difficult right now. He's stepped away... I mean, we're living apart for a while, just until...'

Peg nodded, silently.

Unable to stop herself, Catriona continued, 'He's only been gone a few days. It's worse without him, and yet somehow, it's better, too.' The words out, Catriona realised that this was the first time she'd voiced how she felt about Duncan going. Too afraid to analyse it closely, she had, once again, been focusing her energy on April. 'We both made so many mistakes. I don't even know where to start.'

'Well, I always find that start-at-the-beginning thing such a cliché. Why not start at the end and work backwards?' Peg lifted the teapot and refilled Catriona's mug.

Twenty minutes later, Catriona wiped her eyes and looked over at Peg. 'Well, that was more than you bargained for, I'm sure.'

Peg shook her head. 'Not at all. I'm just sorry you're dealing with so much. And now this wee one isn't talking?' She nodded at April's empty chair, her silvery hair falling over her shoulder.

Catriona swallowed hard. 'No. Not a word for days. Ever since we told her about her adoption.' The words tasted acidic as the emotionally wrought scene replayed in her mind, followed inevitably by Duncan's leaving.

Wanting to shut down that picture show before more ever-present tears overcame her, Catriona lifted her mug and sipped some of the perfumy tea. 'What's in this? Is it some kind of Earl Grey?'

Peg chuckled. 'It's a laxative, of sorts.'

Catriona laughed, despite herself. 'What do you mean?'

Peg rapped her fingernails on the table. 'The recipe includes pure assam tea, a drop of bergamot oil and a dash each of comfort, peace and friendship. All those ingredients tend to ease things out of you, even when you don't mean them to.'

Catriona smiled at her new friend, overcome with gratitude for this gentle soul that had entered the mess that was her life. 'Thanks, Peg.'

Grinning wickedly, Peg fished around in the pocket of her skirt, then pulled out a hip flask. Reaching over, she added a dash of whisky to Catriona's cup. 'A wee tot will do you no harm.'

Catriona laughed again, the release as welcome as the summer breeze that was brushing her cheeks. 'Peg, you are an absolute tonic, but I think you're also trouble.'

Peg chuckled, a deep, throaty sound that heightened Catriona's smile. 'Aye, well, I've been called a lot worse.'

Suddenly reflecting on their arrival, an hour or so earlier, Caitriona frowned. 'By the way. How did you know we were coming over today?'

Peg tapped the bridge of her nose.

Catriona took in the glinting eyes, the remarkably unlined face, and the open smile. It was hard to age this effervescent woman, but she guessed Peg was in her early seventies.

'I'm right here. If there's anything I can do. And if you ever want to talk, just come in. The door's always open.'

Catriona's throat thickened, this abundance of kindness once again taking her to a place where her ability to control her tears disintegrated. 'Thanks. That's really good to know.'

Peg stood up, stretching her arms above her head, revealing a strip of pale skin at her waist, then, startling Catriona, she turned to face the loch and shouted, 'Bruce, you old bugger. The tea's cold.'

A few moments later, the tall, silver-haired man Catriona had seen that morning appeared, pacing across the grass, a gnarled walking stick at his thigh. 'Righto, light of my life.' His voice was warm and filled with humour. Turning to Catriona, he said, 'I married her for her charm, you know.' He smiled broadly, his freckled cheeks folding into two deep dimples, somehow incongruous with the rugged face and pale grey eyes. 'And who are you, m'dear?'

13

The wind was creeping beneath the shingles and making the roof whistle as Catriona huddled under a blanket on the sofa in the living room. Summer storms could be wild in the Highlands and as she focused on the fire in the grate, she listened for footsteps upstairs, April only just having fallen asleep a few minutes earlier.

Just as she glanced at the phone, Duncan's number flashed, so she picked it up.

'Hi, Cat.' He sounded tired. 'How's things?'

'The same.' She scanned the empty room, the lamplight casting tree-like shadows up the wall by the window. 'It's blowing a gale tonight.'

'Are you OK?' His concern felt good, wrapping itself around her weary heart.

'Yeah, just tired.' She pulled the blanket closer across her front. 'What's going on with you? Work OK?' These platitudes felt odd and brittle, a strange way to be communicating with her husband, but if this was all they could manage for now, then it was better than silence.

As had become their pattern, avoiding addressing the seeping wound of their separation, they talked mostly about April. Based on Catriona's report of their day, another where April had not uttered a word, they agreed that it was time to find her some help.

'I'll call the child psychologist that I've been researching. She has a practice in Strathcarron, so it'll be easy to get to.'

'Good. That makes sense.' He sighed.

Sensing that something else was coming, Catriona stayed quiet.

'Cat?'

Her heart rate quickened. 'What?'

A few moments passed as she held her breath, not sure what she wanted to hear, then she felt a dipping in her chest as he said, 'Never mind.'

She let her head drop back against the sofa, the flames from the fire creating a row of shadowy tongues that licked the ceiling. As she tucked her feet under her, searching for something they could safely talk about to fill the awkward silence, she recalled her visit with the neighbours. 'So, we have new neighbours.' She paused, expecting him to be surprised.

'Oh, yeah. Sorry. I meant to tell you, but with everything that happened...'

'You knew about them?' She frowned, sitting upright. 'Since when?'

'Old Jock up at the sailing club told me, a couple of days before Hope...' His voice faded.

'Oh, right.' Catriona gently rescued him, not willing to twist a knife that was already so deeply buried. 'I met them today. They're a sweet couple, called Peg and Bruce, living with their grandson, Graham.' She stood up and switched on another table lamp, walked to the fire and slid a log onto the diminishing pile of embers. The smell of smoky pine whisked her back to her childhood home on Loch Lomond, and her father banking the fire up so high that her mother would scold him. 'Do you know much about them?'

'Jock said they were friends of the people who run the village shop, over in Dornie. He said they were renting the cottage for a year, or something like that.'

'Right. Peg told me that.' She frowned. 'Do you know where Graham's parents are?' Catriona turned her back to the fire, enjoying the creep of warmth up the back of her legs.

'Seems the father wasn't ever around, but the mother died in a car crash down in Glasgow, a few years ago.'

Catriona let the information sink in, Peg's extraordinary compassion for their own loss making even more sense now. 'Oh, that's terrible.' She shook her head, picturing Graham's glittering eyes and easy smile. 'Kids are remarkably resilient, aren't they?' As she said it, an image of April, her mouth clamped shut, her eyes full of tears and her cheeks sunken and grey, made Catriona shiver. 'Do you think she'll get over this, Duncan?' She ran a hand through her mass of hair, her finger catching a knot at the back of her head.

'I'm sure she will, love.' He spoke quietly. 'It'll just take time.' He hesitated. 'For all of us.'

The following morning, having dropped April at school, Catriona headed to the village hall. It was the first time she'd decided to go back to tai chi since losing Hope, and the prospect of seeing the small group of friendly faces who'd been keeping her in casseroles and pies was unsettling. Them dropping off food at the house, while difficult, had been easier to cope with, as she'd been on her own territory, but now, as she walked across the car park towards the hall, her heart began to tick faster.

As she reached the door, feeling the slight tackiness of the rolled-up mat she used under her arm, she tasted salt on her upper lip. The morning was cool and overcast, a thick layer of cloud masking the watery sun as the smell of fresh-baked bread filtered across the road from the nearby café. A dog began to bark from somewhere behind her as Catriona hesitated outside the door to the hall, peeking through the glass panel at the small group that was gathering inside.

Just as she made to push through the door, the teacher, Sandy, turned and caught sight of her, the warm eyes lighting up as she raised her palm and smiled. Seeing some of the other ladies turning to look at the door, each face eager and washed with sympathy, Catriona took a step back, her hand dropping to her side. As she imagined each of these warm-hearted people wanting to squeeze her hand, hug her or ask how she was doing, how April was coping, and how Duncan was, the tightness in her chest became vice-like, her palms growing sticky as she shifted her mat up under her arm. Taking a deep breath, she lifted her hand again, but, as she locked on Sandy's eyes, Catriona took another step away from the door, then turned and began walking back to her car.

The crunch of the gravel under her feet, the distant rumble of a car passing behind her on Harbour Street and the rasp of her heightened breathing all melded together inside her head as she focused on the dark outline of the Land Rover, her hand going into her pocket, feeling for her keys. Clutching the bulky bundle, her vision blurred as she reached the car and fumbled to open the door.

Inside, she tossed her mat onto the back seat, gripped the steering wheel, and let her forehead drop to her hands. As she breathed deeply, trying to slow her racing heart, a tap at the window made her jump. Sitting up, she saw Sandy standing there. She was smiling and pointing at the passenger door, glancing back at the hall, where two of the other ladies were now hovering in the open door.

Suddenly embarrassed by her retreat, Catriona turned the key and pressed the button to lower the passenger window. 'Sorry, Sandy, I just can't, yet.' Her voice was thick, all the moisture sucked from her mouth. 'I...'

'I understand, Catriona. I just wanted to make sure you were OK.' She held Catriona's gaze.

Catriona nodded slowly. 'I'll be OK, and I'll come back, at some point.' She gulped. 'I just can't, today.'

Sandy nodded. 'That's fine. But don't isolate yourself for too long. You need support.'

Catriona saw the genuine concern for what it was and, grateful, she found a smile. 'Thanks, Sandy.'

As she started the engine, the healthy rumble sending a surge of relief through her as it signified her escape, Catriona wondered how long it would be until at *some point* came.

Back at the house, her mother was almost whispering into the phone, as Will was apparently napping in the chair across from her. 'So, do you think this Peg is fey? It sounds like it.'

Catriona smiled at the old-fashioned word – one she hadn't heard for ages. 'I don't know, Mum, but she knew we were coming, and that I'd made shortbread.' She crossed the kitchen and stood at the sink. Outside, the breeze was plucking at the loch, pulling white crests up from the surface as the gorse fluttered, and several birds were pushed back in their progress across the murky sky. She couldn't see the Cuillins today as a soft mist had gathered over the water, masking the view in a wispy grey shroud.

'Your gran was fey, too. She'd always know when the phone was going to ring before it did, and she knew you were a girl as soon as I fell pregnant.' Iris laughed softly. 'She once told me that you'd live on the water and have a daughter of your own.' Iris's voice caught. 'Sorry, love. I still miss her.'

'I know, Mum. I do too.' Catriona nodded, an image of her grandmother, Isabelle, flickering to life, a mass of white hair tamed into a tight bun, her sky-blue eyes, the tiny spider veins on her high cheekbones, the pearly teeth, much like Iris's, and the hearty laugh that drew you in like a magnet, making you want to be close to her. Isabelle had passed away when Catriona was twenty-seven and newly married and her loss still weighed on them all.

'So, you liked the couple?' Iris asked. 'It's so important to have good neighbours.'

'Yes, I did like them. They're kind and warm, and they're actually raising their grandson.' She looked over at the Mackenzie house, the window at the side of the kitchen glowing. 'He's a sweet boy, Mum. He lost his mother a few years ago, poor kid.' Catriona heard her mother catch her breath.

'Oh, that's terrible. I can't imagine.'

'I know. It's tragic.' Catriona tucked the phone under her ear. 'He was so good with April. So easy. I hope they can be friends. She needs someone her own age to talk to.' She sighed. 'If she would just talk.'

'Still no progress there, then?' Iris sounded concerned.

'No. But I've made an appointment for her on Friday with that psychologist I mentioned.'

'Good, Catkin. I think it's time. That kind of pain stays with you unless it's dealt with. It's like scar tissue, or a fingerprint left by what's injured you.'

Her mother using the word *injure* – the same word Duncan had used the night before he'd left – made Catriona shudder, and she pictured his car pulling out of the drive, feeling once again the conflicting sense of loss and relief that she'd felt that morning.

As she made tea, Catriona listened to her mother complain about her father's messiness, the way he left kitchen cabinet doors open, the lid off the jam, his dirty socks on the end of the bed, all the irritating habits that she'd been putting up with for decades but that seldom caused any real tension between them. The list never varied and, as Catriona cringed waiting for the pièce de résistance – the mention of her dad leaving the bathroom door open when he was on the toilet – she closed her eyes.

The things that Duncan did that drove her mad flickered through her mind like a movie reel: him finishing the toilet roll and not replacing it, leaving his sweaters littered around the house like confetti, his muddy shoes perpetually lying at the bottom of the stairs and a line of half-empty coffee cups sitting on the counter, just inches away from the dishwasher. As each action came back to her, she realised she missed his mess, even those sticky cups that she'd rinse and slam into the dishwasher herself.

The anger she'd been feeling towards him was sloshing between a simmer and a raging boil, and as she opened her eyes and looked out at the water – the same water that had taken her darling girl from her – for the first time since it had happened, she felt sympathy for her husband. This glimmer of understanding that had been impossible, just a matter of days before. Neither of them was perfect. They had both made mistakes, and as he had failed Hope that night, was she not now failing April?

14

Two weeks had passed since Catriona had first met Peg, and Catriona had been next door a handful of times to either chat or just deliver more baking. While Peg was a green-fingered gardener and keen herbalist, she wasn't a competent baker, so Catriona's offerings were always gratefully received, especially by Bruce and Graham.

It felt good to be doing something for others, rather than always being the recipient of other people's kindness. It made Catriona feel needed, and that was something that was missing from her daily life right now.

April was still not speaking, her days becoming clones of each other as she withdrew into her own world of silence. She would no longer go to Brownies and Catriona was nervously awaiting the morning when she'd also refuse to go to school. So far, while not exactly cheerful, April would get herself dressed, eat her breakfast, and get her backpack ready as Catriona scheduled her tutoring sessions, wrote shopping lists, and drank her morning coffee. Then, without being asked, April would drag her jacket from the hook and make her way silently to the car.

She had been to two sessions with the child psychologist, a bright-faced woman in her mid-fifties called Nora, who worked from her home and had several cats wandering around during the appointments. Catriona would sit in an adjoining room and observe through a small window, as April nodded, pointed to things in a book, or sometimes put puzzles together while Nora talked to her. After the second session, Nora had told Catriona that April was displaying signs of psychogenic mutism – a form of mutism that occurs when a child who is capable of speech stops speaking. 'While it seems that April is simply refusing to speak, she could in fact feel physically unable to, Mrs Anderson.' Her grey eyes had assessed Catriona from behind narrow-framed glasses. 'The trauma of seeing her sister drown has caused her to seek out something she can control, and this is how she's exercising that control.' She'd smiled kindly. 'However, trying to force her to speak before she's ready is useless.'

'So, what *can* we do?' Increasingly afraid that the more she tried to stay connected to April, the more the child was slipping away, Catriona had crossed her arms and hugged herself as, behind Nora, through the window, April had sat, frighteningly still, staring out of the window, her mouth pinched shut as she'd hugged Hamish and Harvey to her chest.

'Exactly what we are doing. Give her time. Give her the sense that her silence is accepted, for now. She will gradually process everything that's happened to her and, if you're able to keep bringing her for a few weeks, I'll work with her on various techniques that will help her to regain her confidence.' Nora had paused. 'I also think we should try family therapy, with you and your husband here. It can often be very beneficial in finding new ways to communicate with the child while this is happening.'

Catriona had nodded, immediately wondering how on earth they'd organise to have Duncan present, when Nora didn't have treatment hours at weekends. While it wasn't an ideal plan, it was all they had, and having discussed it with Duncan that night, they had agreed to schedule six more sessions over the next couple of months.

Duncan had said he'd make it there, and, while doubtful, Catriona had taken him at his word. They were still not talking about their own relationship, but his commitment to April had taken a step forward, one that Catriona would not question, as it was long overdue and gave her a sense of hope that she was almost afraid to acknowledge.

In the meantime, school was the only thing keeping April from becoming a total recluse and, for that, Catriona thanked the universe daily. The fact that Graham was attending the same school had proven to be a bonus, as April had quickly formed an attachment to the gentle-natured boy.

Despite being two years older than her, Graham was kind and patient with April and displayed a compassion that belied his tender years. Catriona wondered if it was a result of having come through his own devastating loss, but the maturity she saw there was astounding, regardless.

When Catriona and April had gone next door the previous afternoon, he'd asked April if she'd like to see the puppies again, who were almost ready to be weaned. 'Come on, April. They're so funny, all cheeky and fluffy. Like little fuzzballs.' He'd laughed softly, and, to Catriona's relief, April had happily let him take her hand, calmly following him through to the laundry room, where Guinevere was still using a giant basket to nurse the pups. Seeing April enthusiastic about anything at the moment was all that was keeping Catriona from losing hope of ever getting her sweet-natured daughter back.

It was over a month since Duncan had left and July was underway. The loch had turned into a glassy body of water, less turbulent than just weeks before, reflecting the sun in a way that was unique to this part of the Highlands. The early evening light would turn amber as it hit the water, sending shafts of shimmering copper across the garden and licking up the glass of the windows. The sunsets were spectacular now and each evening, having put April to bed, Catriona would sit in the conservatory nursing a glass of wine and letting her palm settle on the empty seat next to her, overcome with the sense of having a piece of her heart out of place.

After an initial break of two weeks, Duncan was now coming back to see them on Sundays, and so far, each visit had been brief, and somewhat awkward. He'd hover in doorways rather than be fully in the room, stand at the kitchen sink to drink his coffee, pace about and then walk down to the boathouse, leaving Catriona feeling conflicted as to whether him being here was helping or serving only to confuse April, who would greet him with a hug, then disappear up to her bedroom again.

On his last visit, Duncan had sat at the piano and begun tapping out 'Chopsticks', his long back curved over the keyboard, his newly cropped hair, freshly ironed shirt, grey cords and polished brogues seeming oddly formal, as if he'd put on his Sunday best as a visitor might.

After a few minutes, the music seeming to draw her in, in a Pied Piper-like way, April had appeared in the door, her fingers in her mouth and Hamish and Harvey, as ever, in her other hand.

'Come and sit with me, April Mactiggiwinkle,' Duncan had beckoned to her, his warm smile sending a ripple of gratitude through Catriona. 'Come on, little one. I need some help here.' He'd pulled a face. 'You know what a brilliant musician I am.' He'd shrugged, then winked at April, who, after a moment or two, had given a tiny half-smile, crossed the room and slid onto the piano stool next to him.

Seeing them sitting side by side had momentarily filled Catriona with joy, but then the glare of the empty space on his opposite side had lifted her from the sofa and sent her out into the back garden, where she'd walked across the lawn and down to the edge of the loch. As she'd clenched her fists and stared at the water – for all intents and purposes innocent and welcoming – she'd let tears tip down her cheeks, the gentle breeze drying them on her face, tightening her skin.

As far as she knew, Duncan was coming back the following day and, as she thought about it, Catriona felt the familiar prickle of nerves at his return. While she missed his company, there was still a tinge of relief when he'd eventually pick up his keys, brush her cheek with his lips and walk out to his car.

Now, having finished a fresh batch of ginger biscuits, Catriona tidied up the kitchen, then went in search of April. She had been watching *All Creatures Great and Small* again after breakfast, but now, while the TV was still on, the living room was empty. Reaching the bottom of the stairs, just as Catriona was about to call to her daughter, something stopped her. Instead, she quietly climbed the stairs and went into the girls' room, expecting to see April either on the bottom bunk or sitting at the small plastic desk in the corner, reading one of the books Catriona had bought her about being adopted, but Catriona stopped short at the sight of the empty room.

Turning into the hall, her pulse quickened as she headed back towards the stairs, then, from behind her, she heard a shuffling noise coming from her bedroom. Frowning, she walked back and very slowly pushed the door open to see April facing the window, her hair tumbling in waves down the back of her bumblebee pyjamas, and her feet, not in her customary slippers, but instead swamped by a pair of Duncan's formal shoes. She was looking down at her feet, seemingly lost in her thoughts, as she shifted her weight from side to side, as if testing the shoes' ability to support her tiny frame.

Catriona stood, frozen to the spot, unsure whether to make her presence known or to back out of the room and leave April to whatever this was – creating a kind of connection with her father, perhaps even trying to understand him, although that thinking instantly felt too profound for a nine-year-old. As she stood, paralysed by what she was seeing, Catriona longed to step forward, wrap her arms around the little girl and tell her that everything would be all right, but Catriona knew that in order to be convincing she had to believe it herself.

As she hesitated, April lifted her head and stiffened, her back arching as if she'd been stung, then she turned her head and caught sight of Catriona. Rather than flinch, or even blush, April stared at Catriona, her turquoise eyes full of questions that Catriona wished she had answers for. Then April folded at the knees and sat on the carpet, carefully removing her feet from the shoes. Her eyes on Catriona, she lifted one brogue, then the other and awkwardly stood up, walked across to the wardrobe, and set the shoes back inside, then closed the door.

Unable to hold back any longer, Catriona's heart was clattering as she crossed the room and opened her arms to April. *Please, April. Please let me hold you.* It felt like minutes until April's shoulders dropped a little and she walked into Catriona's embrace. Overcome, Catriona closed her eyes, breathing in the sweet, powdery smell of her daughter, feeling the little heart beating against her middle as she began to rock her gently, tears clogging Catriona's throat.

After a few moments, April eased herself out of Catriona's arms. Her cheeks were flushed and her eyes full. Seeing the tears waiting to come, Catriona took April's hands in hers. 'You know, it's OK to miss your daddy, April. He misses you too.' Catriona caught a flash of what looked like anger in the blue-green pools. Momentarily confused, Catriona blinked, desperately searching for the right words, for a way she could reassure the little girl that the broken pieces of her world would one day fit back together.

15

The peal of the doorbell startled Catriona. She'd been reading the paper in the conservatory, the incident with Duncan's shoes still playing on her mind, while April napped on the sofa in the living room.

Scanning the hall for any sign that April had woken, but seeing no movement, Catriona walked to the front door. Through the bubbled glass at the side of the door frame, she could see a slender figure in a long dark skirt. The flash of silver hair gave her the last clue as to the identity of her visitor, and Catriona opened the door to see Peg, holding a potted plant close to her middle. This was the first time Peg had come to her door, and Catriona was pleased to see her new friend.

'Hello, neighbour.' Peg held the plant out towards Catriona, the lush, corrugated leaves shining in the afternoon sunlight. 'A peace lily for you. I repotted mine and split it. They're easy to keep.' She held it out a little farther from her. 'Don't need a lot of light either, so they're good in bathrooms and the like.'

Catriona accepted the plant, the rough surface of the

pot grazing her palm. 'Thank you, Peg. It's lovely.' She looked at the plant, seeing two white, cone-like flowers with long stamens. 'I'll try not to kill it.' She smiled, then stepped back. 'Come in. I'll put the kettle on.'

'I don't want to intrude.' Peg glanced behind Catriona. 'Is your husband here?'

Catriona waved her in. 'No, he's coming tomorrow.'

Peg nodded, following her inside. 'What a lovely home you have.'

'Thanks. We like it.' Catriona felt the sharp edge of the word *we*, feeling like a fraud using it, as more than one critical component of that collective term was missing. 'Come through. April's asleep.'

Peg frowned, her hands going into the deep pockets of her skirt. 'It's two o'clock.'

Slightly embarrassed, Catriona set the plant on the kitchen table, walked to the sink, and lifted the kettle. 'I know, it's a bit odd. But this has been happening ever since the accident.' She filled the kettle, then put it in the cradle. 'Nora, her counsellor, says to let her sleep for short periods, then wake her. She's been out for about twenty minutes, so I'll give her ten more. We're going to the harbour later, to get some fish. Would you like me to pick anything up for you?' Sensing that she had sounded rather over-bright, she turned to face Peg.

'Catriona, I'm sorry. I didn't mean to sound judge-mental.' Peg's cheeks were flushed. 'That was thoughtless.'

Catriona patted the air, wanting to relieve her new friend of any discomfort. 'Not at all. I know it's strange, but then our entire lives are at the moment.' She drew an arc around her. 'We are a collective mess.'

Peg shook her head. 'What is it they say, been there and

got the T-shirt?' She smiled. 'There's no right way to do this.'

Catriona nodded. 'That's what my mum says, too.' She took two mugs from the cupboard. Sensing that Peg had just cleared the way for her to ask about Graham's mother, Catriona eased a chair back and sat at the table, watching Peg take her cue and do the same. 'Peg, may I ask you something?'

Peg's eyebrows lifted. 'Aye, of course. As long as it's nothing to do with baking.' She gave a soft laugh.

'No, no. I wanted to ask you what happened with Graham's mum. I mean, your daughter.' Catriona leaned forward on her elbows. 'If it's not too insensitive.'

Peg sat back, letting her hands fall into her lap, her mouth drooping slightly. 'It's not. It's just hard to talk about. No matter how much time passes.' She halted. 'But you know that, pet.'

Catriona nodded, feeling the new bond that had begun to form between them strengthening a little.

'It was a car accident. Emily had Graham in the back, and they were coming home from a birthday party. She was at a traffic light near Sauchiehall Street and a bus hit her from behind. It shoved her car into the junction and a lorry drove through and hit her head-on.' Peg looked at her hands in her lap. 'They said it was instant. A broken neck.' She looked up at Catriona. 'Graham was five. Escaped with some minor scrapes. A miracle really.' Her eyes were full as she nodded sadly. 'Life is cruel, Catriona, but I don't have to tell you that.'

'No. You don't.' She eyed Peg, seeing the effort the older woman was putting into pulling herself upright and breathing away her pain. 'But he has you two. Which is a blessing.'

Peg smiled. 'He's the blessing, believe me. He's an old soul, our Graham. Sometimes I wish he'd be more...' She hesitated.

'What?' Catriona stood up and poured the boiling water into the teapot.

'Childlike.' Peg shrugged. 'He's old beyond his years.'

Nodding, Catriona sat back down. 'He's very mature. So kind and good with April.' She smiled. 'I'm very grateful, Peg. It's about the only time she smiles these days – that and when her dad plays the piano.'

At this, Peg leaned forward. 'You have a piano?' Her face was suddenly alight again.

'Yes, an old family heirloom. In the living room.' Catriona pointed behind Peg. 'It's not great or anything, but my mum gave it to us, so it's special to me.' She paused. 'I always thought I'd take lessons one day, or that the girls might.' She met Peg's eyes, seeing them fill with sympathy. 'April seems to like it, though she rarely touches it now.'

Peg accepted the mug of tea that Catriona slid towards her. 'I used to teach, you know.' She added some milk. 'The piano.'

'Really?' Catriona pulled her own mug towards her. 'That's great.' She paused, an idea flickering to life. 'Maybe you can teach April, sometime?'

Peg sipped some tea, put the mug down and cupped it between her palms. 'I could teach both you and April if you like. My rates are pretty good.' She nodded at the plate of ginger biscuits on the table. 'Let's say a batch of those a week, plus one of those fresh raspberry tarts you made the other day, and I'm your woman.'

Taken aback, Catriona's eyebrows jumped, the idea that this might be a way that she and April could reconnect filling her with hope. 'God, Peg. That'd be wonderful.'

'Well, think it over and let me know. I can work around your tutoring, and Duncan's visits, so it's convenient for everyone. I've got plenty of time on my hands.' She smiled, her soft linen shirt bringing out the blue of her eyes.

Suddenly desperate for something uplifting to cling to, Catriona gushed. 'How about tomorrow afternoon?'

Peg laughed. 'Perfect. Now, let's spice this up a bit.' She grinned as she stood up, pulled her hip flask out of her pocket, and walked over to Catriona. Holding the flask above Catriona's mug, she chuckled. 'One lump or two?'

Mungo looked pleased to see them as he swung himself off the boat and onto the dock. His boots were covered in fishy slime and his hands were grimy, as he lifted a thick palm in greeting.

Catriona smiled at her old friend. 'Hello, there.'

'Hello, yourself.' He grinned. 'How's tricks?' He looked down at April, who was jabbing the dock with the toe of her shoe.

'We're OK, thanks.' Catriona met his eyes. 'Much the same.'

Mungo nodded, wiping his hands on the dirty cloth hanging from his pocket. 'So, what'll it be th'day? Haddock, or I've got some braw prawns?' He nodded at the boat. 'For special customers only, mind. They'd make some great scampi, wi' a few chips.' He winked at April, who now stood next to Catriona, her hair being whipped up behind her by the salty breeze. Seeing the lush chestnut mane, flicking in the wind, Catriona was suddenly overwhelmed by a need to rid herself of her own long tresses, the same deep auburn that Hope's had been. Every time she washed or brushed it, it served as a painful reminder of the little girl she'd lost, making her turn away from the mirror. As the thought circled her mind, Mungo nudged her arm. 'Ship to shore. Come in, shore.' He smiled again, revealing his trademark gap.

'Sorry, Mungo. Prawns sound great.' She found a smile. 'But I'm absolutely paying for them today.' She widened her eyes at her old friend.

Mungo rolled his eyes. 'Aye, OK then. I'll get you a bag.'

With the shopping unpacked and April once again ensconced in front of the TV, watching a nature programme, Catriona raked around the kitchen drawers looking for her long scissors. She couldn't help but think how freeing it would be to cut her hair, to rid herself of the weight and the memories it sparked. Just as she pulled the scissors out from under the wooden spoons, April came into the room behind her, holding out a small stack of mail that she must've picked up from the front doormat.

Surprised, Catriona dropped the scissors back in the drawer and accepted the envelopes. 'Thanks, sweetheart. That's very helpful.' She smiled at her daughter, who simply nodded, then turned back into the hall. Disappointed that their brief interaction was over, Catriona sighed, and flicked through the various pieces of mail, seeing the electricity bill, a bank statement, and a flyer for the upcoming regatta. At the back of the stack, a flat white envelope caught her eye, so she dropped the rest onto the table and flipped it over, noting a vaguely familiar address in Stirling.

She frowned, sliding her finger under the flap, as her memory yielded something that she hadn't thought about for nine years. Pulling the single sheet of paper out, she unfolded it, and her heart stopped momentarily, seeing the distinctive logo at the top of the page. It was from the adoption agency they'd worked with when April came into their lives.

As she scanned the page, going back to the beginning and reading it again, willing what she was seeing to be a mistake, for the words to change miraculously, Catriona began to pant. A sudden wave of nausea made her rock slightly as the room began to close in around her. This couldn't be happening. Not now.

16

Catriona adjusted the laptop screen and checked once more that the bedroom door was firmly closed. April had been in bed for an hour and the wait for Duncan to call back had been interminable. She could see that he was sitting at the narrow kitchen island in the flat above the office in Fort William, the window behind him completely dark and a collection of cups and dishes piled on the counter near the sink. As she tried to read his face, her heart ticked rapidly.

'So, tell me exactly what it said.' He frowned, then took a sip from a tumbler of whisky.

'That April's birth mother wants to see her. That, as per the terms of the adoption contract, we'd agreed that, should this ever happen, we'd allow it.' Catriona's breathing was laboured. She'd always known that this was a possibility, and while leaving the door open to April's birth mother had felt like the right thing to do, for April's sake, now it felt as if their world was crumbling even more – just when there was so little keeping it all together.

As she looked down at the letter again, the words beginning to swim across the page, she knew that deep in her heart, despite all their good intentions at the time, she'd been dreading this moment, for years.

Duncan took another sip and set the glass down. 'OK. Let me call my brother and see what he says. There may be something we can do. Some get-out clause or other.' He raked his fingers through his hair.

Catriona stared at him, the eyes she knew so well somehow shrouded behind an expression of forced positivity. She was grateful to him for his effort, but, suddenly, glowing beneath her mounting fear was a deep moral sense that they didn't have the right to deny this request, regardless of how disruptive it may or may not be for April, or for their family. 'Duncan, I don't think we can go back on the agreement,' she whispered. 'We signed a contract.'

Duncan shook his head. 'There's no harm in asking Ian to take a look at it, before we do anything, especially as I'm away for almost two weeks.' He locked on her eyes. 'Cat, do you agree?'

She watched him rub the top of his head, then clasp the back of his neck. She'd somehow forgotten that rather than coming home, he was leaving for Lisbon the following day, then going straight on to Geneva, and as she sifted through the myriad thoughts that were crowding her head, he frowned.

'Cat. We have to be in agreement. Don't go and say it's OK or something before we find out more.'

She kept her voice low. 'Why do you think I called you?' She shook her head.

'OK. OK. I just want to make sure we cover ourselves here.' He leaned back, his fingers now linked behind his head. 'So, let me call Ian and I'll get back to you, at the latest tomorrow, before I leave.'

'Fine.' She nodded, the sense that everything of consequence in her life was slipping away from her overwhelming. 'Duncan...'

'What?'

She watched his brow crease, his thinner, more angular face still new to her. 'Just call me as soon as you've spoken to him. They've asked us to get back to them within the week.' She scanned the letter again, noting the timeline that had been suggested, a week feeling like no time at all to open their home, and their hearts, to whatever this unknown woman might bring into their lives.

The following morning, having taken April into the village, Catriona was driving home when her phone rang, jolting her from her spiralling thoughts. April had nodded off, but nervous that she might wake up and overhear them, Catriona rummaged through her bag and stuck her earbuds in her ears.

Duncan sounded breathless. 'Ian says there's no easy way round it. We're legally obliged to allow April's birth mother to see her. He said we can request certain conditions, like it has to happen somewhere *we* are comfortable, like maybe on neutral ground, but unless we're willing to go to court to contest the request, we're stuck.' He sighed.

Catriona nodded, her stomach knotting as she turned back onto Innes Road. 'Right. That's what I thought.' She braked to let a car out at a junction, then, a few moments later, turned the Land Rover into their drive. As she turned off the engine, careful not to disconnect the call, she spotted Peg, standing at the front door. 'Duncan, I have to go. Peg's here.'

'What's she doing there?' He sounded irritated, setting Catriona's teeth on edge.

'She's come to give me a piano lesson. And maybe April too, if I can get her interested.' Hearing it out loud, she was suddenly embarrassed by the notion that she had any mental energy left for something that now felt frivolous.

Taking her by surprise, Duncan said, 'Great idea. You need something to...' He stopped.

'To what?' She waved to Peg, who waved back.

'I don't know. Feed your soul?'

The unexpected response made her pause. Duncan had never been one for what he called touchy-feely stuff, but this was exactly what she needed to hear. 'Really? You don't think it's a daft idea?' She opened the car door, her hand lingering on the key in the ignition.

'Not at all. Perhaps you can even help me out, after.' He laughed softly, bringing a half-smile to her face at the image of her trying to teach him what she'd learned, but the implicit reference to the future surprised her – as that was something she wasn't allowing herself to think about, yet.

'I don't know about that.' She sighed. 'Look, I've got to go. Call me from Lisbon?'

'Sure. If it's possible to postpone meeting her until I get home, that'd be best. Don't let them rush you, Cat.'

'I won't.' She shook her head. 'Bye, for now.'

Her first piano lesson had been challenging, the keys feeling spongy under Catriona's fingertips, but Peg had been patient, encouraging her not to be afraid to put pressure on them. 'They'll no' break, pet. Give it some welly.' She'd laughed. 'Scales are damn boring. But get these under your belt and we can start on some simple tunes.'

Catriona had relaxed into the half-hour lesson, deciding not to tell Peg about the disturbing news they'd received, but rather to immerse herself in something completely unattached to her worries. Soon, she'd been laughing at her bungled finger work, trying to remember when to slip her thumbs over or under her working fingers as she moved her hands up and down the keyboard. 'I'll never get this,' she'd laughed. 'I'm a lost cause.'

'Not at all.' Peg had batted the air. 'You'll be playing Chopin in no time.' She'd winced as Catriona had hit a bad note. 'Well, maybe "Three Blind Mice".'

They'd laughed companionably, then adjourned to the kitchen, where Catriona had made coffee to go with the requested raspberry tart that, unable to sleep, she had baked the night before. Now, they sat opposite one another, and Peg leaned back, her hands on her flat stomach.

'Oh, I'm stappit fu.' She chuckled. 'That tart was delish.'

Catriona stood up and lifted the pie dish. 'I'll wrap the rest up for you.'

'Och, no. Just give me a couple of slices for the boys.' She nodded towards the garden. 'They'll hoover it up after their dinner.'

Catriona set the dish down and pulled out the tinfoil. 'No. A deal's a deal. This is payment for the lesson.' She smiled over her shoulder as she tucked the foil over the edges of the tart. 'No arguments.' She turned and put the dish in front of Peg, who was standing up, carefully pushing the chair back in under the table. She looked past Catriona and out of the window, a distant look on her face.

'Are you OK?' Catriona leaned back against the sink, feeling the hard edge dig into her hip.

'Catriona, I have a proposition for you.' Peg folded her arms, looking newly purposeful.

'Oh, yes?' Catriona was intrigued. 'Go on.'

Peg assessed her for a few moments, as if convincing herself of something, then nodded sharply. 'I think April should have one of Guinevere's pups.'

'Oh, no, Peg. I don't think...'

Peg held her palm up. 'Just hear me out, and then, if you still disagree, I'll not bring it up again.'

Catriona frowned, picturing a nine-week-old puppy darting about the kitchen, chewing everything in sight, whining all night long and having accidents left, right and centre.

'The thing is...' Peg shoved her hands into the pockets of her skirt, 'the other day, when she and Graham were with Guinevere, the puppies were tumbling all over the place.' She smiled. 'It's hard not to adore them, that's the truth.'

Catriona nodded, picturing the fluffy little creatures, their pale pink noses and tiny claws, all heartbreakingly new and unspoiled.

'Graham was chasing one that had snuck out of the laundry room, and I was behind the door, half spying, just keeping an eye on April.' She paused. 'Catriona, I'm only telling you this because I think it might help.' Her eyes were full of concern.

Catriona's alarm bells instantly started to clang. What more could possibly happen to shake her crumbling foundation?

'It's just that I think I heard her speak to a pup. One of the smaller ones that has one brown eye and one blue.' Peg eyed her. 'I may have imagined it, but I was pretty sure I heard her.'

Catriona felt the ground shift under her, the air growing suddenly thick and hard to breathe in. 'Really?' she croaked. 'Oh, Peg.'

Peg patted the air. 'I don't want to get your hopes up, but I thought it might be helpful for you to know.'

Her concerns over the practicalities of a puppy disintegrated as Catriona crossed the room and threw her arms around Peg's shoulders, feeling the soft muscles of her arms and catching the trademark scent of lavender. 'Thank you.' She swallowed hard, stepping back and letting her arms drop to her sides. 'I said to Duncan weeks ago that I thought we should consider getting her a pet. Some little companion that she'd have to care for as a way of drawing her out of wherever she goes in her head, but I was thinking a rabbit, or a gerbil.' She coughed, swiping away a tear. 'I don't know what to say.' She scanned Peg's face, the customary calm countenance gone as Peg also dabbed at her cheek, then cleared her throat.

'Right. So, we have an agreement.' She held a hand out to Catriona. 'Let's shake on it.'

Catriona grasped the cool hand in hers. 'Deal.'

Peg nodded decisively. 'I'll get Graham to bring the pup over when they get back from school. It's a boy, and we've been calling him Arthur.' Her eyes were glittering as she lifted the pie dish to her middle. 'Okey-dokey?'

Catriona nodded, wiping her nose with a piece of kitchen paper. 'Yes, totally great.'

17

Catriona had dashed out to the shops to find puppy supplies. Finding most of what she needed around the village, she'd stuffed everything into the back of the car, stopping to pick up a small, lightly used dog bed from a friend. Then she'd collected April from school, a bubble of excitement keeping Catriona's breathing shallow all the way home.

Back at the house, she'd left everything out in the car and gone inside with April, quickly made her a drink and a snack, then unpacked her backpack to check for any spelling or reading homework.

April had dropped her shoes under the coat rack and curled up on the sofa in the conservatory with Hamish and Harvey and a book about reptiles. Catriona's mind whirred as she tried to figure out how to break the good news. What if April spoke to her? What if the puppy was the catalyst they'd been looking for? The thought was like electricity, sending waves of hope through Catriona's jaded soul.

By four thirty, Catriona was pacing around the kitchen, a cup of cold tea in her hand. She'd been scanning the back garden, looking for Graham, who had taken to jumping the fence when he came over, rather than using the front door. Just as she dumped the tea in the sink, she caught sight of him. He was walking across the grass, a blue bundle in his arms and a big holdall slung over his shoulder, the wind lifting the back of his open hoodie up in a navy-coloured sail.

Her heart skipping, Catriona waved at him and opened the back door.

Graham hugged the bundle close to his chest as he strode down the path and stopped at the door. 'Hello, Mrs Anderson. Got a delivery for you.' His eyes were bright. 'Is April there?' He looked behind her as the bundle squirmed, a paw appearing from the folds of the blanket and then a tiny snout.

'She's in the conservatory, but she doesn't know yet.' Catriona held a finger up to her lips. 'Come in, Graham. Let's bring this little one inside and I'll go and get her,' she whispered. He followed her into the kitchen and looked around him, and Catriona realised that he was unsure where to set the puppy down. Feeling silly, she pulled a face. 'Sorry, love. Just him put him here.' She pointed to the back doormat, and just as she was about to walk away, a question that had been floating in her subconscious surfaced. 'Graham, can I ask you something?'

'OK.' He looked confused as Catriona hesitated, suddenly unsure whether this was wise.

Graham dropped the bag on the floor and put the black-and-tan puppy onto the mat, unwinding the blanket from its stubby back legs. It stood still for a second, then shook itself dramatically, the momentum sending a shockwave along the length of its body until the tiny back end plopped down on the mat, making Catriona laugh. As she looked at the endearing creature, all legs and ears and tail, she took a deep breath.

'Does April ever speak to you, Graham?' She locked on his eyes, mirrors of Peg's, seeing no guile there. This was the face of honesty.

'No. She doesn't.' He shook his head, gently guiding the tottering puppy back onto the mat, and before Catriona could ask anything more, he continued, 'Nan says that she will speak when she's ready, and I think that's fine.' He shrugged. 'Sometimes being quiet feels good when things are sad all around you.'

Once again, Catriona was shocked by the depth of compassion and insight coming from this young boy, who knelt there carefully corralling the puppy and smiling up at her.

'Yes, I think you're right, Graham.' She nodded. 'I can understand that completely.'

Graham lurched to the side and lifted the puppy, his hand sliding deftly under its stomach, the four paws dangling over his palm. 'Arthur is a right wriggler.' He laughed. 'You'll need to keep an eye on him all the time.'

Breathing away a sudden flash of doubt over this rash decision, and what having this tiny, dependent creature in their home would mean, when so much else was in question now, Catriona tucked her hair behind her ears and smiled. 'Noted. Right, I'll be back in a sec.'

April was still reading, now lying on the sofa with her legs dangling over one of the arms. As Catriona walked into the conservatory, the sheer length of her little girl took her by surprise. Shaking her head, she stopped in front of the sofa and pressed her palms together.

'April, I have a surprise for you.' April twisted her head to look at her mother, her eyes questioning. 'Graham's here, too. Are you coming to see him?' She held a hand out, wiggling her fingers. 'Come on. I think you're going to like this.'

April let herself be helped up, then followed Catriona into the kitchen. As they walked in, Graham had crawled under the table, the backs of his jeans and his battered trainers protruding from one end. 'Come here, you wee bugger,' he laughed, his legs disappearing further under the table. Next to her, April was frowning, then she put her hands on her knees and bent down to look under the table. 'Got you.' Graham slowly eased himself backwards until his shoulders, then his head emerged, his hair tousled, and his cheeks flushed. He sat back on his hips and lifted Arthur up to eye level as April gasped, a soft inhale but the first sound that Catriona had heard from her in weeks.

Catriona put her hand on April's back. 'It's Arthur, sweetheart. The wee pup you like.'

April looked up at her, the turquoise eyes full under the chestnut widow's peak.

Catriona cupped her cheek. 'Arthur is yours now, April. He lives here, with us.'

At this, April's hand went to her mouth and then she smiled. The sight of a light going on inside her daughter was like a shroud lifting from Catriona's eyes.

'Go and say hello, then.' She gently pushed April towards Graham, who was now laughing, as the puppy squirmed in his arms.

'Better be quick, before he escapes again.' He shunted himself back across the floor until his back was against the door, and his legs stuck straight out in front of him in a V-shape. 'Come and sit here and we can trap him.' He beckoned to April, who walked slowly across the room, her hands now flexing as if she couldn't wait to touch the little dog.

Just as she settled herself opposite Graham, her legs out at a ninety-degree angle, the puppy leaped from Graham's hands and landed in between them, its tail ticking back and forth as it sniffed the air. He yipped once, then again, sending Graham into fits of laugher and April's hand back to her mouth.

'It's OK, you can pick him up.' Graham nodded at the puppy who was sniffing April's kneecap. 'Go ahead.' April tentatively put her hand out and stroked the fluffy back. As she let her fingers settle, the puppy lifted its head and looked at her, as if seeing her for the first time and yet knowing her already. April gently lifted him onto her lap, then while Arthur licked her hand, his tiny pink tongue flicking in and out of his mouth, her eyes slowly filled with tears.

Catriona lay in bed with the laptop propped up on her knees. Duncan had texted when he landed in Lisbon and told her he'd call at nine, her time, so she checked the clock, seeing it was 9.08 p.m.

April had finally fallen asleep, with Arthur wrapped in a blanket containing a hot-water bottle lying next to her on the living-room sofa. Hearing the slow, steady cadence of April's breathing, Catriona had gently transferred the puppy to the dog bed and April to her own bunk. Then she'd carried Arthur into her bedroom to keep him close during the night, until she could be sure he wouldn't whine and wake April.

As she looked over at the dog bed, tucked in close to the radiator under the window, the puppy made a mewling sound that reminded her of a new-born, and it sent a shard of memory through her, like a needle piercing her heart.

April was obviously besotted already, and Arthur seemed to know her, in some deeply calming way that had made Catriona's eyes sting. Watching the two of them playing on the floor in the conservatory had been the most relaxed she'd felt in weeks. While the little dog flopped and lolloped around, investigating his new home, so April became more animated, her eyes filling with light and her mouth twitching into a smile that she didn't fight to suppress, as she had been doing since Hope died. It was as if she felt she shouldn't experience any happiness without her sister, and even as Catriona wanted to take that guilt away from her daughter, she couldn't help but understand it, more deeply than anyone could have known.

As she stretched out her back, making a mental note to source a puppy playpen so that they could contain Arthur, both inside and out in the garden, the laptop jingled. She pulled her knees up closer to her as Duncan's face materialised.

'Hi.' He looked exhausted, his face drawn and his eyes glassy.

'Hey. You OK?' she asked. 'You look done in.'

He nodded, carrying his laptop to the desk at the other side of his dimly lit hotel room. 'I am. I had a yapper next to me on the flight, so I couldn't get much work done, and no chance of a kip, either.' He rolled his eyes. 'So, was today OK?' He adjusted the angle of the screen, and she could see a pretty seascape painting on the wall behind him.

'It was fine.' Catriona nodded, suddenly nervous to tell him what she'd done. 'We had an interesting development, actually.' She tipped her head to the side as his brow creased. 'April has a new friend.' She paused as his eyebrows lifted. 'A four-legged friend.'

Duncan looked puzzled. 'What do you mean?'

Catriona shifted further up against the headboard. 'We have a puppy, one of Guinevere's from next door. His name is Arthur and he's nine weeks old.' She smiled, trying to sound upbeat. She didn't want to give him any sense of her second-guessing the decision or reveal a crack he might wriggle through and convince her she was out of her mind.

'A puppy? Seriously?' he huffed. 'She's far too young to take care of a puppy, Cat.' His face darkened. 'Did you think this through?'

Catriona bristled. 'Yes, I did. And if you'd seen her with him, Duncan, you'd understand.' She shook her head. 'It's a long story, but Peg told me that she thought she'd heard April talk to the puppy, over at their house. She wasn't a hundred per cent sure, but she thought she'd heard her.' She watched his eyes widen.

'She spoke?' He rubbed the back of his head, his crumpled shirtsleeve tightening around his bicep. 'Well, that's encouraging.'

Catriona nodded. 'Right? When I saw her with Arthur today, she was completely engaged, even happy, for a while. I haven't seen her like that for weeks.' Her throat tightened, so she took a deep breath. 'She actually smiled. She sat with him on the floor for over an hour, just being a child with an adorable puppy. It feels right, Duncan.' She shrugged. 'Anyway, it'll be me who does everything for him for the next few months, until he's fully house-trained and April can learn what to do. But it'll be good for her to have responsibilities, to have to take care of him.' She nodded to herself.

Duncan leaned forward on his elbows, the frown gone

as he held her gaze. 'If you think so, Cat. I trust your judgement.'

Relieved, she nodded. 'Thanks. I think it's the right move.'

He ran a hand through his hair and yawned. 'Right. Well, I suppose we are a family of four, again.'

Catriona sighed at the sad reference, missing Hope more than she could bear. 'Yes, four.'

They talked briefly about his planned meetings the next day and then, inevitably, he asked about the adoption agency. 'Are you going to phone them tomorrow?' He lifted the laptop and walked to the bed.

'Yes, I have to get back to them. There's an email address on the letter, but I think I'll call.' Catriona glanced over at the envelope lying on the chest of drawers by the door, its contents seeming to be pulsing inside it. 'What if she's great? A really good person who made the best decision she could for her child but regrets it. What if she wants...'

Duncan held his palm up. 'Don't go down that rabbit hole, Cat.' He frowned. 'April is our daughter now. Legally, and in every other way. If this woman wants to be involved in her life, it will be on *our* terms. How *we* allow it to happen, and how it works for us. That's it.' He flopped back against the bank of pillows behind him.

Catriona's mind was reeling. What if they weren't a *we* anymore? If things were never repaired between her and Duncan, then there'd be no *us*, there would just be fragments of a family held together only by loss, sadness and heartbreaking memories.

18

Two days later, having spoken twice to the adoption coordinator who'd written to her, Catriona paced across the kitchen, on the phone with Duncan's brother. She was anxious about the agency's request that she allow April's birth mother to come at the end of the week, just a matter of days away, and before Duncan would be back. 'Ian, I'm going to let her come here, to meet April.' She paused. 'I was going to suggest meeting at a park or something, but then I thought it'd be better for April if she was on her home turf. She's had so much disruption and change lately.' She willed the knot in her throat to release. 'I checked with her counsellor, and she agrees with me.'

'Yeah, I get it.' Ian's voice was lower and more gravelly than his younger brother, Duncan's. 'Just make sure to keep your cards close to your chest, Catriona. Don't volunteer too much at first, until you get a sense of her.'

'I will. Don't worry.' She scanned the back garden, a flash of white drawing her eye. In the middle of the lawn, a giant seagull was stamping on the dewy grass, one yellow foot after the other like a march, scaring up worms. When her mother had told her about this, years ago, Catriona had thought she was joking, but it had been true, and now, whenever she saw it happening, she thought about Iris.

Knowing that she needed to tell her parents what was going on, Catriona closed her eyes briefly. They had been through so much with her, she'd rather have protected them from this, but her mother was too intuitive to lie to, instantly knowing from Catriona's voice if she was hiding something.

'What does Duncan think about it?' Ian asked. 'How is he?' He paused. 'How are you two?'

Catriona turned her back on the garden, taking in the tidy kitchen. In one corner stood the new puppy pen, inside its colourful walls a pile of toys, the remnants of a puppy chew, an old fabric book of April's, and Arthur, lying on top of a soft blanket, his front leg twitching as he chased something in his dream. 'We're OK, Ian. But it's not easy.' She swallowed hard. Talking about what was happening between her and Duncan was like chewing glass. As they still hadn't discussed their plans from this point forward, finding the words to explain it to his brother was nigh on impossible. 'We're doing the best we can.' She turned back towards the garden, the seagull now tugging a long worm from the grass.

'I know. I just hate to think of you two being apart.' He hesitated. 'You know... separated.'

'I know. But it's what he... what *we* chose to do, for the moment.' She bit her lip.

'He won't say much,' Ian sighed. 'But you know what he's like.'

Catriona nodded, grateful that Ian hadn't acknowledged her faux pas. 'I do. That's why a little distance might be the best thing, for now. Until we both get ourselves back on some kind of even keel.'

'Well, I'm sorry. But you know I'm here if there's anything I can do. Even if it's not legal advice.' He laughed, a throaty sound that reminded Catriona of her grandfather, Jim, Iris's father, a policeman who had smoked for sixty years before he'd passed away.

'You should come and stay, Ian. We've not seen you since the funeral and I'm sure April would love it.' She looked over at the Mackenzie house, noticing Bruce walking across the lawn towards the loch. Behind him were Guinevere and Lancelot, and what looked like three puppies, trailing them like black-and-tan ducklings. Peg had said that they should bring Arthur over to see his parents and siblings as often as they wanted, and as Bruce had decided to keep one of the pups, it would be a lovely connection for Arthur.

April had been a little brighter since the arrival of the puppy, if still silent. However, even the occasional smile made Catriona's day, so she had much to be grateful to Peg for, and to Arthur, who was growing by the day and had quickly taken over the household. Duncan was still dubious about it, despite trying to sound supportive, but Catriona was convinced that as soon as he saw April with the dog, he'd be sold.

Drawing her back to the moment, Ian coughed. 'I'd better go. No rest, and all that.'

'Thanks, Ian. And thanks for the advice. I'll let you know what happens.'

'You take care now, Catriona. I'll be in touch.'

Catriona lay the phone down and checked the time. She had half an hour before her student, Olivia, arrived, so just enough time to call her mum.

· · ·

'Surely not, after all this time, Catriona?' Iris sounded distraught. 'She gave up her parental rights over nine years ago.' Unusually for Iris, she wasn't giving all parties the benefit of the doubt. 'Can't you just say no? April's been through so much.'

Catriona walked around the bed, tucked the phone under her jaw and tugged the duvet flat. 'We can't, Mum. We agreed to an open adoption.' She thumped her pillow, avoiding looking at Duncan's, still as smooth and undisturbed as it had been for six weeks now. She'd changed the cover every week, as she always did, despite knowing it wouldn't be used. 'And that wouldn't be fair to April, or her mother.'

'*You* are her mother, Catriona. Genetics are one thing, but raising a child is entirely another. That's where the real work, the true devotion comes in,' Iris snapped.

'You know what I mean, Mum.' Catriona spoke softly, her mother's panic mimicking her own. 'I just mean that she does have some rights, in this respect.'

Iris tutted. 'Well, just make sure she knows who's boss.'

Catriona laughed, caught off guard. It was so unlike her mother to be territorial, let alone confrontational. 'Don't worry, Mum. She just wants to see April. Maybe just to give her something, for when she's older, or...' Catriona stood up straight, suddenly frozen to the spot. How could she not have asked this question of the adoption coordinator? All this time, she had simply accepted the birth mother's right to see her child, but Catriona hadn't dug into what the woman wanted to achieve. Mortified, she turned and sat on the edge of the bed. 'God, Mum. I don't actually know what she wants.' She blinked, her eyes feeling gritty. 'I need to call you back.'

'Don't take any nonsense, Catriona. April is ours, and that's that.'

An hour later, Catriona was distractedly watching the clock as Olivia completed a vocabulary test. Catriona had been formulating what she would say when she called the agency back, and each time she ran through the script in her mind, it became stronger, her position feeling more solid. Having said she would agree to a meeting this coming Friday, to accommodate the fact that the birth mother, whose name was Lauren, would be in the area, she now wanted to snatch that back, Duncan's words about waiting until he got home gnawing at her.

'I'm done.' Olivia lifted the paper up and smiled.

'Oh, good for you.' Catriona stood up. 'Let's take a look.'

Twenty minutes later, she waved Olivia off, darted into the kitchen and grabbed her phone. As soon as the agency answered, she asked to speak to Annette, the case coordinator.

'Hello again, Mrs Anderson.' Annette sounded pleased to hear from her. 'How can I help?'

Catriona circled the kitchen, the smell of the bread she'd baked that morning lingering in the sunlit space. 'I have some more questions, about this meeting.' She swallowed. 'Things I should've asked before I agreed to it happening this week.'

'Oh, right.' Annette's voice dipped. 'What sort of questions?'

'Well, first, I'd like to know what Lauren's intentions are?' The minute she'd said it, Catriona winced. It had not come out as she'd intended, as she hadn't wanted to sound defensive.

'Um, well, I'm afraid I can't answer that, Mrs Anderson. All we can tell you is that she would like to see April. She's not obliged to tell us any more than that.'

Catriona's stomach lurched, the evasive response fanning her smouldering doubt over the wisdom of this meeting. 'It's just that my daughter has recently been through a trauma, we all have, and I need to make sure we're not leaving her open to anything else... I mean, any more hurt.' Her voice gave way and, frustrated that she felt tears pressing in, she dug her fingers into her thigh.

'I'm sorry to hear that.' Annette sounded sympathetic. 'But there's not much I can tell you, I'm afraid. Try not to be too concerned, though.' She paused. 'Just focus on April. Make sure she understands what's happening and is handling everything OK.'

Frustrated, Catriona rolled her eyes. 'Yes. Of course.' Did they really not think that was her first priority? She just hoped that what she had to tell April didn't widen the growing distance between them even more.

19

April was sitting on a blanket, out on the lawn, Arthur rolling on his back in the grass next to her. As Catriona approached, she heard April laugh, a breathy sound carried to her on the July breeze that made Catriona stop in her tracks, statue-like, as she waited for something more. With only silence following, she sighed, crossed the remaining distance between them and, as April turned to look at her, she knelt on the blanket. 'Hi, sweetheart.' She rubbed Arthur's downy stomach as he snorted, his pudgy legs pumping the air. 'It's lovely out here today.'

April stared ahead, rubbing her nose with her palm.

'I want to have a chat with you, April. I've got something important to tell you, love.' Catriona's voice snagged.

April scowled, as she watched Catriona gather herself. There was no easy way to do this, and no matter how much she had practised, Catriona had ended up in knots over what words to use, what this could mean, and how April might react. Now, she focused on the turquoise eyes, the V-shape peak of chestnut-coloured hair that pointed at the bridge of the narrow nose, and the tightly closed mouth, so many words, and feelings, held hostage inside.

'So, remember when we talked about the lady who... who was your... is...' Catriona almost gagged at the prospect of using the word *mother*, in any context, desperately seeking another description that would do Lauren justice, but not usurp her own position in April's life. She saw April's frown deepen. 'The lady whose tummy you were in, who gave birth to you.'

She dipped her chin lower, holding April's questioning gaze until the frown seemed to lift slightly, as April nodded.

'Well, she would like to come and see you. Just for a visit.' Catriona reached for April's hand, the need to rein-force their connection overwhelming. As was now happening frequently, April snatched her fingers away and tucked them under her thigh, just as Arthur righted himself, toddled onto the blanket and proceeded to crouch and pee, his little back legs quivering with the release. 'Oh, Arthur.' Catriona jumped up and lifted the puppy back onto the grass, his little tail wagging as she gently tapped his nose. 'Naughty boy,' she huffed, a smile tugging at her mouth.

As she turned to gather up the blanket, she caught April's expression, her eyes alight and her mouth twitching. The uncomfortable conversation momentarily relegated, Catriona's insides lifted as she saw a smile crack April's face, as if despite her efforts she couldn't contain it, and the sight of it was like air to the suffocating.

Catriona widened her eyes and pulled a comical face as April clamped a hand across her mouth, her shoulders rising up towards her ears. 'What a little monkey he is.' Catriona smiled behind mock-annoyance. 'What shall we do with him?'

As she waited, her breath held, April's face smoothed of

the smile and she shrugged, her fingers going into her mouth and the vacant look returning to her eyes.

Disappointed, Catriona lifted a corner of the blanket, forcing April to get up. 'Let's get this in the wash and we'll talk more inside.' She gathered the blanket up as April began walking towards the house, Arthur tripping behind her and Hamish dangling from her hand.

April sat at the kitchen table, an uneaten sandwich in front of her and Arthur safely in his pen by the back door. Catriona sat opposite her daughter, and shoving her own plate away, leaned back in the chair. The temporary diversion the puppy had caused was over and it was time to finish what she'd started, out in the garden. 'So, I was telling you about the lady.' She hesitated. 'Her name is Lauren.' She scanned April's face, waiting for her reaction, but all Catriona saw was heartbreaking disinterest. 'She'd like to come and see you.' She paused. 'It'll just be for a little while and then she'll go home again. Nothing is going to change, April, for us, or for you. What do you think about that?'

April stared at the sandwich, pointedly over at Duncan's empty chair, then lifted her eyes to Catriona's, a sheen of something glittering behind them that Catriona didn't recognise. It cut her deeply that her sweet girl, one of the brightest stars in Catriona's sky, was becoming more of a mystery to her by the day. Then, as she waited, willing April to give her a clue, a blink, a shrug, anything to show that she'd heard her, April's face cleared, and she simply nodded.

Surprised, and a little hurt at the ease with which this momentous news was being accepted, Catriona swallowed hard. 'OK, then.' She stood up, lifted her untouched food, set it on the counter by the sink, and scanned the back garden, the golden blossoms on the gorse fluttering in the summer wind coming in from across the loch. 'She's coming tomorrow, so we'll go to the village now and get the shopping done. If we hurry, we might have time to go and see Mungo?'

She turned to face her daughter, only to see the chair empty, and the sandwich still untouched on the plate.

'Damn it, Cat, I thought you were going to wait until I could be there,' Duncan snapped. 'This is really bad timing.'

'I had no choice,' Catriona whispered, her throat raw from keeping her voice controlled now that April was finally asleep across the hall. 'Besides, it won't be the first time I've had to deal with tough stuff alone, even when you *are* around.' She stared at him. 'I'm used to it, Duncan.'

'That was uncalled for.' His eyes narrowed. 'And this is a totally different situation. Work demands are what they are, Cat, but this is something else.'

'Oh, so you mean our family is finally a priority?' Her heart was pounding as she looked away from the screen, determined not to cry.

'Jesus, you can really go for the jugular.' His voice was rough and low. 'Right on target.'

Turning back to face him, Catriona saw the hurt her words had caused. Deep furrows cut across his forehead, and he was fiercely pinching the bridge of his nose. Suddenly seeing the futility of delving any deeper into these old hurts, she took a deep breath. 'Look, I couldn't say no. She was going to be in the area, and apparently, according to Annette, it's not easy for her to get around. I don't think she has a car.' She shrugged.

'So, how's she getting there, then?' He frowned, the window behind him dark, speckled with a smattering of orange and yellow lights, glittering behind the windows of Lisbon's historic skyline.

'Trains and taxis, I suppose. I'm not sure.' Catriona shifted back against the headboard, the cool of the approaching night making her draw her knees up closer to her. Across the room, Arthur was in his bed, noisily chewing, his two front paws clamped around the ragged remains of a plastic bone. 'Look, I'm sure it'll be OK. She'll be here for an hour or so, we'll sit out in the garden, have a chat, she can say whatever it is she has to say to April, and she'll go.' Catriona lifted her palm up, seeing his frown deepen. Failing to convince even herself, she dropped her gaze to the duvet. 'It'll be fine.'

Having closed the laptop on Duncan, Catriona had tiptoed downstairs and poured herself a small brandy and she had just got back into bed when Iris called. Her mother's gentle voice and lilting laugh instantly tugged Catriona back from the unsettled place her call with Duncan had left her. Speaking to Iris was a tonic, and even as Catriona talked about what was going to happen the following day, it began to feel a little less intimidating.

'So, you're feeling OK about it just being you and April?' Iris asked.

'Yes. I just hope the weather's decent, as I'd prefer to sit in the garden.' Catriona tugged the duvet up around her middle. 'That probably sounds daft, but keeping her outside feels safer, somehow.' She nodded to herself.

'I totally understand,' Iris said. 'And you're going to ask

her what she expects out of this, right?' She sounded dubious.

'Yeah, I will.' Catriona felt the knot of tension returning to her chest as she looked around the tidy room. Duncan's absence now felt increasingly normal, which was both sad and surprising. 'Whatever it is, Mum, I just hope she doesn't upset April. She's walking a very fine line between hurt and anger, right now.' Catriona pictured her troubled daughter, the new, distant look in April's eyes, the chilling flashes of contempt Catriona had been seeing. Perhaps she *should* have said no to this meeting? Perhaps, she should have insisted that it happen once Duncan was back, so they could present a united front? But even as she considered it, she knew it was too late for that now.

20

Catriona looked in the mirror, her heart flip-flopping under her crisp white shirt. Her nerves were raw, her hands trembling and her stomach in knots. It was only an hour until Lauren was due to arrive and, as the minutes ticked by, Catriona felt herself sliding into a place of such self-doubt that her head began to ache.

What would Lauren be like? What was her life like now? What would she think of Catriona, and of their home? Would she question Duncan's absence, or be suspicious of the circumstances that had created the silent, distant child that was her daughter – the child she'd given away in the hope of providing her with a better life?

As Catriona tried to picture their family, as Lauren might see it, the image was less than idyllic and it made Catriona sad and then, suddenly, angry. She wouldn't be made to feel bad about any of it. They had done nothing wrong, and everything that had crumbled recently had not been their fault. They had done everything they possibly could to give April a wonderful life.

As she thought about all the happiness and contentment that had surrounded them for years, her eyes stung. Catriona longed for those times; those joyful, carefree moments that they'd taken for granted, assuming there would be so many more to come. Precious moments they had thrown away because they hadn't realised their value – and so many of which Duncan had missed, simply by being distracted. At the same time, her reflex of wanting to exonerate them from any blame over what had happened to Hope, and the damage that had caused to their family unit, gave her pause. With that came an image of Duncan, sitting between the girls at the piano, the three of them laughing as he murdered a handful of Christmas carols, and the mass of conflicting emotions spun inside her, tugging at her middle.

Whatever Lauren thought of them, Catriona didn't care. It was none of Lauren's business what had brought them to their current state, and that was the way it would stay. She would protect their privacy to the extent she could, and this stranger, this cuckoo in the nest, would have to be content with whatever Catriona was willing to share.

Shaking off her anxiety, Catriona had taken the time to dry her hair properly, rather than leaving it to curl into the soft twists that usually surrounded her face, and with a little rouge and a touch of mascara on, she felt less scattered than she had in weeks. Her freshly washed jeans were loose on her, and, with a sunny forecast, her bare feet were in her leather flip-flops.

She took in her reflection, the slender nose, the wide-set blue eyes, the scattering of freckles across her cheekbones dusting the tiny lines that had appeared underneath them. Despite the recent changes that life had brought about, in her own face, she still saw Hope staring back at her.

Closing her eyes momentarily, Catriona's breath caught. Every day, something brought Hope back to her. A waft of jasmine shampoo, a whistle from a robin that had always made Hope smile, the feel of the rough stone path under her bare feet – Hope often being told off for not wearing shoes outside in the warmer weather – and today was no different. It had been almost four months since her darling girl had been torn from her and it was as painful now as it had been that night, sitting in the cold mud, Hope's lifeless form in her arms as she'd rocked her.

Overcome, Catriona steadied herself on the edge of the sink, her pulse filling her ears. That loss, the cavernous hole that tiny Faith, and now Hope had left, was always lurking close by. While Catriona had been necessarily focused on April these past few months, when she let herself think about her lost daughters, the hole still threatened to consume her entirely.

April was out in the garden, with Arthur. Catriona had kept her off school for the day, and without any fuss, or particular show of emotion, April had quietly dressed herself as Catriona made breakfast.

April had chosen her favourite yellow shorts, a ladybird top and a broad yellow hairband that held her hair away from her face. She'd eaten some toast and then, surprisingly, had pulled a chair over and washed Hamish's face in the kitchen sink, rubbing it with a towel as Catriona watched, both touched and hurt at the care she was taking over her own, and her toy monkey's, appearance. Now, hoping that she would do April proud, Catriona blinked at her reflection, pulled her shoulders back and turned away from the mirror.

Down in the sunny kitchen, the tea tray sat on the table, with three of the silver teaspoons her mother had given them as a wedding present lined up neatly by the cups. As she took it all in, the mellow sound of Adele on the radio in the conservatory, the smell of the rosemary outside leaking in through the cracked window, her pulse still tapping at her temple, Catriona exhaled. Everything was going to be OK. It had to be.

The doorbell made Catriona jump. She'd been standing in the conservatory watching April outside chasing the puppy, trying to get him to bite onto a stick she held.

Catriona had cancelled the piano lesson she'd set up with Peg, postponing to the following day, but not feeling comfortable sharing with Peg what was actually going on. Catriona still hoped that she might get April interested in learning to play the piano – any conduit to communication being worth a try.

Passing the mirror in the hall, she gave herself one last look-over, then hesitated behind the front door, listening to the crunch of shoes on the gravel outside, before opening it.

Lauren was looking away from the house, her back to Catriona. She was wearing a long suede jacket the colour of toffee and a pair of black jeans. She was slender, taller than Catriona had pictured, and her hair, cut into a jaw-length, shiny bob, was the same rich chestnut colour as April's. Hearing the door open, she spun around, and Catriona felt the air being sucked from her at the sight of the pronounced widow's peak and the same distinct, turquoise eyes as April.

'Oh, hello. I'm Lauren.' The young woman smiled, revealing a tiny gap between her two front teeth. 'Sorry, I was just admiring the scenery.' Her face coloured slightly. 'What a lovely spot you have here.'

Catriona's legs felt as if they might buckle as she forced a smile and tried to calculate how old Lauren was, landing on mid-twenties. 'Yes, we like it.' She nodded, trying not to stare at the hairline, the eyes, the smile that conjured images of days gone by when April had played outside with Hope and would throw her head back in the wind as she laughed loudly. 'Come in, please,' Catriona rallied, stepping back into the hall. 'It's good to meet you.' She extended a hand, noting the long, cool fingers inside her warmer ones, and the faint scent of cinnamon wafting in on the breeze.

'You too.' Lauren stepped over the threshold, the sight of her trendy trainers, occupying Catriona's hall, blinding. 'Oh, what a beautiful house.' Lauren's voice was warm, filled with genuine admiration.

'Thanks. It's home.' Catriona shrugged, instantly wanting to take back the somewhat inane comment.

Lauren looked past her into the living room and smiled broadly. 'Oh, do you play?' She pointed at the piano. 'I've always wanted to learn.'

'April and I have just started.' The white lie tasted bitter, as Catriona felt her cheeks warming. 'Let's go through to the kitchen. I thought we'd sit in the garden as it's such a lovely day.' She gestured over her shoulder. 'Let's have a quick chat before we go outside.' She walked over to the sink and refolded a clean tea towel, uncomfortable saying 'and then you can *meet* April'. Instead, she found a smile, and said, 'April is in the garden.'

Lauren flicked her eyes around the kitchen, taking in her surroundings, the wide window, the rack of glistening copper pots above the island and the tea tray, then she nodded. 'OK.' Stepping forwards, she gripped the back of a chair, as if she were steadying herself. 'Mrs Anderson, I'm really grateful for this.' Her eyes were full.

'Catriona, please.' Catriona patted the air, the slight apprehension she saw in Lauren's face somehow comforting. 'You don't need to thank me.' She watched the younger woman's forehead release the hint of the frown she'd just seen.

'I know this must be hard for you.' Lauren pressed her lips together. 'And I don't want to cause any disruption to April, or you.'

Despite her nerves, and sense of needing to protect herself, and her family, Catriona was filled with sympathy for this young woman, or was it empathy? Either way, there was something disarming in Lauren's manner that drew Catriona across the kitchen and to her side. 'Listen, Lauren. We're happy you're here. That you wanted to come.' She smiled. 'It's a little nerve-racking for us all, but it'll be good for April, and that's the most important thing.' She took in the flash of surprise and relief on Lauren's face. 'Let's sit for a bit.' Catriona pointed at the chair Lauren was standing behind. 'Please.'

Lauren nodded, returning the smile, and sat down. 'I thought long and hard before I contacted the agency.' She looked down at her knotted fingers. 'It wasn't something I just decided one morning, over a cuppa and a slice of toast.' She gave a half-smile. 'Anyway, I just wanted you to know that I'm not doing this lightly.'

Catriona nodded, circling the table, and sitting opposite her. 'I'm sure you're not.' Surprised at the sense of calm that was growing inside her, Catriona leaned back in the chair. Rather than feel threatened, she felt the need to reassure Lauren, to let her know, and believe, that she was welcome.

'It's just that I've reached a place in my life where I feel I need to go back and, well, revisit some things I did.' Lauren's cheeks began to colour again as she smoothed her palm over her hair. 'Face certain decisions I made. Paths I took.' She sought Catriona's eyes. 'I hope you understand.'

Catriona took in the youthful face, the clear eyes and

smooth skin, noting the lack of wrinkles or shadows, signs of pain, loss, or regret – some of the fingerprints that life had left on Catriona's own face. Seeing only mild discomfort, Catriona dropped her gaze to the table. This young woman must have regrets, surely, or she wouldn't be here. 'I do understand, believe me.' Catriona nodded. 'None of us have lived our lives without *some* regrets.' As soon as she'd said it, she held her breath. She was putting words in Lauren's mouth and opening a door to something that she may not even be feeling. Sitting up straighter, Catriona nodded. 'Please, go on.'

'When I gave my daughter up for adoption, I was only sixteen, and too young to be a good parent. My mum wouldn't support me, so I had no choice.' Lauren eyed her, a new frown creasing the smooth brow. 'Giving my baby away was the most gut-wrenching thing I've ever done, and even if it was the right thing to do then, time doesn't take the edge off that.'

'Lauren, you don't need to explain yourself to me.' Catriona shook her head, the words *my baby* snagging her heart. 'You put April first. That was the ultimate act of love. You did the right thing.' She hoped she hadn't sounded patronising as she watched Lauren shift in the chair.

'I love the name April, by the way. So pretty.' The smile was back.

'Yes, we felt it suited her. She was such a sunny baby,' Catriona said.

At this, Lauren seemed to withdraw into herself again, leaning back and crossing her arms protectively across her middle, the gesture making Catriona want to bite her tongue. She seemed to be saying all the wrong things, despite her wish to make Lauren feel comfortable.

Trying to right the balance, she leaned forward on her

elbows. 'So, tell me a little about yourself, Lauren. Where do you live, and what do you do for a living?'

Lauren seemed slightly alarmed, perhaps expecting to be the one asking the questions, her eyebrows lifting. 'Oh, I live in Glasgow, and I'm a vet.' She placed her palms on the table and stared down at her knuckles.

Surprised at herself for having expected a less confident and accomplished person to be sitting opposite her, Catriona's eyes widened. 'Wow, that's great. How long have you been practising?'

Lauren looked up. 'A year or so. The practice is doing well, though. We're really busy.' She pursed her lips, the same way April did when she was holding something back. Sensing that she might be being intrusive, pushing too hard too fast, Catriona backtracked. 'April is animal-mad. She just got a puppy recently and it's the first time she's...' She caught herself, shocked that she was about to share something that could leave her open to questions she wasn't ready to answer. 'Anyway, she's animal-mad.' She shrugged.

'Sweet.' Lauren smiled, a warmth returning to her eyes. 'Can we go out now?' She leaned forward and looked over at the window. 'I'm desperate to see her.'

Catriona took a breath, the decision to tell Lauren about Hope sliding into place so fast that it made her blink. 'Lauren, I need to tell you something before we go outside.' She paused. 'It's not easy for me, so please bear with me.' She felt the threat of tears gathering behind her eyes, so linked her fingers in front of her and squeezed hard. 'You probably weren't aware that we had another child, a daughter.' She swallowed. 'Hope was our natural daughter, a surviving twin.' The word *surviving* tasted bitter, so she swallowed several times before continuing. 'She was born two days before April, and they were inseparable.' She watched

Lauren's face, the eyes softening even more as her full mouth opened slightly. 'Three months ago, there was an accident, and Hope drowned.' Catriona took a slow breath, willing herself to keep it together and not disintegrate in front of this stranger. 'April was... *is* still devastated about losing her sister, and she's not been talking for a few weeks now.' Saying it out loud made it seem heavier, more damning than it had before. 'We're having counselling, as a family, and we're sure that things will get back to normal, in time. But I wanted you to know so you understand if she doesn't interact too much.' She shrugged. 'We're all learning to adjust to the loss, but April is extremely sensitive. She feels it deeply.'

Lauren slowly stood up and, to Catriona's surprise, she walked around the table and stood in front of her. 'I am so, so sorry, Catriona.' Lauren opened her arms as her eyes glittered in the sunlight flooding the kitchen.

Before she could stop herself, Catriona stood up and then they were hugging, Catriona's eyes filling up as she felt the lean arms around her back and caught the same cinnamon scent she'd noticed when she'd first opened the door. Despite being taken aback by this spontaneous show of sympathy, she realised how badly she'd needed to be hugged, and that it was this person she barely knew, whom she had wanted to keep at arm's length, who was providing her with the comfort she craved, was bizarre.

Comfort slowly shifting towards awkwardness, Catriona stepped away and walked back to the sink, her hands shaking slightly as she filled the kettle. 'So, are you married?' She deliberately kept her eyes on the back garden, searching for April's form out near the row of gold-tipped gorse. 'If you don't mind me asking, of course.' She spoke over her shoulder, spying April walking across the grass with Arthur in her arms, her hair flowing around the yellow band in deep waves.

'Um, yes. I am,' Lauren said. 'Just over a year now, and we have a son, Connor. He's four.'

Catriona froze, blinking and trying to focus on the surface of the loch, the breeze churning up rows of white-topped ripples beyond the slope of the lawn. A son. She had never considered that April's birth mother would have had other children and hearing it now rocked her to her core. April had a half-sibling. An all-important blood connection that she and Duncan couldn't give her. Suddenly, the calm that Catriona had felt earlier seeped away like the receding tide, leaving her heart raw, slashed wide open, and her little family feeling horribly vulnerable.

21

Catriona would never forget the look on April's face when Lauren held her hand out to her, smiling almost shyly. 'Hello, April. I'm Lauren.'

Catriona felt a vice-like squeezing of her insides as April grasped the hand, her curious eyes scanning Lauren's face as if she were seeing herself in the mirror. Then their eyes met, the turquoise irises, duplicates of each other, and the identical, reddish widows' peaks pulling the two of them together with a force that had the potential to bring Catriona to her knees.

She had decided to hang back, to let them have a little time together, but when Lauren hugged April, then asked about Arthur, Catriona had to summon every molecule of strength she could not to inject herself. April accepting the affection of a stranger when she was resisting it from Catriona was a new strike that left her feeling superfluous and heartsore.

'So, this is your puppy. He's very handsome.' Lauren knelt on the grass and stroked Arthur's back. 'Does he like to pay tug?'

April nodded, her fingers going to her mouth.

'You know, I'm a vet, so I'm surrounded by all kinds of animals every day at my practice.' Lauren nodded, flicking her eyes to where Catriona was hovering, close to the rosemary bushes. 'We have all kinds coming in to see us. Parrots, cats, lots of dogs, hamsters, snakes, even a giant lizard or two.'

April gave Lauren a huge smile and seeing something that she craved and yet was being denied, Catriona breathed around the ball of hurt that had been growing inside her.

'You'd love where I work, April. Catriona tells me you like animals, too.'

At this, the hairs on Catriona's arms prickled to attention. Why had Lauren not said *your mummy* tells me? For the first time since this open-faced young woman had walked into her home, Catriona felt threatened and the temptation to step in between them and assert her position in April's life was overwhelming. That position felt tenuous, and fragile, for the first time since they'd brought the tiny infant home, and the realisation left Catriona nauseated.

'When I was your age, I was always reading about animals, drawing them and watching all the wildlife programmes I could.' Lauren smiled warmly at April, who seemed mesmerised. 'So, we're just the same, April.' She sat down, lifting Arthur onto her lap, and then April followed suit, sitting opposite Lauren, her skinny legs forming a wide V in the grass. 'I brought you something that I hope you'll like. It's inside in my bag.' Lauren gestured over her shoulder. 'It's a CD with lots of different songs that have animals in the titles. I thought it'd be fun.' She tipped her head to the side as April nodded, her eyes glowing with pleasure.

'My favourite is "Nellie the Elephant".' Lauren laughed softly. 'It might be a bit babyish for you, because you're so grown-up, but...'

Catriona caught her breath as April lunged forward, grabbed Lauren's hand and shook her head vigorously.

'Oh, good.' Lauren sighed. 'Maybe we can listen to it together sometime?'

April nodded, sitting back as Lauren stroked Arthur's ears. 'What other kinds of animals do you like?'

Catriona held her breath, in anticipation of April actually answering, but when she simply shrugged, Catriona felt a wash of relief so strong that she took a step backwards and closed her eyes for a second. Had April spoken to Lauren, that might have been a blow Catriona would never recover from.

Lauren spent the next half an hour just talking, asking questions that went unanswered, telling April about her work, her home and her daily life.

Having not asked Lauren to avoid mentioning Connor just yet, Catriona felt newly vulnerable, and remiss in that oversight, as she listened from a respectful distance. Her teacup was quivering in her hand as she walked around the path, deadheading pansies and trying to look disinterested.

Eventually, having had all the distance she could take, Catriona crossed the lawn and joined them, sitting on one of the deckchairs she'd set up and refilling their cups from the teapot. She tried to sound at ease, but their conversation felt slightly less natural than earlier. 'So, where in Glasgow are you based?' Catriona focused on the loch, the thickest patches of the grass, the rugged outline of the Cuillins that were clearly visible across the water, anything other than meet Lauren's eyes – April's eyes – again.

'The West End,' Lauren said. 'Hillhead. We moved there after I graduated from university.'

Catriona's eyebrows jumped, Hillhead being a very trendy and expensive part of the city that her Glasgow friends called *the posh end.* 'Lovely. Is it still as busy, at the weekends?' Catriona slipped her sunglasses on, one more layer of protection to hide behind.

'Oh, yes. It gets a bit mad.' Lauren nodded. 'But our house is on a quiet street, and the back garden is lovely and peaceful.' She drained her teacup and set it on the tray that sat on the grass next to her. 'We're very lucky, really.'

Catriona tried to picture the house, imagining a Georgian sandstone with high windows and a pretty rockery at the front, behind a wrought-iron fence. As she squinted into the sunlight, April trotted past them with Arthur following close behind, her yellow shorts bright against the mid-blue afternoon sky. Smiling, Catriona glanced over at Lauren.

'So how long has she not been speaking?' She turned to look at Catriona, her eyes full of sympathy as her glossy hair separated in the afternoon breeze.

Suddenly feeling cornered, Catriona took the few moments she needed to reply. 'As I mentioned, Hope died four months ago, and April stopped talking a week or so after that.' The exact circumstances of the start of April's silence were locked in a place that even Catriona wasn't accessing at the moment. 'As I said, we're having family counselling, and things will resolve themselves, in time.' She nodded decisively, then stood up, a signal, she hoped, that the visit was drawing to a close.

Catching her off guard once again, Lauren's expression softened even more. 'You're amazingly strong, Catriona. I don't know if I could...' She halted, clamping her mouth shut.

Catriona instantly felt bad about having been somewhat clipped, considering that Lauren had experienced the pain of giving her child away – and to them, no less. That must have been the most agonising thing to do, short of losing April to death, and she needed to give Lauren credit for finding the strength to put the well-being of her baby first. 'You know about loss too, Lauren. In a different form, perhaps, but no less traumatic, I'm sure.' She smiled kindly, holding her hand out for Lauren's empty cup. 'Shall we go in?'

Lauren took a few minutes in the downstairs bathroom while Catriona gently put Arthur back in his pen and explained to April that their visitor would be leaving. April nodded, pinching her lips with her fingertips, and then turned and walked into the conservatory.

When Lauren came back into the hall, Catriona suggested she go in and say goodbye. Lauren nodded, went to see April, and spent a few minutes crouched down in front of her, talking in a low voice. Catriona strained to hear them from the kitchen but couldn't catch what was being said, as April nodded repeatedly, her eyes locked on Lauren's.

Now, as Lauren hovered in the open front door, she looked visibly downcast, her eyes glistening as she nervously smoothed her hair. 'Thanks a million for having me. I didn't know what to expect, and you've been so kind.' She smiled at Catriona. 'April is just wonderful.' She paused, a question obviously working its way out, and before Catriona could respond, Lauren sputtered, 'Would it be OK if I came back, in a week or so? I'd love to bring Connor to meet April, if you're comfortable with that?'

Catriona was taken aback. While she'd suspected this might come up, she had not expected it so soon, or quite so directly. As she tried to formulate a response, Lauren talked about her son, his love of aeroplanes, strawberries and *Sesame Street*. Catriona was only half listening as she struggled with what to do, whether this was something she should wait and talk to Duncan, or even Ian, about. But Lauren had been so sincere, warm and accepting of their situation, and she sounded so genuinely excited about the prospect of introducing April to her half-brother that Catriona felt safe in agreeing to the request.

Swinging the door open a little wider, she looked past Lauren, the sky beginning to darken as ominous clouds slid across the sun. 'I think that'll be OK, Lauren, but I'll talk with my husband first. I'd like him to be here the next time you come. He wants to meet you, too.' She hoped she'd sounded genuine, and open to the meeting, despite her stomach twisting into knots.

'Right.' Lauren nodded, slinging her handbag over her shoulder. 'He was working today, of course.' She looked behind Catriona into the living room, another question seeming to hover behind her eyes.

'Yes, he's on a business trip at the moment, but he'll be back tomorrow.' Catriona shrugged, once again the edited truth tart on her tongue. 'So nice to have met you.' She held her hand out. 'Safe trip home.' Suddenly she realised that hadn't asked Lauren how she'd got here, and Catriona's face warmed. 'How are you getting back?'

Lauren pulled out her phone and glanced at the screen. 'I got a friend to drop me. He's waiting in the village, so I'll just text him and then start walking.' She kept her eyes on the screen.

'I could drop you off in the village, if you like,' Catriona offered, hoping Lauren would decline, wanting to get back to April and close the door on this surprising, and emotionally charged, day.

'No need. I don't want to be a bother. And I'll enjoy the walk.' Lauren tapped out a message, then slid her phone away. 'Thanks again, Catriona. Just give me a ring when you've talked to your husband.' She pulled a piece of lined paper from her bag and held it out. 'Here's my contact info.'

'Thanks. I will.' Catriona slipped the paper into her pocket, feeling the weight of its contents against her thigh.

Graham had come over after school and asked if April could go next door with Arthur and have tea with them. 'Nan's made shepherd's pie, April.' He'd grinned at her. Catriona had looked over at April, whose entire body was asking for permission, her face full of light, her eyes huge and her torso leaning towards Graham, like a giant magnet was pulling her away from Catriona. She'd nodded. 'Off you go, then, but don't be too late. Seven thirty at the latest, OK? Will you please walk her home, Graham?' She'd watched April lifting Arthur from his pen, the puppy already a bigger handful than just days before. She'd then grabbed a chew toy and his blanket and smiled up at Graham, with obvious relief.

'Yep. No problem.' Graham had smiled. 'Come on then. Let's go before Pops eats it all.' He'd beckoned to April, who'd followed him out the door.

Her heart aching as she'd watched April so willingly move away from her, once again, Catriona had waited until they'd climbed over the fence and were heading inside the Mackenzie house before she'd shut the back door and returned to the silence of the kitchen.

Turning, she surveyed the tray sitting on the counter, the cups tea-stained and the milk in the jug looking buttery. As she lifted it and poured the contents down the drain, Catriona replayed the events of the morning, her remaining energy seeping away with the milk.

April had been in bed for an hour when the laptop pinged on the side table in the conservatory. Catriona had eaten some leftovers, poured herself a large glass of wine, and talked briefly to Iris about how the day had gone. She had been waiting for Duncan to call so she could fill him in. As she answered the call, her stomach fluttered, a mixture of her reaction to the surreal nature of the day and nerves at his likely response to what she had agreed to.

'Hey.' He was sitting at a desk in a dimly lit office, a lamp glowing next to him and a bottle of water sitting on a coaster.

'Hi. Are you still at the office?' She walked over and quietly closed the door before returning to the sofa.

'Yeah. We had a late meeting, and we're going to dinner with the client in a bit.' He stretched, his arms reaching above his head and his chin dropping to his chest. 'So, how did it go?' He leaned forward and focused on her face.

'It was fine. She was friendly, and easy-going. She was fine.' She nodded.

'That's it?' He sounded irritated.

Taking a deep breath, she continued, 'She's sweet and kind, actually. Pretty young. Around twenty-four or five. She's a vet. Lives near Hillhead, apparently.' Catriona sat back, propping the laptop on her knees.

'Must be doing OK if she lives there.' His eyebrows lifted. 'What else?'

'Married for a year now, and Duncan...' She took a moment, grabbing her hair into her fist and tossing it over her shoulder, trying to picture Lauren's slender fingers and whether she'd been wearing a ring. 'She has a four-year-old son.'

Duncan's face darkened, his jaw slackening. 'Oh, wow. I didn't expect that. But I suppose it's not that surprising, if she's still in her twenties.'

Catriona took in the spidery lines around his eyes, the newly sunken cheeks making his nose seem more prominent. 'She wants to bring him here next week, to meet April.' She sucked in her lip as his frown deepened.

'And you said no, I hope.' He stuck his chin out in the way that spoke volumes.

'Just hold on, before you deliver a lecture.' Catriona held her hand up. 'Let me tell you what happened.'

As she described Lauren's gentle nature, the surprising empathy she'd displayed, the looks of understanding, her apparent sensitivity to their loss and pain, Duncan sat statue-like, his fingers lightly tapping the desk, occasionally distracting Catriona from what she was saying.

When she could take it no more, Catriona tutted. 'Can you not do that, please. It's really loud.'

He looked surprised but drew his hand back onto his lap. 'So, what you're telling me is that you said it was all right for her to bring him over, before I get back. Right?'

Catriona felt like a child caught with her fingers in the jam jar, and it made her clench her teeth, momentarily. 'I said I'd talk to you and then let her know.' She spoke pointedly, holding his gaze. 'But, Duncan, we're talking about April's half-brother. Not some random child coming for a play date. There's a genuine connection here.'

'I knew you should've waited until I could be there.

This would never have happened.' He shook his head. 'You just can't say no to anyone, Cat, and this is all happening too bloody quickly for my liking,' he blustered.

'What the hell are you talking about? I say no all the time.' She forced herself to control her voice, concerned that April might wake and overhear another damaging conversation. Catriona wasn't prepared to handle that right now.

'We don't know what she wants yet. Why she's suddenly shown up after all these years. We need to be careful.' He paused. 'Take it slowly and make sure to protect April from anything...'

'Anything what?' Catriona's voice was growing raspy from forced whispering.

'Unknown.' Duncan's jaw ticked, a sure sign of anger.

'You telling me to delay her to visit and what had to actually happen were two separate things. And why do you think it would have gone any differently if you'd been here?' Catriona felt the burn of tears behind her eyes, so looked away from the screen. 'I'm perfectly capable of handling this without you.' Her eyes flashed as his chin lifted abruptly.

Her message had obviously hit a nerve, as she saw his eyes widen. Then he backtracked. 'Look, I'm sorry. It's just hard being so removed from all of this going on,' he said. 'So, aside from what happens next, it sounds as if you genuinely liked her.' His tone was less accusing now. 'Did you?'

Catriona considered for a moment, then nodded. 'Yes. She was sensitive and thoughtful. She's confident, and obviously intelligent, and she really seems to have got her life together.' Catriona nodded as she processed how she felt about the young woman who had been in their home, surprising her on the one hand with the depth of her compassion, and on the other, leaving a trace of angst within Catriona that she was struggling to squash.

Picturing April hugging Lauren, smiling at her, willingly letting Lauren take her hand, Catriona swallowed over a lump of hurt. If she couldn't reach April again, and soon, was it possible that Lauren could offer April something essential that Catriona couldn't anymore? Not only did April appear to instinctively connect with her, but Lauren had the ultimate trump card in Connor, and the realisation of what that could mean was utterly terrifying.

'She was really good with April. Patient, chatty but not pushy.' Catriona sucked in her bottom lip. 'She's not what I imagined, though.' She eyed him as he waited for her to continue. 'I think I wanted her to be more unsure of herself, maybe even a bit broken, but she seems completely together.'

Duncan leaned back in the chair, shaking his head slightly as he adjusted his screen. 'I still don't think you should let her come back, not until I can be there.'

Suddenly exhausted, Catriona felt a tear welling on her bottom lid. 'She asked a few direct questions, mainly about April's silence, and you being away, and even though she was being kind, somehow she made me feel...' She hiccupped.

'What?' Duncan frowned.

She hesitated, her feelings of earlier only now falling into place. 'She made me feel as if *we* are the broken ones.' Her voice hitched.

Duncan put his face close to the camera, his eyes glinting in the amber light of the desk lamp. 'We are *not* broken, Cat. We're bruised, for sure, but we're healing.' He sounded tentative, unsure, not something she heard in his voice often. 'Right?'

Catriona took in the face that she knew so well, the way his eyes narrowed when he was concentrating, the full mouth that she'd kissed more times than she could count, the taut jawline and the shadow of a day's growth on his angular chin, and all she wanted was to say, yes, that they were healing, but she couldn't find the words. What if she never could?

The following evening, April sat with her back to Catriona, her eyes glued to the TV. Her hero, James Herriot, was tending to a horse in labour in the middle of the night, an episode April had watched at least three times.

Having cleaned up the kitchen after dinner, Catriona was reading on the opposite sofa, keen to be in the same room as April for as long as she could. She missed spending time with her daughter, April's habit of walking away from her, trotting up the stairs to her bedroom and closing the door, becoming increasingly frequent and upsetting.

Seeing the programme come to an end, Catriona put her book on the coffee table and stretched her legs out, feeling the tension in her calves. Missing weeks of tai chi classes was beginning to take its toll on her body.

As she watched, April lifted the remote and switched off the TV, and before she could slink out of the room, Catriona stood up, walked over, and sat next to her daughter. 'I was thinking we could have a spa day tomorrow. Maybe paint our nails, like we used to. Plait each other's hair and spend the day in our jammies watching telly.' She lifted April's hand from the sofa and looked at the perfect little fingernails, the rosy-pink cuticles and bright white crescents at their bases.

As she waited for April to respond, the earth seemed to

shift under Catriona as April pulled her hand away, her eyes dull and her bottom lip protruding.

'What is it, sweetheart?' Catriona battled to control her voice. 'Don't you want to? You used to love spa day.' She scanned the flushed little face in front of her, trying to banish a blinding image of the beautiful smiles that had been gifted to Lauren the previous day.

April tucked her hand into her lap and shook her head, her lower lip now pouting outward.

'It could be fun,' Catriona tried again, leaning in towards April's stiff frame. 'I'll make us chocolate orange mousse.' She smiled brightly, despite the cold fingers of fear that were grabbing at her middle. 'April?'

April stood up, lifted Hamish and Harvey from the sofa and shoved the hair away from her face with her free hand. Catching Catriona's eye, she shook her head again, this time more emphatically, then edged past Catriona and headed for the door.

Catriona stood up unsteadily and followed April out into the hall. 'April, love. Please don't walk away from me.' Her voice threatened to fail her, so she pressed her tongue hard against the roof of her mouth, as April continued her progress towards the stairs.

Her heart splintering, Catriona also climbed the stairs, staying three steps behind April, watching the deliberate way she stared straight ahead, never looking back to acknowledge Catriona's presence. Then, when April reached the hall, she paced along it until she stopped abruptly at her bedroom door.

For a second, Catriona thought that April might look over at her, maybe even smile, but instead she walked into her room and, turning around, avoided Catriona's eyes, then gently closed the door in her face.

Catriona's palm clamped over her mouth as she began to pant, tears instantly flooding her eyes. She bit down on her lip, battling to contain the sobs that were building inside her, then she turned and leaned against the wall, feeling the cool of the plaster through her shirt. As she slid to the ground, her knees coming up to her chest and her chin dropping onto them, she let the tears come.

The following morning, Catriona was hovering outside April's closed door. She could hear Arthur scuttling around and April playing with him. There was music in the background and Catriona leaned in closer to the door to make it out. As she closed her eyes and concentrated on the tinny notes, the tune became familiar, and then she recognised it. It was 'Nellie the Elephant'.

Pressing her eyes tighter closed, Catriona took a shaky breath. Could this be a sign? Was she dismissing April's clear messages, out of her own fear and selfishness? April's repeated rejection was devastating, and while Catriona knew that she was a child, struggling, and ill-equipped to deal with the grief and pain she was experiencing, Catriona asked herself a question that she had been forcing down since Lauren's visit. What if Lauren was the better parent for April, now? What if April would be better off with her, and her half-brother, safely away from this house that was filled with so many painful memories? What if April would simply be happier being away from her and Duncan, and everything they represented?

22

Peg sat at the piano, waves of silvery hair flowing down her flower-patterned back. April sat next to her, her legs swinging back and forth under the long, narrow stool while Catriona sat on the sofa at the opposite end of the living room. This was the first time they'd managed to get April to sit at the piano, and Catriona considered it progress, despite the promise of ice cream she'd had to use as bait.

Since the last fraught conversation with Duncan, several days had passed with no contact other than the occasional text, and rather than miss talking to him, Catriona had been relieved at the hiatus. The tension had been palpable between them over what had happened with Lauren, and as long as they were on opposite sides of the best way to handle her request to come back, and bring the little boy with her, it was easier to avoid talking at all.

April had been consistently silent, and sullen, since Lauren's visit, leaving Catriona increasingly afraid that no matter how many counselling sessions they went to, how many ways she tried to reach her daughter, with every day that passed without the sound of April's voice, it became less likely that they'd ever hear it again.

Tugging Catriona back to the present, Peg's voice was gentle, but firm. 'Try to keep your wrists up, April, like mine.' Peg demonstrated. 'Then spread your fingers a wee bit, like this.' She reached over and helped April span the keys. 'That's right.' Peg nodded, then flicked a glance over her shoulder. 'She's getting it, Mummy.'

Catriona nodded as April leaned forward, focusing on the keys, then pressed multiple fingers down at once, making a clanging sound that caused them all to flinch.

'Oh, cripes,' Peg laughed. 'The trick is to play them one at a time, at the moment. Just until you get used to how the keys feel.' She leaned in, her silvery crown tipping towards the smaller, glossy head. 'Now, press them in this order.' She stretched her hand over April's and guided her. 'One, two, three, four, five, then back the other way, five, four, three, two, one.' Together, their combined hands picked out the beginnings of a basic C-scale.

As she watched, Catriona longed for *her* hand to be the one guiding April's, their fingers connected, their eyes on the same keys creating the same tune, functioning together rather than in the disconnected way they were now existing within their shared space.

Suddenly feeling as if she was intruding, and not wanting to distract April from the sliver of progress they were making, Catriona slid to the edge of the sofa and quietly stood up, just as her phone buzzed in her back pocket. She had given the agency permission to share her mobile number but seeing Lauren's name flashing on the screen still made Catriona's heart falter. She walked quickly into the conservatory and closed the door behind her. 'Hello?'

'Hi, Catriona. It's Lauren.' She sounded bright, and slightly breathless. 'I hope this isn't a bad time.'

Catriona took a moment, then shook her head. 'No. It's fine. What's up?' She cringed at her slightly flippant response.

'I'm going to Fort William tomorrow to stay with a friend for a few days, and I can borrow his car, so I was wondering if I could bring Connor over to meet April. Maybe on Thursday?'

Catriona walked to the window and looked out at the overcast sky, the Cuillins hidden behind a misty veil, and the wind bending the thick branches of gorse down towards the grass, as if they were made of gold-tipped rubber. She shivered, as her thoughts went to Duncan, and their inability to agree on how to handle this situation. They still hadn't spoken to each other since their last argument, and even though he'd got home from his business trip, he hadn't come to see them at the weekend. Catriona had told April that he had a cold, so would be home the following one instead. April had seemed momentarily disappointed, then had eyed Catriona, her narrow brow puckering, as if she was unsure if she believed the story, then she had gently lifted Arthur from the kitchen floor and gone upstairs to her room.

'Catriona?' Lauren's voice tugged her from her thoughts and back to the unanswered question. Thinking on her feet, Catriona cleared her throat. 'Thursday could be tricky as Duncan will be working.' She hesitated. 'He wants to be here next time, I mean, to meet you.' She bit her bottom lip. 'The weekend would be easier, for us.'

Lauren hesitated. 'Oh, right. But I'll only have the car on certain days.' Lauren's voice became muffled as she covered the microphone and, as Catriona surmised, spoke to someone next to her. 'What if I brought him on Thursday, then we could come back on Saturday, too, to meet Duncan? I'm not going home until Sunday, so that would work well, if it's not too much for you.'

A prickle of irritation made Catriona take a deep breath. 'I'll speak to Duncan and get back to you, OK?'

Lauren was silent, indicating either disappointment or displeasure, neither of which Catriona had the energy to handle.

'Lauren, this is a really important meeting. We probably shouldn't rush it, just because of logistics.' Catriona turned her back on the garden and crossed the room, walked into the hall and then halted at the door to the living room.

April was playing the five-note scale by herself now, with both hands, steadily hitting the keys and rocking slightly from side to side, as if her slender body was a metronome, while Peg stood behind her, clapping her hands to keep time. The sight of her daughter being so obviously lost in what she was doing, her hair swinging across her back and her legs kicking out in front of her, synchronised perfectly with Peg's claps, brought a smile to Catriona's face. She was suddenly filled with such a sense of hope, so uplifted, that she softened towards Lauren's request. Would it be so bad if Duncan wasn't there for this next visit, if Lauren was coming back a matter of two days later? Just as she was about to say so, Lauren cut in.

'Of course, I know it's important. I would never want to rush you, or April, into anything.' She sounded mortified. 'I would never presume...'

Once again swayed by the younger woman's uncanny knack of sensing what she needed to hear, then delivering, Catriona exhaled slowly. 'Look, if you can leave Connor with your friend, how about you come by yourself on

Thursday, preferably after three thirty, then I'll be finished with my tutoring sessions. Then, come back on Saturday, with Connor, so you can both meet Duncan then. And maybe stay for lunch.' Having made the offer, Catriona felt a pinch of anxiety, first that she hadn't asked Duncan if he was definitely coming at the weekend, and then as she realised that she hadn't extended the invitation to Lauren's husband. 'Oh, and please bring your husband, of course.' She paused. 'I'm sorry, I never asked you his name.'

Lauren took a few moments to reply, then sounded flustered. 'Oh, it's Greg, but he won't be coming. I mean, he can't. He's away at the moment. I mean, he's usually around, all the time, but there's this thing at work...' She paused. 'Men, right?' She laughed. 'Thanks, though.'

Catriona frowned, the explanation seeming to have some holes in it, but needing to focus on whatever positives presented themselves, she dismissed the thought. 'OK, then. We'll see you on Thursday afternoon.'

'Thanks, Catriona. That's brilliant.' She sounded delighted. 'See you around four.'

'See you then.' Catriona slid the phone back into her pocket, crossed the hall into the living room and stopped beside the piano stool. 'Wow, well done, sweetheart.' She smiled down at April, who had heard her approaching and was now looking up at her. April's face was blank of emotion, her eyes eerily empty, sending a shiver through Catriona that made her wrap her arms across her middle. 'That sounds fab.' Her voice trailed as she looked over at Peg.

Peg, who was standing at the other end of the room now, caught Catriona's eye and winked. 'She's a veritable prodigy.' She smiled exaggeratedly. 'Just like her mother.'

Catriona rolled her eyes. 'Oh, that'll be right.' She tried

to laugh. 'I think April is outplaying me, already.'

Peg came back to April's side, her hand going to the angular little shoulder. 'Well done, April. You get a gold star for your first lesson.' As Catriona watched, April dropped her hands back into her lap, her eyes flicking between Peg and Catriona, as if she was expecting a *but* to follow the praise. 'Would you like me to come back tomorrow? Perhaps we can start to learn a wee tune.' Peg smiled warmly as April nodded, her hand going to her mouth, a smile spreading across her face despite her efforts to hide it.

That she could do that for Peg, gift her with any part of a smile, while Catriona received only blank stares, broke another splinter from her heart.

Peg caught her eye and shook her head slightly, her expression saying *don't take it personally,* but how could Catriona do anything else. Her daughter now stared right through her, seeming to wish her elsewhere, and there was no way to pretend that wasn't true.

Three days later, Lauren was standing in the kitchen, her eyes bright and her voice higher pitched and more brittle than Catriona remembered. There was an almost palpable excitement hovering around the young woman, as Catriona ushered her into the conservatory. 'Come on through.'

The rain pelted the windows and the laden sky seemed to bulge with purple-tinged clouds. 'Not the best of summer, today.' She smiled as Lauren settled herself on the sofa, her eyes flicking around the room, presumably searching for April.

'Pretty crap for July, right enough.' Lauren gave an awkward snort, then her cheeks coloured. 'Sorry, I mean, yeah, not the best.' She lifted her giant handbag onto her lap and began raking around inside it, her hair falling in a glossy curtain over her right eye. 'I brought these for April.' She pulled out a box of Maltesers and a small, hardbacked book. 'I thought she might like this story.' She held the book up.

Catriona took it from Lauren and scanned the cover. It was called *Yes! Katie is Adopted* and the illustration showed a young girl with curly dark hair sitting on a blonde woman's knee, a kitten curled on the floor at their feet and a fair-haired man standing behind them, his hand on the woman's shoulder. The inference that they had not had this conversation by now, or sufficiently explained the circumstances of April's birth, even read her similar books to help her absorb her birth story, was somewhat insulting.

Catriona held the book in her palm and, making an effort to smile, said, 'Thank you, Lauren. We have several in this series. They're great.' She turned and set the book on top of the bookshelf next to the box with the robin's egg in it, the sight of the perfect, sky-blue oval, still nestled in its cotton-wool bed, a sharp reminder of that perfect day, when her family had still been whole.

'Oh, right. Sorry. A friend recommended it,' Lauren said. 'I should've checked with you if you had it.' She blushed. 'Sorry.'

Afraid she'd sounded peevish, Catriona turned the chair at the desk around and sat down. 'No. It was very kind of you.'

Lauren glanced over her shoulder at the door, her mouth twitching in a curious way, as if she were clenching her teeth. 'Where's April?'

'She's in her room, with Arthur. I'll go and get her in a minute.' Catriona found a smile, working to quell the rising defensiveness that was making her want to jump up and pace rather than sit still. Her own insecurities were getting the better of her and, unsure why she felt more threatened today than on Lauren's first visit, Catriona coached herself to breathe them away. She took in the red-brown widow's peak, the wide-set eyes, duplicates of April's, the same suede jacket and black jeans as last time, nothing giving rise to anything to be concerned about. 'So, tell me a little about, um, Greg, was it?' With no prepared questions, and Duncan's warnings still hovering in the back of her mind, Catriona let her instincts guide her.

Lauren looked nervous. 'There's not much to tell, really. He's a mechanic. Works at a garage in Glasgow.' She shrugged.

'It's always handy to have a good mechanic around.' Catriona smiled, sensing that she was entering uncomfortable territory, as Lauren dropped her eyes to the floor. 'And you've been married a year?'

Lauren sat up straighter and met her gaze. 'Yep. Just over.' She nodded. 'He's a really great father. So good and patient with Connor.' She smiled widely, her mouth seeming to disconnect from what was behind her eyes, the statement almost too emphatic.

Catriona nodded, wanting to put Lauren at ease. 'That's great. I'm glad you found him, Lauren.' She scanned the slightly flushed face. 'They're not ten-a-penny, good fathers.'

Lauren sat back and tucked the hair behind her ears. 'I know.' She eyed Catriona. 'I bet Duncan is a good dad.'

The leading statement, with what could potentially have a shaded underbelly, brought Ian's words filtering back to her – *Keep your cards close to your chest, Catriona.* 'He is. One of the best.' Catriona nodded, swallowing what felt like the seed of an untruth, just as the door opened and April walked in. Hamish and Harvey were both dangling from the one hand as her eyes snapped to Lauren, and a beautiful smile lit up April's face.

'There you are, sweetheart. Come and say hello to Lauren.' The ill-thought-out statement made Catriona suck in her bottom lip, then grapple for a more apt follow-up. 'Where's Arthur?' She glanced behind April into the empty hall as April turned and met her eyes, a sullen veil drawing across the little girl's joyful expression. As Catriona waited, feeling as if she'd been stabbed in the heart once again, April pointed over her shoulder. Then she turned to face Lauren and, to Catriona's shock, held her hand out to her.

'Hello, April.' Lauren took April's fingers in hers. 'You look so pretty today.' Lauren beamed again. 'I love your shoes.' She looked down at the bright red flip-flops April was wearing, a giant butterfly attached to the outer edge of each one. April looked at her feet and then nodded as Lauren stood up. 'Did you want me to come with you some-where?' Lauren bent down and, in a gut-twistingly, propri-etary gesture, stroked the hair away from April's forehead, revealing the matching widow's peak.

Before Catriona could step in, April nodded enthusias-tically, her eyes lighting up with excitement. Catriona held her breath, momentarily unsure whether she should let them go off to wherever April had in mind or follow her instincts and keep herself part of this interaction.

'So, where are you taking me?' Lauren grinned as her shoulders lifted. 'Is it a secret?'

April made a soft, snuffling sound and turned towards the door, and as she followed April, Lauren's eyes were sparkling.

Catriona hung back for only a few seconds before making to follow them when, snatching the breath from her, April spun around and held her palm up, like a stop sign, her eyes steely and her message crystal clear. If April had driven a metal rod through Catriona's heart it could not have hurt her any more as she froze in her tracks, every nerve-end prickling under her now clammy skin.

Seeing that she'd been understood, April lifted her chin and gently tugged on Lauren's hand, turning towards the kitchen. As Catriona watched them go, every step April took away from her, her hand locked in Lauren's, drove the painful barb of her daughter's cold indifference deeper into Catriona's heart.

April led Lauren into the kitchen, then out the back door, as Catriona, hobbled by her pain, waited until they were outside, then stood at the kitchen window, tears streaking her cheeks. In all the time that April had been silent and distancing herself, Catriona had never seen such open dislike in her daughter's eyes as she had today. The sight of the narrow palm, held up as a barrier to entry, had brought Catriona to her lowest ebb, and now, as April led Lauren across the garden, to the left of the lawn where it sloped down to the fence by the river, Catriona let the thoughts she'd been quelling surface again.

The harder she tried to hold on to April, the more she seemed to be slipping away, and it hurt like hell. With April isolating herself, the episode with Duncan's shoes, the eloquent if non-verbal messages she'd been sending – it was clear that April blamed her for everything that had gone wrong. Perhaps for stopping her going after Hope that night. Definitely for withholding the truth about her adoption, for Duncan leaving, and their life together crumbling around them. If that were the case, could Catriona regain April's trust and get past those hurts? If April couldn't forgive her, what did the future hold for them as a family – if they had one?

23

As if her need for reassurance had filtered out of her mind, floated across the garden, over the fence and in through the window of the Mackenzie house, Catriona's phone rang on the countertop. Seeing Peg's number, she blinked her vision clear and picked it up.

'Catriona, it's me. I just thought you might want some company. Not now, but after your visitor has gone.' Peg's voice was bright. 'I'll pop over in a couple of hours. OK?'

Catriona smiled through her tears, grateful for Peg's offer. Catriona was lonely and scared, conflicted about this new connection that was forming between April and Lauren, and so quickly. While she wasn't sure if she wanted to talk to Peg about it all, the idea of her company was welcome. 'That'd be lovely.' She croaked. 'Thanks, Peg.'

'Righto. See you then.'

Lauren and April had been outside for over half an hour by the time Catriona had tidied herself up, splashed her puffy eyes with cold water and quickly made up a plate of sandwiches. Now, pulling her shoulders back, she put the loaded plate on a tray, along with some glasses of fresh lemonade, and made her way out into the garden.

As she rounded the house, heading towards the river, she heard the musical sound of laughter. It was April. She knew that sound so well, and the recent absence of it tore at Catriona once more.

Taking a deep breath, she followed the path, crossed the lawn and saw Lauren trotting around the grass with April on her back. Lauren was making clip-clop noises and April's legs were around Lauren's waist and her arms locked around Lauren's neck. April's face was flushed and radiant. They hadn't seemed to notice Catriona standing there, so she waited, fingers tightly locked around the handles of the tray, forcing a smile that made every muscle and tendon in her face ache.

After a few moments, Lauren turned and spotted her, a look of embarrassment wiping away her carefree expression. 'Oh, hi. Sorry, we got a bit carried away.' She stopped in front of Catriona and, bending back, gently lowered April to the ground. 'We were horse riding.' She laughed, an airy sound that seemed to linger between them.

'No, it's fine. I'm glad you're both having fun.' Catriona smiled at April, who was tucking her T-shirt back into her shorts. 'I've got a friend coming over in a while, so I thought we'd have a quick lunch.' She tried to sustain the smile. 'I'm not chasing you away, but...'

'Oh, right. Of course.' Lauren nodded. 'You didn't have to feed me.' She ran her fingers through her hair, her cheeks the same flushed pink as April's. 'But thanks. I'm starving.'

April was hovering behind Lauren, her fingers now covering her mouth.

'Are you hungry, sweetheart?' Catriona carefully

lowered the tray onto the grass as April shook her head. 'I made tuna and mayonnaise. Your fave.' Catriona tried to sound casual. 'You know you love them.'

April was nibbling the skin around her thumb, her eyes flicking between Catriona and Lauren. Just as Catriona was about to coax April again, Lauren cut in. 'If you don't want them, I'll eat the lot.' She turned and poked April gently in the tummy, causing April to drop her hand from her mouth and grab Lauren's fingers. As Catriona watched, April's face melted into a smile and she shook her head. 'Oh, yes I will,' Lauren laughed. 'Just watch me.' She flopped down on the grass, crossed her legs and reached for a sandwich.

Within moments, April was sitting next to Lauren, in an identical pose. Their knees were touching as they both bit hungrily into their sandwiches and the sight of them together, matching hairlines, identical blue-green eyes alight with joy, and cheeks pulsing as they chewed in unison, was more than Catriona could bear. Forcing a swallow, she turned towards the house. 'I'll grab a blanket for us to sit on.' Hoping her shaky voice hadn't given her away, she walked quickly away, her vision blurring again and her throat on fire.

Two hours later, having waved Lauren off, and then April instantly running back out into the garden, with Arthur, Catriona was sitting in the conservatory.

Peg sat on the rug, her nimble legs crossed beneath her long, linen skirt and her leather sandals discarded by her side. She'd been uncharacteristically quiet as, despite herself, Catriona had spilled all the events of the past week and Lauren's unexpected arrival in their lives. Now, Peg's eyes were bright as she scanned Catriona's face, her tanned finger crooked through the handle of her coffee mug. 'So, what's your impression of her?' Peg sat up straighter, her long hair splitting over her shoulder.

'She seems genuinely nice. Extremely sensitive and kind. Clever, then also a little naïve – which is quite endearing.' She paused. 'I don't know exactly *what* to make of her, actually.'

Peg blinked several times. 'I'd listen to my inner voice if I were you. It won't guide you wrong.'

Catriona sat back against the cushion, her bare feet flat on the cool floor. As she took in Peg's expression, she shivered, involuntarily. 'I try to, but sometimes I talk myself out of what it tells me.'

'My sense is that you should take your time with all this.' Peg nodded to herself.

'You sound like Ian, Duncan's brother.' Catriona sighed.

'Wise man.' Peg smiled, tipping her head to the side like Arthur did when he was listening intently to April. 'I'm just worried that you're dealing with so much, on your own.'

'I believe she's a good person, Peg. She's made April smile and laugh again, which is more than I can anymore.' Catriona shook her head sadly. 'She really seems to care about April, and April is totally taken with her.' She shrugged. 'There's a definite connection there, and maybe it's simply nature versus nurture, but it's undeniable.' She paused. 'It's hard to compete with that.'

Peg massaged her jaw, then extended her legs out in front of her, the suntanned feet and ankles a sharp contrast to the pale skirt. She looked as if she wanted to say something, then thought better of it.

Suddenly feeling drained, rather than ask, Catriona sipped her coffee, seeing April dash past the window. Her hair was lifting in the breeze and a smile splitting her face as she spotted Graham climbing over the fence. Before Catriona could even say, 'Here comes Graham,' Peg heaved herself up from the floor.

'Ah, that's Bruce after his tea.' She set her mug on the desk. 'I'm just next door. Happy to be a buffer, bouncer, or escape route any time Duncan's not here.' She held her palms up. 'Just call.'

Catriona smiled. 'I will. And thanks for coming over.' She followed Peg out into the hall. 'I'm so glad you moved in next door.' She touched Peg's shoulder.

'Aye, us too.'

Behind Peg, Graham had reached the back door and was waiting on the path as they walked out. He smiled at Catriona just as April sidled up beside him and slid her hand into his, Arthur following close to her heels. 'Hello, Ape-face.' Graham gripped April's hand as she smiled up at him, the new nickname making Catriona's eyebrows lift. 'Pops says are we having any tea th'day, or should he go for fish and chips?' Graham's eyes twinkled as he looked at his grandmother.

Peg huffed. 'I knew it. That man. I'm coming now, and there'll be no fish and chips.' She pulled a face, then turned back to Catriona. 'Remember what I said, pet. I'm just next door.'

Catriona nodded, the hairs on her arms standing to attention. Whatever it was that Peg wasn't saying was slightly concerning, but more than that, Catriona was growing increasingly anxious that no matter how hard she tried, the reality was that she couldn't compete with Lauren, and everything that was coming into their lives as a result.

24

Three days later, Duncan was in the living room at the piano. They'd agreed that he'd stay overnight – in the spare room – after Lauren's impending visit, so his rucksack and laptop sat in the hall, and his jacket and trainers had been dumped at the bottom of the stairs, as if he'd never left.

April was sitting next to him, and the sight of their backs, so unevenly matched and yet seeming to fit together so naturally, made Catriona's chest ache, Hope's absence looming large.

'So, what tunes have you learned, April Mactiggiwinkle? Can you play something for me?' Duncan looked down at April who shrugged, then lifted her fingers to the keyboard.

Sensing her behind them, Duncan glanced over his shoulder, but Catriona pressed her finger to her lips and shook her head, so he turned his attention back to April's hands. He seemed to be enjoying a new kind of connection with April, being more confident around her, and the last thing Catriona wanted was to distract him from that.

April shifted further forward on the stool and reached

her feet towards the floor, her toe catching the join in the floorboards. Seeing it make contact, Catriona realised how much April had grown in the past few weeks, and it sent a snake of sadness coiling through her. Even as the world felt suspended, their lives in a sad hiatus, her daughter was growing up, in silence, and in pain. While April's voice was stalled, the rest of her was blooming into a leggy, angular young girl that Catriona barely recognised.

April leaned away from Duncan and began to play 'Three Blind Mice' – the first tune Peg had taught her where she used both hands. Her right hand carefully picked out the melody, as her left held a three-note chord, then switched to another, as she stuck her tongue out and nodded in time with each beat of the tune.

Duncan tapped his lean thigh, the blue-black jeans new to Catriona, as the glint of his wedding ring drew her eye. Instantly spinning her own around her thinner finger, its presence, that had always felt like a given, now felt more like a decision to be made. Catriona wondered whether Duncan felt the same.

'Nice work.' Duncan clapped his hands as April finished playing. 'You're a mini-Mozart.'

April bumped her shoulder against his arm, the gesture fond, if somewhat awkward, and Catriona felt a surprising flicker of jealousy. While it was good to see, how was it that Duncan didn't provoke the same kind of cold indifference in April that she did? Had they both not let April down, Catriona holding back the truth and Duncan saying hurtful things, that surely were equally punishable? But perhaps as Catriona's bond had been deeper with April, her crimes were more heinous. There were so many questions that demanded answers and yet all Catriona could do was look at her husband and daughter and wish for this moment of peace, of something close to normality, to last a little longer.

April had gone next door with Arthur, so Duncan and Catriona sat across from one another in the conservatory, a pot of coffee on the desk and a Billie Holiday CD playing in the background. The moody sky had cleared since Duncan had arrived that morning, and now the outline of the Cuillins was visible across the loch, behind a layer of lacy clouds.

They had around half an hour left until Lauren was due to arrive and Catriona was nervously picking at the skin around her thumb. 'Try not to make her feel uncomfortable, Duncan. She was a bit wound up, initially, the last time she was here.' Catriona ran a hand down each thigh, smoothing her denim skirt.

'So, the husband's not coming?' Duncan frowned. 'Seems a bit odd.'

Catriona shrugged. 'She said he was a mechanic, so perhaps his garage is too busy at the weekends.'

Duncan sipped some coffee. 'But you'd think this was a big enough deal that he'd have organised the day off.' He eyed her across the room. 'Don't you think?'

Catriona nodded, recalling Lauren's vague explanation as to why Greg wasn't able to come. 'Yes, I suppose so. But who knows what's going on there?' She met his eyes. 'We're not exactly the poster child for family togetherness right now, either.' Her throat began to narrow as it always did when this subject came up.

Duncan frowned. 'Well, I suppose we'll see what happens today. I presume you've told April about the wee boy?' He leaned forward and set his cup on the side table next to the sofa.

'Of course. We talked about it yesterday.' Catriona sighed. 'Well, I talked, and she listened.'

'How did she take it?'

Catriona recalled the impassive expression on April's face, the slight twitch at her mouth when Catriona had explained that this little boy, Connor, had the same birth mother, so was her half-brother. She'd also used one of the children's books she'd bought about blended families to help illustrate the connection. The genetic map seemed potentially confusing, but April had simply nodded, adjusting the broad blue ribbon she'd tied around Hamish's neck. 'So, you and Connor are related, sweetheart. It could be fun to have a little brother, don't you think?' Catriona had scanned the smooth face, the blue-green eyes, taking in the glossy widow's peak that each time she saw it now brought an image of Lauren with it.

'Cat?'

Tugged back to the moment, she sighed. 'She seemed nonplussed. No reaction either way.' Catriona felt the rise of tears that she had no intention of giving in to. 'I feel like if the house was on fire right now, and I was stuck inside, April would just shrug, walk out the door and not look back.' She held her hands out, palms up. 'I know that sounds self-pitying, but I'm running out of ideas, Duncan. I just can't seem to reach her, to break through this wall of silence that she's raised around herself.'

Duncan leaned forward, linking his fingers between his knees, his sympathetic expression making Catriona swallow hard. 'I know, love. I wish I knew what to suggest, but you were always better at this stuff than me.' He shook his head.

'How's the counselling going? Do we have any more family sessions booked?'

Catriona shook her head. 'No. Just her one-on-one appointment next week. Though I'm not sure how much longer we should keep going. Nora told me last time that we should perhaps consider a psychiatrist at this point.' The idea that her daughter was in such a dark place that medication may be the next step was frightening.

'She doesn't need that.' Duncan sat back, running his hands over his hair, the dark mop shorter behind his ears than the last time she'd seen him. 'She'll come back, Cat. She almost smiled at me in there.' He jabbed a thumb over his shoulder. 'At the piano.'

Catriona took in the lift of his eyebrows, the slight hint of a smile and the way his eyes were scanning her face – a look of hope there that both lifted her and then set her down in a place that she was tired of being.

'I'm glad for you, Duncan, but she doesn't smile at *me*. She stares right through me. Sometimes it makes me shiver, because I see the sweet, warm-hearted little girl we raised slipping away.' She gulped. 'You're not here, so you don't see it, but it tears me up that she's consistently shutting me out. She's broken, and we've only made it worse.' She drew a line in the air between them.

Duncan stood up and crossed the room, hunkered down in front of her and took her hands in his, the unexpected contact like a spark of electricity fizzing through her. 'You are the most wonderful mother, Cat. Don't ever doubt that.' He rubbed his thumb over the back of her hand, leaving a smudge of heat on her skin. 'This isn't about you doing anything wrong. This is about April, and her being in survival mode.' He released her hands, stood up and walked to the window. 'We all grieve in our own way, and I suppose we have to accept that locking up her voice is April's way of coping.'

Catriona stood up, her skin feeling oddly numb where his hand had been. The tables seemed to have suddenly turned, and Duncan giving *her* parenting advice was surprising. What he'd said was true, though. They were each grieving in a different way, and Duncan's way of coping was to do what he always did, isolate himself, not with silence, but with distance. 'I know that, Duncan. It's just hard to feel so utterly unwanted, and unneeded.' She paused. 'Superfluous.'

He held her gaze, his eyes flooded by something she couldn't quite identify. 'You are wanted, and needed, Cat. More than you know.'

Lauren had been ten minutes early, and the doorbell had made Catriona jump. She'd rushed into the kitchen, dumped the coffee things in the sink, then checked the quiche that she'd put in the oven. Turning down the temperature, she'd flashed a final *be kind* stare at Duncan, who was standing in the hall.

Seeing Duncan's overnight bag still sitting there, she'd hesitated, momentarily concerned that it might give something away, but rather than tell him to move it, she'd opened the door.

Now, Lauren was standing on the front step, her face flushed and her hair held back by a bright red bandana. Her soft cotton skirt skimmed her ankles and she wore a tight-fitting T-shirt, with an impressionist image of a tiger's head on the front. Her big hoop earrings, a new, dramatic swoop of eyeliner and a touch of rouge on her high cheekbones made her look fresh, carefree and confident, reminding

Catriona of everything she was not – which made for a hard pill to swallow.

On Lauren's hip was a little boy, with white-blond hair and the biggest sky-blue eyes Catriona had ever seen. His cheeks were rosy and his nose dotted with freckles. He sucked his three middle fingers, his chubby legs swamped by a pair of loose tartan shorts. 'Hiya. Sorry we're early.' Lauren beamed, hitching the child higher up her side. 'He needs the loo. Do you mind?' She looked past Catriona into the hall, where Duncan was now standing by the living-room door.

'Oh, sure. Come in.' Catriona stepped back as Lauren walked past her, leaving a trace of the now familiar cinnamon scent.

'Thanks.' She walked quickly past Duncan. 'Hi, I'm Lauren. Back in a sec.' She flashed him a brilliant smile, then ducked into the guest toilet, as Duncan gaped at Catriona.

Catriona closed the door and whispered, 'Just give her the benefit of the doubt. He must've been desperate.'

Duncan followed Catriona into the kitchen, then stood at the table, a deep frown cutting across his forehead. 'A bit familiar, though.' He eyed Catriona, who held her finger to her lips.

'Shh, she might hear you.'

He rolled his eyes just as the toilet door opened and Lauren, Connor once again on her hip, breezed across the hall and into the kitchen.

'That was close.' She gave a breathy laugh, her eyes going straight to Duncan, who had shoved his hands into his pockets and was leaning back against the sink. 'You must be Duncan.' She let Connor slide to the floor, then extended her hand. 'Nice to meet you.'

Standing behind Lauren, and seeing Duncan's guarded expression, Catriona widened her eyes at him, willing him to be civil.

Duncan caught her eye, stood up straight and took his hands out of his pockets. 'Nice to meet you, too.' He gripped Lauren's hand. 'And this must be Connor.' He looked down at the little boy, who was hugging Lauren's thigh.

'Yes, this is Connor.' Lauren eased the child around her leg, turning him to face Duncan. 'He's four and full of mischief.' She held Connor's shoulders as the little boy again stuffed his fingers into his mouth.

'Aren't they all, at that age.' Catriona crossed the room and stood next to Duncan, feeling the need to present a united front. 'Hello, Connor.' She smiled at the child, who closed his eyes and leaned back against Lauren's legs, as if trying to submerge himself in the material of her skirt.

'I don't suppose you've got a plain biscuit he could have, do you?' Lauren looked over at Catriona. 'He ate all the fresh fruit I packed ten minutes into the journey.' She laughed.

Catriona nodded. 'Sure. I've got some Rich Tea or a digestive.' She turned and pulled the biscuit tin down from the shelf. 'I've made us some lunch, but it won't be ready for about half an hour.'

'Thanks.' Lauren took a digestive biscuit from the tin and handed it to Connor, who grabbed it and hungrily bit into it, crumbs cascading down onto the stone floor as Catriona watched the almost manic chewing.

'Gosh, you are hungry,' Catriona laughed, as Connor stuffed the last piece of biscuit into his mouth. 'Would you like another one, sweetie?'

He nodded shyly, then reached out a hand.

'Thanks, but I think one's enough.' Lauren tutted gently. 'He'll spoil his lunch, the wee gannet.'

Embarrassed by the gentle rebuke, Catriona clamped the lid on the tin and shoved it back into the cupboard as Duncan's frown returned.

'Say thank you to Catriona.' Lauren brushed a crumb from Connor's cheek.

'Fanks.' He spoke quietly, his middle three fingers already back in his mouth.

'So, shall we sit in the conservatory, until April gets back?' Catriona pointed at the door. 'She's next door with her best pal, Graham.'

Lauren looked surprised. 'Oh, OK.' She lifted Connor back onto her hip. 'How old is Graham?'

Catriona led the way, eyeing the overnight bag in the hall and wishing she'd taken the time to get Duncan to move it. 'He's ten, nearly eleven. He lives with his grandparents, and he and April are thick as thieves.' She smiled over her shoulder as Duncan, and then Lauren, followed her into the conservatory.

'Does she go over there a lot?' Lauren set Connor down on the floor and scanned the room, as if deciding on the best vantage point.

Seeing Duncan's eyes narrow, Catriona jumped in. 'Yes, quite a lot. Graham comes to get her, and they walk over together. They just jump the fence at the end there where I can see them, then he either brings her back, or I go and fetch her.'

'It's so nice that she has a friend nearby.' Lauren smiled, sitting on the sofa. 'Kids need other kids around them, don't they?' She nodded to herself, then smoothed her skirt over her knees as Connor knelt down and began pulling books from the lower shelves, dropping them in a pile on the floor.

Duncan perched on the edge of the desk chair and leaned his elbows on his knees. 'So, Catriona tells me you're staying with a friend in Fort William for a few days.'

Lauren's eyebrows lifted, a sightly alarmed expression making her look very young again. 'Yeah, a friend of Greg's. My husband.'

Duncan nodded. 'Whereabouts in the town?' He gave a half-smile as Catriona frowned, picking up on the tone of interrogation rather than polite enquiry.

Lauren smiled brightly. 'Oh, his flat is right near the high street, behind The Red Lion pub.'

Duncan nodded, something behind his eyes making Catriona feel the need to intervene before he dug any deeper. 'Why don't I pop next door and get April, then we can make the introductions before lunch.' She stood up, forcing a smile as she flashed Duncan another warning glance. 'I'll be back in a minute.'

April sat on the floor with Arthur between her legs. Her jeans were muddy from being in the garden, and her Pokemon T-shirt was pooling over her hips. Connor sat opposite her, a smile lighting up his face as he reached out to pet the puppy, but rather than stroke Arthur's soft fur, Connor grabbed a handful, making the puppy squeal.

'Oh.' Catriona jumped up from the chair, but before she could intervene, April reached over and lifted Connor's hand away from Arthur, then, to Catriona's amazement, April smiled at the little boy. Rather than bat him away, she covered his fingers with hers and guided his hand back to Arthur's neck, gently stroking the soft fur in a trail down towards his tail.

Looking up at April, Connor smiled shyly and let her

move his hand along Arthur's back as the puppy's tail flicked back and forth. Catriona marvelled at the gentle maturity of what she'd just seen, the natural way that April had taken on the role of big sister, another profound connection that Catriona and Duncan could no longer provide for her.

As a surge of longing for her lost children, past and present, tugged at Catriona's centre, Duncan and Lauren came back inside, from where, at Catriona's suggestion, he'd been giving Lauren a tour of the garden.

Blinking furiously, Catriona turned to face them. 'Everyone ready for lunch?'

'Yes, please.' Duncan nodded, looking down at April and Connor. 'How's it going in here?'

Catriona nodded. 'Fine. We're getting on fine.'

Lauren immediately sat on the floor next to April. 'Aww, he's so sweet.' She tickled Arthur's ears. 'We have so many puppies at my practice. The come in practically every day.' She eyed April, who was looking up at her. 'Maybe one day you can come and visit me there?'

At this, Catriona halted her progress towards the door, flicking a glance at Duncan who was standing next to the French doors.

'I don't think...' He halted, a dangerous shadow clouding his eyes, and once again, Catriona injected herself back into the scenario.

'That might be fun, April. If we all went to see some of the animals at Lauren's work.'

Without turning to look at Catriona, April nodded enthusiastically, as Connor, having become bored with stroking Arthur, stood up and walked towards the still-open French doors, grabbing Harvey, who lay on the windowsill.

As Catriona hesitated, unsure whether it was safe to

leave Duncan in the room with Lauren, Lauren said, 'Oh, yes, please come sometime. That'd be lovely.' She beamed at Duncan, who was looking at Connor as he plucked at the toy rabbit's ear. 'I'd just need to clear it with my business partner.'

Catriona nodded. 'Of course.' She looked over at Duncan, who had begun following Connor out into the garden. 'Duncan, can you keep an eye on him while I serve up the food?'

Just as Duncan turned around, Lauren jumped up. 'No problem. I'll go with Connor.' She smiled. 'It's so nice outside, and that view is to die for.'

Catriona nodded. 'Of course. You go out and enjoy it.' Lauren was obviously not comfortable being left alone with Duncan, and Catriona could understand why. While he'd been polite, he had been less than warm, despite her asking him to try to make Lauren feel welcome.

Fighting a swell of disappointment in him, as she walked into the kitchen, Catriona was struck by something else that made her catch her breath. What if Lauren had learned the details of Hope's death and was anxious about Connor being out in the garden without her? As a mother, Catriona could understand how that might be the case, and the idea that Lauren was naturally being more cautious and responsible than she and Duncan had been brought a bloom of shame to her cheeks.

Catriona had said nothing about the exact circumstances surrounding Hope's drowning, her instincts to protect them from speculation on high alert when she'd told Lauren about the accident, but now, a deepening sense of their inadequacy as parents chilled her, like the creep of hardening ice.

25

April had taken Lauren's left hand and was leading her into the kitchen. On her other side, Lauren also held Connor's hand, as the threesome moved across the room, halting at the table.

Duncan was hovering behind them, his eyes locked on Catriona, as she sliced up the quiche. Just as she was about to put April's plate at her usual place, on the left of where Catriona normally sat, April released Lauren's hand and began shifting her chair, scraping the wooden feet noisily across the stone floor.

Catriona was on the point of asking what April was doing when she saw Duncan's eyebrows jump. Her chest tightening into a knot, she bit her lip, as April continued to shove her chair over, next to where Lauren was standing. Then, April wriggled awkwardly onto her seat.

Appearing not to notice, Lauren plopped Connor onto the chair on her opposite side and sat down. Then she leaned in, her shoulder touching April's. 'Hello, missy.' She stroked April's cheek as April smiled up at her.

Seeing the gentle contact, so happily received, Catriona's heart contracted. April never willingly touched her anymore or accepted any kind of affection. She never ran into her arms or slid her hand into Catriona's like she used to. Any contact was initiated by Catriona, and rarely accepted, and having that rubbed in her face was torturous.

Just as Catriona thought she might scream, Lauren looked over at her and smiled gratefully. 'This looks really lovely, Catriona.' She pressed her palm to her chest. 'You're spoiling us.'

Taking a few moments to gather herself, Catriona nodded. 'You're welcome. It's just quiche and salad.' She set a plate in front of Lauren. 'Enjoy.'

Sitting opposite Duncan, Catriona reached for the salad bowl, her hands shaking as she served herself. Having no idea how she would swallow anything, she held the bowl out to Duncan, who was staring out of the window, his brow deeply furrowed, and his mouth clamped shut. How would she get through this lunch, this visit – this ongoing nightmare – being consistently snubbed and shut out of her only remaining daughter's life?

Catriona stood in the open doorway as Lauren was putting Connor into his car seat. Behind her, Duncan hovered in the hall, having said a stilted goodbye and April was standing next to him, cradling Arthur to her chest. Above the drive, a pair of seagulls flicked past, leaving their calls lingering on the breeze behind them.

Connor had been crying for the last ten minutes, after Lauren had tried to take Harvey from him, telling him that it was April's rabbit and he had to give it back. The little boy had turned scarlet, making fists, and then screaming, as

Lauren had eventually pulled the threadbare toy from him and handed it back to April, who'd looked vaguely horrified.

Connor was still sniffling loudly, his mouth curled around his middle fingers and his wet cheeks glistening in the afternoon sunlight.

'Thanks a million for lunch and for letting me bring him.' Lauren nodded towards Connor. 'He's not usually such a bother.' She shrugged, her mouth dipping.

Seeing Lauren's discomfort, Catriona wanted to end the day on a positive note. 'He's no bother, Lauren. I thought he was very good, actually. It's been a big day for him, and for us.'

Lauren opened the driver's door, got in, then lowered her window. 'Well, hopefully we can do it again soon.' She dragged the bandana off her hair, letting it fall across her cheek. 'This was really special, seeing them together.' Her eyes were full. 'Truly.'

Just as Catriona was about to give her a final wave and close the front door, April eased past her with Arthur under one arm and Harvey tucked under the other. As Catriona watched, April approached the car and stood at the back, where Connor sat, then she tapped the window with her elbow. Lauren smiled and lowered the back window, and once it was fully down, April held Harvey up and kissed his head, then leaned in and handed the rabbit to Connor.

Catriona felt as if her heart would explode, first with pride, then with the sheer poignancy of this unselfish act – another undeniable indication of the sibling connection, the innate need to protect, and share, that is rooted in one's DNA, and that April was obviously feeling with Connor.

As Catriona's eyes blurred, April patted Connor's chubby arm, then wordlessly walked back in the door and headed for the stairs.

'We can't take it. Really.' Lauren shook her head. 'It's April's bunny.'

Catriona turned to look at Duncan whose eyes were glittering, a stunned look on his face. She held her palms up. 'April obviously wants Connor to have it. She's the kindest soul.'

Lauren held Catriona's gaze, her eyelids flickering as if she were seeing something that she couldn't process, then she nodded. 'Well, thank you, and please thank April. That was incredibly sweet of her.'

Catriona nodded. 'I will. And drive safely.'

Lauren closed the window, and momentarily, the car was gone.

Catriona followed Duncan into the kitchen, where he was opening a bottle of Chianti. Much as after the last time Lauren had left, Catriona was emotionally wrung out and having the house back to themselves was a relief. She sank into a chair and kicked off her flip-flops, enjoying the cool sensation of the stone under her feet.

'That was interesting.' Duncan waggled the bottle in her direction. 'Want some?'

'Yes, please.' She nodded, raking her hair into a rough ponytail, and securing it with the band from her wrist. 'Interesting?' She accepted the glass he held out to her.

'I'm not sure whether I like her or can't stand her.' He dragged a chair out and sat opposite her.

'Come on, Duncan.' Catriona sipped some wine. 'She's bright, sweet, thoughtful and she's clearly a good mother.'

Duncan shrugged. 'She's good with April. I won't deny that. It's her manner with us that bothers me, I think.' He took a long draught of wine and set his glass down. 'Like we're up for approval, or something.'

While she wasn't entirely sure she disagreed, either

with his observation or, indeed, Lauren's right to assess them, Catriona swirled the deep-red wine around the glass. 'I don't think so. She's just unsure of herself around us, so she's kind of tightly wound.'

'Well, I suppose time will tell,' he grumbled.

'She seems to genuinely care about April, and that's all that matters.' April had obviously formed an attachment to Lauren, and having to see it, over and over, stung Catriona badly, so she diverted the conversation. 'What did you make of Connor?'

Duncan's shoulders bounced. 'Seems like a nice wee lad. Kind of young for his age.' He paused. 'The screaming fit was different.' He pulled a comical face.

Catriona laughed softly, his expression one that always amused her. 'Yes, not too much fun, but lots of children at his age have tantrums. I don't think it's anything she's doing, or not doing.'

Duncan eyed her, the dark irises working up and down her face as he tipped his head to the side.

'What?' Catriona cupped the glass in her palm.

'You. You always see the good in people.' He gave her a sad smile. 'I wish I was more like that, sometimes.'

Catriona batted the air. 'Well, she really seems to have her life together. All the pieces are in place.' She shrugged.

'Unlike us, you mean.' Duncan pushed his glass away from him, his eyes dipping to the tabletop.

As she took a slow breath, the ominous questions she'd been asking herself took on a new dimension. After everything that had happened to their family, were they doing the best thing for their daughter by keeping her only blood relatives simply as occasional visitors in her life?

Catriona's heart felt weighted, Duncan's question demanded the truth, a truth that was painful to give. 'Well, we're not exactly in a great place, Duncan. This whole arrangement with you dropping in and out. The weekend parenting. Us being so... divided.' She halted as his head came up sharply, the familiar look of conflict – a mixture of being trapped and lonely at the same time – washing over his face. Catriona sighed, sipped some wine, and waited, letting the silence carry her thoughts to him, thoughts she knew he could hear, loud and clear.

After a few moments, he spoke quietly, his voice rough. 'What are we going to do, Cat?'

As she met his eyes, Catriona wished – she wished that she was able to say *just come home. Let's get through this together. Let's be a family again.* But even as she tried to form the words, something held her back, a ripple of anger that still twisted under her desire to repair their lives, as an image of Hope flashed brightly behind her eyes.

After a few moments, he nodded slowly, as if accepting that whatever it was that he wanted to hear would not be forthcoming. 'Right.' He shook his head. 'You know, I think I'll go back to Fort William, tonight.' He pushed the chair out from the table and stood up. 'I've not drunk enough of that to worry about, and I've got an early start tomorrow.' He pointed at the still full wine glass.

Catriona frowned, this not being what she'd hoped for, even though it was Duncan's MO. 'If you want.' She met his gaze, seeing the conflict behind his eyes. 'You don't have to go, you know. We can talk some more. You could spend time with April, maybe put her to bed.' She tried to smile as he shook his head.

'No. I think it's probably best, for now.' He shoved the chair back in under the table, poured the wine down the drain and set the glass on the counter. Then, taking her by surprise, he swung around, a look of angry determination on his face. 'We're never going to get past this unless you forgive me, Cat. You know that, right?' He held his palm up. 'If you can't, we won't survive. This marriage won't survive.'

Overcome with a rush of such mixed emotions that she could barely breathe, and unable to stop herself, Catriona whispered hoarsely, 'You've never asked me to.'

26

An hour or so after Duncan had left, April had disappeared with Graham again, leaving Catriona wandering around the house, her heart heavy and her mind reeling. The events of the day were spinning in a recurring loop inside her head and rather than fixate on all the hurtful incidences of April's obvious bonding with Lauren, Catriona padded up the stairs looking for something to distract her.

As she walked into April's room, the tidy top bunk with the smooth bedding made her catch her breath. She still expected to see Hope's messy duvet, hanging off the edge of the bed, pyjamas strewn across the pillow, her latest book or favourite cuddly toy sometimes tangled in the sequined drapes that skimmed the edge of the bed frame.

It had been weeks now since Catriona had relented and washed the bedding. All the while, she had stood, numb and frozen to the spot in the kitchen, watching the washing-machine drum spin, the sudsy water taking away the sweet scent of Hope that had lingered within the cotton threads.

In contrast to the pristine top bunk, April's bed was a jumble of pillows, the T-shirt she'd worn the previous day, one bright red sock half-on Hamish's left foot and the *Mulan* book, half-open like a bird on the wing. Tutting, Catriona began picking up the items and putting them back in their designated places, a mild sense of purpose making her feel less adrift.

Deciding to change the sheets while she was at it, she lifted April's pillow and began pulling off the cover, when a sliver of paper fell out. It was folded into a square and she could see that it had dark markings on it, so purposefully drawn that the paper felt thick, almost embossed. Catriona hesitated for a second, held back by a flicker of guilt at this intrusion into something that April had obviously intended to be hidden. But curiosity won out and Catriona carefully unfolded the paper.

As she looked down at the picture, what she saw was an image that she instantly knew would never leave her. April had drawn herself, wearing yellow shorts and her ladybird T-shirt. Her face was long and narrow, her hair a reddish-brown cloud that reached her waist, and her eyes were large blue-green circles. She was holding the hand of a tall, slim female with identically coloured reddish-brown hair that ended sharply at her jaw. The woman had the same distinct blue-green discs for eyes and was wearing a long, triangular-shaped skirt. On the woman's other side was a little boy, with sunflower-yellow hair and large pale-blue discs for eyes. He was wearing oversized red shorts and was also holding the woman's hand. Underneath the drawing, April had neatly written, *My family*. Catriona took it in, her eyes darting back and forth from one figure to the next, then back again. Her heart thumped so wildly that she began to feel light-headed as the last, fragile remnants of her broken family seemed to float away from her like dust motes, carried away in a sunbeam.

Turning around, she sat on the edge of the bed, the paper dangling from her hand as she folded at the waist and began to pant. April had drawn herself with Lauren and Connor, the imagery so searingly clear, and eerily accurate in its detail, that Catriona couldn't bear to look at it anymore. This was the final sign. There could be no other way to interpret what she'd seen, and as her heart threatened to explode, Catriona stood up, grabbing the bed frame to steady herself. Then, suddenly sure of what she must do, she pulled her phone out of her pocket and walked towards her bedroom.

Duncan had taken a few minutes to answer the phone. He'd been in the supermarket in Fort William, but, hearing the tone of her voice, had abandoned his shopping and walked quickly back to his car so they could speak.

Catriona was now lying on the bed, her head pounding and April's drawing, face-down, next to her on the duvet.

'What's going on, Cat? You're scaring me.'

'I need to show you something.' She hiccupped. 'Can we switch to a video call?'

'Sure. I'll call you back in a few minutes. Just sit tight.' He hung up.

Catriona heaved herself up and laid her palm on the drawing, not needing to see the image that was already burned into her brain. After what seemed like an age, as her heart pattered alarmingly, her phone rang. Picking it up, she saw that Duncan's face was drawn and his eyes were wide.

'Talk to me. What's happened?'

'I found something in April's room. I need you to look at it.' She adjusted the phone, then lifted the paper and positioned it in front of the camera. 'Can you see it?' Her voice cracked. 'Duncan?'

After a moment, Duncan said, 'Yes, I see it.'

Catriona dropped the picture on the bed and looked at her husband. He was sitting in his car, one hand at the back of his head and his lips tightly pursed.

'That is a picture of April's perfect family, and we're not in it, Duncan.' She coughed. 'It's absolutely breaking my heart, but I'm afraid that we're not what she needs anymore.'

Duncan looked stunned, his mouth gaping open. 'What are you saying, exactly?'

Catriona sat back against the headboard, every muscle, tendon, and sinew in her body screaming for relief from the pain that had been coursing around inside her for so long now that it felt as if it had permeated her blood. Pausing to make sure that her door was fully closed, she took a breath and continued, her voice not much more than a whisper. 'Remember when we brought April home, how we both stood at the girls' cot and made a vow that we would always put their needs ahead of our own? That we would never lose sight of what was best for them and their well-being, first and foremost?'

As Duncan nodded, the edges of his mouth drooping, she pictured April, smiling at Lauren, holding her hand, shifting her chair closer to Lauren's at the table, then gently taking Connor's hand and helping him pet Arthur. Next, Catriona saw April glowering at her, turning her back, grabbing back the flannel in the bath, closing her bedroom door in her face – pulling away from her in every sense and refusing to let Catriona mother her. The trough all that had dug, deep inside her, filled with a new, toxic swell of pain, that seemed to slosh around with every movement she made.

'Lauren is a good person, and a loving mother, Duncan. In fact, she's in a better place to...' She halted, terrified that if she said what was in her heart, there would be no going back.

'To what, Cat?' His voice cracked.

'To give April what she needs, now everything's changed.' It was out – the barbed thought that had been churning inside her for days – and now, she held her breath as she waited for him to react.

'That's insane,' he barked. 'Total crap.'

'Duncan, listen to me.'

'She doesn't know what she needs, Cat. She's a kid. And she's not even talking to us, so how can you know what's going on in her head?'

'Duncan, she *has* been talking to us.' She held up the picture. 'In so many ways. But we're just not hearing her.' Catriona's throat knotted as tears trickled down her face, sliding between her lips. '*She* is the priority in this entire mess.' She panted. 'Just think about it before you snap to judgement. Put April first in this scenario, then tell me if you don't agree with me?'

Seconds ticked by as, suddenly craving fresh air, Catriona stood up, carrying the phone with her. She walked out into the hall, heading for the stairs, the wooden treads feeling oddly spongy under her socks. As she passed through the kitchen, catching the faint scent of coffee and the fresh bunch of basil she'd hung above the island the previous day, she wiped her wet face with her palm.

Outside, a briny breeze instantly lifted her hair from her damp neck, and the sound of Bruce's lawnmower hummed behind her. As she paced across the lawn, heading for the river, she finally heard Duncan sigh. 'No, I don't agree with you. We just need to battle on. April will come back from this. It'll just take us time to work through it, together.'

Catriona shook her head, her heart aching as she focused on his chocolatey eyes. 'That's just the point, Duncan. We're living apart. You're not here. She needs stability, a real family, parents who are united and able to guide her, and that's not us anymore.' Her voice trailed. 'I'm sorry, but I think we should consider letting her be with Lauren, at least for a while. Until you and I...' Her voice failed her as the statement ripped her breath away with it.

Duncan cut in. 'You can't be serious?' he sputtered. 'Cat?'

Fresh tears slid down her face, instantly drying in the cool breeze. Even saying the words felt like an agonising surrender, a white flag that should never have been raised, and yet she knew there was also bravery, and truth, in what she'd said – truth that Duncan had to hear and acknowledge.

After a few moments, he spoke again. 'Cat, please don't do anything hasty. Let's think this through and talk more before you make any moves.' He paused. 'I promise to think about what you've said, if you promise me that you'll wait until I can get home and we can decide what's best, together.'

'That's exactly what I'm trying to do. What's best for April.' She turned her back on the river and stared at the house, the gently gabled roof, the wide windows over-looking the water, like pairs of gentle eyes taking in the stunning vista. The row of gold-topped gorse, the tidy lawn, the rosemary bushes leading to the back door, all making up a picture of domestic bliss. And yet, under the surface, much like the loch to her left, the waters were tangled with seaweed, tugged to and fro by invisible currents, threatening to suck them all under.

Before she could answer him, he continued. 'I think we should call Ian. Ask him to see if he can find out anything more about Lauren's situation, her story, so to speak.' He paused. 'There's just something about her that makes me think this idyllic scene she's painting of her life might be too good to be true.' His voice sounded far away, pensive. 'Ian can confirm exactly what the picture is before we do anything.'

The inner voice that drove Catriona's actions so often was whispering that if they were to consider letting April be with Lauren, this was the right thing to do, even as her conscience twitched at the idea of digging into Lauren's private life, her past. As the two forks of the dilemma jabbed at her, Catriona focused on the fact that this wasn't about Lauren as much as it was about April and protecting her, as best they could. 'Yes, I suppose it's wise. But I don't want this to turn into a witch hunt, Duncan.' She sucked in her bottom lip. 'Whatever she has or hasn't done, or not told us, Lauren made April, and she also made hard, unselfish choices for her baby. So, there's a deep good in her. I know it.'

'I'm not suggesting we hire a PI or anything,' he grumbled. 'Just ask Ian to look at whatever is on public record. If there's anything to be worried about, we should know. Because I'm not going to let anyone, or anything, hurt you both, not anymore.' His voice cracked, sending a needle of pain through Catriona's heart. 'Whether we are together or not, yours and April's happiness is everything – all that matters to me – whatever happens next.'

Catriona leaned into the statement, hearing the heart-breaking honesty in his voice. As she counted her rapid breaths, a dark shape moved in her peripheral vision, pulling her around to face the river. Squinting into the early evening light, she shielded her eyes and focused on the spot. A few moments later, a sleek head surfaced, two giant black eyes seeming to lock onto her as she stood still, afraid to move. The seal looked to be mature, judging by the size of its head, and as its whiskers twitched, Catriona held her breath, willing it to stay a few moments longer. Being July, it could be a pregnant female, looking for the perfect spot to have her pups – maybe even coming back to the same place she herself had been born, as was common with harbour seals. Then, the creature rose out of the water with such grace that Catriona gasped, before it dived again, its shimmering, speckled back arching as it slipped soundlessly beneath the surface. Its rear flippers appeared and then disappeared in seconds, cutting a clean line through the water, leaving no trace of its presence except for a circle of tiny bubbles, that separated and drifted away with the current. Perhaps this had been the same seal that had drawn Hope to the bank, all those weeks ago?

'Cat, are you there?' Duncan's voice snapped her back to the moment.

'Yes, sorry. There was a seal.' She looked at the surface of the river, the same, white-topped ribbon of water that had borne her daughter away from the bank, sucked her into the current and then tipped her out into the loch, breathless, scared, cold and perhaps even knowing that this was her end. Catriona forced a swallow and clenched her free hand into a fist until her fingernails bit into her palm.

'Do you want me to come back?' He sounded breathless now. 'I can get back up there tomorrow evening.'

She shook her head. 'No. There's no need for that. I just thought you should know what's going on, and what I'm thinking.' Rather than escalate things yet, she needed some time to delve deep inside and see if she could find any possible way to live with this devastating decision, that would, without doubt, irrevocably change the rest of their lives.

'OK. I'll call Ian now. And I'll come back home next weekend. In the meantime, don't take her calls, Cat. Please.'

27

April was eating a slice of toast and jam at the table when the clang of the doorbell made Arthur bark.

'Who can that be, on a Sunday morning?' Catriona frowned, looking down at her tracksuit bottoms and baggy T-shirt, wishing she'd got dressed properly after her shower an hour ago. 'Back in a minute.' She smiled at April, who tore a corner off her toast and held it out to Arthur, who was sniffling around the leg of her chair. 'April, love, don't feed him at the table, please. We've talked about that,' Catriona sighed, then padded through the hall to the front door.

Half expecting to see Peg standing there, her eyebrows jumped as her old friend Mungo stood on the doorstep, a bulging plastic bag in his hand, and a self-conscious smile revealing the trademark gap.

'Gosh, hello, the boat.' Catriona smiled. 'What brings you here?'

'Hello, the shore.' His voice rumbled. 'I didnae want to disturb you, but I was just passing and thought you might like these wee prawns.' He held the bag out. 'They'll no' keep.'

Catriona took the bag from his weathered hand, noting the frayed sleeve of his peacoat and the ubiquitous muddy boots sticking out from under his waxed trousers. 'You're not disturbing us. Come on in. I've got coffee made.' She stepped back and beckoned to him.

'Naw, I won't stay. I just wanted to...' He halted, his rheumy eyes full of what looked like worry, sending a zap of concern through Catriona.

'What is it, Mungo? Is everything all right?' She beckoned again. 'Please, come in have a quick coffee. You can't be in that much of a hurry on a Sunday.' She lifted her eyebrows comically as he hovered on the step, then she saw something change in his expression as he stuffed the holey, woollen hat he'd been holding into his pocket.

'Aye, a quick one then.' He stepped to the side and began tugging off his boots.

'Don't worry about that. I'm cleaning tomorrow, anyway.' Catriona patted the air, but Mungo shook his head.

'Naw. They're honkin'.' He pulled each mud-caked boot off and stood in his thick socks, one with a hole big enough to reveal a horned toenail, making Catriona hide a smile.

'April's through here having breakfast.' She walked into the kitchen, where April was now sitting with Arthur on her lap, feeding him bits of toast crust. 'April Anderson,' Catriona tutted. 'Put him down, and don't feed him at the table. I've told you a dozen times.' She rolled her eyes at Mungo, who was grinning.

'Hello, April. How are you th'day? Up to mischief as usual?' Mungo patted April's shoulder as she lowered Arthur to the floor and smiled back at him. 'I had tae come and see you, because you havnae been to see *me* in ages.'

His mouth dipped comically. 'I can see why, now. I've got competition.' He bent and scooped Arthur up from the floor, the pup's fluffy legs dangling from his big, calloused hand. 'Well, he's a fine fellow, right enough.' He ruffled Arthur's head as the puppy's tail beat back and forth with the speed of a hummingbird's wings. 'What's his name?' Mungo gently set Arthur back on the floor and looked at April, as Catriona, standing by the sink, held her breath.

April stared at Mungo, her mouth twitching in what had become a sadly familiar way, then she flicked a glance at Catriona.

Catriona exhaled, releasing the mixture of hope and disappointment that followed every time she thought she might hear her daughter speak again. 'Arthur.' She smiled at Mungo, who stood behind Duncan's usual seat. 'Sit down, Mungo.' She poured a large mug of coffee and set it in front of him. 'Milk's there.' She pointed to the jug.

Mungo added a generous splash to his mug and then lifted it up between his big paws. 'So, how's tricks? What've you all been up to?' He sipped some coffee, his eyes twinkling.

'Nothing much.' Catriona sat at the far end of the table, her casual dismissal of everything that had been happening feeling like a betrayal not only to her, and her family, but also to Lauren, and even Connor. 'Same old stuff, Mungo. How about you? Fish still biting?'

'Aye, well enough.' He nodded. 'Enough tae keep me and young Harry out of trouble, anyway.' He chuckled, then glanced at April, who was wriggling out of her seat. 'Off tae change the world, lass?' He smiled fondly as April nodded, her fingers going to her mouth. 'Course you are.'

Catriona watched April lifting Arthur, then raising a hand to Mungo in goodbye as she walked out of the kitchen.

The lack of a goodbye to Catriona left her with the familiar twinge of hurt, as her daughter disappeared down the hall.

When Catriona looked back at Mungo, he was staring at her, a strange look on his face. 'What is it, Mungo? Is there something wrong?'

The old man carefully put his mug down, his cheeks puffing slightly as he pouted momentarily. 'Aye, well, there's something I think you should know, lass. It might be nothing and it might be something, but you can decide.' He shoved the mug to his left and linked his big, meaty fingers in front of him. 'I was in the Harbour Arms last night, about half-eight or so. I was wi' old Stan, just chewing the cud, and I went to the bar to get another round when I heard this young thing asking about you.' He frowned, as Catriona's insides flipped.

'Go on.' She leaned forward. 'Who was it?'

Mungo shook his head. 'A young, brown-haired girl. Nae idea who she was, but to have a wee bairn out with her at that time of night, I thought it was a bit off.' His frown deepened. 'Anyway, she was asking Sheryl about you, and Duncan, and wee April, and then she asked about Hope.' His voice caught as Catriona's breath faltered.

'What was she asking about Hope?' The idea of Lauren, leaning into the bar with Connor on her hip, peppering sweet-faced Sheryl, the landlady of the pub, with questions about Catriona and her family felt deeply invasive.

Mungo shifted in the chair. 'She asked about the accident, what happened.' He hesitated. 'Sheryl was busy, and I could see she was uncomfortable when the girl kept on at her, so Sheryl just said it had been a tragic way to lose a daughter, and then...' Mungo shook his head.

'What, Mungo? Tell me.' Catriona fought to keep her voice level. 'Please.'

He steadied himself by leaning his elbows on the table and blinked. 'Sheryl was hassled, mind, so don't be cross with her, but she said that with everything else you were dealing with, it was an awful shame that Duncan had moved out.' His face coloured as Catriona's hand went up to cover her mouth. 'Sheryl didnae mean to blab your business, Catriona, but that wee bism just wasn't letting up.' He looked down at his hands. 'None of us can possibly understand what you pair have been through, and you know we'd no' judge you, or Duncan, regardless. You're all family to us, in the village.' He lifted his eyes to hers, a telltale glint betraying his genuine fondness for them all. 'But this girl seemed almost chuffed when Sheryl said that, as if it was what she was wanting to hear.'

'Surely not, Mungo. Are you certain?' Catriona shook her head, unable to believe this was possible.

'It was strange, Catriona, but aye, she looked as if she'd won the bloody lottery.'

28

Having mulled Mungo's story over for an hour, Catriona called Duncan's number. It was 10.45 a.m. and as she listened to the rings, each one seeming to drag, she paced in front of the kitchen window.

Across the loch, the hills were clearly visible, and the sun dappled the water as if thousands of silvery fish were circling beneath the ripples. The gorse flickered in the breeze as the scent of fresh-cut grass seeped in the half-open window.

April was still upstairs, and Catriona could hear Arthur's distant yapping, so felt sure that she could talk freely, if Duncan would only answer the phone. Just as it would have clicked over to voicemail, she heard his voice. 'Hi, Cat. What's up?' He sounded tired, as if she might have dragged him from sleep.

'Did I wake you up?' She frowned, trying to picture him still lying in bed in the top-floor flat above his office in Fort William, with a view of Ben Nevis behind it and only steps from the high street where Lauren and Connor were staying.

'No. I'm just leaving the gym. The phone was in my bag, so I didn't hear it at first.' He coughed. 'What's going on? Are you OK?'

Catriona spoke quietly, keeping her eyes on the hallway in case April materialised. As she repeated everything Mungo had said, the situation felt less threatening than he had made it sound, but as soon as she stopped talking, Duncan cut in.

'What was she still doing up there? And what was Sheryl thinking?' He sounded furious. 'Our business is none of her concern.'

'Don't be angry with Sheryl.' Catriona opened the back door and walked outside, the path pleasantly rough beneath her bare feet as she passed the fragrant rosemary bushes and turned left, heading towards the river. 'The way Mungo described it, Lauren kind of cornered her.' She felt the spongy grass sliding between her toes as she walked across the lawn, ahead of her the long fence protecting them from the unpredictable river.

'So, what's she up to?' Duncan asked. 'I knew we shouldn't be so trusting.' In the background was the sound of a busy road, then some young voices shouting something Catriona couldn't make out.

'I think Mungo might have misunderstood what he saw. I'm sure there's a simple explanation.' Catriona closed her eyes momentarily, recalling the impromptu hug that Lauren had given her at their first meeting, the compassion shining from behind the blue-green eyes, the gentle way she'd handled April, none of which gelled with this new, somewhat sinister picture that Mungo had painted. 'It just doesn't seem like her to be up to something, or at least what I know of her.' Despite defending Lauren, Catriona couldn't help but second-guess herself, as she watched the surface of the river breaking across a large rock at the edge, just feet from where she'd sat, her daughter's limp form cradled in her arms and her heart breaking into millions of pieces.

Two hours after her call with Duncan, as she sat half-listening to some classical guitar music, and distractedly flipping through a French textbook, trying to focus on preparing for her tutoring session with Olivia the following day, Catriona's phone rang on the living-room coffee table.

April had been lying on the other sofa watching James Herriot tending to a sickly piglet but had happily left to go next door as soon as Graham had knocked on the back door, twenty minutes earlier. Peg had sent a message asking Catriona to come over too, for coffee, but wanting to just sit and try to unwind, she'd asked Graham to please thank Peg but tell her that she was working and would pop over tomorrow.

As she looked at the phone, seeing Lauren's name flashing made Catriona's pulse quicken, and Duncan's words came back to her – *don't take her calls*. While she knew she should probably take that on board, especially after what Mungo had told her, a deep-rooted instinct caused her to disregard the advice. Whatever was going to happen, she wanted to treat Lauren with the respect she deserved, as still, deep down, Catriona couldn't believe that she could have been so wrong about her and her motives.

'Hello, there.' She kept her voice even. 'How are you?'

'Oh, great. I hope I'm not disturbing you. I just wanted to thank you again for yesterday. You were all so kind and welcoming to Connor. And the kids got on so well.' She paused. 'I'd never take that, or your hospitality, for granted, Catriona. I just wanted you to know that.'

The words were carefully chosen, the message sincere, and even heartfelt. Could this possibly be the sound of deceit? 'You are welcome. You both are welcome here, Lauren.' She looked out of the window, seeing a tractor bumping along the road, hay bulging over the back of the trailer behind it. 'How's Connor? Was he awfully tired after the long day?' Catriona opened a door, willing Lauren to come clean.

'Yes, he was bushed.' Lauren laughed. 'I actually met up with a friend there in the village, and we went to get some dinner. Ended up staying longer than we'd planned, so by the time we got back here, it was pretty late.'

Relieved, Catriona sat up straighter, letting the book slip onto the cushion next to her. 'I didn't know you had a friend around here?'

'Oh, yes. She's a nurse at the Mackinon Hospital, over on Skye. We went to school together, but we never get to see each other anymore,' Lauren laughed softly.

'I'm glad you got to see her, then,' Catriona said. 'So, what can I do for you?' She looked at the clock on the mantel, the hands showing 12.20 p.m.

'It went so well yesterday, I was hoping to come back once more before we head back to Glasgow, if it's not too much to ask?'

Catriona let a few moments pass, then, Duncan's words echoing inside her head again, said, 'I think perhaps we should leave it a little while longer before we do it again. April's been through a lot, and we don't want to overwhelm her.' She held her breath, waiting for what came next, not sure what to expect.

'Oh, OK. I totally understand. I just don't know when

I'll be up this way again.' Lauren sighed. 'But that's OK, Catriona. It must be difficult for you, with Duncan not...' She stopped.

'With Duncan not what?' Catriona stood up, her heart instantly thumping under her shirt.

'Look, I'm sorry. I don't mean to be rude, or insensitive, but I know that he's not living there at the moment.' She hesitated. 'Since Hope drowned, I mean.'

Catriona pressed her hand over her mouth, her eyes prickling as she stared out at the driveway, picturing Lauren standing next to the car, her wholesome appearance, the shiny hair skimming her smooth jaw, the widow's peak pointing down towards the narrow nose, the kind eyes, the open smile.

Despite Catriona's doubts about their ability to be what April needed now, the instinct to pull it together, before she gave anything more away about their fractured family, overtook her. She spoke slowly and steadily. 'It's been a difficult time for us, since we lost Hope, as I'm sure you can understand, Lauren. We've had some very tough patches, for sure, but we're getting through it.'

'I do understand, of course. I didn't mean to be intrusive.' There was a weighted pause. 'Oh, God, I hope you didn't think I was judging you, or suggesting anything.'

Catriona dipped her chin. 'Not at all. I'm just saying that that kind of loss gets inside you so deeply, it wrecks you, basically, and you do whatever you have to, to get past it and heal. For us, it's taking a little space so we can each grieve in our own way.' She paused, afraid that she'd already said too much.

'I know we don't know each other that well, Catriona, but you can talk to me. I mean, you can trust me, because I know how hard it is, to feel alone.'

Catriona heard genuine compassion, and she couldn't help but respond. 'Thanks, Lauren. It's been a hellish time.'

'I can imagine.' Lauren's voice was warm. 'If there's anything I can do to help, or to make things easier for you, or April, you just have to say.'

Catriona let the offer circle for a few moments, conflicting emotions roiling inside her. As her mind flicked between Mungo's story and what she'd seen with her own eyes, she couldn't help but want what Lauren had said to come from a place of honesty. 'Thanks, Lauren. That means a lot.'

A few seconds passed, then Lauren spoke softly.

'Is there no way I could pop over, just for an hour tomorrow? I promise not to stay too long.'

Catriona pressed her eyes closed, wanting to be strong enough to say no, but her mind snapped back to April, and the easy smiles she'd given Lauren. The way she'd taken Lauren's hand so naturally, accepted her touch, then given Harvey to Connor. Wanting to give her daughter whatever tiny slivers of happiness she could, Catriona sighed, 'OK, Lauren. Oh, but wait. It's Monday tomorrow. Don't you have to get back for work?' She opened her eyes and watched an encroaching thick band of cloud suck the light from the room, casting a purple-tinged wash across the wooden floor.

'I've checked, and my partner can cover for me, so it's fine,' Lauren said. 'We're always covering for each other.'

Catriona took a few moments, letting the decision percolate, then nodded. 'Fine. If you pop in at noon, perhaps we can go for a walk, now April's on her summer holidays?'

'That sounds lovely,' Lauren gushed. 'Thanks a million, Catriona. I'll see you then.'

Catriona put the phone down and instantly second-guessed herself. What would Duncan say when she told him? She knew he'd be furious, so as she walked through the hall and into the airy kitchen, she decided not to mention it, just for now.

Catriona and Lauren sat on a blanket on the sand. Having lunch at Coral beach had been a last-minute idea when Catriona had seen the clear sky earlier that morning. She had packed a simple picnic, texted Lauren directions of where to meet them, and now April and Connor were standing a few feet away, at the edge of the water, in the gentle curve of the sheltered bay.

The sand, made of calcified seaweed, was a pale amber colour, a series of soft ridges lying one behind the other, echoing the line of the shore. Dotted about were several large rocks, each low and smooth, resembling basking seals. They provided perfect spots to sit and watch the undulating water and the groups of seabirds circling overhead. The sharp smell of the seaweed, floating in clumps on the surface of the water, always took Catriona back to childhood holidays on Skye, when her parents would take her to a similar beach, for chilly summer picnics.

As she pictured them, her parents and her huddled together, their backs to the wind as laughter surrounded them, a closely bound family, she was once again overcome by the fear that had been keeping her awake at night, the gut-wrenching question that seemed to raise its unwelcome head every time April snubbed her with silence. And while Catriona couldn't bear to admit it, each time she thought about it, she was growing closer to making a decision that made her physically sick.

As she looked at the water, gently lapping the sand where the children stood, now hand in hand, Catriona watched the midday light bouncing off the rippling surface, giving it a greenish tint. Behind them, the moss-coloured slopes of the Applecross mountains seemed to slide right down into the loch, as lacy clouds broke up the bright sky with wisps of grey that gave the whole scene such an ethereal quality that it brought a lump to Catriona's throat.

'It's so pretty here.' Lauren leaned back on her hands, her legs stretched out in front of her and her bright-red toenails shimmering in the sunlight.

'Yes, we love to bring the girls here.' Catriona halted. When would she stop including Hope in the present tense, in her every thought, or statement? Perhaps never. 'April and Hope could sit here for hours, just watching the birds.' She closed her eyes for a second, feeling microscopic granules of sand, gritty beneath her lids.

'It must be so hard for you, and April, to go back to places Hope loved.' Lauren spoke softly. 'I can't even imagine.'

Catriona looked over at the younger woman, the scarlet tank-top and tight-fitting jean-shorts in stark contrast to the more conservative shape and palette of her outfit on the previous visit. As she took in Lauren's shiny bob, the dark sunglasses hiding her eyes, and the high, wedge sandals sitting in the sand next to the blanket, Catriona felt dowdy in her beige linen Capris and white T-shirt. Suddenly conscious of her ragged toenails and unshaven legs, she sat up and crossed her feet under her, dragging her hair away from her face and shoving her sunglasses up onto her head. 'It is hard. I don't know if it will ever *not* be.' She swallowed. 'But we take it a day at a time. There's no other way.'

Lauren nodded sadly. 'Poor April. No wonder she's so sad all the time.'

Catriona frowned. She wanted to snap, *She's not unhappy all the time*, but even as she tried to say it, she knew that Lauren's statement was closer to the truth than she, Catriona, wanted to admit. Taking a moment to gather herself, she focused on the horizon. 'It's not that she's sad *all* the time. She is grieving, like we all are, and only time, patience and love will get her through it and back to the sunny little girl we know. But it will happen.' She glanced over her shoulder, at Lauren.

Lauren's eyes were hidden behind the dark lenses. 'I know that, Catriona.' She paused. 'And I know you're doing absolutely everything you can for her.' Lauren stopped, pressing her lips together and looking over at the children, who were hunkered down, poking in the sand with matching sticks. As Catriona followed the line of Lauren's view, a sound floated across to them on the breeze, a light-filled, uplifting, musical sound that Catriona had not heard since she'd seen April riding on Lauren's back, out on the lawn. April had laughed again, openly, her hand going to Connor's back as she brushed the sand from his bottom and helped him stand up.

The air leaving her in a rush, Catriona snapped her eyes back to Lauren, who was staring ahead, her sunglasses now holding her hair back from her face. Catriona felt the weight of what she knew in her heart was coming, settling on her like a mass, so heavy it pressed her down into the sand beneath her. April was happier when Lauren and Connor were around. She'd seen it multiple times now and couldn't deny it. Could Catriona do what she'd suggested to Duncan – put her own needs aside and let April go? Perhaps stay with Lauren, until things settled down, or until more healing could take place? Was it selfish, keeping April somewhere that made her deeply unhappy? As the recurring thought took on more water, so the ground seemed to part under Catriona, sucking her towards a place she knew she might never escape. If Lauren could give April a real home life, her little brother around for company and a break from having to miss Hope every time she saw something, or went somewhere that reminded her of what she'd lost, didn't April deserve that?

Catriona's insides were quivering now, the ability to speak having escaped her. As she stared at Lauren, this person who had, in a matter of two weeks, turned their lives on their heads, the stark materialisation of the very thing that Catriona had been dreading, and yet was unable to stop herself thinking about, was so shocking that she felt as if she was going to pass out. The piercing sound of the seagulls overhead faded to a dull squawk as the light began to dim behind Lauren, her shape becoming blurred against the skyline.

'Catriona, are you OK?' Lauren sounded panicked.

Catriona sucked in a deep, salty breath, forcing herself to rally, channelling all her energy into her voice. 'I'm fine. Just a bit overtired. Sleep doesn't come easily these days.' She tried her best to sound casual.

As Lauren nodded sympathetically, Catriona was flooded with another series of what ifs that plucked at her insides, like a hungry vulture. Loudest of them all, overpowering all the rest, was this. If she did the right thing, and lost April too, would there be anything left worth living for?

29

By the time they'd made it home from the beach, Catriona had been an emotional mess. She'd dumped their picnic things in the kitchen, run a bath for April and fed Arthur, all in a haze. Then, she'd watched her daughter, head down and mouth clamped shut again, shed her sandy clothes and slide into the bath. Catriona had knelt down and made to dip the flannel into the foamy water, when, wrenching the breath from her, April had taken the cloth from her hand, her eyes bright and challenging.

'Do you want to do it yourself, sweetheart?' Catriona had tried to keep the hurt from her voice as April had nodded, then lifted the soap from the dish on the side of the bath and begun rubbing the flannel across it. Catriona had sat back on the bathmat, but after a few seconds, unable to bear yet another form of rejection, she'd reached out and touched April's bony shoulder. 'April, I know you're angry with me and Daddy. Especially me. I know you're sad and I know you miss Hope, and the way things used to be, so much. But you mustn't ever forget how much I love you.

Daddy and I both do.' The knot of emotion in her throat had felt as if it was choking her. 'April, you are my little girl, and I want you to be happy more than anything in the world. You know that, right?'

April had stopped soaping the cloth and met her eyes, the turquoise pools seeming to clear of their resident fog and see Catriona for the first time in weeks.

Encouraged, Catriona had continued. 'If you can tell me what it is that would help you, what might make you feel better, I'll do everything I can to give that to you.' Catriona had swiped at a single tear that had slid over her eyelid. 'Whatever it is, April, you can tell me. Do you understand, sweetheart?'

April had taken a few moments, then simply nodded, her eyes emptying again as she'd gone back to soaping the cloth in her hand.

Disappointment had held Catriona still for a few minutes, her limbs feeling leaden and useless, until she'd heaved herself up from the floor and walked slowly out into the hall. 'I'll be back to check on you in a few minutes, love.' She'd fought to keep her voice level as she'd bumped along the hall, her vision blurred and her head beginning to pound.

Now, April was lying on the sofa with Arthur next to her. The puppy was already so long that his back was the length of her thigh, and his fur had begun to thicken around his throat and shoulders. His colouring was becoming more distinct, and his baby teeth had started to show up in the pen, tangled in his blanket and in the fur of his toys. April had retrieved a couple of them and put them in the soap box, with the robin's egg, and while Catriona found it a little grizzly, she'd left them there.

The TV was on, and April was sucking her three middle fingers, the exact way that Connor had, and seeing it surprised Catriona. 'April, love. Can you please take your fingers out of your mouth?' She smiled as April started, then looked over at her, her hand sliding back to her thigh. 'Thanks, sweetheart.' Catriona stood up and walked over to the sofa, settling herself next to April. 'It's getting quite late. I think it's bedtime.' She stroked Arthur's back as the pup wriggled onto his side, lifting his legs up to give her access to his tummy. 'You are a cuddle monster, Arthur. I swear you're going to be bigger than both your parents when you've finished growing.' She gently tugged on a paw as Arthur made a snuffling sound, then gave a high-pitched sneeze. Caught by surprise, Catriona laughed. 'Bless you.' She ruffled the puppy's stomach as, next to her, April covered her mouth with her hand to hide a smile, the now familiar gesture giving Catriona hope that the moment of recognition, up in the bathroom, might not be the last opportunity to connect before the day was out. She gently took April's hand in hers, noting the warmth of the narrow fingers. 'You can laugh, April. It's not a bad thing to be happy. It's OK.'

April blinked several times, then dropped her hand to her stomach. Her eyes were full of a question, something heavy, cumbersome, and as Catriona held her breath, April sucked in her bottom lip and nodded. The action felt momentous, as if a message had finally been received as opposed to ignored, as if a tiny window had opened and a sliver of light had penetrated the shadowy place her daughter now resided.

Buoyed up by hope, Catriona squeezed April's fingers. 'Would you like to sleep in beside me tonight?' She smiled.

'We can read a story and have hot chocolate in bed.' She wiggled her eyebrows comically, sending all her energy into her fingers, hoping they would convey to her daughter how much she wanted this.

After a few moments, April slid her hand away and sat up, then she lifted Arthur onto her lap.

'April?' Catriona felt the moment slipping away, the wall between them rising again, and as she watched April get up, the legs of her bumblebee pyjamas now ending halfway down her calves, April shook her head.

Suddenly exhausted, and soaked in defeat, Catriona nodded. 'OK, then. Come on. Let's get you and Arthur into bed. We've got an early piano lesson with Peg tomorrow.' She held a hand out to April, who hesitated for a second, then turned and walked out into the hall, heading for the stairs.

As she pulled the duvet up around her shoulders, Catriona shivered. The call she'd just made to her mother had been somewhat stilted, Catriona not willing to share all the details of Lauren's visit, or her growing fears about the future, but, predictably, Iris had seemed to sense that she was hiding something. The more Iris had pressed her, the more Catriona had tried to resist, but not willing to let her off the hook, Iris had forged on until Catriona had shared some of her thoughts.

'You just need to believe in yourself, Catkin. You are the best thing that ever happened to that little girl. And don't you forget it. And we are one hundred per cent behind you, whatever happens. If you need moral support, or for us to come back, love, or if you need money...' Iris's voice had faded, as if she'd sensed that was reaching.

'Why would I need money, Mum?' Catriona had frowned. 'We're totally fine.'

'Och, I know. It's just that we feel so helpless down here, and your dad worries so much about you, and wee April.' She'd sighed. 'How's Duncan taking all this?'

Catriona had grimaced, awash with fresh guilt over keeping the last, and most upsetting, meeting yet, a secret from him. 'He's doing the best he can, Mum. He's not a particularly trusting person, in general, so he has his reservations about Lauren.' She'd shaken her head, hearing the distant chiming of the clock down on the living-room mantel and counting to nine as the musical sound had filtered up the stairs.

'Well, he's maybe not the most sensitive man in the world, but he's got his head screwed on.'

Caught off guard, Catriona had laughed. 'Mum, that's the first time you've ever said anything less than complimentary about Duncan. You've finally acknowledged that he is human, not perfect, fallible even.'

Iris had hesitated for a few moments, then she'd spoken gently, but with a clear message. 'Catriona, I know he is fallible, as we *all* are.' She'd paused. 'He is human, and therefore, by definition, he makes mistakes.' She'd waited for a few moments, and Catriona had known what was coming next as well as she knew that night followed day. 'You need to remember that *no one* is perfect, love. However much we want or expect them to be.'

Catriona had nodded, scanning the empty room, taking in the chair in the corner devoid of Duncan's rumpled clothes, the pillow next to her smooth and vacant, his bedside table empty of the ubiquitous pile of banknotes and coins, the old diver's watch with the missing dial and the dog-eared engineering books that were permanently stacked there. All the signs of her husband's presence had been neatly tidied away, both physically and from her heart, rather than being visible, loud, messy and alive in her life.

She'd suddenly felt a momentous shift inside her, a bone-deep yearning for Duncan, for his company, his touch, his gravelly voice to wake her from a dreamless sleep as he leaned in and kissed her, the smell of coffee on his breath, and before she could stop herself, she'd given in to more tears. 'We are broken, Mum, and I don't know if we can fix things.'

Iris had taken her time to respond, then she'd said quietly, 'The question is, Catriona, do you want to?'

Catriona had rolled onto her back and nodded, as tears slipped down her cheeks and trickled into her ears. 'I think so, yes.' She'd choked out the words. 'I want to fix it all. I want my family back. I want April to open up to me again, to let me in like she used to. To need me, like she used to, Mum. I want it all back. But I think it's too late.' She'd sobbed as Iris had tried to comfort her, ease her back towards solid ground. 'I don't want to lose another daughter, Mum. But I simply must do what's best for April.'

'Take a breath, Catriona. Step back from any decisions until you and Duncan have really talked it through, sweetheart. I know in my bones that that little girl is better off with you two,' Iris had crooned.

'I wish I felt as certain as you,' Catriona had gulped. 'If you could see the way she looks at me now.' She'd shivered. 'I've got to go, Mum. I think I hear her up.' The white lie had released her from the conversation, and now, all she could focus on was that she had to talk to Duncan.

. . .

Twenty minutes later, her cheeks tight with dried tears and her arms wrapped around her middle, she paced in front of the bedroom curtains blocking out the night sky, her heart pattering under her long T-shirt. Duncan's phone was ringing interminably and just as she was about to hang up, she heard a clatter downstairs.

Her stomach flip-flopping, afraid that April had got up for something and had perhaps fallen or hurt herself, Catriona grabbed her robe and rushed along the hall, then down the stairs.

As she flicked the light on in the lower hall, she saw a large shape by the front door, broad shoulders, a head of thick hair, and before he could turn around to face her, she wrapped her arms around him, burying her face in the back of his sweater. 'You came back,' she gasped, tears once again masking her eyes as she breathed him in, the smell of car, of dust, of musky soap and of understanding, an under-standing that went beyond words.

He turned and wrapped his arms around her, breathing into her hair. 'Cat, I had to come home. There's something I need to tell you. I didn't want to do it on the phone.' His voice was thick, and she caught a whiff of stale coffee, as her mind took flight as to what was so urgent that he'd driven almost two hours at this time of night. 'Let's go and sit down, love.' He eased her away from his chest. 'Come on.' As she focused on his face, he was blinking repeatedly, his jaw twitching and his lips pursed as if he was chewing on something bitter.

'What's wrong?' Catriona raked her hair away from her face and tugged her robe closer around her. 'What, Duncan?' The silence was unbearable. 'Tell me.'

He led her into the kitchen, pulled out her chair for her and then sat opposite her, his palms flat on the table in front of him. 'Ian called me earlier this evening. He'd done a bit of digging, about Lauren.' He paused.

'And?' His tone was telling her that whatever was coming was not good, so she braced herself, but no amount of preparation could have saved her from being blindsided by what he said next.

30

Duncan pulled his hands into his lap. 'Ian said that the records showed that April was taken from Lauren by the courts, because she'd repeatedly left the new-born baby alone in the flat, while she was out with her friends.'

Staggered, Catriona's heart flipped, conflict at wanting him to keep talking, and not, instantly roiling inside her. 'Go on,' she croaked.

'He said that her neighbours had called the police to report the baby crying, for hours on end, day and night. So, apparently, April was taken into foster care, only briefly, until Lauren decided to give her up.'

Catriona let the shocking information sink in, horror and sadness sickeningly mixing in her gut as she conjured an image of April, tiny and alone in a shadowy bedroom, crying, afraid, hungry, perhaps needing to be changed. As Catriona tried to banish the image, the hairs on her arms lifted from her now chilled skin. Lauren could not have done that. Surely Ian was mistaken.

Duncan was watching her, waiting for a cue to continue, so she took a deep a breath and nodded at him.

'Ian said that there's no record of her having been married, either, but apparently she had a boyfriend, who seemingly scarpered a few months ago. She was staying with her mother, in her flat in Govan, so presumably she's still there. And she is not a vet, Cat, but she works as a receptionist at a veterinary hospital.' He let his hands drop into his lap. 'She lied, love.'

Catriona felt the air leave her with a rush, as grim images of one of the roughest areas of Glasgow flashed behind her eyes. The picture of the pretty terraced house with the neat garden she'd imagined, when Lauren had told her she lived near Hillhead, disintegrated as Catriona tried to focus on Duncan, waiting for the next bombshell.

'Cat, are you OK?' He frowned, leaning forward on his elbows.

'Yes,' she whispered. 'Just shocked and disappointed. No, hurt. Well, all of the above.' Her mouth dipped. 'Why would she lie, Duncan?' Hurt crept up the back of her throat. 'I trusted her. I even thought she might be the better mother for April. Be able to give her more than I could.' Her voice caught.

Duncan linked his hands in front of him, the long fingers forming a mesh of skin and bone. 'I know you did, love. That's why I came home, to tell you in person.' His eyes were full of sympathy. 'I won't let her hurt this family, Cat. That's the bottom line.' He paused, scanning her face. 'So, what do we do now?'

Catriona leaned back, letting the chair support her as she tried to breathe away the anxiety that was bubbling under her ribs. How could Lauren lie so blatantly? Did she not think they'd find out the truth, eventually? Had she, Catriona, done something to make Lauren feel bad about herself, feel the need to create an imaginary life that was better than her reality? As question after question flickered through her mind, she remembered Lauren's kind turquoise eyes, her gentle manner with April, the compassion and understanding she'd shown Catriona, all making up a picture of someone who cared about others, someone who did the right thing, who could be trusted. As her feelings catapulted from disbelief to anger, then back to hurt, despite everything she'd just heard, Catriona couldn't conjure up hatred for Lauren. Whatever had made her do what she had done, there must have been a reason, and until Catriona knew what that was, she would file away her hurt and try to give Lauren the benefit of the doubt.

Duncan stood up and moved to her side, then gently pulled her to her feet. He wrapped her in a hug, his chin resting on the crown of her head, then, after a few moments, he spoke slowly and carefully, as she leaned back and took in his face. 'Cat, I want to be here, more than anything. Not just for the weekends, but always.' His voice was clogged with emotion, his eyes brimming. 'If you can forgive me, let me back in, I won't let you down again.' He shook his head, a single tear rolling down his cheek and dropping onto Catriona's chest. 'I won't let April down, either. She deserves better from me, and I intend to give her that.' He paused. 'Can you forgive me, Cat? For Hope. For it all. For this entire bloody mess.' He released her and swung his arms out wide. 'Please?'

The angles of his face blurred as she sniffed, then swiped at her eyes. This was all she'd wanted to hear, for months, and as his words filled her head, and heart, she gulped. 'It wasn't all you, Duncan. I helped make this mess, too. But we can get through it.' She nodded, wanting to surrender to this, even as a sliver of doubt sliced its way into her centre. Could she trust him not to flee again if things got tough? She didn't think they'd survive that. 'Duncan, I want you home, but to stay. You can't retreat again when things get hard. I need to know you'll talk to me, that we'll work things out together, whatever we face.'

He studied her, taking in each feature as if seeing it for the first time, then nodded slowly. 'I'm not going anywhere unless you and April are with me.'

Relief taking the air from her, Catriona closed her eyes and walked into his arms, her mouth craving his. 'I'm so glad you're home.'

Lying in the dark, their clothes scattered across the floor and the curtains opened wide so that they could see the star-studded night sky, Catriona and Duncan were whispering to one another. She had told him everything about Lauren's last visit and while he'd been visibly upset, he hadn't taken her to task on hiding it from him. Everything in his manner spoke of him having changed, opened up to the significance of his family, how fundamental they were to his happiness, and Catriona could feel her own trust, and contentment, begin to rekindle, a low glow that promised to get brighter if they could just stay on course.

Her head was on his shoulder and her leg draped over his thighs, as she stroked the line of hair that ran down the centre of his chest. 'I seriously asked myself, what if April needs to be with her and Connor? I thought perhaps that was what could bring April back from this silent place, this self-imposed isolation.' She rolled onto her back and stretched her legs out, her toes finding a chilly section of the duvet.

Duncan shook his head against the pillow. 'What she needs is us, Cat. Us to be a family again.' He reached for her hand, wove his fingers through hers and held it against his chest. 'The more I thought about Lauren, and what she might want out of this, the more afraid I became that she could say exactly that, that we're not in the position to give April what she needs anymore.' He paused. 'When you told me what Mungo said, I was afraid that she was shoring up her own position. Trying to build a case. We should have been more cautious. Not let her come here so much.' He whispered, more to himself than to Catriona, 'I think we need to put this all to bed, once and for all.' He lifted her hand and kissed the knot of fingers. 'What do you think about asking her to come back, so we can clear this up, face to face? I'm not sure this is something we can do remotely.'

Catriona shook her head. 'I think we all need a break from each other, just for a while. Let things settle down a bit.' She eased her hand from his and turned onto her side, seeing his profile, a clean, strong line against the pale wall behind the bed. 'Duncan, the most important factor in all this is April. What we need to do is win back her trust, and her love. Whatever it takes to make that happen, we have to do it.' Catriona pictured April earlier that evening, taking the washcloth from her hand, and whatever Catriona didn't know, she finally knew this, April was her daughter. Nothing would change that, and even if it took weeks, months, or years, they would repair their family.

Half an hour later, while Duncan went downstairs, to pour them each a nightcap, Catriona went to check on April. As she tiptoed along the hall, she saw the dim, greenish glow coming from the dinosaur night-light in April's room. She had spotted it at the Superstore a few weeks earlier and had lifted it from the shelf, turning it back and forth until Catriona had said, 'Would you like it for your room, sweetheart?' April had nodded, then slid it into the basket, her fingers covering her mouth as she kept her face turned away from Catriona. Catriona had pretended she hadn't seen the glimmer of a smile as they'd finished their shopping, then, when they got home, April had dug the night-light out of the bag and bounded up the stairs with it.

Now, as she approached the half-open door, Catriona stepped inside the room, letting her eyes adjust to the partial darkness. The butterfly-covered curtains were open, and the moon was gigantic, a pale disc hanging low in the sky, perfectly framed between two patches of ghostly clouds. The window was cracked open, and the scent of rosemary filtered in on a wisp of cool night air.

Arthur was curled up in his bed, under the window. His nose was tucked under his front paw and his tail twitched, and Catriona imagined him dreaming of the seagulls that he loved to chase, and see off, in the back garden.

Across the room, the sequins twinkled on the gauzy drape above the bed. April was sprawled in the bottom bunk, her hair spread across the pillow in a dark fan, her right arm hanging over the edge of the mattress, and the duvet bunched up at her feet. A broad strip of milky-white skin was exposed between the top and bottoms of her pyjamas and, making a mental note to buy her some new ones, Catriona tiptoed to the side of the bunk.

Holding her breath, she leaned in, gently moving the duvet from under April's legs, trying to cover her up without waking her. The scent of soap mixed with mint, and innocence, made Catriona pause for a second, as this evocative cocktail always did, and she let the familiar images of her two beautiful daughters playing together come. She could almost hear Hope's laugh, the distinctive sound that would bubble up from her middle, inevitably giving birth to a snort, which would then set April off, her laughter higher pitched and breathy. Together, they had created the perfect harmony, a symphony of mirth and abandonment, freedom, and trust and, most of all, of utter joy, altogether a heady sound that Catriona missed more now than any other sound she could imagine.

Taking a moment to let her heart settle, she gently pulled the duvet up and tucked it around April's shoulders, and then, seeing a tiny flicker of her eyelids, the dark lashes quivering ever so slightly, Catriona whispered, 'Hi, sweetie.'

April lay motionless, her lips slightly parted and her breaths coming slow and steady, but something in the way her eyelids rippled made Catriona go on.

'April, I want you to know something. It's all right if you don't want to speak to us yet. Daddy and I understand. We know that when you're ready, you will. And when that day comes, we'll have a party. A giant, happy, April's-voice-is-back party, with cakes and balloons. Nana and Gramps, and Graham, Bruce and Peg will all come, and Peg will play the piano. We'll eat until we burst, and we'll play games, and sing songs, and dance all over the house, and then, when we're all full up, and tired, and happy, we'll talk about Hope. We'll remember all the lovely times we had together, all the funny and clever and silly things you two did. All the running around in the garden, and watching the seals in the river, and going to the beach, or into the hills for picnics.' She took a breath, scanning April's eyelids, hopeful for more movement. Seeing nothing, Catriona leaned down and kissed April's forehead. 'You are such a good girl, April Mactiggiwinkle. The best daughter anyone ever had. You are so incredibly loved. Always carry that with you, sweet-heart. Always know it in your heart.' She lay her palm gently on April's chest, then backed slowly out of the room with the comforting sense that she had been heard.

Despite the late hour, Duncan had called Ian and had put the phone on speaker so that Catriona could hear, with the volume turned down low. They'd been sitting next to one another on the bed, their heads tilted towards each other as they'd listened, their hands linked on top of the duvet.

Wanting to reconfirm their legal position, as regards Lauren's right of access to April, and future visitation requests, they'd asked Ian to clarify the situation once again.

Ian had told them that, based on the terms of the adop-tion agreement, they could stipulate how often any visits took place and also say no, within reason, if it was becoming intrusive or affecting the stability of April's life. 'It's basi-cally up to you, guys,' Ian had said. 'You can't deny her access if she's not posing any threat to, or visibly upsetting, April, but she has to comply with your decision as to when and how often she comes.'

'I thought that was the case, but it's good to have it confirmed. Thanks, bro.' Duncan had nodded, keeping his eyes on Catriona.

'So, don't be bullied into anything you're not happy about,' Ian had chuckled. 'Though I seem to remember you were the one who protected me, in school, Dunc.'

Duncan had smiled. 'Well, I might've been the younger by a few minutes, but I was a whole half an inch taller than you, big man.'

Catriona had been surprised by this, never having heard Ian or Duncan speak of it before, and the knowledge that he had come to Ian's rescue that way made her proud. In that same spirit, it was clear that he had also come to hers and April's rescue, this very night, more than he might ever know. He'd come home when they needed him. The only question was, would he stay this time?

31

The next evening, the call had come at 7.30 p.m., when April had been in the bath. Catriona had been hovering at the open door, trying not to let April see her. Seeing Lauren's number again had set Catriona's heart pattering as she'd darted along the hall, down the stairs and into the kitchen, where Duncan was reading the paper.

She'd held up the phone. 'It's her. So, we're agreed?' She'd seen him nodding, their conversation of that after-noon still fresh on her mind.

They had decided that when Lauren called again, asking to visit, they would agree to her coming at the week-end, giving them time to prepare. They had decided that their best tactic would be to present a calm, united front, not corner her right away, but to let things unfold gradually. Then, they'd pick their moment and ask her why she'd lied to them. Their hope was that whatever Lauren's reason, faced with them being obviously, and firmly, together again, she'd come clean, without the need for any uncomfortable confrontations.

Now, Catriona kept her voice light. 'Hi, Lauren. How

are you?' She slipped into the chair opposite Duncan and switched to speaker mode.

'Yeah, great. Great. How are you, and April?'

Catriona looked at Duncan. 'We're *all* really well, thanks.' She deliberately widened the circle to include Duncan. 'It's been a busy few days.' Catriona let the silence linger until Lauren spoke again.

'So, I was wondering if we could come back at the weekend. Saturday maybe? Greg's away again, so it'd just be me and Connor.' She cleared her throat. 'Perhaps we could do another picnic or something?'

Catriona locked on Duncan's eyes, the two of them shaking their heads in unison, having also agreed that this time, they wanted Lauren on their home turf. 'I think it'll be fine for you to come, but I'll make us some lunch here. It's just easier, with there being more of us. Come around eleven thirty, if you can, then we can make sure you get away at a reasonable time.' She sucked in her bottom lip, hoping she hadn't sounded too brusque, as, across the table, Duncan gave her a thumbs-up.

'Right. OK. We'll see you then.' Lauren sounded pleased. 'Give April a hug from me, will you?'

Catriona waited for a second or two, then nodded. 'I will. Bye, Lauren.'

She lay the phone on the table and eyed Duncan, who had put the paper down and was watching her, his eyes warm and gentle, the way they used to look whenever he'd see her walk into a room.

'So, Saturday it is.' She circled her head, feeling her neck grind. 'Are we ready?'

'I think we are.' He walked around, stood behind her and began kneading the taut muscles along the top of her shoulders. 'Ready as we'll ever be.'

As he worked on a knot, sending sparks of what her mother referred to as *good pain* up her neck, and into the base of her skull, Catriona leaned back into the pressure of his fingers. They were ready, she just hoped that Lauren wouldn't take them to a place where things got unpleasant.

The next three days sped by as Catriona had doubled her tutoring sessions. With the universities and local schools on their summer holidays, she'd taken on two new students, twin brothers of eighteen, both needing help with German.

Duncan worked until late each night, taking a break for a family dinner, piano time and then April's bedtime story, which he and Catriona were now reading to her on alternate nights. While still silent, April had seemed a little more engaged since Duncan had come home, something that even as she was glad to see it, hurt Catriona, her still being unable to elicit a similar response in her daughter. With April tucked up in bed, and while Catriona prepared for her lessons the next day, Duncan would stack the dishwasher, then go back to his desk for an hour or so, before joining her in the living room for a night cap.

These new rituals felt good, and each day that passed, Catriona found she was trusting that Duncan was more committed than ever to being part of their little family, which somehow freed her up to think about Hope, more than she'd allowed herself to before. Now, she could occasionally think about her without crying, even though the smallest, random reminder could still send her rushing off to the bathroom in search of tissues, or into the garden, letting the late-summer breezes coming off the loch dry her tears before Duncan or April would notice them. Hope felt as present to Catriona as she had when she'd been alive, and that feeling was as comforting as it was painful.

The morning of Lauren's visit, buzzing with nervous energy, Catriona had got up early to do some weeding in the garden as the sun rose behind the house, then she'd roasted a chicken, made a fresh raspberry tart, cleaned the kitchen and guest bathroom, then taken a sleepy April for a bike ride around the village.

All the activity had been a welcome distraction and as she and April biked back down the drive, Catriona hoped there would be no drama today. There had been more than enough of that, for all of them, for a lifetime.

Now, Duncan was in the conservatory with April and Arthur. They were sitting on the floor and playing tug with the puppy, who, as they'd been getting dressed, had grabbed a sock of Duncan's from the floor of the bedroom and dragged it down the stairs. April had stifled a laugh as she'd followed her father, and her dog, and Catriona had smiled at Duncan, as he'd rolled his eyes, comically.

As Catriona set a freshly ironed napkin at each place at the kitchen table, the doorbell rang. She snapped her eyes to Duncan, who had jumped up from the floor and was speaking to April. Nodding to him, Catriona went to open the door.

Lauren was in a long, floaty summer dress, her feet in flat, gladiator-style sandals and her hair was loose, the sun highlighting the rich chestnut of the sleek bob. Seeing Catriona, she smiled. 'Hiya.' The now familiar tiny gap between her two front teeth was somehow endearing, as Catriona smiled back.

'Come in. Where's Connor?' She glanced at the old Ford Fiesta that Lauren was driving, parked next to the house.

'He's in the car. We have something for April.' Lauren clasped her hands together under her chin, like a child who'd been given a secret that they were struggling to keep.

'Oh?' Catriona tried not to frown. 'What is it?'

'It's a surprise.' Lauren dropped her hands to her sides. 'Where is she?'

'She's in the conservatory with her dad.' Feeling awkward, Catriona slid her hands into the back pockets of her jeans. 'Is Connor not coming in?' She looked over at the Ford again, trying to spot the little boy's outline behind the mottled glass of the back window.

'As soon as we know April is ready.' Lauren grinned. 'Can you keep her inside until we get organised?' She lifted her eyebrows, as her expression, one of pure excitement, made Catriona second-guess herself, wondering if they'd been wrong in thinking this person could be such an accomplished liar.

Desperate to ask more about the surprise, but not wanting to burst Lauren's bubble, Catriona nodded. 'OK. I'll go in, then give me five minutes or so.'

In the conservatory, April was sitting on the sofa with Arthur, as Duncan stood at the open French doors. His hair was freshly washed and slicked back from his face, and the light tan he'd acquired from being out in the garden with April most lunchtimes made the whites of his eyes seem startlingly bright. 'What's going on? Aren't they coming in?' he frowned, looking behind Catriona at the empty hall.

'Lauren and Connor have a surprise for April.' She held her hands out, palms up. 'They want to bring it in, together.' She looked over at April, whose chin had lifted at the mention of her name. 'Are you ready, sweetheart?' Catriona smiled at her daughter. 'I've got no idea what it is.'

April nodded enthusiastically, standing up and gently

tugging Arthur's collar to get him off the sofa. Having refused help from Catriona to dress that morning, April had chosen a white T-shirt with a huge giraffe's head on the front and her cut-off jean-shorts. Her legs and arms were now lightly gilded, and her hair shone, a sheet of deep waves swinging between her shoulder blades.

'You look lovely, sweetheart.' Catriona walked over and kissed the top of April's head, smelling the new lavender shampoo they'd started using.

Moments later, Lauren walked into the room carrying a large cardboard box. Behind her, Connor was dragging a plastic bag, with long strands of hay sticking out of the top, some of which floated onto the floor as the bag bumped over the threshold of the door.

'Hi, April, love?' Lauren beamed at April, who immediately smiled back at her. Lauren seemed not to notice Duncan, who was now standing by the desk. 'We've brought you a wee present.' She lifted the box up a little higher, a rustling sound coming from underneath the open flap. 'Do you want to sit down, then we can open it?' Lauren nodded at the rug, shifting the box up higher, then twisting to balance it on her hip. 'Sit on the carpet, then.' She dipped her chin, as April, looking momentarily confused, sat down and crossed her legs. 'Catriona, could you hang on to Arthur for a bit?' Lauren glanced over at Catriona.

Caught up in the suspense Lauren was creating, Catriona lifted Arthur from where he stood next to April and held him in her arms.

'Great. OK, April.' Lauren bent over and set the box in front of her. 'You can open it now.' She stood back.

April glanced up at Catriona with what looked like a request for permission, and her heart twitching gratefully, Catriona nodded. Her anxiety was rising, the longer she was in the dark about what was in this box. Judging by the rustling, it was some kind of animal, and the possibilities began to crowd Catriona's mind, as she imagined hamsters, rabbits and even a kitten, clambering out of the box and straight into April's heart.

April gingerly lifted one of the open flaps, then sat back and gasped, her hands clamping over her mouth as she smiled widely behind them.

'Do you like him?' Lauren was bending over, folding back the remaining flaps, as April edged forwards and looked inside again. Then, she nodded, reaching her hand inside.

Catriona caught sight of Duncan's frown, his hands diving deeper into his pockets as he stared at April's back. Unable to take it any longer, Catriona walked over and looked inside, keeping a firm grip on Arthur, who was wriggling, straining against her grip.

On a bed of hay was a large tortoise, its head pulled inside its shell until only the tip of its nose was visible, and its four scaly legs completely retracted. 'Oh, April. It's a tortoise.' Catriona looked back over at Duncan, whose face had darkened as he crossed the room and joined them, just as Lauren moved around and stood behind April.

'His name is James. You know, like James Herriot?'

April gasped, her eyes snapping to Catriona's and a look of utter disbelief on her face. Catriona's heart faltered as she tried to brush this odd coincidence aside. See it for what it was, this time, simply a coincidence, rather than a sign.

'Someone found him at the side of a main road, near the practice, so they brought him in to us. He needs a new home, so I thought you could take care of him, April.' Lauren let her hands rest on April's shoulders, her scarlet nails like drops of blood on April's T-shirt.

Shaking the disturbing image away, Catriona watched her daughter, waiting for the moment when April would shrug away from the contact, lean forward or even stand up and move somewhere else, as she had been doing for weeks now if Catriona pulled her into a hug that lasted more than a second or two.

April was rapt, her fingers gently stroking the tortoise's shell, and she seemed not to notice, or mind, Lauren touching her, and seeing it, Catriona felt a familiar stab high up under her ribs. Determined not to spoil April's obvious pleasure, she backed away, and heading for the kitchen, called lightly over her shoulder, 'I'll put Arthur in the pen for a bit.'

In the kitchen, she put Arthur in his bed and closed the gate of the pen, her heart aching as if she'd been punched in the chest.

'Sorry, little man.' She bent over and stroked Arthur's back. 'You're still her number one guy. Don't worry.' The tiny, mismatched eyes seemed to hold hers, then Arthur shook himself, energy rippling down his back like an electrical current and ending at the tip of his tail. 'I'll let you out soon, I promise.' She stroked his soft ears, gently rubbing the tips. 'You're such a good boy.'

Back in the conservatory, Connor was hunkered down next to April, his nose shiny and needing to be wiped, as he patted the back of the tortoise that April had lifted out and set on the rug in front of her.

'Good boy,' Connor crooned, as April smiled at him. 'Want some?' Connor held a wilted lettuce leaf under the mostly hidden nose, as one leathery foot emerged from the shell, causing both the children to move in closer to the timid creature.

'Don't crowd him too much,' Lauren warned them.

'He's shy and it'll take him a while to feel comfy coming out to say hello.' She smiled at Catriona, whose eyes slid to Duncan, now leaning his hips against the desk, intent on watching the children.

Just as Catriona was going to suggest they take James out onto the grass, Duncan stood up. 'You need to wash your hands after you've touched him, April, love. Don't put them near your mouth, OK?' He waited for April to turn around and acknowledge him, but she was transfixed, staring at James, who'd popped another leg out at the back of his shell. 'April?' Duncan tried again.

April flicked a glance over her shoulder and gave a single nod, then lifted the tortoise up to eye level, peering at the opening where the head had now completely disappeared.

'Be gentle, love.' Lauren walked over and guided April's hands down towards the floor again. 'He'll need lots of TLC, and fresh veggies, and he'll like being on the grass, so do you want to take him outside for a while? I think he needs some fresh air.'

Having Lauren assume control in this easy manner sent a spark of irritation through Catriona as she crossed the room and held a hand out to April. 'I think we should wash our hands and have some lunch first, then we can all go outside for coffee.' She looked over at Duncan, who was nodding, his mouth twisted, a sign that there was so much more he wanted to say but was keeping locked in. She gave him a look that said, *Breathe, everything is fine,* and seeing it, the tension visibly released from his jaw.

'Good plan, Cat. I'm starving.' He patted his stomach. 'Let's eat.'

. . .

Throughout lunch, Lauren had seemed slightly wound up, fidgeting in her chair, chattering about all the animals at work, how April would make a great vet, then about the shocking price of petrol, nervously twisting her hands together in her lap. Her eyes had seemed oddly bright and at one point, when she'd gone to the bathroom, Duncan had cleared the plates from the table, then leaned in and whispered to Catriona, 'What's going on. Do you think she knows we know?'

Catriona had whispered back, 'She's just nervous. Trying too hard, that's all.'

Duncan's mouth had dipped, and he'd been about to say something else when Lauren had come back in, laughing at the sight of April, feeding Connor a carrot stick. 'You look like a little rabbit, Con.' She'd tugged the chair out and sat down, curled her fists under her chin and mimed exaggerated chewing. 'Munch, munch, munch.'

Now, with the lunch things put away, Catriona had set the coffee machine up, the rich smell of the freshly ground beans cutting through the warm air of the kitchen. 'Shall we have coffee outside?'

'Connor needs a nap.' Lauren sounded almost apologetic. 'Can I put him down in there?' She pointed towards the living room.

Caught off guard, Catriona nodded. 'Um, sure. But you can use the spare room if you prefer. The bed's clean.'

Lauren shook her head, already up and rounding the table to where Connor sat, his bottom lip protruding as she hefted him out of the chair.

'Noooo,' he whined, his eyes filling up.

'He'll be fine down here, thanks, and then I can keep an eye on him.' Lauren bumped him up on her hip. 'Back in a bit.' Connor began to whimper as she walked out into the hall. 'Shhh now. Just a little nap, and you'll have lots more fun after. OK?' She shushed the little boy, who was shoving himself back from her, his palms flat on her chest. 'Connor, stop. It's nap time.'

As her voice faded away into the living room, so Duncan moved in close to Catriona's side, his body language clearly communicating that he was wired and ready to break the seal on the difficult questions they'd agreed to ask Lauren, when the right moment arose. 'Let's get April to play outside for a while. Then we can talk to Lauren in there.' He nodded towards the conservatory. His voice was barely audible, as April walked over and lifted Arthur out of the pen.

Catriona's stomach flipped. 'All right, but, Duncan, tread carefully, and don't be too aggressive. Give her time to reply. To explain,' she whispered. 'Promise?'

He held her gaze, then nodded, 'OK, Cat. Trust me.'

No sooner had he lifted the tray from the counter than Lauren came back in. 'He went out like a light.' She laughed softly. 'He always fights me, but he'll be a happy boy for the rest of the afternoon, now.' She scanned the empty table. 'I was going to help you clear up, but you beat me to it.' She flashed a dazzling smile at Duncan, who gave a tight one back.

'Let's go through, and perhaps April can take James outside for a while now.' He looked over at Catriona, as if the idea had just come to him.

Not letting Lauren have time to weigh in, Catriona quipped, 'Great idea. Let's get him some fresh lettuce, and you can see if he'll eat it.' She spoke to April, who was standing near the back door, with Arthur at her feet. 'You take Lauren through, love, and I'll get April sorted out, then join you.' Catriona smiled as Duncan turned and walked into the hall, with Lauren, looking slightly unsure, trailing behind him.

Catriona handed a mug of coffee to Duncan, one to Lauren, then sat on the edge of the chair at the desk. Duncan was standing near the open French doors, his hand dwarfing the mug as he lifted it to his lips. Outside, the sound of Bruce's lawnmower drummed behind a symphony of birdsong, and the occasional yip from Arthur. Catriona could see the puppy, out on the lawn, nudging James with his nose, his tail wagging furiously as April gently eased him away from the tortoise.

Lauren sat back, her mug on her lap. 'Is April any better? Has she spoken at all?' Her eyes were wide as she glanced from Duncan to Catriona, her mouth slightly open. 'She seemed to brighten up a lot when she saw James, and don't you love the way she mothers Connor? It's so sweet to see them together. Kids just blossom around other kids, don't you think?' She sipped some coffee. 'We need to make sure they see each other more. Maybe she can come to visit me in Glasgow, sometime?'

Catriona instantly knew, without even looking at Duncan, that Lauren's remarks had flipped a dangerous switch inside him and, consequently, this was the moment that could change everything.

32

Duncan pulled a stool up next to Catriona and sat down. Across the room, Lauren looked suddenly nervous, as if she'd like to take back what she'd just said, knowing some damage had been done.

'We'd like to talk to you, Lauren.' Duncan kept his voice low, controlled.

'Is everything OK?' She flashed a bright smile, her mouth disconnected from what was behind her eyes. 'Looks like an intervention.' She laughed, a harsh bark of a sound that made Catriona wince.

Duncan took a deep breath and, linking his hands between his knees, began to talk. As Catriona focused on what he was saying, and keeping her breathing even, she still hoped that Lauren would have an explanation that would justify the upsetting facts they'd discovered, a story to tell that would make her deception forgivable. Knowing that Duncan would think her naïve for fanning the dying embers of that hope, she laced her twitchy fingers together in her lap and waited.

Duncan had stopped speaking and Lauren, her coffee

abandoned on the table and her hands gripping her knees, was crimson in the face. Her eyes were darting between them, as if looking for an allied force, from the middle of no man's land, and her shoulders had risen up towards her ears.

'We'd just like to know if these things are true, Lauren.' Duncan leaned back again, crossing his legs. 'And, if so, why you weren't honest with us.'

As Catriona watched, the calm façade that Lauren had been struggling to maintain disintegrated. She stood up abruptly, her hands going to her hips as she shook her head. 'OK, so it's true. It's all true. But that was a long time ago, and I'm a different person now. Plus, my personal life has nothing to do with you. And I don't have to explain myself to you, either.' Her eyes were flashing, her voice quivering with anger. 'You shouldn't judge people for their pasts. God knows, you two haven't exactly got a shining track record,' she snapped, her fingers going to her mouth.

'Lauren, just calm down. We're not attacking you. We just want to know why you...' Catriona stood up and made to cross the room, as Lauren held her hands up.

'No. Don't.'

Catriona backed away, her heart racing.

'If you'd known everything, do you honestly think you'd have let me see April?' Lauren glared at them, her mouth working on itself. 'My mum died last month.' She gulped over a sob, the sound sending sympathy spearing through Catriona, as she imagined the agony of losing Iris. 'She wasn't much of a mum, but she was all the family I had.' Lauren's breath hitched. 'I told myself that I'd be better off, but then I felt so alone, so incredibly alone, that I knew I needed to find April, to see her, because she is my family, too.' She eyed Catriona, tears streaking her face. 'You of all people should understand, Catriona. You can't rub a child out of its mother heart, ever.' Her face melted as her mouth fell open, and tears began to slip down her cheeks. 'April is my daughter, whatever you think about it. And whatever piece of paper we have signed. You know it, and so do I.' She gulped down a sob. 'You're obviously not who she wants anymore. That's clear. What she wants, and needs, is me. I am her mother.'

Catriona felt the words like a slap to her face, and her determined sympathy for this distraught young woman slipped beneath her hurt at the bitter attack. 'Lauren, you lied, not only about the past, but about your life now. That's the worst kind of betrayal when we welcomed you into our home, into April's life. We trusted you with our child, with our story, our struggles and even our loss.' Her voice cracked, but seeing Duncan stand up, ready to intervene, she held a hand up to him. 'No, please, Duncan.'

He hesitated for a second, lifted his hands in submission, then gripped the back of Catriona's chair.

'You lied to me when I was at my most vulnerable. I trusted you, but now I can see that you deliberately played on what I told you – what I confided in you about losing Hope, even about our pain – trying to use our time apart against us, somehow.' Catriona took a shaky breath. 'You know, I wanted you to have an explanation that would excuse it all. Some justification that might've meant we could still be friends. Right up until about five minutes ago. But what you've done, what you're saying, is cruel and unforgivable.' Tears broke over Catriona's bottom lids and she angrily swiped them away. This was not a time for tears. This was a time for truth, no matter how painful.

Lauren sank onto the sofa, her face dropping into her hands. Her back shook as she panted into her palms and, despite everything Catriona was feeling, all the anger and pain and disappointment, she couldn't stand to see Lauren's abject agony.

Catriona walked over, sat next to Lauren, and gently put her hand on her back, feeling the juddering breaths Lauren was taking. 'Lauren, just try to breathe,' she said, as Duncan flopped down onto the desk chair, his eyes full of concern.

Lauren didn't jerk away, as Catriona had expected she might, instead she let Catriona's hand stay there, until, slowly, she stopped crying. Sitting up, she wiped her nose on her palm, then Catriona pointed to a box of tissues on the bookcase, so Duncan pulled out a few and handed them to her. She gave the tissues to Lauren, who accepted them, blew her nose loudly, then tucked them in her pocket.

'You have no idea what it was like for me.' Lauren's voice was ragged. 'I never had a proper family. My dad was gone by the time I was three, and my mum was always working, or out drinking, palming me off on neighbours. Then, when I got pregnant at fifteen, she threw me out.' She shoved her hair away from her face. 'April's dad was fifteen too, and his family packed him off to boarding school abroad as soon as it came out that I was expecting.' She coughed. 'So, I lived with a friend until the baby was born, and after they took her from me – once I gave her up – I had nowhere to go, so I moved back in with Mum.' She shook her head. 'A few years later, I got offered a place at the veterinary school, at Glasgow University, but then I got pregnant with Connor, and I couldn't afford childcare.' She gulped. 'I had a place at uni.' She sniffed, miserably. 'It was my dream.'

Duncan was shifting in the chair, his eyes glued to Catriona's as she sat still, afraid to move now. 'What about

Greg?' Duncan's voice was softer now. 'What happened there?'

'That wasn't my fault. He just couldn't cope with Connor.' She sniffed, then, as Catriona was about to empathise, Lauren stood up again, as if she'd suddenly found a second wind, an edge to her voice now. 'I did my best with April, and I'm doing my best with Connor. You weren't able to stop your own daughter from drowning right outside your back door, so I don't think you'll win any parenting awards any time soon.' She coughed again, as her words scattered across the room, like a million shards of broken glass, bouncing up and piercing their skin. 'I've asked April if she wants to come with me and Connor, and she does.' She turned to face Catriona, her cheeks on fire. 'She wants to be with *me.*'

Shocked to the core, Catriona took a few seconds to find her voice. 'How do you know that when April isn't speaking?' She stared at Lauren.

'She spoke to me when we were at the beach, while you were packing up your car.' Lauren spat the words out. 'She spoke to *me.*'

As she replayed the events of that day in her mind, Catriona remembered a brief moment or two when April had been standing next to Lauren, holding her hand, smiling and nodding, as the two of them faced the water. So damaged by the continuous series of rejections, Catriona had not set any particular store on yet another jab at her heart and had turned away to hide her tears.

Now, every protective, maternal instinct in Catriona fired up into high gear. The idea that this woman had manipulated her, all of them, with her sweet-natured comments, her empty sympathy and practiced compassion, was more than Catriona could stand, but that Lauren had

had the audacity to speak to April about this was the last straw.

Taking a deep breath, Catriona stood up and faced Lauren, noting the overly bright eyes, the widow's peak, the wide mouth. 'Lauren, I am sorry for the hard and painful life you have had, and that you've lost your mum, I truly am. But I feel utterly let down by you, by your lies and manipulation of me, and of my family, when we were nothing but open and welcoming to you, and Connor.'

She took a moment before delivering the truth that had taken her a while to remember, to rediscover, under the sea of self-doubt that had plagued her since Hope's death – since April's withdrawal into silence, and Duncan leaving for weeks, feeding all her fear and guilt over what had happened in the past and what might happen in the future. Now the answer to the most fundamental question of all, that she'd asked herself over and over during the past few months, was crystal clear. There was no longer any doubt about what was best for April, and knowing it so profoundly gave Catriona courage.

A wave of something settling, and sure, washed up inside her, and as she held Lauren's gaze, she spoke, Catriona's own mother's words coming to her when she needed them the most. 'You know, Lauren, being a mother is about more than giving birth, it's about nurturing, being selfless, putting the child first regardless of what you need yourself.' She paused, as Lauren flinched, Catriona's words seeming to pepper her skin. 'You gave birth to April, and for that, we will always be grateful to you. And you made an unselfish decision about what was best for her.' Catriona paused. 'It was the right decision then, and it's still the right decision. We are her parents, Lauren, and nothing will change that. Not now. Not ever.' She exhaled, and while a great weight lifted away from her heart, she was still aware of the pain that saying those words had created in Lauren. But she had to go on. 'We are her family and being here, with us, is what's best for April.'

Spent, Catriona walked to Duncan's side and took his hand, the press of her fingers an eloquent thank-you for him letting her take this on, handle it her way and follow her instincts.

Lauren seemed to take a few moments to process what Catriona had said, then, rounding on them both, her face scarlet, she snapped, 'That's exactly what I'm *saying*. You're not doing what's best for April. *You* are the ones being self-ish. She is bloody miserable here. She hasn't spoken to you in months, she's surrounded by sadness and bad memories, and the only time I've seen her smile is at me or Connor.' She gripped her waist, her knuckles turning white. 'She wants to be with *me*, I'm telling you.'

A rustling sound behind her made Catriona swing around, to see April, standing on the back path, her face ashen, and James tucked awkwardly under her arm. Her eyes looked huge as she sucked in her bottom lip, her chin quivering.

Her heart forcing its way up into her mouth, Catriona gasped, 'Oh, April, sweetheart. Are you OK?' She held a hand out to her daughter, her fingers numb and her insides turning icy cold. *Take my hand, April. Please, take my hand.*

April hesitated for a few, agonising moments, as if she were a sail, floating above the path, waiting for a strong wind to guide her to the safest shore. Then, as Catriona felt the air leave her in a rush, April carefully put James on the ground and calmly walked into Catriona's arms, burying her head in Catriona's middle and gripping her around the waist, like a drowning man would a log.

The next few minutes became frozen in time, April holding her so tightly that Catriona had to take shallow breaths, until Duncan was also next to them, his arms around them both. Catriona began to rock her daughter, a gentle swing from side to side, that soothed April, her gradually loosening her grip and lifting her head to reveal her flooded eyes.

As Catriona wiped her cheeks, April smiled at her, a gentle, eloquent smile that wrapped itself around Catriona's frayed nerves, calming her so utterly and completely that she simply nodded when April stepped back and turned to face Lauren.

Lauren was now perched on the edge of the sofa, wide-eyed and breathing shallowly. She was a pitiable sight, and Catriona's heart was breaking for her as April walked over and stood in front of her. Then, April took Lauren's hand. 'You are really nice to me, Lauren, but you're not my mummy. I don't want to go to your house because I live *here*.' Her voice was rough, rusty from lack of use. 'Thank you for visiting me, and for bringing Connor to play. I like him being my brother. And thanks for James, too.' April swallowed, as Catriona felt her heart triple in size, tears blurring her vision as April's voice, the sweet sound that Catriona had been waiting for, for months, seemed to fill the room.

Reaching for Duncan's hand, she felt him move in closer behind her, his chest behind her shoulder blades, his legs against the backs of her thighs, his breath on her temple, his whole being behind her, with her, body and soul.

April released Lauren's hand and walked back to Catriona and Duncan, her eyes clear and some colour having returned to her face. She eased her hand in between their clasped ones and lifted her chin as she spoke. 'I'm sorry I was so grumpy and sad. I promise to speak again if you let me stay here. And please still be my mummy and daddy because I love you.'

A single fat tear trickled down April's cheek, so Catriona wiped it away with her thumb. Unable to hold it together any longer, her arms going around her daughter and her tears falling freely onto April's shoulders, Catriona let all the hurt she'd been burying inside break free. All the months of silence melted away as she held her child against her heart.

Mother and daughter clung to one another until Catriona could control the force of her tears and finally choke out the words, 'We love you too. And of course, you can stay here, April. This is your home. And we will always be your parents. No matter what.'

33

Lauren had collapsed back on the sofa, her face ravaged by April's words. Catriona had asked Duncan to pour Lauren a brandy while she settled April upstairs, with Arthur, and put James in his box, then had made her way back to the conservatory.

Now, Lauren sat with a flushed Connor on her knee, rocking the little boy as she hummed something tuneless, while he sleepily sucked his middle fingers. The distraught look on Lauren's face tugged at Catriona's core, as having lost two beloved daughters, she knew only too well the agony that she saw coursing through Lauren's body.

As Duncan set a brandy glass on the side table next to Lauren, Catriona reached for his hand. 'Thank you, love. Let me sit with her for a while if you don't mind.'

He frowned slightly, then his face cleared. 'If you're sure.'

'I'm sure.'

As he left the room, gently closing the door behind him, Catriona pulled a stool close to the sofa and sat down. Dragging her hair into a ponytail, she tied it up and waited for

Lauren to meet her eyes. When Lauren finally looked at her, there was recognition there, the anger had faded, and in its place was pain, and resignation.

At Catriona's suggestion, Lauren had taken Connor up to the spare room to lie down for a while before she drove home. Catriona had been relieved, as having drunk some of the brandy Duncan had poured her, Lauren had instantly seemed exhausted.

Catriona had helped her upstairs, given her a soft blanket to throw over her and Connor, and drawn the curtains, leaving them alone, Lauren's face buried in the little boy's hair.

Now, Catriona and Duncan sat at the kitchen table with April, who was drinking some chocolate milk. She had a thin, milky-brown line along her top lip that was making Catriona smile as she waited for April to put the glass down and speak again. Hearing April's voice still felt like a gift that could be snatched away, leaving Catriona on tenterhooks, anxious that April might slide back into silence at any moment. But from what she could see, April seemed present again, where there had been vacancy, for so long, and witnessing that re-engagement was worth all the trauma that this day had brought.

Circling her stiff shoulders, Catriona stood up and put her empty cup in the sink, just as a robin landed on the fence between them and the Mackenzie house. It began preening itself, the tiny beak leaving narrow trails along its mink-coloured wing, its trademark crimson face and chest fading into the soft white of its underbelly. Seeing this little bird was like Hope letting them know she was with them, and rather than say anything, Catriona stood still and watched the tiny creature, hopeful that Hope could hear her thoughts, know that she would be forever loved and part of this family.

As the robin ruffled its wings, then took off into the breeze, Catriona said a silent farewell, then turned back to April. 'So, do you want to call Nana and Gramps later? They'll be so happy to hear from you.' She smiled at her daughter's profile, the long hair now in a loose plait down her back.

April nodded, putting her glass down and licking her lips noisily. 'Yes, but later, when it's just us.' She glanced over at Duncan, who was nodding his agreement.

'Good plan, April Mactiggiwinkle.' He smiled. 'You are a very kind and thoughtful girl. Did you know that?'

April seemed to glow, the colour in her cheeks rising as she dipped her chin coyly. 'No.'

'Well, you are. Isn't she, Mummy?' He stood up and joined Catriona. 'She gets that from you.'

Catriona felt his arm circle her waist, his fingers finding her ribs and the prickle of his chin pressing into the muscle of her shoulder. 'I'm not so sure about that.' She laughed softly, cupping his cheek in her palm. 'But thanks for the compliment.' She winked at April, who rewarded her with a grin. 'How long shall we let her sleep?' Catriona pointed at the ceiling as Duncan released her and walked to the back door.

'An hour or so?' He shrugged. 'She hardly drank anything.'

Catriona nodded, taking April's empty glass from the table, and rinsing it. 'I think it was more shock than brandy, Duncan.' She watched him put on a baseball cap with a fish logo on the front. 'I'll leave her a while longer.'

'Right. I thought I'd go and brush out the boathouse. Do

you want to come and help me, April?' Duncan shoved his feet into a pair of old running shoes.

For a split second, Catriona wanted to say *no*, shadows of a nightmare she would never forget flickering through her mind's eye. As she battled with the images, Duncan was staring at her, his mouth slightly open and his hands on his hips. Then, realisation seemed to dawn as he closed his mouth, took off the hat and raked his hair back before replacing it.

'Actually, perhaps you'd better stay inside, love, just in case Connor wakes up, or something.'

Hearing the painful regret in his voice, Catriona rallied. 'She can go with you. It'll be more fun that staying here with boring old Mummy.' She pulled a face, instantly rewarded by the obvious relief and gratitude that filled his eyes.

'OK, then.' His voice was gruff. 'Let's go, kiddo. Get your shoes on.' He pointed at the two pairs of trainers tucked under the coat rack, Hope's still sitting next to April's.

April walked over to the rack, reached down, and lifted Hope's shoes, gently touching the laces. Then, turning to her father, she spoke quietly. 'We're not going to stay angry with Lauren anymore, are we?'

Catriona's heart faltered for a second until she saw Duncan's initial surprise transform into a look that could only be described as love. 'No, we're not, sweetheart.' He shook his head. 'While Lauren didn't tell the truth about everything, she has a good heart and she cares about you, a lot, and that's what matters to your mum and me.'

April nodded, her fingers lingering on the tangled laces. 'And can Connor still come to play sometimes?' She looked over at Catriona, her eyes full of hope. 'I think he likes having a big sister, like I did.'

April's statement was simply heartbreaking. 'Yes, he can, love. We'll figure it out.' She gently took the shoes from April and began untangling the laces. 'Whatever happens, we are a family, and now Connor and Lauren are part of that.' She set the shoes on the floor at April's feet. 'And family sticks together, no matter what.'

April sat on the floor, and put Hope's shoes on, taking her time to tie the laces and meticulously do a double loop, something Hope always did, but April, seldom. As she focused on what she was doing, the tip of her tongue visible between her lips, Catriona let the peace of this simple, perfect scene, something that she had been craving for months, fill her up.

As she looked over at Duncan, he mouthed, *Thank you,* absorbing the same priceless moment that Catriona had, their hearts in lockstep once again.

Twenty minutes later, Lauren appeared in the hallway as Catriona was putting away the last of the dishes. Lauren's eyes were swollen, her face flushed, and her mouth pinched as she gripped Connor's hand. The little boy's middle fingers were once again in his mouth as he leaned into his mother's thigh.

'How are you feeling?' Catriona pointed at a chair. 'Please sit down, Lauren.'

Lauren hesitated for a few moments, her eyes darting between the window and Catriona's face, then she slid the chair out and sat, drawing Connor onto her knee.

'Do you want some water, or tea?' Catriona hovered by the sink, unsure what kind of response she'd get.

'No. We need to go.' Lauren combed the soft hair out of Connor's eyes with her fingertips then met Catriona's gaze. 'But thanks.'

Catriona nodded, folding the tea towel over the handle on the oven, half wishing that Duncan and April would come back in, but also grateful that they were still safely outside. There were things that she needed to say and having April present might turn them from purely practical, and inevitable, to cruel in Lauren's eyes.

Catriona spoke gently. 'There was never any need to lie to us about who you are, or how you live. None of that matters to us. You made April, so we will always be grateful to you.' She paused. 'You did your best by your daughter, back then, and you are doing a wonderful job of raising your son, now. We all just have to have the bravery to tell the truth about ourselves, even the mistakes we've made, because believe me, we've all made them.' She saw Lauren's eyelids flicker, as if her words had hit home, and wanting to forge on while she might continue to be heard, to open a window where the door had been firmly closed, Catriona crossed the room and sat next to Lauren. 'You may feel that you haven't had a real family, but you are part of *this* family now.' She tentatively touched Lauren's knee, feeling the tremble of residual shock still rippling through her. 'You will always be welcome here, and so will Connor, but you must agree that there will be no more talk of April going with you.' Catriona sat back, careful to frame the next sentence in as sensitive a way as possible, while still holding firm to what she knew must happen. Lauren met her eyes, an all but imperceptible nod making Catriona exhale. 'I think we all just need a little distance from each other for a while, then, after some time, if you still want to, both you and Connor can be part of April's life. One way or another, Lauren, we'll always be connected.'

The high colour had faded from Lauren's face, a last trace of pink on her cheekbones highlighting the turquoise eyes that brought April's face to mind every time Catriona saw them.

'Lauren, did you hear me?' Lauren's blank expression unnerving, Catriona sat back and ran her clammy palms down her thighs.

Lauren lifted her chin, cradling Connor close to her chest. 'Yes, I heard you.' She nodded. 'But you don't know how awful how this feels.' A tear oozed from her left eye and trickled down, clinging to her jaw.

'Actually, I think I do.' Catriona smiled sadly, then stood up, carefully pushing the chair back in to the edge of the table. 'Do you want to say goodbye to April?' She tipped her head towards the back door.

'No. I can't.' Lauren shook her head. 'I can't bear it.'

Understanding, at such a bone-deep level that she couldn't find words to express it, Catriona simply nodded.

34

To Catriona's surprise, Duncan had been almost coy when Peg arrived, shortly after breakfast the next day. She'd breezed in, all wind-blown and fresh-faced, a basket of eggs from the chickens they'd recently installed in a large coop in the back garden looped over her arm. 'Hello, Duncan. So glad to meet you, finally.' She'd held the basket out to him. 'The missing piece is found.' She'd smiled over at Catriona, as Duncan had jumped up, taken the basket from her, and given Peg his chair. He'd then poured her some coffee and asked after Bruce, Graham and even the dogs. As he talked, warmly, thoughtfully, Catriona had stood with her back to the sink, a secret smile tugging at her mouth. Not only was she surprised that he'd retained all this information about their new neighbours, but she was overcome to see the re-emergence of the man she'd married, the one who'd won her heart with his quiet, if intense intelligence, his self-effacing humour, his unshakeable focus when something important was being said. Seeing him back had sent a jolt of love through her that had made her catch her breath.

Now, Peg was at the piano with April, teaching her two-handed scales, as Duncan hovered behind them, tapping his thigh in time with April's playing and glancing back at Catriona who stood in the doorway, smiling at the scene.

'That's really good, April. Well done.' Peg put her arm around April and drew her close. 'We'll make a pianist of you yet.'

April made a soft, snorting sound, then swivelled around on the stool. As Catriona watched, April beckoned to her father, and then slid to the edge of the seat.

Understanding, Peg stood up and made room. 'Dad, your presence is required.' She mock bowed, gesturing towards the stool.

Duncan's face coloured, as he patted the air. 'This is April's lesson. I don't want to muscle in.'

Peg assessed him for a few moments, then circled her hands towards her middle. 'A bit of muscle is exactly what's called for.' She winked at him. 'I won't charge any extra pie, for a few more minutes.'

Duncan turned to Catriona, frowning. 'Pie?'

Catriona laughed. 'We have a special arrangement, Peg and I.' She smiled at his confused expression. 'Lessons in exchange for pies, biscuits, fruit tarts, shortbread et cetera.' She shrugged. 'It's a bargain.'

Peg chuckled, drawing Duncan's focus back to the piano, where April was still staring at him, expectantly. 'Will you join us?' Peg held her hand out again.

Duncan hesitated for a few moments, then walked over and eased himself onto the stool, next to April.

'How about I teach you a duet? You'll have to practise, mind. Every day.' Peg gave an exaggerated frown as April looked up at her, her eyes wide. 'No excuses from either of you, and I'll be checking up on you regularly.' She pulled her shoulders back, her hair falling away from her face.

'Bruce calls me the sergeant major, so I might as well live up to the title.' She grinned. 'Now, let's give it a whirl.'

Catriona watched Peg, guiding her husband and daughter, occasionally tapping their wrists, pointing to the sheet of music propped up on the stand, her skirt swishing between her tanned ankles as she walked behind them, then turned in a circle as she laughed when Duncan's huge hand and April's tiny one got tangled, and the resultant clang from the piano was jarring.

'Oh, it's enough to drive me to drink.' She smiled over at Catriona, who nodded, unable to speak in case her voice gave way. The sight of these two people, who meant the world to her, sitting side by side again, leaning in towards each other, their heads inclined as they struggled with the finger work, was exactly what she needed, right at this moment.

Graham and April were out in the garden, running around on the lawn. Graham had brought Guinevere and Lancelot over, after April's lesson was finished, and now Arthur had joined the melee, gleefully chasing his mother's tail as Graham and April chased him.

The mid-morning light was watery but bright, as big, tufted clouds covered and then slid away from the sun, while clusters of seagulls cut across the skyline, their calls left hanging behind them like the echoes of a discordant choir.

Inside, Catriona, Duncan and Peg sat around the kitchen table, the windows open and the smell of damp grass filling the air. The last few crumbs of a giant cream-filled meringue sat on Peg's plate, as, outside, Lancelot barked, making Graham laugh loudly and them all smile.

'Oh, that was brilliant.' Peg patted her flat stomach, the sleeve of her striped linen blouse flapping around her bony wrist. 'Your wife has a gift.' She smiled at Duncan, who was looking affectionately over at Catriona. 'In turn, I tempt her with a wee nip, now and then.' Peg patted the pocket of her skirt. 'Duncan?' She eyed him, a sly smile making her eyes wrinkle at the corners.

'Ha, no. A bit early for me.' He shook his head, smiling. 'But feel free.' He nodded at Peg's teacup. 'Whatever floats your boat.'

Peg chuckled, poured a generous dash of whisky into her cup and tucked the flask away in her pocket. Then her eyes seemed to cloud over as the smile slipped from her face. 'So, now that the introductions are over, can I speak plainly to the pair of you?' She took a sip of tea and sat back in the chair.

The sharp change of tone took Catriona by surprise as she met Duncan's questioning eyes across the table. 'Um, yes. Of course.' She watched as Peg rubbed her jaw, her fingers massaging the flesh of her cheek.

'Right. I won't sugar-coat it, as I think you know me well enough now, Catriona, to understand me.' She eyed Catriona, whose nerves had begun to tingle. 'It's about that young woman, Lauren. I've felt it all along, but now there's energy here that needs to be cleared.' She swept a hand in an arc around her. 'She's mixed up, poor thing, like she has good and bad doing battle inside her.' Peg paused, nodding to herself.

Duncan shifted in the chair, discomfort flooding his face. For a second, Catriona thought it might be because Peg had gone straight for the jugular, regarding something so private to them, but as Catriona studied his expression, she saw that it was more at the significance of Peg's words.

Catriona and he had talked about Peg's *fey-ness*, as Iris called it, and, surprisingly, Duncan hadn't tried to logic her out of it, or deny the phenomenon of this kind of *sight*. He'd simply nodded, taking it all in, as he was now.

'Peg, we know. We discovered some upsetting information and we handled it yesterday.' He traced a line in the air between himself and Catriona. 'Cat and I have things under control.'

Catriona smiled at him gratefully, not only for his acknowledgement of their partnership, but also at his unaccustomed willingness to be so open with Peg, whom he'd just met. Catriona considered it another testament to his determination to be on her side from now on, a team, as they used to be.

Peg absorbed what he'd said, her lips pursing as she narrowed her eyes. 'Well, thank God. I've been dying to talk to you both, but Bruce held me back.' She exhaled. 'My teeth have been aching something rotten.' She opened her mouth wide, her palms on her cheeks. 'It's a sign of a lie being told.' She held Catriona's gaze. 'I'm so relieved. And all I can say is that the truth always surfaces, eventually.' Turning to Catriona, Peg's eyes cleared and she smiled widely. 'Your husband wants to take you out, somewhere special.'

Duncan's eyes widened as he mouthed, *What?*

Catriona laughed, relieved that the conversation had come back to a lighter place. 'Oh, really. And where might that be?' Her eyebrows lifted.

Duncan raised his hands in defeat. 'You got me. I booked a table at The Waterside, at the Kyle of Lochalsh, for tomorrow night.' He looked mildly embarrassed as Peg shoved her chair back and stood up. 'I was going to tell you.'

He looked over at Catriona, whose heart swelled at the gentle way he said, 'It's our anniversary.'

She sucked in a breath. She had completely forgotten, for the first time in seventeen years, and that it was nearly August was a startling reality to face. Hope had been gone almost five months, and give or take a week or so, that was how long it had been since April had spoken freely. While she'd had a couple of short conversations with her delighted grandparents, April still wasn't speaking in front of Peg, but when Catriona had called Nora to ask her advice, Nora had said that this was normal, that April would gradually feel more confident in her voice, and as that happened, she would feel able to talk in more situations.

As the thought of any more silence threatened to pop Catriona's bubble of happiness, she consciously set it aside. They were getting back on track, and with time, and patience, April would rediscover her confidence, so, for now, Catriona would allow herself to enjoy feeling valued, seen and loved by her husband.

'So, what time do you need me to come over?' Peg lifted her plate and cup and walked to the sink. Catriona frowned, still caught out by Peg's uncanny ability to pre-empt things, so artfully. Peg caught the frown and tutted, theatrically. 'To babysit?'

The restaurant was right on the water at the Kyle of Lochalsh, the long building, a former railway station, floodlit and glowing warmly against the darkening sky. The station platform, and rail tracks, both ran the length of the structure, and across the water, the outline of the Skye Bridge stretched from the mainland to the island, dotted with bursts of headlights glittering, like tiny stars, as the cars crossed the Loch.

It was a cool night, and Catriona was glad of her jacket as they walked quickly from the car to the entrance of the restaurant. Above them, the sky was a marvellous, midnight-blue, streaked with the beginnings of a midsummer sunset, amber, gold and green waves a backdrop to the kyle.

Duncan held her hand as they walked inside, where a young man, with cropped blond hair and eyes the colour of moss, greeted them and showed them to a table tucked into a corner by a window. The compact bar sat across one corner of the room, draped with twinkling lights, and the handful of antique tables, each unique, with a set of mismatched, heavily carved chairs, were carefully placed, to create atmosphere without being crowded. An open wine-wall was stacked with bottles and a series of antique mirrors bounced the light from the candles on the tables around the room, like the sun sparkling on the loch outside.

Duncan had had a haircut, was clean shaven, and his skin was glowing from the walk they'd taken to the beach at Loch Carron, with April, that afternoon. They'd paddled at the edge of the chilly water, picked up empty scallop shells and taken them home to wash in the bath. As she swished the shells around in the water, April, unaware that they were still standing behind her, had begun to hum to herself, a tuneless sound that nonetheless had brought Catriona to tears, as she and Duncan had backed silently out of the bathroom and left April to her moment of innocent pleasure.

Now, Catriona sat back and looked out the window, a perfect frame for the glorious colours emerging in the sky, the entire painting reflected in duplicate on the surface of the water below. She sighed, as Duncan reached over and took her hand. 'Happy anniversary, Cat.' His eyes glittered in the candlelight. 'Seventeen years today, and we're still here.' He smiled, in the gentle, almost self-conscious way that always gripped her heart. 'I love you.'

She shook the hair from her eyes and squeezed his fingers. 'Seventeen years is not too shabby.' She smiled. 'And I love you too, by the way.'

He laughed softly, releasing her hand. 'You better.'

'Thanks for thinking about this. For booking the table.' She looked into his eyes. 'I can't believe I forgot.' She grimaced. 'I'm sorry.'

He shook his head. 'Don't. You've been to hell and back these past few months. There's nothing to be sorry for.'

Catriona leaned forward on her elbows and lowered her voice. 'There is, actually.'

He frowned. 'What do you mean?'

Catriona took a breath, this moment had taken its own time coming, but now that it was here, she wasn't going to let it slip away. For the first time in months, she knew exactly what she wanted. The certainty that everything would be all right the simple touch of his hand had always given her.

She extended her hand, palm up, until he slid his fingers back into hers. 'I'm sorry I blamed you, so utterly and completely, for what happened to Hope, that I couldn't see you anymore, or how much you were hurting, too.' She swallowed. 'I'm sorry I shut you out, just as much as April did.' Duncan made to stop her. 'No, please. Let me finish, love.'

He nodded, his eyes holding hers.

'And I'm sorry that it took letting you go to realise that I can't do this without you.' Her throat threatened to clamp shut, so she took a shaky breath. 'We are a team, Duncan.

Through good and bad. We are in this life together and that's the only way I want to move forward.'

As she let herself exhale, feeling lighter than she had in months, he looked down at the table and surreptitiously swiped his cheek.

'OK. Shall we order now, Mr Anderson? I'm starving,' she whispered.

His head snapped up and he laughed, a crisp, hearty sound that filled her with a warmth that had been missing for so long, it felt like a welcome friend returning from a long absence. 'Yes, Mrs Anderson, let's eat.'

The house was quiet when they let themselves in, Peg already standing in the hall with her coat on as they opened the door. 'All quiet on the Western Front.' She smiled. 'Had a good night?'

'Lovely, thanks.' Catriona nodded. 'Just what the doctor ordered.'

'Great stuff.' Peg patted her arm as Duncan eased past her.

'Thanks a million, Peg. So, how many pies do we owe you?' He suppressed a smile, as, behind him, Catriona laughed softly.

'Cheeky,' Peg tutted, a glint in her eye. 'I'll see you on Wednesday for your next lesson. I've never taught en famille before.' She squinted at Catriona. 'And don't think *you're* getting off the hook, madam. I hope you've been practising?' She walked out the door, then turned back, her expression almost wistful. 'April's going to be fine, you know.'

Catriona stepped forward and wrapped her arms around Peg's shoulders. 'Thanks, Peg. I know she will.'

'Aye, well. Goodnight, now. Oh, and if you marked the whisky bottle, I can only apologise.' She gave a mischievous wink, as Duncan came back outside, his hands in his pockets.

'Can I walk you back, Peg?'

'Heavens, no. It's but a few steps.' She shook her head. 'Goodnight, one and all.' She raised a palm, then turned and headed into the moonlit night.

Catriona went to check on April, who was sleeping soundly, her cheeks flushed and a half-smile curving her full lips. The sight of the smile sent a bolt of joy through Catriona, a gift that she would never take for granted again.

Having recently graduated from the dog-bed, Arthur was curled at April's feet, his nose tucked endearingly under his front paw. The window was open a crack and the dewy night air was heavy with the scent of the loch.

Catriona gently moved a twist of hair from across April's face, leaned in and kissed her forehead, then lingered for a few moments, reluctant to let this moment of peace slip away, until she finally tiptoed out of the room.

Downstairs, Duncan was waiting for her in the conservatory, two brandy glasses sitting on the table near the window and the French doors open to the night. 'I thought we'd sit in here. The moon is unbelievable.' He smiled as she came in. 'Come and sit with me.' He shifted over to make room for her on the wicker sofa.

Lifting the glasses and handing him one, Catriona sat next to him, welcoming the pressure of his thigh next to hers, and the warmth that spread through her insides at his closeness. Gently touching their glasses together, they sipped their drinks, then Catriona closed her eyes momentarily, breathing in the same briny scent that had floated up into April's room moments before.

'Let's have some music.' She pressed her shoulder against his. 'How about some classic Billie Holiday, or Astrud Gilberto?' She opened her eyes to see him smile, then he got up and chose her favourite Billie Holiday CD and, as the opening lyrics of 'At Last' began to float across the room, he settled himself next to her and took her free hand in his.

Catriona leaned her head against his shoulder, the soft cotton of his shirt cool against her skin, just as a noise behind them made then both turn and look at the door.

April stood in the doorway, the light behind her turning her into a silhouette, her hair tousled, and Arthur wriggling in her arms.

'Hello, there. I thought you were asleep.' Catriona held her hand out. 'Come and sit with us.'

April padded over to the sofa, set Arthur on the floor, then squeezed in between them, her slender legs seeming impossibly long in her favourite, too-small pyjamas that she still wore, despite having two new pairs in her drawer.

'Did you have fun with Peg?' Catriona lifted April's hand in hers as April nodded, winding her fingers through Catriona's. Sensing that this would be a quiet moment, no words necessary, Catriona kissed April's temple, then looked over at Duncan, who was smiling down at their daughter. Catriona caught his eye, her vision beginning to blur, as he leaned in and kissed April's other temple, the gesture so touching that Catriona closed her eyes for a second to savour the image.

Feeling movement, she opened her eyes to see April take Duncan's hand in her free one, lift it and place it over her and Catriona's entwined fingers. The gesture was so eloquent that Catriona locked eyes with Duncan, seeing his as full as her own.

As they sat in silence, bathed in milky moonlight, their hearts in tune once more, Catriona knew that while there would always be Faith- and Hope-shaped spaces in their hearts, together they were strong enough to heal, to make new memories – even strong enough to hold the door open to Lauren, Connor and to forgiveness.

EPILOGUE

December had been the coldest on record for years, the loch freezing in large sections and snow coating not only the Cuillins and Applecross mountains, but the roofs and gardens of Plockton. It was picturesque, if slightly hazardous for driving, and the prospect of a white Christmas was undeniably exciting.

Catriona was relieved to have finished her tutoring, until after the new year, and with Christmas just a few days away, she had a list of last-minute things to do. Duncan had done most of the shopping, but there were a few remaining gifts that Catriona wanted to pick up in the village, specifically for her parents, and something for Graham, Peg and Bruce, who were all joining them for lunch.

Earlier that morning, as Catriona had checked the time, then pulled on her coat, April had come running into the kitchen. Her cheeks had been flushed, and beside her, as ever, stood Arthur. Having reached his full height, his handsome head was now level with April's hip. His new tartan lead had been clamped between his teeth as his tail had noisily slapped the kitchen cabinet. 'Can we go with you, to see Mungo?'

Over the past five months, April had steadily been gaining in confidence, speaking more often, enjoying school again and making more friends – even going back to Brownies. She and Graham were still thick as thieves, and Catriona would joke that Peg should just give April a bedroom, as she practically lived next door anyway.

Catriona had zipped up her coat and dug into the canvas bag that hung on the coat rack, stuffed full of all their gloves, scarves and biodegradable bags for Arthur's walks. 'Sure. Get your coat and scarf on though, as it's bitter out on the pier.' Grateful for the gradual re-emergence of April's former, sunny energy, that lifted all their spirits, Catriona's eyes had blurred as she'd smiled at her daughter.

Bundled up in coats and scarves, mother and daughter had dashed around the village, their noses growing crimson and whisps of icy breath escaping them as they talked through the plans for the next few days. They'd popped in and out of the shops, with a growing collection of bags filled with bright wrapping paper, more tinsel for the tree, and the last few gifts that were on their lists. Throughout their excursion, Catriona had juggled a sense of happy anticipation at having all the people she loved around their table once again, while also dreading the painful void that Hope's absence would inevitably leave in the room.

When they'd got back to the house, April had eaten two mince pies, had a hot bath, and was now tucked up in bed with a book, and Arthur at her feet.

Downstairs, Catriona and Duncan were sitting on the floor in the living room, wrapping presents and listening to Nat King Cole croon, 'I'll Be Home For Christmas'. The Christmas card they'd received from Lauren lay on the coffee table, its presence a silent reminder of just how close they'd come to losing April, something Catriona couldn't bear to think about, now.

They'd had little contact with Lauren since the summer, other than an initial letter of apology for how she had behaved, followed by a series of colourful, animal-print postcards that, with their permission, she'd been sending to April each week. In the cards, Lauren's tone had been warm and kind, and her obvious respect, and acceptance of the situation, had touched Catriona and Duncan, prompting them to want to help her, in some way.

Their decision to offer to supplement Lauren's income, so that she could go to university, had felt right, to them both, and having agreed on how to best present this to her, they had just decided to invite her and Connor to join them for Christmas. So, when April appeared in the doorway, wearing Hope's robe, and with Arthur padding behind her, they both jumped. 'Hey, sweetheart. What's up?' Duncan carefully tucked a half-wrapped present for April behind the tree.

'Can I ask you something?' She looked shyly at them, then walked in and slid onto the piano stool, her feet now easily touching the floor.

'Of course, love.' Catriona dropped what she was doing and beckoned to April, who crossed the room and sat on the rug next to her.

'Can Connor and Lauren come for Christmas?' April leaned into Catriona's side, her hair smelling of lavender and her cool fingers finding Catriona's.

Catriona looked over at Duncan, who was smiling and shaking his head as he pulled the heavy curtains across the window behind the Christmas tree. That they had been talking about this very thing, just moments before, obviously struck them both as uncanny, but the longer they'd been around Peg, the less instances like this seemed to faze them anymore.

Catriona hugged April tight. 'Actually, we were planning on calling Lauren tomorrow to invite them.'

April beamed. 'Oh, ace. I saw a fire engine in the Tiny Toy Box shop in the village. Can we get it for Connor?' She clasped her hands together, her eyes bright.

'Yes, that sounds like a great idea.' Catriona smiled at her daughter, the sweet open face, the lively eyes, the gentle-natured child who filled their lives with so much joy they had no way of measuring it. Pointing at the piano, Catriona laughed softly. 'You better get practising "Away in a Manger", because Peg says you've to play it for us all on Christmas day.'

April nodded, leaned back on her hands, and sighed. 'I really miss Hope.' She paused, her eyes glittering as she took in the brightly decorated tree. 'But it's going to be a lovely Christmas, isn't it?' She looked at them both in turn, a tentative smile curving her mouth.

'Yes, sweetheart, it is.' Her insides flooded by a curdled mixture of loss, and overwhelming love, Catriona smiled, locking eyes with Duncan. 'The first of many.'

AUTHOR LETTER

Dear reader,

Thank you, from the bottom of my heart, for choosing to read *Someone Else's Child*. I hope you enjoyed it. If you would like to keep up to date with all my latest releases, just sign up at the following link. Your email address will never be shared, and you can unsubscribe at any time.

www.bookouture.com/Alison-Ragsdale

The seeds of this story came from a conversation I had with a friend about a child she had once taught who was a selective mute. I was soon deep in research mode, where I learned about the various forms of mutism and the different causes and ways the condition manifests in children. Everything I learned, coupled with my fascination for the mother-daughter relationship, formed the beginnings of this book.

While Catriona's story is one of heartbreaking loss, it is also about the incredible strength of a mother's love – a force that can endure, even during the most unimaginable circumstances. Catriona and April's story touched me deeply because it's reflective of the remarkable spirit and determination of two women whom I greatly admire. So, it was a privilege to write.

Thanks again for taking the time to read *Someone Else's Child*. If you enjoyed it, I'd be grateful if you would take a moment to write a review. They are a great way to introduce new readers to my books, so it would mean the world to me if you did.

I love to hear from my readers, and you can get in touch with me via my Facebook author page, through Instagram, Twitter, Goodreads, or my website. I look forward to it.

Thanks again for reading.

All the best,

Alison Ragsdale

www.alisonragsdale.com

 facebook.com/authoralisonragsdale
twitter.com/AlisonRagsdale
 instagram.com/alisonragsdalewrites

ACKNOWLEDGEMENTS

My heartfelt thanks to the wonderful team at Bookouture for their generous support, expertise and refreshing sense of humour when it is most needed. Special thanks to my brilliant editors, Maisie, and Kelsie, for being the best champions an author could hope for and for helping me step back, dig deep, and get the absolute best out of these characters and their stories. Thanks also to Alex, Natasha, Lauren, Noelle, Peta, Jade, Jon, and everyone who helped this story make its way into the world. I am so fortunate to be working with a group of such genuine and professional individuals.

As always, a special thank you to Lesley and Carly, my best friends, first readers and most patient think-tank cohorts. Everyone deserves sisters like you.

Thank you also to all the friends, readers, reviewers, book bloggers and my wonderful Highlanders Club members who support me and my books. I will never be able to express how much that means to me. Every one of you is a treasure, and you make this writing journey so special.

Finally, and most importantly, to my incredible husband. Thank you for always being prepared to listen – and for keeping that old business card for a year. I love you.